NEW YORK REVIEW BOOKS
CLASSICS

W9-ASF-384

THE COMMUNIST

GUIDO MORSELLI (1912–1973) spent his youth in Milan, where his father was an executive with a pharmaceutical company. When he was twelve his mother died from Spanish flu, an event that devastated the reserved child. After attending a Jesuit-run primary school and a classical secondary school, Morselli graduated from the Università degli Studi di Milano with a law degree in 1935. Instead of practicing law, however, he embarked on a long trip around the Continent. Though he wrote consistently from the remote town in the lake region of Lombardy where he lived alone, Morselli succeeded in publishing only two books over the course of his life: the essays *Proust o del sentimento* (Proust, or On Sentiment, 1943) and *Realismo e fantasia* (Realism and Invention, 1947). His many works of fiction, journalism, and philosophy were repeatedly rejected by publishers, and, frustrated by his perceived failures, he committed suicide in 1973. Hanging in his library was the motto *Etiam si omnes, ego non* (Though all do it, I do not). In fact, Morselli's nine posthumously published novels, among them *Roma senza papa* (Rome Without the Pope, 1974), *Divertimento 1889* (1975), and *Dissipatio H.G.* (The Dissolution of the Human Race, 1977), enjoyed considerable critical success. Morselli left his farm and lands to the town of Gavirate in his will, and today Parco Morselli looks south onto Lago di Varese and north toward the Alpine foothills.

FREDERIKA RANDALL is a writer and a translator of Italian literature. Her translations include Luigi Meneghello's *Deliver Us*; Sergio Luzzatto's *The Body of Il Duce*, *Padre Pio*, and *Primo Levi's Resistance*; and Ippolito Nievo's *Confessions of an Italian*, named among the best books of 2014 by *The New Yorker* and the *New Statesman*. Among her awards are a Bogliasco Fellowship, a PEN/ Heim Translation Fund grant, and, with Sergio Luzzatto, the Cundill Prize. She lives in Rome.

ELIZABETH McKENZIE's novel *The Portable Veblen* was longlisted for the 2016 National Book Award for fiction. She is the author of the novel *MacGregor Tells The World* and story collection *Stop That Girl*. Her work has appeared in *The New Yorker*, *The Atlantic*, *Best American Nonrequired Reading*, and other publications. McKenzie is senior editor of the *Chicago Quarterly Review* and the managing editor of *Catamaran Literary Reader*.

THE COMMUNIST

GUIDO MORSELLI

Translated from the Italian by
FREDERIKA RANDALL

Introduction by
ELIZABETH McKENZIE

NEW YORK REVIEW BOOKS

New York

THIS IS A NEW YORK REVIEW BOOK
PUBLISHED BY THE NEW YORK REVIEW OF BOOKS
435 Hudson Street, New York, NY 10014
www.nyrb.com

Library of Congress Cataloging-in-Publication Data
Names: Morselli, Guido, author. | Randall, Frederika, translator. | McKenzie,
    Elizabeth, 1958– writer of introduction.
Title: The communist / Guido Morselli ; translated by Frederika Randall ;
    introduction by Elizabeth McKenzie.
Other titles: Comunista. English
Description: New York : New York Review Books, 2017. | Series: New York
    Review Books classics
Identifiers: LCCN 2016059772 (print) | LCCN 2017017105 (ebook) | ISBN
    9781681370798 (epub) | ISBN 9781681370781 (paperback)
Subjects: LCSH: Communists—Fiction. | Labor—Philosophy—Fiction. |
    Meaning (Psychology)—Fiction. | Belief and doubt—Fiction. | Italy—Fiction.
    | Soviet Union—Fiction. | Political fiction. | Psychological fiction. | BISAC:
    FICTION / Political. | FICTION / Psychological. | FICTION / Literary.
Classification: LCC PQ4829.O714 (ebook) | LCC PQ4829.O714 C5713 2017
    (print) | DDC 853/.914—dc23
LC record available at https://lccn.loc.gov/2016059772

ISBN 978-1-68137-078-1
Available as an electronic book; ISBN 978-1-68137-079-8

Printed in the United States of America on acid-free paper.
10 9 8 7 6 5 4 3 2 1

CONTENTS

INTRODUCTION

IN THE aftermath of World War II the Italian Communist Party found itself in a position of significant power and prestige. With the third-largest membership of any Communist Party in the world, surpassed only by those of the USSR and the People's Republic of China, the Partito Comunista Italiano, or PCI, had survived repression under Mussolini to play a central and decisive role in the partisan resistance to the German occupation. Under its charismatic leader Palmiro Togliatti, it went on to contest elections in the newly founded postwar republic, and though it never succeeded in gaining control over the national government, it did over many of Italy's regions and towns, especially in the industrial heartland of the north.

The "good Fascist" is taken to be a contradiction in terms, but in Italy on the local level the "good Communist" truly existed, organizing workers' cooperatives and sponsoring art festivals that were enjoyed by many people other than the party faithful. Divided from the Eastern Bloc by the iron curtain, Italian Communists pledged themselves to Marxist/Leninist ideology without having to endure totalitarian control, while dismissing news of the gulags and other barbarities as so much capitalist propaganda. Stalin helped to fund the PCI and remained an inspiration to its members. When he died in 1953, the party paper *l'Unità* published the following panegyric:

GLORIA ETERNA A GIUSEPPE STALIN!
Fellow citizens, comrades! A grave, irreparable disaster has struck us all. Joseph Stalin, the man upon whom millions of

Italian workers, peasants, and intellectuals looked with trust and affection as their leader and their hope, is dead. Our sorrow is deep. The powerful of the earth bowed before Stalin's immortal genius. The people cry for him as they'd cry for the loss of a father...

Fascism's defeat was the beginning of our national redemption...

Eternal glory to Joseph Stalin!

Long live the Communist Party of the Soviet Union!

Long live the Italian Communist Party!

Long live the indestructible friendship of the Italian and Soviet peoples!

(translation by Mitchell Abidor)

Three years later came Khrushchev's speech to the Twentieth Congress of the Communist Party of the Soviet Union, in which he denounced the Stalinist cult of personality and disclosed some of Stalin's many crimes. For many committed Communists in Italy and elsewhere, the subsequent de-Stalinization of the party was bewildering, a fertile time in which to set this novel.

The Communist begins in 1958. Its central character, forty-four-year-old Walter Ferranini, is a devoted party member. The son of an anarchist who revered Sacco and Vanzetti, Walter pores daily over *Avanti!* and *l'Unità*, content to be participating in the "Marxist picture of reality."

As a deputy in parliament he represents the region of Emilia-Romagna, which, with the highest per capita party membership in Italy, is a model of cooperativism, arguably the most successful adaptation of Communism anywhere, ever. As a young man Walter had worked tirelessly as an activist, forming the Reggio Cooperative League and Inter-Agraria. But now as a bureaucrat, he's mothballed: "In five months he had not opened his mouth ... he, once so combative in Reggio, so inclined to take responsibility." A labor organizer at heart, Walter is eager to draft a bill for worker safety, but his friend and fellow deputy, the union leader Reparatore, reminds him that such action is incompatible with party policy: "Communists do not take part in the life of the parliament, they observe and remain outside!" Walter feels more and more separated from the hands-on work that gave his life meaning in the past, with less and less room to maneuver. The threat of punishment in the unforgiving, hierarchical party always looms.

The only things that do still give Walter pleasure are his "pastoral visits," when he goes out to meet his constituents and hear their concerns and complaints. They are the fabled "base" and their "petty, combative, concrete" experiences were "part of his life." Visiting a factory that produces rosaries, he notes that the circular saws have no safety devices, and must scold the owner for taking short cuts: "To be a Communist means to be willing to make sacrifices, not play the gangster. Do you understand? This comes to you from Comrade Ferranini, someone who still makes sacrifices himself." He is proud to think that "Communism was something he had earned. Temptations, large and small, had presented themselves, but he had resisted." Nevertheless Walter remains troubled by the inside dealing and political favoritism that are turning the activity of the cooperatives into business as usual.

In spite of his Marxist piety ("Humanity's bible, Marx, his guide, and a guide for all mankind"), his disenchantments begin to pile up. Walter is ordered by his superiors in the party to travel to Turin to question a young comrade accused of "deviationism (easy to say, but it was a serious charge, something that could sink a man)." The visit confirms the comrade's claims that the local deputy is "corrupted by the bourgeois leprosy" and "rotten with personalism." In this idealistic young deviant Walter sees himself, and he begins to wonder how he has gotten to this point.

Walter is stubborn, earnest, self-critical, and increasingly isolated. There is something heartbreakingly lonely about Comrade Ferranini as he circulates among the parliament in Rome, his favorite tratto-ria, his stark room in a pension, moving from his daily duties into the vaults of the past, troubled by pessimistic thoughts: "We're keeping death at bay from the moment we enter this world." He suffers from a heart condition—possibly psychosomatic—that fills him with existential dread, and he sees his life's path as resembling a parabola: "A sharp uptick loaded with hope and initiative, then the inevitable plunge? The downstroke of the parabola went deep into despair, but then came charging out for another ascent, in turn condemned to reverse into another dive."

Unbeknownst to himself, Walter is also a romantic, though he works hard to suppress his urges. He maintains an ambivalent relationship with a "lady friend," Nuccia Corsi, a single mother who has long been separated from her husband. Nuccia, kindly, intelligent, tolerant of Walter's foibles, is an editor at a publishing company who, during the war, joined the partisans and distinguished herself with her bravery. (Partisan stories are legendary in Italy to this day; for instance, tourists can follow "partisan resistance itineraries" in the north.) Nuccia's tenderness for Walter softens the man, opens him up. He tells her about his disappointing pilgrimage to Spain in the 1930s to fight Franco and his subsequent exile to the United States, where, notwithstanding his unrepentant leftism ("The Central Command of Capitalism, not just Chicago but America itself, had failed to tame him"), he found himself marrying Nancy, his boss's daughter and an all-American beauty with that most bourgeois of attributes, a family property—Old Laurel Farm, a place he grows to love.

The descriptions of Walter's unexpected American idyll in *The Communist* are gorgeously youthful, conveying the initial ecstasy of Walter's marriage. The tone of the novel is generally precise and pragmatic—the tone of a good Communist—but it grows lyrical when Walter succumbs guiltily to the illicit pleasures of remembering times past spent in the heartland of capitalism, especially since the marriage did not last, and he now sees his whole American foray as a temptation barely escaped. Reminiscing about those days, he

tells Nuccia: "Nature is an enemy reality I must struggle against...
to keep it from prevailing, from subjugating us.... I would abandon
myself, allow myself to be enchanted. And then at Old Laurel there
was something else, something worse: the countryside, the sly
weapon of a bourgeois world intent on dominating me."

Walter scours his motives for ideological indiscretions at every
turn. Nuccia teases him a bit: "You do go in for self-criticism....
Such a dedicated Communist. Can't you just say you were in love?"
Well, how can he, he who loved America so much, while his friends
and colleagues at home were "starving, getting shot at from every
side."

Walter is a seriously lonely man whose only outlet for his loneliness is the party, a person trying to understand himself and play a
role in the world, to make sense of things, but what he believes in
gives him no language with which to understand his loneliness, and
his efforts to square the circle of the personal and the political will
leave him ever more dissatisfied with the party and the party ever
more dissatisfied with him. This predicament will pose an increas-
ing threat to his relationship with Nuccia and, before the end of the
book, will lead Walter to take the strangest of adventures.

Born in Bologna in 1912 and raised in Milan, Guido Morselli, the
author of *The Communist*, would have been familiar from an early
age with what it means to be a "party man." His father, a scientist
and executive at one of Italy's largest pharmaceutical companies, was
a member of Mussolini's National Fascist Party, serving two terms
in parliament.

Morselli was by all accounts a lonely, antisocial child who struggled at school but found a world to his liking in writing and books.
At age eight, no less, he started his first novel, *La mia vita* (My Life),
and wrote prolifically ever after. The death of his mother in 1924,
when he was twelve, devastated the boy and his three siblings, who
were then raised by a housekeeper in a period of acute national flux.
In the fifty-odd years that Italy had existed as a nation-state, it had

been host to zealous throngs of Fascists, anarchists, syndicalists, re-formists, interventionists, socialists, and Communists, ever splintering into yet more polarized subgroups and unexpected new formations. Walter's near-religious allegiance to Marxism can be seen both as a manifestation of this situation and as a psychological refuge from it, a way of surviving the constant political convulsions of the era in which he, and Morselli, came of age.

Morselli, as a young man, sought to please his father by studying law and taking a marketing job at a chemical company, but eventually he asserted his natural bent by writing reviews, essays, and a study of Proust, which came out in 1943. During World War II, he served in the Italian army; after the war, his father provided him with an allowance to support his intellectual pursuits.

At first he holed up in the family summer home in Varese, but in 1952 he bought a parcel of land and built a house near the Swiss border, just outside Gavirate, where he would live alone for the next twenty years. He collected a large library (in addition to Proust, he favored Flaubert, Musil, Kafka, and Svevo). He had intense liaisons with women, proposed to one who refused him, never married. He also wrote nine novels in all. None of them was published in his lifetime.

The Communist, written between 1964 and 1965, was his fourth full-length work of fiction, and it was soundly rejected by Italo Calvino for lack of verisimilitude when Morselli submitted it to the publishing house Einaudi. (Calvino had been a member of the PCI for years, but resigned in 1957. His collected letters reveal the extent to which his membership consumed him.) The *Encyclopedia of Italian Literary Studies* describes "Italo Calvino's letter of rejection, dated 5 October 1965 ... as one of the most embarrassing documents of shortsighted literary judgment." Further: "According to Calvino, one does not write a good political novel by demystifying the untouchable reality of the Italian Communist Party." Shortly thereafter, the publisher Rizzoli accepted *The Communist*, but a change in management led Morselli to pull it and return to his solitary discipline.

There's a great comic scene toward the middle of *The Communist*, when Walter pays a visit to his friend and doctor, Amoruso, an educated and cultured man with a sophisticated wife. While Walter's there, Amoruso's friend Alberto Moravia drops by. Moravia of course is the author, then at the height of his fame, but Walter doesn't have the least idea who the great visitor is, the one asking him what he thinks of "socialist realism." Walter replies that "realism is not confined to socialists. Everyone, socialist or not, has relations with reality. It can't be eliminated from life. Whether it can be eliminated from literature, I don't know, but it doesn't seem to me a requirement for literature." Moravia, who knows that Walter's views are unorthodox, not to say positively heretical, asks Walter to write a piece for the journal he edits. Walter, exhilarated, obliges by turning in a piece in which he wonders whether the Communist Party shouldn't seek to liberate the working class from the burden of labor, an even more heretical proposition. It will be the source of many problems for him afterward.

It's hard, in any case, not to hear Walter's reply to Moravia as Morselli's own retort to the gatekeepers of Italian fiction. Italian publishers could not appreciate any of the veins he worked in, not speculative and dystopian fiction (Rome Without the Pope, written in 1967; *Dissipatio H.G.*, written in 1973), not counter-history (*Past Conditional*, written in 1970), and certainly not the naturalistic, astute, psychological portraiture of *The Communist*.

Then again, Cosimo Stifani has noted in his paper "Morselli Antimoderno": "Morselli's intellectual isolation allowed him to explore different directions . . . an otherwise difficult task to achieve within the Italian literary milieu, so rigidly driven by Marxist mythologies."

Brave Morselli. While working on *The Communist*, he wrote to Alberto Moravia. Did he mind being mentioned in the novel Morselli was working on? Moravia's brief reply was hardly encouraging, and epically condescending. No, he didn't mind, he wrote, but: "It's usually difficult to introduce living persons in a work of the imagination."

Morselli paid him no heed, introducing not only Moravia but Togliatti and several other grandees of the Italian political land-scape.

In 1973, shortly after finishing the novel *Dissipatio H.G.*, in which the protagonist spends Italian Republic Day in a cave pondering sui-cide only to emerge and find a world destroyed and empty of human beings, Morselli shot himself in the family house in Varese. He left a simple note: *Non ho rancori*. (I bear no grudges.) A folder full of re-jection letters was found on his desk, a flask drawn on the cover. *Un fiasco*—a symbol of failure.

With ironic inevitability it was only now that this neglected writer's compositions were at last found to be stunning, varied, bril-liant. Morselli was said to have been ahead of his time, a genius, and the publisher Adelphi brought out his novels, one after another, in the course of the 1970s. Several were translated into foreign lan-guages. Pierre Ysmal, reviewing the French translation of *The Com-munist*, went so far as to say that Morselli's "rigor and probity better explain Communism than all the books written by 'exes' who too often attempt to even the score. With this book Morselli joins the ranks of the rare great writers of the Communist world."

In *After Words: Suicide and Authorship in Twentieth-Century It-aly*, Elizabeth Leake discusses how Morselli's suicide has shaped in-terpretations of his work, and how his failure to publish any of his novels came to shape their making. For instance, *Past Conditional*, an ingenious alternate history of post–World War I Europe, is inter-rupted by a lone chapter titled "Critical Intermission—Conversa-tions Between the Publisher and the Author." It's an eight-page self-immolation. The "publisher" demands: "Do you honestly claim that this blatantly apocryphal version of contemporary history which you have submitted, so full of questionable theses and so short on appeal from every angle, can go by the name of a novel?"

Morselli may have had the most bourgeois of upbringings, but he and Walter Ferranini have a good deal in common. Walter Ferranini is a martyr to Communism. Guido Morselli was a martyr to art. *The Communist* is, among other things, an exercise in self-portraiture.

I'd like to recognize Frederika Randall's graceful and nuanced work on this novel's behalf—a literary feat in its own right. No matter how great Morselli's novel, it takes a master translator to cast the spell afresh.

For the English-reading public, there's still a great deal more to know about Morselli. There are novels yet to be translated and the soulful diary he kept for decades. Once you have read this novel, you are likely to care much more about this. You might even decide to visit Morselli's haunts, such as the property he left to the city of Gavirate, where to this day one can visit Parco Morselli. By the fields and forests through which he walked and spent his days, looking over Lago di Varese and beyond to the foothills of the Alps, the house still stands where Morselli wrote this profound, restless work.

—Elizabeth McKenzie

THE COMMUNIST

I

DEBATE (repose) in parliament. It was question time and the conditions, dreadful, of the State Railways were the subject at hand. The chamber's population, already sparse, had shrunk further as always happened when technical matters were being discussed—all but on the left-wing benches, where the questioner sat. Despite the back and forth between questioner and minister (Angelini) the atmosphere was drowsy, and a weak polemical note introduced by the far right brought only a flicker of mirth and annoyance. The interruption came from the neo-Fascist benches; the voice, with its stout Sicilian cadences, strove for irony.

"You complain that the trains arrive late. You understand, Honorable Boatta, do you not, that your criticism necessarily takes us back to those days when there was one man above all who could make Italian trains run on time?"

"And it cost us dearly," was Comrade Boatta's swift reply.

But the other man persisted. "Not only the trains ran in those days. Sad to say, this pusillanimous *Italia* of ours—"

Here Boatta lost his patience. "Learn to speak Italian, Fascist! In Italian, we do not say *Itahl-yah*."

"Right, I should learn from you. You, who say *Itaglia*, with the *g*. Peasant."

There was a titter from the center benches. Dini, the deputy from Lucca, growled, "Oh, come on, you think we haven't noticed you don't even know how to say Italy?"

From his high seat as president of the chamber, Leone leaned forward to make his presence felt and (a stab at wit) said that "from regionalisms" it was time to move on to "rails." Comrade Boatta raised his clipped gray beard once again, and observed that there was nothing in the least bourgeois about wanting trains that respected timetables, railcars that were modern, conductors dressed in decent cloth and not some shabby worsted.

"It is not only the bourgeoisie that uses trains but above all the workers, just as it is workers who make them run. With toil and sacrifices, as Ferranini, here next to me, can tell you, being the son of a railwayman who died on the job, and a railwayman himself.

"Furthermore," the elderly Boatta plowed on, to the revived indifference of his colleagues, "beyond the railroads we have other public services that are backward and badly organized. Is the telephone system, so important for production and by extension for the workers, at all satisfactory? The Italian postal service is the slowest in Europe. This morning I received a letter here in Rome. My niece mailed it two days ago in Turin."

Now Leone intervened. "You asked to question the transport minister," he croaked, "not the minister of posts. And spare us your personal correspondence, it is of no interest!"

Comrade Ferranini, who was just barely listening, smiled, feeling pleasantly lethargic. Sitting at his bench and resting his elbows on his desktop, he ran his hands though his graying hair. He was taking his repose and he didn't even need to reproach himself: how pleasant. When Comrade Boatta had said his name, he had for one incongruous moment been afraid he would be called on to speak; he, who in five months of parliamentary session had never even spoken once. He had been assigned to a committee that met rarely, the most pacific and least-industrious committee in parliament, in which his silence was no more remarked upon than it was in the chamber. The party, too, asked little of him, perhaps because in Rome, where he had never set foot at party headquarters before his recent election, nobody knew him. Apart from a few inspections on behalf of the administrative offices, he had no duties at all. On Sundays, there were the rallies assigned to members of parliament on a rotating basis; so far, he had led no more than three or four.

Ferranini, Walter. From Reggio Emilia. The last to know that "Italy's Kiev" was well represented by him. Both the shortcomings and the merits.

A real man of the base, accustomed to the base's lively, immediate, human political contact. By no means free of any personal ambitions, Ferranini had always confined them to his home territory and satisfied them there. When he had agreed to stand for parliament it had cost him some considerable regret, a fear of betraying his real calling, an unease from which he was just beginning to recover. To his comrades in Reggio who had put him on the list, he said, "So, you are sending me into retirement." And in some ways, he did feel he had been set aside. He could not pretend, in those intervals he spent back home, to recover that connection between himself and his people that had been interrupted, nor could he resume his previous responsibilities. In Rome (and this he had predicted) no opportunities presented themselves in the party hierarchy, and quite honestly, he recognized he was neither prepared nor keen to take on such a role. The twelve years of work behind him were not relevant, and his experience organizing was too specialized to employ in a much larger sphere, far from the situations and the men familiar to him.

In other ways, he hadn't been unhappy in Rome, and he had ended up settling there. When he returned to Reggio or to his native Vimondino, some twenty kilometers from Reggio, he stayed one day at most. He didn't mind the parliamentary routine, the way that deputies in a great party clung together ("Here, we are choristers with our mouths shut," he wrote to the faithful Oscar Fubini). There were no decisions to make, no initiatives; however, he told Fubini, there was much to learn and much to understand. He had come to terms with parliamentarianism. He no longer thought of how, during the electoral campaign of '53 in the days of the *legge-truffa*, the fraudulent new voting law, he had called parliament (employing a certain scientific slant that ran through his speeches) the "locus of points" of phony formal democracy. Study had always been a passion, and he had nearly always had too little time for it. Now, with many free hours a day, he was able to satisfy that desire. His knowledge of Marxism, although it was firsthand, was disorganized, inconsistent. He applied himself to perfecting it, tenaciously, scrupulously; it seemed to him a way to resist inertia and conformity; it was what a good socialist would do. Those few who tried to flush him out at his lodgings on vicolo del Leonetto, lodgings that were not very inviting, and he even less so, found him taking notes on the classics, intense and ruffled, in shirtsleeves, like a student preparing for his exams. A thermos full of coffee and—that final touch that completed the modest genre painting—a birdcage on the windowsill. He was growing lazy; it annoyed him to have to drag himself out to Civitavecchia or Rieti for the Saturday or Sunday rally, he who back in Reggio would travel the length and breadth of the province all week, running automobiles into the ground, and coming back at night hoarse and exhausted.

All too aware of his inertia, and perhaps the only one there who didn't attribute his idleness to the sirocco or Roman ways, he wondered if it wasn't a symptom of premature aging. Or worse, far worse, the first sign of petit bourgeois regression. One night he rose from his bed and paged uneasily through his texts to see whether sloth was not one of the symptoms by which one could recognize those whom Marx called "vacillators." Luck was with him and he found the passage right away ("The vacillators are the weak, half-hearted, and irresolute") and went back to sleep peacefully.

It was his enduring good fortune that he paid only moderate attention to his own private ego. Soul-searching and inner dialogues were neither lengthy nor frequent with him; it was just that after forty-four good years, the fatigue had become too much. He had played out his role. Started out as a kid slaving and toiling away; never enjoyed even a bit of the good life; well, now he felt the need to take it easy instead. A man past his prime, no; now that he'd been in Rome for a while things were improving, although a few little troubles remained: that ache at the base of his neck, a few signs of hypertension, some shortness of breath, a bit of arrhythmia, which one of his parliamentary colleagues, Comrade Amoruso, an internist, had diagnosed (informally, without having examined him because Ferranini preferred not) as chronic fatigue accompanied by mild functional heart disease, in part psychogenic. The party, by bringing him to Rome to rest, had shown him its providential participation in the life of the individual, and so he would use the leisure to fully restore his health. A new call to action might come at any moment, and in the meantime, to sit there in the chamber with his comrades and his superiors was not to do nothing. Even there, one served. There was certainly nothing wrong with that. If anything, he thought (but not sanctimoniously, that wasn't his way) it was a privilege he didn't deserve.

Boatta had finished. He stated that Angelini's reply was unsatisfactory, and in fact it was not very satisfactory, and then other questions were raised, now by the Christian Democratic side, in collusion with the government. Sham, of no interest. Ferranini sat back more comfortably in his seat and gave up looking through the newspapers he'd brought with him. Two rows below him, Palmiro Togliatti was going through his mail, writing undisturbed; there was a little pile of books on his desk and Ferranini was able to make out the title of the one on top: Montaigne, *Essais*. For a long time he gazed respectfully at what he could see of the person of his leader. The thick, still-dark hair on his head; the motionless, firm shoulders and forearms, which bespoke a serenity and a force that seemed to him majestic, uniting ideas and action. Then he gave a start: Togliatti had stopped writing, turned halfway around, and was staring at him through thick lenses. But he didn't recognize him. He was famous for not recognizing faces, and they had only had the briefest of contacts. No matter: Ferranini savored the composite pleasure of trust and subordination; he felt happy that he somehow belonged to this man.

Among the newspapers on his desk he picked out a telegram that had been delivered to him at the beginning of the session. It came from Reggio, from home, in short, the only (large!) family he had. It informed him that two friends were coming to Rome, leaders of the Farmers' Cooperative of Guastalla, and he had to smile because the two had signed themselves "Amos and Vittorio Bignami, directing

Italy's first kolkhoz." What did you want to bet they had already arrived and were there in the chamber? He looked up, and there they were, in fact, the very same. The sole spectators to that colorless assembly, fists up to salute him, two scrappy cousins with red carnations in their buttonholes sitting in the public gallery. He signaled them to remain calm; they were capable of shouting out loud and making themselves obvious, and Togliatti wouldn't like that. He waited, leafing through the newspapers, until the other man moved. Togliatti continued writing, sitting at his place for another half hour, until eight o'clock, and meanwhile those two up there could be seen talking back and forth and pointing out the various party benches in the chamber.

Outside, they embraced, and not long after, examining him by the light of a shopwindow on the street, Amos Bignami reassured him: "You haven't changed." Ferranini misunderstood.

"Should I have changed? You mean parliament, maybe? Or Rome?"

"No, no, don't be silly. You're still thin, sure; still have that look of a kid, or a poet. Our Ferranini, you are. Hey, we came here for you, you know, to tell you about Vimondino, that little town of yours half submerged by the river Po."

"Always under water in November, our hometown. Why don't you ever come to ask for help against the Farm Owners Consortium instead?"

"Well, so you know we're fighting them, like mad. *Como los moros.* Kruger against Lopez, remember in Spain? Like that! We don't have a choice, believe me. They're going after us. There have been some changes in the Federation, but you know about that."

"And how are things going with Inter-Agraria?"

"Not so smooth there, either. We'll tell you about it."

He led the way to his trattoria on a side street near via dei Coronari, a place not haunted by his parliamentary colleagues and so to his liking. The two Bignamis, Amos more than Vittorio, reported at length, in that polite and deferential way of resourceful subordinates (Ferranini had never had to do much more than outline the political directives with them) and then went on to tell him the town news. They didn't live there but each of them had a piece of land nearby, and they knew everyone and everything. They spoke at length, not eating much. Ferranini ate happily, as usual. Bent over his plate, his left hand pressing a napkin to his chest, with great concentration, although he listened and asked a question now and then. A frugal man—with a liking for simple things, that is—who enjoyed his food, in silence if possible, it seemed (and it wasn't just semblance) that when he ate, he thought of nothing else. His lady friend Nuccia (or better, Annuccia) had decided that though there was no hint of sensuality to it, he was a "serious eater," that is to say, profound, even in that, and scrupulous, while he pointed out to her that he came from a family that had suffered from pellagra—from hunger, in other words—right up into the twentieth century.

Vittorio Bignami, abstemious although he had the purple cheeks of a wine drinker, had been Ferranini's first aide back in '46 when he began working in the cooperatives, and he wanted to know whether he was still dealing with the co-ops here in Rome, and if they'd given him duties in that regard, and what they were. He was astonished to hear they hadn't.

"Okay, but really, Ferranini, you have nothing to do with them? You, one of the greatest cooperativists of our times?"

"Sure. And the Farmers' Cooperative of Guastalla is a kolkhoz," said Ferranini. He had finished eating and now resumed speaking.

"They don't appreciate you? What about Il Migliore, doesn't he know you? You were sitting near each other."

"There are a hundred and forty of us in the lower house alone. But look, you ought to know that the base is one thing, the center is another—two worlds, like water and air, you might say, and the man who lives in one isn't made to live in the other; he doesn't have the organs."

"It's not right."

"It's perfectly right. I'm here to represent the base, not to advance it from above. Different functions, different capacities. I go to the head office a couple of times a month and I still haven't learned how the departments are divided up. You have to understand that the party here is a huge, complex structure. But let's talk about what we know, my friends. Vimondino. Honest territory, rich territory, but a bit dull, eh?"

"Oh come on, Ferranin'! Dull. Dull!"

It was a territory of landowning farmers, and not even such very small farmers; many of them had twenty, twenty-five *biolche* or more (1 *biolca*, about 3,000 square meters). The town was flanked by the railway that ran from Reggio north to the Po; around there they called it the land of priests and poplars, something of an exaggeration when it came to priests, of which there were only two—the parish priest and the chaplain of San Donato—but certainly it was a politically thankless place. Scarce in support for the progressive parties, more open to the Christian Democratic side, not without a putrid residue of Fascism, with 290 votes (out of 1,200) for the neo-Fascist party in the '53 election. Landownership in Vimondino had begun in the twentieth century. That is, with the demise of the feudal lord, a certain Count Giarrentani for whom the Vimondinesi had worked as sharecroppers.

Around 1902, his appetite whetted by the fortune one of his former tenants had made manufacturing cured meats in Modena, Giarrentani opened his own cured-meats company in Reggio and engaged in a brisk competition with the other man, even imitating his brand name. The first contemplated revenge. He waited until the bully count had expanded and put all his capital into the company, then in a few short months, lowering his prices week by week, he drove him to the point where he had to sacrifice his factory and then his lands. Giarrentani was barely able to hold on to the villa where he lived in Vimondino, and he had to endure the humiliation of seeing his old sharecroppers become his peers, for the winner of the match, who had no interest in keeping the lands, sold them one after the other at very convenient prices, and so for once, a war between capitalists brought good fortune to the workers.

The town was the only one in the province of Reggio to produce hemp, a hemp famous for its quality; the buyers arrived from England and snapped it all up. Under King George, the ropes on more than one of His Majesty's ships were woven with Vimondinese hemp. The sharecroppers-turned-bosses recruited field hands (going up in the Apennines to find them) for the hardest work. And they basked in their indolence, their miserly well-being, quite foreign to the political energy of the rest of the province, and for that matter to Emilia as a whole. The impatient socialist Ferranini once held a rally in Vimondino; no one showed up, and he refused to go back there. The town produced a couple of interventionists between March and May 1915, and later quite a few *squadristi* ready to take part in the tamer exploits of the Bolognese Fascist boss Leandro Arpinati.

Amos, the older of the two Bignami cousins and older than Ferranini himself, could remember a thing or two from those earlier days.

"Arpinati treated the people from Vimondino like chicken thieves. His exact words were: 'You people are only good for stealing chickens.'"

Among the few people there, none of them natives, who kept his eyes open politically was Mirko Ferranini, Walter's father, who had come from Cesena to Reggio in 1910 to work as a fireman on the Reggio–Guastalla line. As a young man he'd belonged to a cell of anarchists, an offshoot of that Bakunin League of Young Romagna that had given the movement some of its least hotheaded and most coherent men, such as Capriani. But even Mirko, who had married in '16 after being promoted to engineer, grew tame. A railway engineer is a precision instrument, he would say, and it was clear that meant a man of order. The Red leagues after the war, the popular uprisings in Emilia against the growing forces of reaction, had little effect on Vimondino, or on Mirko Ferranini either. Only in the spring of '21, when in America, in Dedham, Massachusetts, Sacco and Vanzetti were charged and threatened with the electric chair (not a vain threat, as it turned out), did Mirko begin to come back to life. They were martyrs of his old faith, and suffering with them, although far away, he finally felt himself redeemed. He wrote to the elder of the two, Bartolomeo Vanzetti, and some months later he had a reply from prison. He wrote again, and Vanzetti replied, and in the last of those letters he said, "Yes, all power to anarchism, but now we must close ranks. It would be wrong to spend our forces and squander our hopes. The revolution that has triumphed over the tsar is a worthy cause for the sons of Bakunin." The engineer, who had decorated the kitchen and bedroom of his house with photographs of the martyrs cut from the newspapers, did not understand poor Vanzetti's counsel, or decided not to speak about it, but the seed bore fruit in his son. Walter Ferranini (one of the few Italian Communists of today to have read the works of Malatesta and other masters of anarchism) was a socialist even before he became a man.

He got there all by himself, without knowing (without any way of knowing, in Italy between '29 and '34) that socialist doctrine existed—or socialist reality. He glimpsed certain truths—that liberty was merely a formal right; that capitalism depersonalized human beings—on his own, in a sudden burst of revelation, the way a fifteen-year-old boy will guess what a woman's body is like. But he was, and would remain, a simple soul, despite a crude speculative instinct that pushed him to seek out ideas, to dig into them; and he was modest, although spontaneous and direct, qualities that usually didn't accompany modesty. He never made much of his political education, although it was certainly precocious. More than once Ferranini had thought, and said, perhaps even to one of the Bignami cousins, "If I am a good socialist, I cannot take the credit. I couldn't lean to the right because that was to go against nature. Nor to the left in the sense of an anarcho-syndicalist, because that made me think of Vanzetti; I'd been immunized for life against that side." (He had kept those three letters, and promised himself he would go and pay homage to the tombs of Sacco and Vanzetti, wherever they might be.)

He too suffered from temptations. But not of the faith; if anything, it was his vocation as a militant that was threatened. His greatest temptation was tied to a peculiar, vital craving, of mysterious origin but already quite overwhelming when he was just a child growing up in the country, a child who in summertime would lie on his stomach looking down into the pits where the hemp was retted (giving off a stink worse than the sewer), brooding on the worms and larvae that swarmed on the water's green slime. That same craving sent him into town to search the book stalls for tattered old editions of Fabre's insects or Maeterlinck's life of termites. A craving to flush the spiders out of the attic and the toads from the ditches and classify them. A magnifying glass he'd been presented by Zanasi, the teacher in Vimondino (from Ferrara and a Fascist, the same Zanasi who at Porta Po in Ferrara in '27 foiled the attempt on *ras* Italo Balbo's life), that poor magnifying glass was to hang from his neck for years on a piece of twine.

Finally the craving became conscious, and thirteen-year-old Walter understood that to satisfy it would mean sacrifice, and, what was harder, asking others to sacrifice. "All I can do," his father said to him, "is to let you keep on studying without considering you crazy or a slacker." The boy was persistent, and lucky, too, for a while; he knocked on many doors and in Reggio found a pharmacist, Bignami (another one), who had many children and took him in as a babysitter and shop boy, and in return gave him room and board and allowed him to continue his education. He grew fond of him and looked after him and even got it in his head the boy might study to be a pharmacist. Ferranini turned to Amos who was taking his coffee.

"Oh, remember the pharmacist near the hospital? A widower, with a lot of children?"

"I certainly do; he was a relative of ours," said Amos. "Distant relative. One of those pale-faced socialists like Turati. You know what happened to him right after the Great War, in Bologna?"

"No."

"You, Vittorio, did you ever hear about it? The thing was that the Socialist Congress was being held in the Teatro Brunetti in Bologna and Bignami the pharmacist, who was the organizer, met Anna Kuliscioff, and fell in love with her. And she with him, at the time. And you know, she was over fifty years old! All hell broke loose. Turati was as jealous as a wild animal; it almost led to another split among the Socialists."

With the pharmacist's help, young Ferranini had finished the gymnasium and was in the first year of liceo. His goal was approaching, it was becoming clearer before his enchanted eyes: Bologna, university, biology. "Biology," said Ferranini; it was a word that had once set him shivering like the name of a first love, just the sound of it. Then came that terrible December of '29. In just one month his father was dead of pneumonia and Walter had said farewell to school and was back in Guastalla working as a loader at the railway warehouse, to help out his mother. She'd been left with a pension of ninety lire, her mind was undone by misfortune, and the neighbors were afraid she would throw herself under a train. But it was her heart not her head that went to pieces; she died in '31, not even forty years old, of an aneurism. That same year the carabinieri found a packet of leaflets in the station depot where the young man was working, leaflets he was supposed to take home that evening. To distribute among his apathetic, sometimes hostile fellow townsmen.

"Emilia Was and Will Be Red," was written at the top of the leaflet. Fired on the spot, an orphan without relatives or a home, young Walter had learned, directly, painfully, what real labor was. At the station warehouse he sometimes loaded six thousand kilos of milk all by himself and all in one day. Fatigue had marked him permanently, and had clarified certain aspects and problems of labor that no theoretical study can ever teach. They took him on at a small shoe factory at San Donato (he stayed for seven years), and there too it was all toil: packer, driver, porter, loader and unloader of crates, heavy rolls of leather, great demijohns of acid, from six in the morning to seven at night. He didn't have the constitution for heavy labor, and the weariness wasn't just in his mind. When he was called up and went for his medical exam, they found a heart murmur.

That was a nice piece of luck, wasn't it; it meant they gave him an exemption. (He had finished eating and was going over that chapter of his life with the two cousins, letting the hour pass until it was time to get up from the table.) Because if the army hadn't rejected him, Abyssinia awaited, and perhaps Spain.

"Instead," said Vittorio Bignami, "we went to Spain on the right side." He plowed on, certain of what he was saying. "Which is why, you see, it makes no sense that you aren't getting ahead here in Rome too. In the party. You've played all your cards right."

Ferranini, however, was annoyed by his insistence. "First of all, remember that I wasn't here during the Resistance. Someone of our age who wasn't a partisan is a second-rate communist."

"You weren't a partisan because you were in America. How long was it?"

"Five years."

"And it wasn't your fault. You went there after fighting in Spain because you couldn't come back here. And you've also been to the USSR. There aren't many like you."

"Come on, friends, let's be serious," said Ferranini, not very nicely, his temper souring. "I spent forty days in the Ukraine, nearly all of it in the countryside. What I know of the USSR is just about enough to be able to say that our cooperatives in Reggio Emilia—"

"*Your* cooperatives."

"Let's put it this way: there's night and day between them and a real collective enterprise. I mean in terms of mentality. I've said it over and over: what we do here gets done for our own filthy interests."

The Bignami cousins looked at each other and tried to laugh.

"My friends, there's little to laugh about. We are individualists, the opposite of socialists; we think about the land the way we think about a girl's titties. We lust for ownership, although we use the language of collectivism."

He grew heated as he went on. His seriousness was all out of proportion; that wasn't unusual in Ferranini.

"In Russia they may be less advanced than we are in terms of technology, say, machinery and seed, fertilizers, insecticides, silos and dairies, baling, but let me say this, they have gone way beyond our concupiscent mentality. That's the difference, and get it into your heads, otherwise all my preaching is for nothing."

"It's the world we live in," said Vittorio, "the capitalist system."

"What the hell, boys, are we supposed to change the system or not?"

"We've had our coffee," said Amos, gently trying to distract him, "and we forgot the cheese course. What kind of Reggio natives are we?"

The waiter came to clear the table and they asked him to bring cheese. Once again they ate in silence, although Vittorio did take the opportunity to admire the "titties" of two flowery, out-of-season female tourists (Germans? English? you had to be in Rome to see them) who were just then sitting down not far from their table.

Amos was commenting on the cheese, a Reggiano, with his mouth full. "This is the genuine stuff, made in winter, from two milkings. Once upon a time there was hardly any of it on the market; it didn't get as far as, I won't say Rome, not even Bologna. After the war, it was the steel vats instead of the wooden buckets, the electric heaters in the dairies, that made production expand, and for that to happen, as you know, Ferranini, we had to have workers' collectives like the farmers' cooperatives, and the other cooperatives, we needed Collina, Maccaferri, and (say it proud!) the Bignami cousins. We've done a lot, even if you're not content. There are billions that don't go in the bosses' pockets, billions shared by the workers."

Ferranini, still eating, shrugged his shoulders.

"You," Amos went on, "have always been too modest, in Spain, at home, here, everywhere. Did you tell them, at the party, that you can speak Russian? Did you tell them you correspond with the top scientists of the Soviet Union?"

Ferranini glanced around the room. "Get out of here, Bignami. Hush. Soviet scientists have better things to do than write to me."

"Oh, we learned about it from Fubini in the Federation, isn't that right, Vittorio? What was he called, that big-shot professor at the University of Moscow who wrote to you? Bosciàn?"

His face clouded once again. "Stop this nonsense. I wrote to him; I learned some Russian just for that. I wrote Oparin, Bosciàn, Lepeshinskaya, back in '47 when I was still a kid. I had a passion for biology, and I used to study on my own. Oparin had just discovered the Koatszervatnyi mechanism, coacervates, it's a bit difficult to explain."

"Hey, Fubini told us they wrote to you too."

"Fubini should mind his own business. They replied to me—that was it. Bosciàn, one of the greatest biologists who ever lived, wrote: 'I don't have much to tell you; I'm only a veterinarian.' And you call *me* modest? Give me a break! Bosciàn had understood the mysteries of the cell, the origin of life itself."

The second Bignami, Vittorio, the chief organizer inside the Federation, now spoke up. Animate matter and its cells had brought to mind those cells, equally important, that were his daily bread: the party cells of Reggio and the province. The ever-perfectible science of organization was just what he wanted to talk about, and the conversation picked up and became animated. Ferranini saw that he could have been more indulgent with them. He was quite happy to see his two comrades, and in any case he would gladly have done without his reputation as difficult (utterly honest, true-blue, but hard to know how to deal with and so avoided by many). In the end, it was always the politicians who needed politics more than politics needed them.

Close to 10:00 p.m., as they were getting ready to leave, the owner came to say that the Honorable Ferranini was wanted on the phone. Nuccia? Could it be? It was rare that his friend called him in a public place, even at the trattoria. He had so often warned her to be careful.

But yes, it was Nuccia. She was at the station, waiting for a train, summoned to Milan by her publishing house. They were concerned about the store. (They had sent her to Rome a few months earlier to manage a bookstore in the center.) And there were going to be complaints because, it was true, she wasn't selling much, although she'd gotten herself sent to Rome promising to salvage a business that was in trouble. But it was not her fault; the bookstore was a hole, the staff transient, and Romans didn't read, or only newspapers on the bus, over people's shoulders.

"It's all right; I can take care of myself. Believe me, they won't budge me from Rome. I'm worried about Giulia; she's in bed with a fever. I got a letter today from my father."

Nuccia was separated from her husband, and her parents looked after her child. A girl of seven. Too young, Nuccia said (quite candidly) for a mother like herself who was "too old."

"It's the flu, I think. In any case, I can't stay for more than two days. I leave Saturday night and I'll be back Sunday morning."

"Except for the fact," said Ferranini, after hearing her out, "that you can't go because the trains are canceled. There's a rail workers' strike."

He himself had been sent to speak to the Union of Railway Car Workers at Trastevere station. And Boatta had announced the start of the strike during his speech in the chamber. Three hours ago.

"No, Walter. The word came in: counterorders, comrades. No strike. I'm here and the trains are arriving and departing. Unfortunately. I was counting on it."

"That's impossible."

"Surprised, my dear? This is the way things always go for us."

"Come on, you cynic. *Qualunquista!*"

"As you like," said Nuccia cheerfully. "But we lack method, decisiveness, toughness. And you know who said that. Gramsci, of course. But also the man from Predappio." Mussolini.

"Enough foolishness," he said sharply.

There were certain matters Ferranini refused to joke about, and in any case he never joked. Not about anything. There was no getting around it: Nuccia had a streak of *qualunquismo*.

"Sometimes you lack all sensitivity. You were a partisan. Aren't you ashamed?"

"Sensitivity I have in bed, where it's more useful to you. Ah, listen. I have an idea you might like. That you *should* like, rather." Her voice was low. "Saturday night, come over to my house. You can get the key from the doorkeeper. I made the bed for you with fresh-ironed sheets."

A pause. Was she waiting for him to say, You didn't have to do that?

"I get in at seven the next morning; I'm home at seven thirty. I'll just clean up a bit. At a quarter to eight, you know Walter, we'll be ... happy. You know?"

It wasn't much. Except that Ferranini was faithful to his habits (so very faithful!) and felt at ease only in his own room, no frills and no heat. Changing beds bothered him; he was no longer young.

"So you don't want to. Oh, Walter."

Ferranini looked around to be sure the phone closet was tightly closed. "That stuff is for the luxury-lovers. Too refined for me."

"What kind of vows did you take to get into the PCI?"

Silence.

"Watch out, Walter, you'll lose me."

He laughed, finally. "No, I won't lose you. Sunday morning I'll be at the station to meet you, and we'll go home right away. We'll take a taxi."

"Well, good thing you're not proposing to take the bus," she said, knowing he was not only austere but a bit stingy.

"Ciao. Think about your daughter."

It was the longest phone conversation they'd ever had. He put the phone down with a sigh and, relieved, went back to the Bignami cousins.

2

FERRANINI, a nature uncorrupted by (bourgeois) culture and even (measured by some standards) virginal. That Saturday afternoon at the home of his friend and colleague Reparatore, he'd heard the soprano Renata Tebaldi on the record player aching with love for Alfredo. He knew opera and opera singers, and yet, as if for the first time, love *croce e delizia al cor* warmed his blood, and as he left he thought of his lady friend and felt sorry to disappoint her. He made up his mind; she lived on via Ovidio behind the Palazzaccio, the big, heavy palazzo that housed the high court. He went there on a scouting expedition (it was after all a building full of magistrates, and the two of them were illicit lovers), and found a pretext to look at the concierge's lodge and see what sort of person she was. He returned that evening, pajamas and slippers wrapped up in paper, and told her that Signora Corsi was expected after midnight and that he would wait for her upstairs. It was a stratagem dictated by the clandestine nature of their affair, and even more by his shyness, which lay beneath his skin like a second nervous system. (The simile, which irritated him, was Nuccia's. While she loved him even for this, and protectively, vigilantly.)

There was that convoluted side of Ferranini, so forthright and sincere in practical matters. Once inside, the door closed and locked (two small furnished rooms, so furnished you could hardly move), he left the light off and removed his shoes, so that others in the building wouldn't notice his presence. With all this, his heart was at peace and he slept no worse, despite the radiators, than in his chilly room on vicolo del Leonetto.

Sunday, Nuccia was right on time; when she didn't see him at the station she ran up the three flights of stairs, breathless, hoping she would find him there.

"My Walter, man of my life."

"What about the child?"

"She had a fever yesterday too, but it's the flu."

"What if you had stayed there today?" he said while Nuccia opened her bag.

"No, there was no need. It's just the flu, and there are her grandparents. I wasn't worried. Listen, do you think I'm attached to my daughter?"

"Yes."

"Good. But I don't want to hear about it now. Right now I'm focused on what I'm getting ready to do."

Five minutes later, emerging from the toilet after splashing and flushing, she was still wearing her suit. Walter, back on the bed, was quizzical.

"You're not taking off your clothes?"

"Yes, here, in front of you. What, you don't want me to, you don't like it?"

"An appetizer, you mean? I don't need it."

He never managed that kind of talk very elegantly, and it made Nuccia unhappy. But he did make up for it with genuine hunger, that he did. After the "revival" (her word), Nuccia started talking, grown expansive and clearheaded with that special gratefulness that opens a woman's mind while it numbs a man's. Sitting on her knees on the bed in the faint light of the bedroom they'd helped to overheat, she looked thinner to him, there was something infantile and at the same time tense about her, something unpleasant. Nuccia, who'd suffered in life, looked every one of her thirty-eight years. *Fèimna magra, fèimna agra*, Ferranini thought distractedly. Skinny woman, sour woman: a saying he'd heard from his father.

"So the train begins to move and I go to my compartment and lie down to sleep on the top berth. Down below is a woman in her thirties, fat, working on a portable typewriter. Business correspondence.

She apologizes, says, 'The commendatore'—she called him by his honorific—'is traveling to Milan with me,' and goes on typing. Meanwhile I'm trying to sleep. Then a fellow comes in, little guy, I can barely see him from where I am, he takes the letters, they talk, he signs them one by one. Now he's going to leave, I say to myself, it's midnight. But no. Now that the work's done, it's time for recreation. She's lying on the bunk, and he, I suppose, is groping her. Like in their own house. Wait, Walter, listen to this. She's playing hard to get. Snuggling, yes; grabbing, no. Snuggling, get it? I'm about to explode. The man, who's standing, is supporting himself with one hand on the edge of my bunk. I turn on the light behind me and look at his hand. I know that hand! Can you believe it? I recognize the gold signet ring. You know who the commendatore was? It was Cesare."

"Who's Cesare?"

"What do you mean who is he? Cesare Lonati!"

"Your husband."

"Right. I should have beat him on the head, there on the spot. But instead, listen to this, I got the giggles, coughed hard, and not too long after that he left. In the morning when we got to Milan luck was with me and I didn't run in to him. Now can I open the shutters?"

"Yes, but put on a bathrobe!" he barked. "This Lonati of yours," he went on pensively, "someone mentioned him. In the party here in Rome, it seems they think highly of him."

"You know when he joined? Before we got married, in '48, the era of the Great Fear. The PCI was taking in industrialists by the dozen, people getting their party card as insurance. And you know why they think highly of him? Because he contributes. Every year he buys eighty, a hundred memberships. And that's not all; he's in the ink business, supplies the party paper *l'Unità*, and in December he sends them the bill with, written in own hand: 'Void. Best wishes from Comrade Cesare Lonati.'"

"I'd like to know why you married him."

She pressed the backs of her hands against her eyes. "I really can't say, Walter. And to think I was already twenty-eight at the time! He persisted; he had a good position (I have to confess). I didn't get along with my mother. And I was already in love with you, as you know. I would look at you, back in those days at the prefecture, and the more I looked at you, skinny as you were (and are), the more I liked you. I told Cesare when we separated: I know a guy named Ferranini, I love him, he's the man for me. You remember that day in December '47 at the prefecture in via Monforte. Those were great times. A year later things were already slack, deflated. And I was slack too. I let myself get married, went back to being the bourgeois I was born. Now I'm paying for it."

Like her father, the mayor of Monticello, Nuccia Corsi had been a partisan in the north: the Brianza and Val d'Ossola. After the war, slogging away at some job "to bring home a university degree," she became active in the communist movement without ever joining the party, and in 1947 she ended up with the bands that occupied Milan city hall, staying to the bitter end, in what would be the extreme last action of the Resistance. From all across the Po valley members hurried to Milan in aid of those bold comrades, and among them Ferranini, at the time the PCI section head for Porta Castello, in the city of Reggio Emilia.

Instinctively he distrusted and felt annoyed by her nostalgic tone, most likely because, unknown to himself, he was even more susceptible to feverish recollections than she was. He straightened out on the bed, stretched, and said, "Better to change the subject. Come over here."

By noon he was home, where he opened some canned meat before getting down to work, and ate it sitting on the windowsill, a thin stick of bread on his knees and his feet aimed toward the table covered with books and newspapers. Comrade Ferranini's tastes were simple, those of a worker, slightly bohemian, like a student of once upon a time. Nuccia had been upset when she saw him getting dressed to leave.

"Why don't you relax? And you call yourself lazy. Let's spend the day together."

"Lazy? That's the least of it, and why I have to keep busy. I spend my life trying to be just the opposite of what I am."

Or doing the opposite of what he liked.

He had always liked study, though, and given the opportunity here in Rome, he indulged. There was plenty of time, no shortage of subjects, and that old room on vicolo del Leonetto overflowed with silence. I had to wait for my hair to turn gray in order to *sgurèr*, he thought, sitting down at the table. (*Sgurèr*: In the dialect of Vimondino and the Bassa it meant "to polish up, become less rough.")

Just recently he'd been told by D'Aiuto from the Rome Federation that they were looking for an MP to give lessons on the relationship between Marx and Mazzini. Maybe he could do it? Ferranini replied that the theme was interesting (and an issue for bourgeois propaganda as well) and that he'd be delighted to hear someone lecture on it. In short, he was there to learn, not to teach. Sincere modesty. And not excessive either, he was an autodidact. But not, mind you, superficial, not a dilettante, anything but. His knowledge was profound, maybe even excessively ruminated on, made his own. Ever since '46 Ferranini had spent most of his few hours of leisure in the public library of Reggio trying to measure up to the classics, at first in old editions of the Socialist paper *Avanti!*, large, yellow, and fragile like some ancient tome. All that fragmentary, somewhat erratic, and aggressive reading had not brought him erudition. But the Marxist picture of reality that remained an extrinsic concept for many had become vision, an optic, a natural way of seeing.

Ferranini didn't have to translate events into historical materialism. They simply presented themselves to him in that light.

On the other hand, he had to align that perspective with another that was no less natural and necessary to him but unfortunately not always congruent, although it seemed to him as rigorous: biology, vital knowledge for him in all senses. And then (it pained him although it wasn't very clear to him) there was the further problem of reconciling those two perspectives with an abnormal, furtive ambition to build abstractions that led to imaginative syllogizing above and beyond his premises and data. An aberrant instinct, somehow congenital. Which was oddly rooted in this man, if you considered the rough, practical realities he'd struggled with from birth.

After settling in Rome, Ferranini had decided (a planner, like all impulsive people with a will) to reread Marx and Engels line by line—the longest and most difficult course available to any intellectual of the last hundred years. He began with the correspondence and works after *Kapital* (paying particular attention to Engels's naturalistic-scientific treatises), taking the trouble to calculate a course of study that would last through the legislative session, and he'd been at it for four months. He'd also added Marx's just-discovered juvenile writings, a recent acquisition for all Italians. Meticulous, he always wrote a summary of what he'd studied to review the morning after, his notebook on the sink while he shaved.

He measured Engels against Cope, de Vries, Mark Baldwin. Authors equally eminent in his eyes.

He was in fact rereading a chapter of Baldwin, the positives and negatives of that definitive discovery (as he saw it), the doctrine of evolution, easily comparable to that of Marx. He was coming back to it for the second day in a row. (In the pages of Baldwin, beside the roughness of the text, there was a snare that wasn't exactly theoretical, a memory that sank into him bringing other memories, more bitter than sweet. It was the Camden, New Jersey, library, and he was young. He ordered up the book and went to read it lying on the lawn in front of the library. Now, at a distance of five thousand kilometers and thirteen years, he had to be careful to chase away the smell of that grass, the glimmer of that sky layered with white and green, white and gray clouds, never seen again.)

His juvenile crush on the life sciences had matured into a belief that science was honest, valid. Keeping close track of their results helped develop Marxist consciousness; it wasn't mere intellectual curiosity. He exacted an accord between the two poles of his interests: truth could not be sharecropped; it was inadmissible to owe one truth to Engels and another to Darwin. In his somewhat scholastic, somewhat rigid way of thinking, the numbers must add up on both sides, except when he took off on one of his chaste flights of speculation. In judging reality there were different languages, of course, different orientations. But they must all be interconnected. The reward and comfort of the scholar who bothered to get to the bottom of things was that language and orientation must finally be in accord, must merge. Without this assurance, he was unable to make peace with the apostles, the commentators, the critics. He ventured diffidently into the immense underbrush of Marxist literature, convinced, above all, that the only way to get the wider view was to perch on a treetop, *zum Wipfel stehen*: the phrase had struck him while reading Marx.

At four o'clock he changed the water for the two goldfinches, dozing puffed up with the November sun in the cage on the windowsill, and shuffled the papers on his table. (No better break than alternating tasks.) He stood by the window for a moment; from the facing window half a story up, the same two girls began their Sunday air raid on the birdcage with pellets of bread crumbs. "Good evening, *professore!*" they called out. When she was alone the eldest of the two would sometimes try out some tempting moves with her legs and skirt. On the street a noisy bunch of kids passed by with a flag, the banner of a football club. The pellets changed target, but the boys didn't notice.

"Hey, you fanatics!" the girls yelled.

Right now he had to finish examining a small mountain of tracts and documents he had obtained after long insistence (he was an MP, yes, but a Communist) from the Institute of Statistics and the Labor and the Interior Ministries, and some gleaned with less trouble from France, Switzerland, or Belgium.

Information, numbers, laws on industrial accidents. A subject he'd always been drawn to as part of the practical side of his work, but now he had to master the judicial and legislative aspects and develop a plan of action. He'd gotten to parliament and now he had a chance to act. "Accidents" (the term itself was ambiguous, unfair) were one of the most eloquent indexes of the way labor continued to be treated. And how the workers were treated exposed, with sinister clarity, the ills of the whole country: the shortage of modern equipment, confused and inconclusive guidelines, inability to predict needs, subservience to ruling-class interests. In short: Italy. Without a change in the present state of things (in the Marxist sense, without overthrowing the system), the workers would never achieve their right to be reasonably certain, when they entered the factory or the building yard, that they would come out in one piece at least physically, anatomically. To Ferranini, this was clear. In the meantime, something could be done—and must be done. He'd spoken to those party colleagues with whom he was on friendly terms. Reparatore and Amoruso. Amoruso urged him on, but he was just a doctor and saw the question strictly from a professional angle. Reparatore, who was a union leader, advised him not to entertain illusions.

"A bill of this importance introduced by the Communists won't pass. We're the opposition. Are you joking?"

"I don't joke."

"Communists do not take part in the life of the parliament, they observe and remain outside! You know the principle, you even support it."

"And if the immediate interests of the workers are involved?"

The worst came when he realized he would have little or no backing from the party. He had contacted the Research Department and received a pretty clear reply: "We've been looking into the question for some time and it's unlikely there are any genuinely new proposals to be made. In any case we are overwhelmed with work now, so it's a matter for later." He turned to the Legislative Department. The reply was much the same.

It was a hard blow for Ferranini and for several days he was seen looking sour and gloomy. Or not seen at all. Whether or not he was contradicting his principles (anyway, the one Reparatore had reminded him of), he felt useless, and felt that the hundred and forty comrades in his group were useless and idle. "Ergo, we are only here to waste time."

Amos had just written to him; the Catholics and their workers' association were raising their ugly heads around Reggio, and now a Bignami, that is, not a *no one*, had to compete with these Christian activists, loudspeakers on top of their cars and tons of paper to hand out. (Christian Democratic emissaries they were, from Verona, Brescia.) He decided it was reason enough to go up there, and only sent a telegram to justify his absence forty-eight hours later ("Chamber in session").

Back in Rome, he thought it over. Nothing, he decided, prevented him from dealing with the question of worker safety; he could study the material on his own. At some point, someone would probably even listen.

He wrote up a draft bill. It seemed pretty thorough to him, divided into three sections, his bad handwriting filling ten pages of lined notebook, the kind used in school. One: institutional reform of the agencies concerned. Two: creation of a dedicated Labor Police; creation of local technical review boards to oversee and approve all plans to build new workshops and industrial plants. Three: improved policing, stiffening fines, and penal sanctions; creation of a "black book" of employers who repeatedly violated the laws in question; the requirement that employers post public notices, outside their plants and yards, of any and all transgressions committed. Ferranini read it aloud, one hand tapping on the written pages to establish the rhythm.

Publicizing this ugly category of social crimes: would that not be the simplest and most direct way to win the battle? In his mind he saw himself speaking one on one with Togliatti (he always imagined his interlocutor was the party secretary), spelling out his ideas in detail.

"You see, Togliatti, in France, a harshly capitalist country as you know, the Bureau pour la Sûreté du Travail sends out a complete list of industrial accidents to the newspapers twice a month. And here? The Automobile Club prints up statistics of road accidents. The obligation to post notice boards outside building sites to report casualties for which employers are responsible (today effectively the norm) you found in Spain twenty years ago under the Republic. Comrade Togliatti, pardon me if I address you so heatedly. But you know, when I think of the workers who every hour of the day are victims of the careless Italian state, not just the bosses' egoism, I have a bad conscience about sitting here so comfortably, in such safety, my chest pressed to the desk."

He stopped; he was repeating the words of a letter from Marx to Lafargue. A letter about the textile workers of Manchester. Well, so what? Even a century later a socialist could feel the same dismay, the same contempt the Prophet felt. It was a sign that socialism was as timely today as always. A sign there was always something to do, to struggle against.

"Ferranini...." The soft voice at his side was softened further by a head cold.

Giordano, the cabinetmaker in the courtyard who served as doorman, spared himself the many stairs by sending his little girl to bring messages or the post.

"There's a lady downstairs. She wants to come up."

Nuccia. They were supposed to meet in the trattoria, weren't they? It was half past four. This was a breach of their accord.

"Tell her to come up."

The door opened a few minutes later and a long, mannish figure came in, wrapped up in a raincoat over a dark pullover. Came in and sat down, no bones about it. Self-assured, and apparently young.

"I come from Reggio, sent by Dottor Viscardi. I'm Ilde ——." Here the girl said a name that Ferranini didn't catch. She went on, calmly freshening up her hair: "I'm from the Press Office of the PCI Federation. Dottor Viscardi wanted you to know something confidential. But first, if I may, I'd like to speak to you about a small matter that means a lot to me. Something personal. Will you hear me out? May I speak?"

He adjusted the papers on his table. He'd never been introduced to or even seen her before.

"Go ahead," he said without lifting his eyes from the table.

"I write," the girl said, her voice shrill. "I have an article in *Poetry and Industry*. I'm writing one on structuralism. I contribute to *Menabò*. Do you like *Menabò*?"

"What's that?"

"Well, now," the girl went on unperturbed, "I'd like to get Carlo Levi to look at something of mine, now that I'm already in Rome. I'd like to see him tomorrow. I wanted to ask you to give me an introduction to Carlo Levi."

"No idea who he is," said Ferranini. He went on: "I'm a former worker, you know, not an intellectual."

Meanwhile he was thinking: "Oh, great; our people in Reggio are taking on people like this, so the workers' cause is in good hands. Delighted about that." Ferranini was one of those men who lacked a sense of humor even when it was most called for. His thoughts grew darker; the way this stranger had slunk into the Federation suddenly seemed to speak of decadence, betrayal. The fifth column of fool intellectuals in northern sections, something he'd already noticed.

"Oh what a shame you don't know Carlo Levi!" the girl went on. "I can hardly believe it."

"Would you mind telling me what this chatter of yours has to do with the Federation?"

"Sure, right away. Well, Viscardi is only interim director. That you already know. They're making his life difficult. He wants you to intervene and back him. He asked me to remind you of the support he gave you last May."

"In the elections, you mean. Well then," Ferranini replied with considerable composure, "you remind Viscardi that I earned my voters all by myself. It was the workers of Reggio who elected me to parliament. The seven thousand voters who wrote my name on the ballot were seven thousand workers who trusted me."

"Oh sorry, I didn't explain myself well. Viscardi appeals to the friendship between you. Some people in Reggio are going after him, you know, smearing him. There's Caprari of the Porta Castello section who's spreading slander. They're saying Viscardi bought himself a Giulietta sports car when in fact it was just luck, he won it as a prize last year with one of those boxes of bottles they give out for Christmas. It's Caprari who had better look out. Everyone in Reggio knows that Caprari went to Campione d'Italia this summer to gamble. At the Casinò."

Here, Ferranini lost his patience. Attacks on him as a private person (if there were any) slid right off, that cost him little, but this gossipy muck infuriated him; it was a stain, a threat, to an organization dear to him, in which he'd come of age and spent his years, and he was offended to see how coarse, how foul, were the men preparing to replace him in his work. The girl saw him glower, the muscles in his face twitching, and understood she'd approached him the wrong way. She tried to repair the situation.

"You know how things work. Caprari is ambitious, he'd like to run the Federation. And Viscardi is pro tempore, to boot."

Ferranini exploded: he was choking with rage, and he had to loosen the knot on his tie to speak. He leaned over the table.

"Ambition, you say! That's the game of politics! The dialectic produces the best. Viscardi is ambitious, Togliatti the chief is ambitious, I'm ambitious. But sports cars, gambling dens, filthy stuff, that is not ambition. It is squalid, sordid."

"Please, calm down, I'm sorry."

"Let me speak! These things are concessions to bourgeois customs; we turn our backs on the workers we're bound to defend, and who *drop dead*—do you follow me, they *die*—while we sport the symbols of a rotten class and rot in turn because they're corrupting us. And now get out of here, fast. Out, out, out!"

It wasn't easy to regain control. He was rattled, upset, mostly physically, as happened with him.

That he had a reflective bent helped. He began to rethink what he had said. He ran his eyes over the notes for his draft bill, but a different and more difficult problem came to mind. This justifying, this lionizing of others' ambitions, of his own. What gave him the right? Yes, ambition was a necessary ingredient in the political struggle, but it also opened the door to petty rivalries, individualism. And the dialectic of ambition, assuming ambition had a dialectic, was rife in bourgeois parties, too. The Communist Party, however, was only formally a party; in reality it was a church called to found the reign of collectivism. Could this task be performed by men whose prime motive was to stand out, to set themselves apart from others?

He wasn't at all sure that you could collectivize a system by doing away with equal footing for all. In the USSR they had understood that when people built cults of personality around their leaders, it thwarted the free growth of collectivism. The problem, thought Ferranini, was that the leaders themselves risked developing cults of personality; the leaders or those who aspired to be leaders, who sought and took on the responsibility of power. Yet let's be honest, people would never aspire to leadership if they were free of any tendential cult of personality. Lacking that, you might keep the faith, and maybe even be a genius, but you would always remain in the ranks. While up above where leaders were needed, the "personalities," the guides and the bosses, would be in short supply. To have leaders, you had to accept ambition, but ambition negated the spirit of collectivism.

Perhaps there was some simple way out of this logical impasse. But Ferranini could not see it. These thoughts thrashed about in him for a long while, querulous and contradictory, while he studied the two goldfinches, now awake and scuffling in a cage that was too small.

Still in turmoil, he left the house and was irritated not to find Nuccia waiting for him in via dell'Orso. She showed up late. They went off to eat.

At least he wasn't a man of petty vanity. The lavish welcome he received from the owner of the humble eating place where he took his meals annoyed him, the way the man showed him off to other customers (this way, Deputy; pleasure, Deputy), so as always he went around to the back door off the courtyard. Across the way stood the San Salvatore Cooperative Printshop, and often, before he ate, he stopped by to talk to the typesetters (there were twenty of them, and they owned the business together); he loved newsprint and watching them work. Though it was Sunday, the shop was lit up and they were working. Ecclesiastical dispensation, said Gennaro, laughing, who served as a sort of boss. Although he was indistinguishable from the others in his dress and his duties.

"The priest came over to bring us the galleys of the bulletins for this parish and five or six others. He edits them for his colleagues. And they have to be ready by tomorrow."

Gennaro, in his thirties, fleshy, pale, intelligent, had been born and brought up in Brooklyn by Roman parents from Trastevere. The fact increased Ferranini's interest in him.

"Would you go back, Ferranini? Go back to America?"

"No. What I have to do is here."

"See," said Gennaro, "here maybe something will change. There, nothing's going to change."

He was right.

"I meant to ask, Gennaro. Pella, Gonella, Togni, and company—they still giving you work?"

The printshop produced press material for some of the various factions of the Christian Democratic Party, an awful task, Gennaro had confided. There were nights when they had to set the type three times. Second thoughts, rectifications, about-faces, nervous, furious telephone calls, messengers from party headquarters, the Ministry of the Interior, parliament.

"We're buying a third linotype," said Gennaro, sounding cheerful, hoisting himself up on the stock to rest for a moment. "You're the one, Ferranini, who doesn't give us enough work. Don't you have factions in that party of yours?"

"We're all in accord," said Ferranini, bitter.

When they sat down at the table, Nuccia looked hard at him.

"Walter, you would go back to America, wouldn't you? Tell the truth." To tell the truth, he was absorbed in other thoughts.

"Look, I'm a deputy for the third-largest Communist Party in the world. But when I want to have even the least contact with proletarian life, I have to go and bother the boys at the printshop. All the PCI deputies I know are bourgeois; they're muck-a-mucks, not workers. Amoruso is a doctor. Boatta is a teacher. Reparatore used to be a notary. Which is why I feel so uneasy about staying in Rome."

"What did you do today?" Nuccia thought his face looked gray and drawn. "Don't you feel well?"

"I studied."

"Why do you have to slave over the books half the day? You don't need to study so much just to keep in touch with the workers."

Silence. Ferranini "strolled" around his plate, as they say: a piece of bread on his fork, he pushed it around and around cleaning up the sauce, having finished his portion (the first, because he always ordered the same dish a second time) of the baccalà alla veneta they made for him every Sunday.

"You know," Nuccia said after a while, "you're not in the chamber. There's no need to be so silent."

"When you're eating, you are keeping death at bay. Not to mention that we're keeping death at bay from the moment we enter this world. Sorry if that isn't a cheerful thought."

He attempted a laugh and Nuccia was sorry she'd been impatient. She couldn't say she knew her friend terribly well; they had been together some thirty times, maybe not even. But right from the start she'd had a sort of intuition about him, like the dream where you're able to recognize and read a person's mood without even being able to see his face clearly. Just now she thought she'd grasped a fundamental insight, a confession of some deep, irremovable frailty.

"What's the matter, Walter?"

"Nothing."

"I've never seen you so down. You're not well, why let them bring you more food?"

"Let me eat. I got rattled today, that's all. A girl from the Reggio Federation came to see me." He told her about the visit, leaving out the worst gossip.

"Brazen hussy," said Nuccia. "And quite capable of coming back."

"No, she's just one of those who want to call attention to themselves. One of us. All of us in politics (or at the margins) go a little too far in that direction. It's already a lot if we're not corrupt. Is Ferranini different? What do you think? I ask, but it's just a formal question, because I can judge myself, I don't need your opinion."

"And you're wrong about that. You need my opinion. I know how different you really are."

"I can judge myself," he said firmly, digging into his second serving of polenta, deep in steaming sauce glossy with fat. "Those people are my comrades. Nobody forced me to come to Rome."

"Well if you were ambitious you could have come here ten years ago. But listen, Walter, remember when you went to Marcinelle, to the mines in Belgium? Did somebody call you, send you? You were just an obscure activist deep in the provinces. You went hoping (I imagine) to give a hand to poor people in trouble. You set out from one minute to the next, without even a suitcase."

It was true: he hadn't taken so much as a razor or a change of collars. He had stayed three days. First at the mouth of the number 6 mine shaft, where the fire was worst. Then at the home of a miner from Calabria, where he waited with the man's wife and her mother-in-law until the fellow returned.

"And do you remember how I learned you were there? I read it in *l'Unità*." The party paper.

"Well, *l'Unità* gave my name. So you see, I didn't go there for nothing."

"What's that supposed to mean? You're strange. You had no way of knowing when you left home that the paper would mention you. Was it your fault that the reporter they sent came from your parts, from Modena?"

"Okay," he cut her short. "Let's move on."

They were sitting in a side room where a table was reserved for Ferranini. Nuccia moved closer to him.

"Take it easy; there's nothing calculating about you. You're true-blue, pure. Of a purity that's theoretical, out of fashion, straight from a manual for young proletarians. All too pure for my purposes!"

He laughed.

"Fine, laugh. Are you ever going to say, I'm in love? I love you too?

If I were to tell you, I've got a baby in the works, I'd like to see how that purity of yours would react. Would you say, I have to get permission from the party leadership?"

Ferranini raised his eyes to study her.

"Walter, now I can tell you: Last month I was worried for quite a few days. Or rather, not worried at all. I wouldn't be afraid of having a child with you."

"This is 1958," said a serious Walter, "and we are building socialism; the next generation will see communism arrive. My father used to say that socialism in those days, you could sum it up in *bandiere, bande, e banchetti*. Flags, feasts, and marching bands."

Nuccia, who really did love him, accepted him for what he was. She thought, "What matters is that he's not ill."

But when he got home and into bed, Ferranini *was* ill. Very ill. So much so it was a wonder the "pump" was still working.

3

WORSE than the last time.

When was the last time? March, or April. Always when the season changed. But worse this time, much worse, and those great, familiar Po valley oaths, *porca vita, porca matina*, did not come to his aid. At midafternoon his friend arrived (she'd been waiting for his usual phone call and was worried). He was in bed, his face had taken a sharp edge that made him look younger in a pitiful way. He lay on one side, the nape of his slender neck white under the bare lightbulb, and she nearly didn't recognize him.

"Walter, this is crazy, what's going on?"

The eyes that met hers wore an expression of fear and wonder. Nuccia would never forget it.

He'd been afraid. The crushing sensation had gone on too long, it was really bad. Desolately alert, he anticipated and weighed every symptom: the pain from neck to shoulder he'd felt before (the warning, even before he'd gotten into bed), the collapsing blood pressure, the heaving and the squeezing of the "pump." Breathlessness becoming suffocation. He'd been lucid, repeating the technical terms to himself: bradycardia, dyspnea. Desperate.

He didn't want to drop dead in that room. In the dark. Alone, without a helping hand: it was pure misery. The sound of his breathing did not seem to be him but a machine. He had sugared water and Coramine by his side. But he couldn't even sit up to take them. Still, everything was sharp, clear; at midnight he heard the shutters banging downstairs, someone had come home.

The dark tormented him; he was sure it was dark, unaware of the light on behind him. He listened attentively to the church bells marking the hours, heard them chime every quarter hour up to 1:00 a.m.; his sense of hearing was intact, acute: the drop of water that fell on the landing outside the front door; sometimes in hallucination, a voice that kept repeating words of reproach (he knew he shouldn't take it seriously, that it was a dream), a voice he knew, it must be Nancy. What was she saying to him? Air, meanwhile. More air.

After 1:00 a.m. the feeling that he was suffocating grew even worse. And, he saw, the muscular force of his breathing was slowly declining, the spasm that raised his chest. He thought: Now I'm at the end.

He was sweating, his brow and chin. He passed a handkerchief across his face. And then he could no longer raise his arm. The damp handkerchief lay on his shoulder.

When morning came (no one having come to wake him or bring him coffee), he was asleep, slumped on the chair next to the table, his forehead pressed onto the table, his arms forlornly spread over his papers.

He woke, and the surprise of finding himself there in that posture was greater than the terror he was coming out of. He was already forgetting. His breathing had returned to normal; there was only the weakness and a great chill. The pain in his neck was now just soreness. The *crushing* (the attack) had passed and Ferranini, a cardiopathic recidivist for the last quarter century, now had a good physical recovery, and a psychic rebound that was all too quick.

He was a man prepared for anything, not passive, fatalistic; he was even a natural optimist. He couldn't make up his mind to seek treatment. Nor to take precautions or look for medical assistance. (He'd never thought of it before, but in March when it hit him at Oscar Fubini's house, the coffee that Oscar's mother had brought to his bedside had worked, by power of suggestion, to shorten the attack.) He felt he could rely on his generally simple habits and the mediocrity of the fate that had been handed to him. Convinced that disease is in no hurry to carry off people who don't enjoy this world too much. Sometimes the attack came with warning signals, usually that pain in his neck, his shoulder, and so he would get in bed with a glass of water into which he stirred a couple of sugar cubes. It was his primary heart tonic, along with the Coramine, which he'd added after the last experience in March.

He went back to bed. He didn't feel able to open the window, the weakness was in truth exhaustion, his pulse (he tested it) was not much more than feeble. He spent hours trying to decipher the words he'd dreamed, words in another language that must mean something. *The busiest muscle, the busiest muscle.* In his cold room, he heard off and on the sounds of Giordano's tools at work.

Finally, the words came into focus. One winter evening in '42 he'd been returning from work to Camden, and it was snowing. He'd fallen ill in the car and they had taken him to a police station. They thought he was drunk and had called a doctor. Now the episode was coming together in all its minute details: the doctor was Polish, a poor devil with a threadbare necktie and a shabby bag. He examined him very thoroughly, as if he were a paying patient, and then, index finger pinned to his chest, said, "Well, mister. What's wrong with you is the busiest muscle in your body."

The busiest muscle, his worn-out heart. At twenty-eight years old. He attempted an ironic "Oh yeah?," but he didn't mean it.

The doctor was looking at him sympathetically, wanting to be forgiven for the bad news.

"Did you do heavy labor when you were younger?"

"I worked as a loader."

"Be careful. If there's a blizzard you try to stay put."

In the dream (and there were those who took dreams seriously) he was saying the Polish doctor's word to his wife. He, a man who would rather have been hanged than confess to Nancy that he was ill. In two years of marriage Nancy had never once asked how he was with even a tiny speck of interest. For half a day, in the clammy darkness of his room, Ferranini ruminated over these bitter thoughts.

When Nuccia arrived, the doorman's little girl was there. Sitting on a chair next to the bed staring at him in silence, immobile, her eyes wide. He, on his side, staring at the girl in scowling silence. They had been like that for quite some time, two creatures with nothing in common who in some way understood each other.

Nuccia had straightened up the bedclothes and turned on the electric heater. She sent the girl away. And meanwhile she tried to get him to talk.

"Nothing," said Ferranini, the negation providing him a way in. "Just some fatigue. What's the matter with you?"

"Your colleague Amoruso is a doctor. Get Amoruso to examine you."

"I already know what I have. I'm decrepit. I'm past forty-five years old."

"You can't let yourself go this way. Those eyes of yours are begging for mercy, you're unrecognizable. Promise me—"

"I make no promises to anyone. Rather, you should tell them down at the bar to send up a glass of milk and a couple of sandwiches. Damn, tomorrow I want to go up to Reggio."

And the following day, with the chamber adjourned till the end of the week, he left town.

At Termini station, the ticket collector, who was in the Quarticciolo section of the party and knew him, reminded him that this train didn't stop at Reggio Emilia.

"But don't you worry. I'll tell the conductor and they can make a special stop. You be ready—"

Ferranini was furious. "Are you kidding? Trains do not stop for individuals. Not even for Comrade Khrushchev, understand?"

He changed trains at Bologna. The north welcomed him with fog, but it was not a pleasure, that fog of his, which he usually longed for and would ordinarily have come north just to savor.

When he arrived at Reggio he got down from the train at the very same spot on the platform where one evening, maybe it was in '49 or '50, he'd come to speak at a rally for some rail workers on strike. He'd wound up his speech saying, "Today there are two dynamic points in Western communism: Catalonia and Emilia." Even that didn't please him. That was rhetoric. Him, too.

He went right off to the Federation, straight to his friend Fubini.

Fubini was signing up members. Young, intelligent, an ex–insurance man, he was quite well-informed about the question of work injuries. He asked about Ferranini's project and promised him statistics and information. But Ferranini had come to get a sense of the atmosphere inside the Federation. Where, despite everything, he still felt himself the father and patron, tenderly but also inconveniently. The position of local party chief was open and Viscardi, who'd been in the Bologna leadership and had been doing the Reggio job ad interim for three months, was up for confirmation. But Viscardi was a candidate not everyone liked, there was opposition, there were reservations from various sides, from Fubini himself.

"He's from Bologna," Fubini observed in a low voice because Viscardi was in the next room. "The environment's different here; here socialism is in ferment, the masses are different, problematic. We need energy. He's nervous and has a persecution complex, sees enemies where there aren't any. Here? Here, he probably would have enemies."

"He's spineless. And as a matter of fact I know; I know him fairly well."

"That's not true, he did his duty as a partisan and he's anything but a coward. At home in Bologna he's quite popular and Dozza is behind him."

"And his personal life?"

"He's crazy about harness racing; you can find him at the Arcoveggio track every Sunday."

"Great! Some Communist. And of course he goes there in the Giulietta."

Fubini offered to take him to Vimondino. But he was tired and decided to stay in town, to spend the night at the Scudo d'Italia. He woke late in the morning, in time for Vittorio Bignami, who had telephoned, to arrive. Polite, open, extremely well-informed as usual, Bignami filled in the picture that Fubini had sketched out the night before. At the base things were going well, even going forward; up above they were going less well because of deficiencies, interference, disagreements. And the same was true in those areas that Ferranini considered his own province: the Reggio Cooperative League and Inter-Agraria, founded by him in '53 and his creature even in the name. Inter-Agraria was set up to be an alternative to the odious, pro-government Corsorzio Agrario. For a month now Inter-Agraria had been headed up by Asvero Ancillotti, well-known accumulator of titles, city assessor for education, local metalworkers' union rep, vice president of the Chamber of Labor, and now the man behind all the sports clubs. In Reggio he was known, among other things, for his appreciation of the female sex and because he was stepbrother to the bishop of Modena.

"Ancillotti? You put him in?"

"He put himself in."

And that was not all. Before he'd gone to Rome, Ferranini had taken the trouble to name someone he trusted to head the Cooperative League, an older woman, a retired teacher both capable and modest, who'd been a Communist since the PCI was founded at the Livorno Congress of 1921. Luigia, whom he visited and wrote to, and who was, in effect, his *longa manus*, so that he did not feel entirely excluded and maintained an entry point should he wish to return. But now Luigia had confided to Vittorio Bignami that she was fed up. Ancillotti was digging the ground out from under her feet. Now that he was set up at Inter-Agraria, he'd decided—by now it was common knowledge—to gobble up the Cooperative League too.

Half an hour until noon.

"I'm going to go speak to him," said Ferranini.

"Forget it. He's at Rovigo with our football team, Reggiana, for a rescheduled match. He's our sports Duce. Anyway you mustn't seek him out, you who are altogether superior to him. After lunch he'll most likely be back, and I'll let him know you're here and see if he doesn't come over. Oh, don't forget that tomorrow you're at Favellara with us. We're celebrating the sixtieth anniversary of Workers Mutual Aid and we need you."

The "Red Hunchback" kept him waiting until evening came. The nickname was due, deformity aside, to Ancillotti's heated political eloquence in a city that itself was neither tepid nor rosy pink. And then there was the energy he'd devoted to fighting the Nazi Fascists in the winter of '44–'45. But with Ferranini he behaved as if he were shy, made a show of acting subordinate.

"Ferranini, it was you who taught us how to build socialism. We used to go to the section at Porta Castello to listen to Radio Prague and you provided the commentary. There's no third force either in foreign or domestic politics; it's either reaction or socialism, with us or against us. That was your byword. We were kids—me, the two Bignami boys, and Caprari—working with you. Here's something I remember: Saragat was supposed to come up for a rally, and the town was plastered with long, narrow posters spelling out his name. And you had as many posters printed up that said 'Is Looking Fat' and sent us out to stick them up below the others."

"I wasn't the greatest slogan-writer," Ferranini said dryly.

"What brings you here from Rome once again?"

"Again? It's a month since I last showed up."

Ancillotti saw he had been clumsy and corrected himself. "Sure, you don't come often enough. Really."

The flattering tone turned Ferranini's stomach, worsening the effect of that silly voice, the evasive gaze. He wanted to get this over quickly.

"Okay, enough chitchat. I invited you here to say two things. One, the Cooperative League needs to go forward in full liberty and autonomy, because it serves a different function from that of Inter-Agraria (which you now control), and any attempt to limit that autonomy is a strike against its very existence—an act of sabotage against the agrarian and worker masses. Two, in defending the existence of the league, I, Walter Ferranini, will use all my determination and whatever influence I may have in Reggio. And beyond."

Beyond where? In Rome? He hadn't previously caught himself bluffing like that. He was angry with himself, and even more with the other man. Who had meanwhile grown indignant.

"What are you on about? I don't get it! Ah, Luigia, you're think-ing about old Luigia Sanguinetti. A couple of days ago we were to-gether with Viscardi at the Federation. And then I put her in my car, we stopped for a coffee at Caffè Boiardo, and I took her to her house on via Vignanella. Luigia and I are bosom buddies (sorry!), even if she's a Jew and I keep my distance from Jews. A while back, at the Caffè Boiardo in fact, they were saying she'd gotten herself into a land speculation mess, outside town...."

The insinuation just gushed out, there was no escaping it. These Reggio swine fed on polenta and grana padano cheese, on polenta and innuendo. He had a copy of *l'Unità* rolled up in his right hand and he pointed it at Ancillotti's chest, forcing him back a step.

"Not another word. I warn you, not another word!"

The other man adjusted his necktie, a resounding red, gold, and blue. They said he got his way with women on account of the over-bearing flashiness of his ties and shirts in green or blue, as well as the largesse with which he dispensed gifts, and the irresistible appeal of his hunchback to the purblind sex. But with Ferranini, Ancillotti sensed he would get his way by displaying calm, a guarantee of supe-riority before a man who was weak enough to lose his.

"You wave *l'Unità* at me. And that suggests my reply to you. Very good then, we must seek unity, which builds strength. I do nothing to threaten the league's autonomy, but certainly it's unnecessary, a mistake; it's contrary to keeping our masses unified. Two different organisms are too many. Sooner or later we will have to think about unification."

Ferranini had foreseen the objection and considered it sophistry. But he admired the other man's command of his nerves and could only imitate him: "Nossir. The league does political organization. Inter-Agraria—and I can say this because I created it myself—is purely commercial. It sells seed and fertilizer, machines and tools at good prices. It makes things difficult for the local farm producers' syndicate. And in order to make things difficult, it has to work on its own. If it were openly Communist, we'd lose our non-Communist clients, the Christian Democratic growers in Coltivatori Diretti, one after another. Get it?"

"Perfectly, my dear Ferranini, perfectly. I couldn't agree more. And in fact, I repeat, I don't in any way want to see the two confused. What I'm thinking of is a close coordination like you might have if the two things were under one management, which could even be joint. I'm not building a cult of personality, are you kidding? Aren't we de-Stalinizing?"

Jerk, thought Ferranini. Who contained himself this time.

"However," Ancillotti continued, "the two things must not be in competition, as is the case now. Nor should there be confrontation. Policies must be closely coordinated."

Et cetera. He'd retreated, without altering the substance of things; the hunchback's disguised intentions were evident. At the first opportunity, he would annex the league to his own person, taking charge the way he'd already become the boss of Inter-Agraria. But Ferranini was weary; this twisted, slippery character made him feel physically ill, and the other man, in turn, was in a hurry to get away, having no interest in pursuing a discussion that seemed to be going his way. And so he was off, one grotesque fist pumping the air as a goodbye salute to his opponent.

Via Vignanella. Ferranini hadn't known Luigia Sanguinetti lived in via Vignanella. A road at the edge of town; there was an old tavern where he used to go to eat *rudéla*, country sausage and bread, back in '38 before he went off to Spain. I want to go and see if I can find it, he thought. He went out to get a car in the piazza; via Vignanella must be pretty far. But the fog dissuaded him. He wasn't well yet, and he couldn't tolerate the cold. And then, he thought: What for? Spain, and the Reggio of once upon a time, were distant, lost, like his youth.

So he went back to the Scudo d'Italia to eat something and go to bed. Lenin's view of music and music lovers was ever with him. "Unconvincing" was how he judged (and ideally dismissed, following Lenin's example) frivolous and inopportune activities: clinging to memories, reading novels, taking an interest in sport, falling in love when your hair was gray (nor did he appreciate anyone who tempted him either). As for memories, better to forget them, and in any case to leave the dead in the cemetery and the mistakes at the bottom of their slippery slope.

In the morning, the plan was Favellara. At ten the two Bignami boys came to pick him up and he was getting into Vittorio's Dauphine when someone came over. Wearing tweed and flannel, tall, elegant, breezy. Viscardi, the would-be party leader.

Here, in Italy's Kiev, guys like this were leading the proletariat.

"Ferranini, darn it! You come to Reggio once a month and don't stop by to see me? Come inside a minute, we need to speak."

"What about?" he said, by now cautious.

"Politics. You know. Today I'm going to see the prefect and you'll come along. I'll explain. Let's sit down a moment in the entry hall." He put an arm around Ferranini's shoulder and pushed him inside.

"While we're at it, let me tell you about the situation in the Federation. I've found it to be a hostile environment, I've got to defend myself on all sides. Now is that a good thing? Is it in the party's interest?"

"I'm not interested in personal matters. You wanted to talk about politics. So let's hear."

"But if I speak about myself, that's politics too! Call me to Reggio, give me a role. Give me the means—"

Ferranini got to his feet. "Goodbye. I'm off."

"Damn! One minute, there's the other issue. Look, the quarters we're in are too cramped, old-fashioned. As you know. In order to work we need space, breathing room, and some amenities. I've had a plan drawn up to build another floor. But city hall won't give us a permit, on the pretext the zoning law prohibits it. And damn if the mayor isn't a Communist, and the council too. I'm skirting the problem by getting the prefect's backing. He needs to keep us happy. But that takes the cake, no? Having to go through the prefect."

Ferranini's smile was a bit thin. "Are you familiar with the *Communist Manifesto* of 1848? Yes? Maybe you're more familiar with the betting card at the track?"

"I've always been a reader."

"I suggest you study it. There's a page where they say: The bourgeoisie is a powerful force of co-optation. It creates a world after its own image. Even among those who should be opposing it." Ferranini was at the door. "Goodbye, Viscardi!"

He got into the car next to Bignami and signaled they should depart immediately. He was pleased he hadn't lost his temper. As the automobile wove through fog and traffic on the via Emilia, he went over what had happened, avoiding undue pessimism. He'd been unlucky, his return home had not been a success. No. However, in the end, Reggio could still be the Kiev of Italy despite a Viscardi or an Ancillotti. The cult of personality could also diminish and depreciate, if a couple of people abusing their offices was all it took to expose it.

Bignami recalled him to Favellara, where they were headed. The town, with its three thousand inhabitants, was a hive of cooperativism—although not long ago a fiefdom of Turati followers who encouraged workers to act like entrepreneurs. The masons, well organized in mutual-aid societies and in accord with other local groups, were setting their prices higher than those of private companies, and they had become a local monopoly, as petty and coercive as any capitalist monopoly.

"Have no fear," said Bignami, "that's finished. When Communists replace reformers, the atmosphere changes."

"Are you sure?" said Ferranini. He laughed, but without bitterness.

They were met by the mayor and other local notables, including the priest. A worker's association, one of the oldest in the province, was observing its sixtieth anniversary and the town was celebrating. They visited a brickworks, a furniture factory, and several newly built livestock barns. All were cooperatives. After lunch there were refreshments at the Casa del Popolo. Ferranini had no desire to speak. He was hoping to get by with a few remarks in dialect, but then he remembered what he'd discovered before: the men younger than he, workers and farmers, shunned dialect and that way of speaking, even among themselves. They saw it as a mark of backwardness, of a segregation they wanted to be done with, like bicycles and those old cloaks with the rabbit-fur collars. When Mingoni, a young man in his thirties he'd known as a kid who was now a union rep and the manager of the Casa del Popolo, came forward, his manner of speaking was simple, friendly, appropriate.

"Don't feel you have to give a speech, Ferranini. Anyway, your ideas are the same ones we hold. It's enough for us to see that you still remember us now that you've gone off to Rome. And we thank you. Sincerely."

"Do you know, boys," said Ferranini taking Mingoni by the arm, "what I was thinking? That now all of you around here speak Italian, and that's a good thing. Because, proletarians of the world, unite—and to unite you must understand one another, at least at the level of the national language, and so forget about speaking Reggiano, or Modenese, or Piedmontese. It is bourgeois thought, in the guise of left-wing rhetoric, maybe, that portrays the world of labor as picturesque, that confines it to the picturesque, to dialect or slang. Therefore, no remarks in dialect, and no speeches about high politics from me. I'll just say this: If we of the cooperatives want to resist the private companies, we must do two things—"

"Ferranini," a voice interrupted, "you know we still have the portrait of Comrade Stalin hanging in the party section."

"And if you're waiting for me to tell you to take it down, you'll be waiting for a while. So, there are two things we must do. One: educate ourselves, avoid positivism and improvisation. Two: remain united, avoid rivalry on our own side. And there's another thing to guard against: being mere administrators, aping the idolatry of profit and property that are typical of capitalism. We must care about one another and avoid getting too attached to things, to money. That's the main thing. Conserve the proletarian spirit of your organizations; they must remain proletarian at the top as well as at the bottom, in purpose as well as in appearance, and the party will help you, and I, for what I can do, will help you."

One of those present, there were hundreds of them, raised his hand: a young man in overalls, with a southern accent.

"We're not all party members here. I'm not a Socialist and I'm not a Communist either."

"Are you a worker?" Ferranini shot back. "Fine, that's enough. Work and the worker come first, then the party. Listen: Camillo Prampolini was born near Favellara, a name you've at least heard. A socialist, someone who you might think was old-fashioned, but an honest, sincere man. Prampolini once said, 'If I had to choose between political coherence and the well-being of the workers, I would choose the good of the workers.' For the theoreticians, that's heresy, because socialism and the well-being of the proletariat must coincide. I guarantee you, though, only one thing matters: Act so that the workers suffer a bit less than they have always suffered ever since collective humanity existed. All workers have a right to this, even if they don't think the way we do."

Applause. More glasses raised. Bignami appeared and introduced Ferranini to a man of about fifty, big, well-dressed.

"It's Sigfrido Minelli, my friend and yours. Recognize him?"

He barely did.

"Spain, Paris, and America together. And now you snub me, Ferranini?"

It was true; for nearly two years Sigfrido Minelli, a onetime schoolteacher from Favellara, had shared his fate in Spain, in Passy, and finally in America. When Ferranini married Nancy, Minelli had been his witness. No, he didn't mean to snub him. They went to his sister's house, where he was staying, having arrived a few days earlier from New York with a wife and a U.S. passport.

Two hours, and for Ferranini a forced immersion in troubled waters. Minelli stirred them up without mercy, with the foolish pleasure of a man who's extremely pleased about his past (yessiree! among other things he'd become rich). "Remember where I lived in Queens?" "Remember that Italian place in Camden where we went for Easter?" It was destiny, it seemed: yesterday, via Vignanella; today, his companion in exile. It was to cost him, this return to Reggio.

And of course he wouldn't be free of these memories anytime soon.

Bignami left him at the hotel, with the understanding he would take him to Vimondino the following day, and Ferranini went up to his room with a bunch of newspapers. He hadn't read them yet. But he put them aside. His weary mind spooled out people, places, things, seeking some sense, some order. An up and down of slumps preceded, however, if that was a consolation, by hopeful ascents. His was a history (so said Ferranini) without a dialectic, without forward motion. Without progress, just a cycle of pointless repetition. It began, or began again, with Spain. The summer of '38 was at its height, that furious summer of '38 so hostile to the hemp pits of Vimondino, when he decided he must go and fight for socialism. Desert the entrenched battlefield that was Italy, no small task for a man of twenty-three who had eluded military service but was in the police records as a subversive. He spent months thinking, researching how to proceed. Until finally he decided he had found the way. And in fact it was the path other comrades would follow after him, like the Bignami cousins themselves.

One October Sunday in Milan, he joined a crowd of Borletti workers boarding a People's Train for an outing to Lugano. He wore a jacket, no hat, and had three hundred lire in his pocket.

From Switzerland, he was soon in France: from Geneva to Marseille to Toulouse, he followed the chain of clandestine recruitment points for the International Brigades, all of them ill-supplied, poor in everything except enthusiasm and confusion. He wandered from one to another, wasted time, found himself penniless, and was forced to stay over in Marseille, where he worked in a shipyard to put together the hundreds of francs needed to travel onward to Irún. And beyond—for once across the Spanish border he found there was no way to enlist and he had to proceed toward Madrid unaided and on his own steam, undetected in the midst of great confusion. (The whole north of the country was a huge, roiling supply chain for the front.) At Segovia, not far from Madrid, he was finally taken on by the Thaelmann Battalion and there he met Minelli, the teacher from the next town over to his. The city government was evacuating artworks from the Prado, and he and Minelli and some other Italians were attached to the soldiers carrying out this operation. (It took many weeks; his comrades nicknamed him El Letrero because on his back he had sewed a piece of cloth on which he'd written: "When the owners die, the workers live.") Then he fell ill. The pneumonia he'd come down with, spending his nights in the back of the truck under the rain, put him in the hospital at Burgos until January, and because he had a constant high fever, they moved him from Burgos to San Sebastián. Once out of the hospital, he waited for a train at the station for almost a week, until he fainted. A heart condition, as it turned out. This time they took him to a villa that had been requisitioned in Santona, where dozens of sick or wounded foreign volunteers were recovering (one of them was Palmiro Togliatti, then going by the nom de guerre Mario Ercoli), and they held him there by force. By the time they let him go back to the front, it was the end of February. He caught up with Minelli in Madrid, in time to see the Republicans fall, after a day and two nights barricaded with a bunch of others in the carcass of a German truck, and then in a cellar. A euphoric interlude, quickly deflated. They had to get out. After a desperate march to a snowbound León and Asturias, the men of the Thaelmann, nearly all foreigners, made it to the coast. They boarded a ship at Santander, among them the Bignami cousins, Minelli, and himself, Ferranini, returning inglorious (in his view), skin and bones (down to forty-seven kilograms), embittered, and dazed.

They landed near Arcachon west of Bordeaux, and passed through the countryside, where they could have found work if they'd been willing to take jobs as farmhands, for the region was quite short of labor. But the little group (Italians, Poles, some Rhineland Germans) had decided on Paris, and they proceeded on foot, stubborn, starving. At Passy began days of demoralizing inertia inside a sheet-metal hut for Ferranini, the Pole Weiss, Minelli, the Passarin brothers from Bosco Chiesanuova, and the younger Bignami. Each day one of them in turn went to offer their services at building sites or Les Halles. Weiss was the luckiest; a mechanic, he was taken on by a compatriot in a garage. By the end of the month the two Passarin brothers and Bignami were working as dockers at a river port on the Seine. In those days Walter was not strong enough for heavy jobs, as anyone could see right off when he showed up for work. And worse, he was starving. There were times that winter when five or six days went by and he and Minelli had nothing to eat but onions and a few ounces of bread. Salvation came in the person of a certain Brighenti from Modena, who had a shop and traded in wine from Barletta, Trani, and Squinzano, which he imported and used to cut better French wines. Brighenti had a brother in North America, in Chicago, where he produced canned meats, who had long been looking for northern Italians, if possible from Emilia, to work in the warehouse and as guards. Returning to Italy was out of the question. Ferranini and Minelli got written offers, and accepted. Ferranini hadn't forgotten Sacco and Vanzetti. The trip cost two thousand francs; they earned half working behind the counter at the shop, and Brighenti loaned them the rest, his guarantee the future wages his brother would pay.

It was the great holiday of the French people, July 14th, when they sailed from Le Havre, and Ferranini sent a postcard to a friend in Vimondino, with the words: "Back soon, give my regards to Nella." Before he came back with regards for Nella (at the cemetery, for she had meanwhile been mowed down by machine-gun fire on via Emilia) seven years had gone by. And he would be old when he returned, his heart damaged in every possible way. Lying on the bed, his newspapers still folded up, Ferranini remembered and grew irritated. He was irritated with himself and by himself, even as he paid involuntary homage to two impersonal and opposite abstractions: chance and inevitability. As he reviewed his own history, what he'd already understood for some time seemed confirmed. A monotonous adverse pattern ruled his life. Superficial variety concealed a rigid geometry, and the first time he'd made love to Nuccia (they were in the bedroom, just getting up from their labors), to her amused astonishment he'd told her: "The worse for you that you've attached yourself to a man who's parabolic." Okay, you could laugh, but wasn't it true that his life looked like a parabola: a sharp uptick loaded with hope and initiative, then the inevitable plunge? The downstroke of the parabola went deep into despair, but then came charging out for another ascent, in turn condemned to reverse into another dive.

No trace of any dialectical progress. Nothing but repetition in his life. As a boy, the prospect—he had sweated to create it—of study, the university, libraries, laboratories. In just four weeks, he went from sitting at a school desk to loading cars in a railway station. Spain. Sacrifice, a cause to defend, a hopeless but noble war, and a lot of high-sounding talk. Though for him Spain would come down to various hospitalizations and a desperate flight to the absolute misery of life in Passy.

Then—America. Boston, where he arrived at the place he idealized, the prison yard at Charlestown, the goal toward which until then everything had seemed to be arching, never mind the fatigue and isolation. Under the patient gaze of a guard he had meditated at length on the tombs (empty) of Nicola Sacco and Bartolomeo Vanzetti. The patient, maybe ironic guard had not told him that the two men had been cremated.

After which—the collapse.

He landed on July 19th; Minelli remained in New York, but Ferranini kept going all the way to Stickney, near Chicago. Brother Brighenti was happy to see him and set him to work packaging. Hard work, no fixed hours, but he was happy, a worker among other workers, and soon he had won them over, although they were of two races and three or four nationalities. Brighenti, who was stubborn and rough, didn't share some of his Passy brother's Socialist ideas. Employees, be they white or black, were there to be exploited. Ferranini knew that the most vigorous capitalist is the one from proletarian origins. And yet, the man had a certain instinctive sense of justice; he paid his workers well and on time. It came as a shock to all when, at the end of '39, Brighenti died of pneumonia.

A period of strikes followed. The Vogelers, two naturalized Germans who had bought the company from the widow, were highhanded with the blacks and the Italians, and when they cut the workforce, Walter was one of the first to go. He got a job with a hauling company, but with half of Chicago blocked by the strike, that shut down too. He went to a shipping company that moved grain across the Great Lakes, and they took him on as a casual worker, hiring anyone they could get to replace the strikers. But on the third day the dock was ringed with pickets, and he refused to cross the line. Ferranini the socialist was going to be a scab? The sad truth was, his meager savings were shrinking, and because he was an outsider he got no support from the unions. Everywhere he tried, the story was the same: the companies unaffected by the strike were still in trouble because the others were paralyzed; they were laying off. Where strikes had been called, companies were paying double, but you had to accept the status of scab and a police escort. In short, it wasn't from a book that Ferranini learned about the material and psychological dynamics of the strike. He went back to the Vogelers and worked for several weeks as a janitor in the warehouses and offices. In the meantime public services had also become paralyzed: cold and inertia hung over the great city. He felt secure, though; he had expectations. The "ascendant curve" (of the usual parabola) was still on the rise. He felt his life was just now beginning and that difficulties only buoyed him: He learned something from each one of them, measuring his strength, sharpening the positive qualities he sensed were emerging. He weighed the value of the general strike as an instrument of worker action, but also as a symptom of the decadence inherent in the system.

Solitary, without a friend or a woman, suffering from the cold (that winter the Hudson Bay sent blizzard after blizzard down onto the plains), he took comfort in the works of Lenin written during his hard, anxious years in Bern. He spent hours studying in the public library and he was happy. For three reasons: because he was spending his time with the father of the Revolution and the greatest thinker of modern times (after Marx); because he could improve his English by reading the texts in translation (know your adversary, know his language too); because it was a way to avenge himself for all the cold he'd endured outside. He made do with a meal and a half a day and was able to put some money aside, thanks to the stopgap jobs he found here and there: selling tickets in a cinema, working in a garage. He felt privileged; for the first time he was independent, without a boss. When he was ready to undertake the pilgrimage to Sacco and Vanzetti's tomb, the decision to leave was made as a free individual; he didn't have to demean himself by asking permission. He had money to travel and live for a few days. The Central Command of Capitalism, not just Chicago but America itself, had failed to tame him. Quite the contrary, he felt even more critical and antagonistic than before. He knew its instability, its innermost weakness.

On the train east, he contemplated the rite he was carrying out without emotion. (He had set aside two dollars for a black tie and flowers to lay on the martyrs' grave, poor thing.) Pious enthusiasm flushed with pride. *In those plush newspapers of yours, O bourgeois, one day you will read my name among the founders of socialism.* Such were his thoughts.

Ferranini got out of bed, listless. He opened the newspapers, the modest papers from Rome and Milan, his daily bread. They too had never had reason to mention him, not once.

"Good times," he thought aloud. "Good times, great foolishness."

4

THE KID had been waiting at the door for a few minutes. Ferranini hadn't noticed.

"Signora Corsi has arrived."

"And who would that be?"

"She asked for you. Shall I tell her to come up?"

"Ah. Let her come up."

He greeted Nuccia with no sign of surprise at her unexpected arrival. "I almost think I like Rome better now" were his words, and Nuccia, fearing a different reception, was pleased. In truth he was very happy to see her, a spot of warmth in all that fog, her reassuring voice.

The first thing Nuccia did was inspect the room. A diffident female gaze.

"You've been lying in bed, you're not well yet. I knew it, and so I came."

"I was just thinking. The usual sloth. What's new?"

"What's new is that there's something for you to be pleased about, and that's another reason I'm here. Yesterday they were looking for you. The party."

"Who?"

"Someone high up, it seems. Apparently someone very high up."

He was shaken. Togliatti? Well, why not? They might have told him about the project he was working on. After all, reforming the industrial safety law was important, urgent. Worthy of his attention. But hope faded quickly. None of his friends had access to the chief. And Togliatti had always ignored him. Come on! Impossible. Among other things he'd heard Togliatti was abroad at the moment.

"I learned about it from Deputy Amoruso."

"Amoruso knows about you?"

Nuccia burst out laughing. "I'm not a germ! He came into the bookstore."

"And so Amoruso knows that you and I—"

"Well, if he doesn't know, he can imagine. Does that worry you so much?"

Ferranini was holding his head between his hands.

"The train to Rome comes through here at ten forty tonight, "he said. "We can still make it."

"You want to leave now?" Nuccia sounded wretched. "We're going tomorrow."

"We have to be very cautious. This town is a hotbed of gossip. Tomorrow people will be saying that I invited my mistress for the night."

But he backed down. In any case, why get excited? To set himself up for another disappointment? If they were looking for him, it was just for a chamber group meeting. Or some similar foolishness.

They had supper early, in the hotel, and then Ferranini went to his room because (he didn't say so) he was beginning to feel tired. After taking a room herself, Nuccia came up to his, where he'd just undressed. He was getting into bed, and he pointed at the settee under the window.

"No intention of crawling under the covers with you, don't worry!"

"Come on, Nuccia, none of your silliness. It's one of those days."

"And none of your playing, Comrade Ferranini. You're wearing pajamas, a bourgeois invention."

Obedient, however, she took her place on the settee, thinking she would leave in a few minutes and let him sleep. She and Amoruso hadn't just talked politics. From some symptoms, some involuntary hints Ferranini had let drop, the doctor had guessed that his colleague had a heart ailment (of nervous origin, he thought) and he meant to find out more if Ferranini consulted him. Meanwhile, though, it was advisable to keep a cautious eye on him. Upset, she wanted to know more, but Amoruso simply held up his open hands, an eloquent gesture. (The doctor was from Foggia, but had lived in Naples.)

"Signora. What more can I say? I would need to examine him. I suspect our friend is a chronic cardiopath, perhaps not serious. But I may be mistaken, both in under- or in over-estimation."

"Do an electrocardiogram," she said.

"As if electrocardiograms can't be mistaken too! Anyway, if he's the nervous sort, exams and worrying may just make the situation worse."

And so she had decided to join Ferranini; she had to see him right away. On the way, in the train, she continued to think about him. And by unconscious transposition (better that than unreasonable jealousy) her friend's heart problem (now she was certain of it) got mixed up with a quite different heart problem. Walter is fond of me, but that's all. I'm valued, but superfluous to his life. He's still suffering over his ex-wife. Suffering, and silent about it.

Ferranini studied her, his hands clasped behind his neck.

"Walter, it would do you good to be honest, to talk a little. What were you thinking about when I came up here? Your wife, right?"

"You want to know what I was thinking? About America, about the disaster those last four years in America were for me."

"Only America?"

"Tomorrow morning I'll be skipping a meeting with a certain Minelli, a guy who was there with me. Sigfrido Minelli. He was the one who introduced me to Roger Demarr, the firm I worked for. When I came to the United States, I was a free man, alive, but once I joined Demarr, I began to flounder. I sank into a reified, dispossessed world that completely transformed me. It was the great crisis of my life. You know about that. A betrayal."

"You were betrayed, poor thing," she said.

"I mean that I betrayed my faith. Don't you see? The young socialist caught in the cogs of the wheel, become a wheel myself."

Nuccia's thought was: First comes the ideological preamble, then he'll move on to his wife, Nancy. But Ferranini wasn't pursuing that train of thought.

Roger Demarr (on the birth register as Ruggero De Marco, born in Altamura in the province of Bari) had been, was until a few years ago, the owner of a grocery business in Camden. Just across the river from Philadelphia. He already had too many Italians around the shop and didn't want any more. When Ferranini showed up, he only made an exception because the job-seeker came from Alta Italia, the north, and couldn't speak much *Americano* so would not waste his time on chatter. He hired him as a second clerk to supervise the itinerant sales vans that went out to sell sugar and coffee, chocolate and soap door to door. In six months Ferranini had become a confidential clerk responsible for dealing with the suppliers and receiving important clients.

Ferranini's was no mere belated ingratitude. The truth was that in those six months the young socialist, the last living worshipper of the tombs of Sacco and Vanzetti, had become a diligent (if at times somewhat distracted, slightly surly) employee of Demarr, an affable family-owned company that, however, boasted sales of $500,000 per year. In those first days, Ferranini was busy keeping afloat. Too plainspoken a man to go about things in secret, he obtained permission to leave Camden on Saturday afternoon and Sunday to seek out Italian immigrants of his faith, get them together with Minelli's help, hold lessons in anti-Fascism and elementary Marxism, give them courage and take heart himself. He began to think about contacting the local trade unions. Here Minelli, better informed and cannier, advised him not to: the unions in the East were even worse than in Chicago; they knew nothing and wished to know nothing about socialism as we understand it. But the lessons he was giving to his compatriots, all of them southerners, did not satisfy him as he'd hoped. Rather than the preacher that Ferranini aspired to be, they wanted a helper, an employment agency, and when they didn't sense that was Ferranini's strength, they took part in the theoretical discussions only listlessly or not at all, until finally they stopped coming.

And what was more, liberty, which the famous statue at the entryway to the continent had promised him as well as millions of other fugitives, did not reveal itself to be all that abundant. One Sunday afternoon in a small town in Massachusetts (all night on the train to get there) he was speaking to a small group of Sicilians—cobblers, tailors, and barbers—and one of them got up to inquire (in excellent *Americano*) whether anyone not backward still read the Bible. Ferranini had been talking about the Marxist concept of superstructure, and thought the question so posed allowed him to speak clearly. He replied that an intelligent person could at the most tell those stories to children. Was the Sicilian an agent provocateur? A police warning from that town was sent to Camden. Ferranini was ordered "not to occupy himself with the Christian religion using disrespectful language and intent, in a Christian state and a Christian nation" if he wished to avoid criminal sanctions, including imprisonment, imposed by anti-blasphemy laws.

Ferranini was speaking in a soft voice; the hotel room was dreary and the heating low. A single lightbulb over the sink left both of them in the shadows.

"You can't imagine how gloomy I'm beginning to feel," said Nuccia, huddled up on her settee.

"So go to bed. I'm only talking about these things because you brought them up."

As often with men unused to talking about themselves, Ferranini was less concerned to make himself understood than he was to be consistent. In that unplowed field that was his memory of those years, he cut a long, straight furrow without paying attention to all that went unexplored at the edges.

"If I may advise," he said to her, "the empirical individual is of no importance in what I've been telling you. Only one thing is of interest: the degeneration of a consciousness."

Nuccia laughed. "Well, I'm interested in the empirical individual, yes I am! You can't imagine the goodwill a woman needs to put up with one of you, however mediocre."

Ferranini, recalling those years, felt less than mediocre. But she had been right: to reveal himself had made him feel better and was the right thing to do, however much there was to pay in shame and discretion.

Because there was reason to be ashamed.

It was during the first months of 1940. He had held a few more lessons, three or four, and then quit. He gave up.

It wasn't fear of police violence that dampened his enthusiasm, nor did he feel slighted as his audiences melted away. Worse. Other interests were worming their way into him, regressive interests; he was being assimilated by his environment and estranged from himself. Bourgeois society's powerful digestive system.

In just less than a year since he'd been hired by the Camden firm, he'd had a raise three times without asking. Three. Now it wasn't enough to go to the public library in Philadelphia and borrow books; he began to buy them. It was the illusion of appropriation, alienation in practice: the books had to be his. Weary of his rented room and meals in the house of an Italian on Edgeware Road across from where he worked, he found a small apartment for sale at the end of the road and moved in, paying the first two installments with nonchalance. America the leveler—the appealing prosperity of its *way of life*—flattened the aspirations of the young socialist until his aims seemed distant and worthless to him. Sacco and Vanzetti, class doctrine, atheism, and the unpleasant surprise of the anti-blasphemy laws all sank into the silt of disagreeable memories. In early spring came the inevitable purchase of an automobile: a modest Chevy, secondhand.

War had set fire to the world, and millions of men like him were being consumed by it. While he was peacefully scraping by and looking after his career. One of the Demarr clerks, a German, had been interned in a camp. He wrote to them to say they were treating him handsomely, and thanked this great nation, generous even with the children of the enemy. Ferranini was forced to agree, and admire, but he foresaw that Italy would ally with the enemy and feared the time would come when he would be sent to keep the German company. Instead, even after Italy declared war, Ferranini and most of his fellow Italians weren't harassed at all. He went on living as before, and no one bothered to restrict his movements. Minelli lived in New York and was friends with a girl who worked at the Italian consulate; he came to visit Ferranini and told him that the consulate was shutting down. "Now they're going to round us up, you'll see." But Demarr reassured them, said he knew better. "Relax, guys. Look after your health!"

"In other words," Nuccia tried to interject, "Demarr did care about you."

"Did I say he didn't? Meanwhile, though, he got me to disavow my past. He set the machinery in motion. Not that I wasn't aware; I kept saying to myself, 'Walter, watch out, you're losing your way, you're lost.'"

Demarr. A skin-deep American in the way he held his cigar and even to the extent of decorating his office with a portrait of the Quaker William Penn (next to that of Pius XII). With an Irish American bride fifteen years younger than he, past fifty-five now and an unhappy husband and father. He was convinced his wife and the two older children (there were four in all) barely tolerated him, and sought to even the score outside the family. As his business flourished he had acquired various titles in the parish and around town. These seemed too little to him. "Wholesale grocer," the title with which he figured in the Camden chamber of commerce yearbook, didn't gratify him either. He liked to call himself a "landowner" and he had the right to do so ever since he had acquired a nice piece of land during a bankruptcy liquidation, land he measured out in his own way, not in acres but in *tòmoli,* the southern Italian unit of measure for farmland. He had two farmhouses, two barns, and a small sawmill powered by a waterwheel. Thousands of trees, pasture as far as the eye could see. Each summer he spent a couple of weeks there. And then he could no longer go there; the distance was too great, he was obese, suffered from emphysema, and automobile travel was too much for him. When he learned that Ferranini was a country boy and knew something about agricultural work, he began to send him in his place. Those expeditions, which

Ferranini adored (too much!), tranquilized his boss. Old Laurel Farm, as it had been called since Civil War days, stopped losing money. Oats and potatoes were planted, the hay was harvested and sold. Even the maple and oak woods, thick and untended, began to earn money. Here Ferranini's tale grew elaborate, impassioned.

"Saturday before dawn I would leave Camden, and it was four hours before I could see the lake. Lake Erie, as big as a sea. When I arrived I would walk out into the fields. Do the accounts with the men. I had hired two on salary and took on two jobbers to bring in the hay in season. I would spend hours in the barns. At midday I'd lie on the grass in front of the empty, closed-up house. And I'd stay there for hours, sprawled out looking at the fields of 'my' estate, the meadows that extended right down to the shore of the lake. There were no houses in sight. Far away, a rail line with a single track cut across the landscape, the rare train heading past with its plume of smoke."

Nuccia had never known Walter to show interest in the landscape. His quite lyrical description astonished her.

"I had what they call *un'infognatura*. A fixation, a crush. I would hurry to Old Laurel as if I were going out with a girl. I lived for that. I had forgotten I was a man for that."

"And you were happy?"

"I was driven by remorse."

"Oh, come on."

In Lenin's *Sočinenija*, his *Works*, it is written that music is sweet, pleasant, and dangerous. Like all things that distract from reality.

"I believe," Ferranini went on, "that nature is an enemy reality I must struggle against (and labor is this struggle) to keep it from prevailing, from subjugating us. At times nature can take on a sweet and attractive appearance, like music as Lenin speaks of it, and I would abandon myself, allow myself to be enchanted. And then at Old Laurel there was something else, something worse: the countryside, the sly weapon of a bourgeois world intent on dominating me. Why is it that in America they give so much importance to the landscape, to wildlife reserves, national parks, the wilderness? To make people forget the true conditions of society. When you demystify the cult of nature and the propaganda around it, you find it is one of the various social narcotics, like sport and cinema.

"But meanwhile I was allowing myself to be ensnared and I knew that perfectly well; a day didn't go by that I didn't say to myself: Beast, you are a beast! I would dream of my father; he was taking me to task. Outwardly I was like a person who'd lost his memory, but inside I was constantly putting myself on trial. I went around divided in half, a schizophrenic. When I'd meet Minelli from time to time, he'd say, 'Damn, you're doing well for yourself, no worries' (he was married and already had a little girl) 'you ought to be croaking with good health, but you're as scrawny and ugly as a bad debt.' He didn't understand that it was all a load of rubbish, all misery."

Nuccia was puzzled too. Among other things, wasn't this just before he met the love of his life?

"I was like a spectator watching myself. Watching myself degenerate. I realized I was imitating the way the boss Demarr talked, out of the side of his mouth. I figured that if Demarr was the paternalist, I would be the neo-capitalist. I had gotten into the habit of looking at the stock prices on the blackboard outside the Chase Bank branch where I'd put my savings. I walked by every morning on my way to work. Nobody was going to stop me buying a half-dozen shares of Rio Tinto, or some other little sliver of capitalism. And afterwards, I went even further, I began to eye the daughter of the owner, as you know. I wasn't yet thirty years old; America had taken me in when I was naked as a worm, and I'd worked my way up. But then there was my fate. You know, first up, then down, and even the neo-capitalist was going to take a dive, if God willed it. You know what I mean. You know about these things, I've already told you."

Nuccia already knew, more or less, the rudiments of what had happened next, a not very happy tale: ordinary, frequent, and hopelessly bourgeois. She had spent some time putting it all together by herself.

"What I don't know is the most important thing. You've always told me this story as you experience it today, as you interpret it now. I'd like to know how it felt then."

How it had been to be him.

But that was asking too much. To go back and dig up his marriage, their courtship, to relive those events and feelings was to expose another person (his wife, his Nancy) to a judgment that would not be impartial. Someone Ferranini himself had never wanted to judge. No. Impossible.

"It's time to call it a night. Go sleep, it's late."

After all was said and done, Nancy typified perfectly the world she'd been born into and belonged to. As much as he might have suffered, that was her only fault.

Meadville, with its elegant Catholic girls' boarding school (Academy of Saint Thérèse of Lisieux), was the town closest to the pastures of Old Laurel. The Demarrs, husband and wife both devoted Catholics, if in different ways, had sent their eldest daughter there. Or rather, they let her stay, for at the respectable age of twenty-two she had preferred to stay on with the nuns (who practiced a not very ascetic way of life themselves), teaching physical education and calisthenics, rather than live at home in close proximity to her mother, whose nervous troubles and Irish accent she couldn't bear. Sundays, Nancy would show up at Old Laurel with a noisy trail of friends or students, and when it wasn't cold they would eat lunch outdoors. At some distance from him. He would meanwhile pace about the estate keeping busy, or pretending to; months would go by when there was nothing to do and he would simply walk around that exotic countryside.

The countryside of Emilia, the one he was used to, was either inhabited or cultivated everywhere, while here Ferranini felt he was wandering about in a boundless public park without benches or guards and above all without a public that by its presence would justify all that beauty—although it would spoil it (hadn't he become selfish now!). It was precisely that uselessness that he liked, that great, mellow spread of green, unused and without a purpose. A new individual, overbearing and deaf to the voice of social conscience, stopped instead to listen to the voice of the water as it ran over the sawmill waterwheel down in Blue Creek valley, a sawmill that hadn't been working for seventy years, that was no good to anyone. That individual wished that Old Laurel belonged to him. It grieved him to see the house opened up in mid-July, and that proprietary tribe invading: Demarr, his wife, his children, the black maid, the delivery boy who served as chauffeur for the huge Graham-Paige, loaded up like a stagecoach. For three or four weeks, until Old Laurel returned to being his, Ferranini would look for pretexts to stay in Camden.

He and the girl were in sympathy on this. She rarely put in an appearance in summer. When the rest were gone, they would meet again, as if by agreement, barely acknowledging each other. But those imperious tones (of the gym teacher) that she used even with her friends didn't interfere with autumn's restored silence, and that hair of hers, how warmly it seemed to reflect the gold and brown of the beech trees around the house. He struggled to look critically at those specious capitalist appearances (which they undeniably were), and those beeches of changeable color, Blue Creek, the various glints of auburn that played in Nancy's hair. But more, he had to resist their conniving charm, which was something else again. Pointless to pretend he hadn't heard the mistress's orders. "I could use some mistletoe for decoration." "You'll be here tonight to load the skis on the car." When he saw her coming he would say to himself: Remember, this is surplus value's daughter. But it was useless; as saints of another caliber know, you don't exorcise the devil with common prayers.

The fact was (mistletoe, hedges, pretty girls aside), it is easier to play the hero than to be coherent over the long haul, and that piece of wisdom, which now at age forty-five Ferranini was ready to accept, he still struggled to apply to others of his species and faith. Cases like that of Viscardi and Ancillotti would not have derailed him so much had he been sure that a man who'd risked being shot fighting the Nazi Fascists was not necessarily immune to the temptations of everyday life, or the good life.

One winter morning (he was by then the permanent administrator of Old Laurel) he met Nancy Demarr coming out of the barn, the two of them looking like the cover of *The Saturday Evening Post* with the snow, the rustic backdrop, her elegant short pink coat, he in his checked flannel shirt. She was holding a pitcher of milk warm from the cow, and whether on a whim or out of sudden friendliness, she took it from her smiling lips and offered him some. He gave her a disdainful look. And she insisted: "Go ahead, be my guest." Was he going to let that simperer boss him around? He turned to go. Luckily for him (or unluckily), the simperer did not take umbrage. She called him back. "Where do you take your meals? Why don't you join us?" He said something brief, cool, and correct in thanks. He ate, and slept, in the room next to the storehouse, along with a Pole he'd hired as a farmhand and who, although he'd been in America for a number of years, still didn't speak *Americano* and communicated in grunts. This was the proper company for him.

Nancy didn't insist, but the next Sunday there was an extra pair of skis on the roof of the car from Meadville. Ferranini accepted them willingly. He was lean and agile and it didn't take much for him to learn to use them; he made his trial runs where the others couldn't see him, though. It was Nancy who sought him out. Expert in many things (and even too much in one that we shall learn about), she was no less ingenuous than he in that field.

Things went the way they would. In mid-December came a phone call from Saint Thérèse of Lisieux to say that the girl had the flu. She wanted some green China tea, imported exclusively by Demarr. It could not be found in Meadville. Of course her father, to be sure she got it quickly, sent Ferranini. Fifteen-year-old Salvatore, the eldest Demarr son, went along, and the two of them entered that little sickroom bursting with flowers, so many wildflowers and potted plants that it looked as if someone had died. (Salvatore told him it was one of his sister's manias to sleep surrounded by flowers, even at home.) Ophelia among the flowers, the ex-militant in a convent. Not to be believed, thought Ferranini grasping for his sense of humor as she waved him closer. Then, when he was sitting down and she had smiled at him, and a bored Salvatore had gone out to take a walk around Meadville, he no longer entertained ironic thoughts. He no longer thought at all.

They listened to the radio, she asked him to read her the paper for a bit, and then they fell silent. He didn't permit himself to look at her but let his eyes roam around in the half-light of her little room: a place, a girl's bedroom, that to Ferranini (he hadn't had sisters or lovers) was strange and daunting, like a church. He was astonished to find the Stars and Stripes on the wall at the head of her brass bed. The Virgin, a crucifix? No, neither.

He would have been even more astonished if he had known what this Ophelia's vocation was. She was an activist, which was laudable, although he didn't like her cause. A daughter of immigrants, the adolescent Nancy had embraced "Americanism": a sort of inward-looking nationalism worshipping the customs, memory, and "heritage of the stock," a creed espoused by people whose patriotism-cum-social conservatism verged on racist idiocy. Nancy had become a "distinguished member" of a couple of Americanist societies through her proselytizing in school and out. When that didn't satisfy her, she had founded her own league called August Americans, with some hundred members, both boys and girls, who during the war began collecting magazines, records, and trinkets to send to the soldiers. Now Nancy, languorous under her Stars and Stripes, stretched out a hand on her bedcover to touch Ferranini's. The hand of that *alien* who'd dropped in from God knows where, as foreign and probably as irreconcilable with Americanism as *maccheroni* or the fandango.

They were engaged four months later, spring already budding. Nancy, in crinoline and a straw hat, appeared at Old Laurel in a two-horse landau. Pink and smiling, she was the picture of old Colonial charm, under some cherry trees that were opportunely heavy with blossoms. The wedding followed at the Camden town hall; Minelli was best man and there was no party, those being hard times. The day before she had told him, frankly but nicely, what other women may think but don't say: "I'm marrying you because I like you, but I like my freedom too and I'm marrying you to have more of it, not to give it up." Her mother, the pale, faraway, sensitive Clementine, did not pretend to be happy, but she did not oppose the marriage. Demarr was too fond of his own peace of mind to object, although his sights had been set higher. "You're a lucky guy," was all he said, in *Americano* as always, because beyond that he spoke only the dialect of Altamura, which was impenetrable to Ferranini. Besides, the young man seemed to be serious, he was a confidential clerk (not a salesman), and there was Salvatore, Demarr's firstborn son, to inherit the company one day. Ultimately, Demarr looked upon his daughter's choice with favor.

To Ferranini, it was all somewhat unreal. Old Laurel's meadows seemed to flower just for him; other people barely existed, they didn't touch him. "I had no idea what real happiness was. That's why I was self-centered." His energy pierced the lazy clouds of that mild Pennsylvania spring day like an airplane shooting straight up. When he was alone in his office at the firm, he would beat his fists on the desk and sing to blow off steam. At first, right after the engagement, he was halting, timid. He seemed to persist in avoiding her. But every day brought new euphoria. Not just contentment but timorousness, triumphant anxiety, and amazement. "I can't believe this. I don't get it." In short, it was happiness, not real if it didn't overflow, if it wasn't muddied by worries, if it didn't question itself, incredulous.

Even so, he couldn't see himself in it. "I've died and come back to earth as someone else." It was not just the would-be builder of socialism who had disappeared; it was his supposed Italian and Emilian convictions. *Oxen and wives from your own tribe. Before you do marry, thrice fill the granary.* Gone, too, was his own familiar diffidence and fierceness; that supremacy of *ideas* over sentiments he had so often boasted of. (At twenty-three, twenty-four years old!)

After they married, naturally enough he calmed down, in part because the responsibility, in the most solemn sense, fell entirely on him. He had to be all that was needed for both of them. His makeshift experience was enhanced by his own tenderness, yet experience taught him that his wife was neither very tender nor anxious to conceal the fact. "Your interests for you, Walter," she said, "and mine for me." A rule that might even have been fine, if beyond their separate interests they had been eager to be intimate, but Nancy didn't bother with that. Their wedding landau had but one horse, as it were. He was the one who must follow, must understand her and make himself understood, a double task. When she came back, and sometimes she came back a day late, from Meadville (from the school where she was still teaching three days a week), Nancy was pleased to find the house warm, clean, well-stocked.

Honestly convinced that this happened miraculously and without any effort, she decided it was "absurd" to waste time on domestic duties ("like Mrs. Brown and Mrs. White do") because things exist to serve us and not vice versa. And as she was in love's intimate matters, so she was in her everyday affairs: it was he who took care of her when she had a cold, or reserved a seat on the plane for Boston where she had to go once a month. She was sincere as could be, and so helpless it made a man's jaw drop.

A great expert, however, in areas that to Ferranini seemed less essential. For example, in Camden town politics, where she was keen to encourage certain of her father's political aspirations. But when her husband complained that she left him alone on Sundays, or instead filled the house with people, Nancy would say quite seriously, "What do you expect? I don't have a clue; you're the first man I've had in my life."

A year went by in those three rooms they'd grown into, a bit dark and low-ceilinged on the top floor of the Demarr mansion; meanwhile out in the world, the war grew wider and more disastrous. Ferranini resigned himself to putting his feet back on the ground and tried to go less often to Old Laurel; it made him feel gloomy. He continued to be in love, with that pathetic certainty that stokes love, that Nancy would make him suffer. And yet he was sure that he knew her. He made lists of her merits and defects.

"You are honest, not very demonstrative. You're proud, you are sincere. Stubborn."

He wasn't so very wrong, but he was far from knowing her. Surprises lay in wait.

"I'm not stubborn. I simply married a man who is different from me. If you knew how to carry me off...."

She wasn't entirely wrong, not that she herself knew how she wanted to be carried off, either. Her character, impervious and tough as it usually was, was also supremely contradictory, and she would suddenly, unpredictably turn tender. Whisper in her ear in one of those receptive intervals (brought on by some state of mind or body or who knows what other imponderables) and she would be docile and utterly available. An hour later, no one could budge her, not without hearing about it. Some casual suggestion made at just the right moment would become compulsory behavior for herself and others. A psychologist might have been curious about this dangerous, if deeply hidden, peculiarity of hers. Her family, not only poor Walter but also her parents, never saw it, although they sometimes bore the brunt.

A girl who wanted a life of her own, who dimly sensed she was physically frail and insisted from the beginning they would have no children. Something—certainly not her upbringing—also made her insist against her parents' wishes on a civil rather than religious wedding. For poor Clementine this was scandalous; for Demarr, a heartache. Her stubbornness remained a mystery and they blamed it, quite wrongly, on the bourgeoisifying Ferranini. But they did give in.

Rosaleen, a sister of Clementine Demarr, lived in Boston. Her husband had been a local reporter for a New York newspaper, but he had died years earlier. Nancy had gone to visit her aunt after she married Walter, and the visits became a habit. She didn't say much but from what Ferranini was able to learn, she was drawn to Boston by friends, perhaps friends she'd recently met, intellectuals, people who wrote in the papers. She also went to conferences, or classes, what sort it wasn't clear. In April 1945—it was their anniversary— she went to Boston and immediately came down with a cold. She phoned to say she would be late in returning, and in fact they waited all of fifteen days. And when she did return, she was no longer herself. Walter scarcely recognized her. She spoke a different language.

It didn't quite dawn on him that it was English. A King's English that obeyed the diction of Harvard and the accent of Boston's better sort. She would no longer be going to mass, she told the Demarrs. She had converted to Presbyterianism (a fashionable denomination, also of the better sort), producing a certificate signed by the minister of St. George Chapel in Boston. As for Walter, she expected him to enlist in the army as soon as possible, so as to earn American citizenship right away, and in the meantime she wanted him to apply to change his surname: it wasn't respectable; it needed to be Anglo-Saxonized.

While she was down with the cold, someone had seized the moment to expose her to another virus. One well-known and widespread in the States, raw material for sociologists and amusing to people of good sense. It took the form of abhorrence of anything that wasn't highborn Yankee, that wasn't descended from Anglo-Saxon Old America. Although in New America, those distinctions were as rarely to be found as Cato's sturdy Roman spirit in the wealthy new quarters of Rome.

Ferranini had already thought of enlisting, and now that the USA was fighting alongside the USSR, he could earn Nancy's approval with a clean conscience. One morning he went down to the army enrollment office in Germantown, Philadelphia. The physical exam was rigorous. Though he was careful not to breathe a word of his old heart murmur to the army doctors, they flushed it out immediately. As a foreigner, he couldn't be taken on in the civilian corps. So there was nothing to be done, and as for the new name, there wasn't much point in that. Nancy was displeased, and angry at him about the physical, as if the murmur were his fault and he'd wasted time trying to hide it. Ferranini wasn't offended; he was in love. And he always found a reason for his indulgence: Nancy had inherited an irritable nervous system from her mother; you had to be patient. (Hadn't she also inherited those copper streaks in her hair, those bewitching green eyes?)

Now patience is the key to marital happiness, if there are two to practice it. Nancy was as smug about being peevish as she was about her small round breasts. Even with her parents, with old Demarr, things weren't going smoothly. One evening, in front of them and some of their friends she proudly announced she had joined the executive committee of American Heritage in Boston. This was another league (far more powerful than those she'd been part of at school) of political conservatives, or rather political extremists, with plans for a "restoration" of government institutions, of manners (and race relations) to what they'd been at the time of the Civil War if not before, and with a special veneration for Southerners and slavers. Old Demarr knew little about American Heritage, but he'd heard it was anti-Catholic. He protested that his daughter would end up in the Ku Klux Klan.

"In any event," replied Nancy, "I shall live and die an American."

"And me? I've been an American for thirty-two years!"

And in all those years, he was told, he had never learned that on Thanksgiving Day you ate roast turkey and not boiled capon.

Such was her infatuation—and things would get worse. In their bedroom she kept a recruiting poster for the Marine Corps, showing a tall, slim soldier with sandy hair and a close-fitting uniform, captioned "The Only Country That Never Lost a War." Dark and not very tall, Ferranini nightly undressed in front of the poster while his wife watched, the unhappy comparison implicit. Meanwhile she read the *National Review*, a bellicose, chauvinist weekly for which, she told him, she hoped to write. For Nancy Demarr and her fellow Americans, even some who were older, better educated, and wiser, snobbism was becoming ideology. Right-wing opinion, or prejudice—it would culminate in McCarthyism—was gathering strength. Reaction against Roosevelt, the New Deal, the alliance with the Soviets, and the ideals of peace and international unity mingled with the East Coast and Southern bourgeoisie's everlasting contempt for and dread of the blacks and the immigrants.

Because of the war effort, the propaganda was subtle and contained, but it was unflagging. Nancy was one of the many conquests, and victims. A victim who, without meaning to, spread disorder among all those close to her. She couldn't forgive her parents (always referred to as "the old folks") for their Irish and Italian origins. Her mother, Clementine, then decided that her husband, Demarr, was too old and too simple to "understand" her, and that her son-in-law, Walter, was a sly one who had gotten himself a rich wife. One sorry day she affirmed that she was gravely ill (in spirit, the others were so insensitive and small-minded), and she took herself off to an ocean-side clinic and spa at Vanport that treated illnesses like hers and of-fered psychoanalytic care. And there she remained. Demarr, in a fit of vexation and misery, then grief, telephoned her and blurted out that he was glad she was gone. He quickly repented, begging her to come back. Perhaps offended but certainly hysterical, as introverts can be at menopause, she proclaimed he had crushed her soul: he would never see her again. Every evening at the table ready to eat, Demarr broke down in tears. Only Ferranini was there to console him. Nancy neither defended nor disapproved of her mother; she was neutral. And yet old Demarr, left with the children, and Car-melo the youngest not yet seven years old, really did deserve some sympathy. Nancy was the eldest and she loved her siblings, but she had no time or inclination to look after them. Instead, they had to take on Mrs. Esposito, an elderly employee of the firm who minded them in her spare time. She was the unwitting cause when matters took another turn for the worse for Ferranini and for all of them.

Mrs. Esposito's husband taught at the elementary school of St. Paul's Academy (private and Catholic) of Camden. When school reopened in September 1945, she decided to enroll the children there, and Demarr incautiously agreed. His eldest daughter learned about it too late, and Mrs. Esposito was fired on the spot. Nancy then drove to the school to pick up her two brothers, and she scolded them, too. Afterwards she laid into her father. The kids were meant to go to an American public school, not debase themselves studying with Poles, Puerto Ricans, and Italians. Demarr, who had learned his lesson in the debacle with his wife, gave in right away this time.

It was past midday. Ferranini was in the kitchen. Busy stirring polenta in a pot, when he caught the end of her tirade. He strode out, tearing off his apron, grabbed her by the arms, lifted her up, held her suspended above the floor, then dumped her in a chair. Demarr intervened, not to defend his daughter but to come to Ferranini's aid. Livid, his eyes glazed, Walter was in a state. He staggered to the door to leave, to be gone, but he couldn't open it and stood there frozen to the doorframe.

He came back two days later (from the South where Demarr had sent him to sell off some stock; the company, growing large, was always short on liquidity). The words he had to say were already in his head, pulsing like veins. He asked her pardon; he spoke to her, patiently. Told her that she was mistaken, and how she was mistaken. (He had come to some conclusions on the road. It was not her fault. She was a good person, she had accepted him when she saw he loved her, poor devil that he was. She was good, and therefore she could be reclaimed; he must clean off the mud they'd splashed on her; he could do it, he'd have her back, he'd make her new.) He took her face between his hands, spoke to her calmly and gravely, his lips on her hair. It was sweet to reason with her that way. She was young and fresh and had too much love coming to her to give in to these crooked, old, foolish, inhumane ideas. Yes, America had won the war, but more important, notions of humanity—really just one notion, that we are all one race, all of us, even the Puerto Ricans, and all men need the same things, bread, a house to live in, a woman—those notions had to triumph inside America.

And finally poor Ferranini had only this to say: "When we were engaged, you asked me if I was a Commie." A Communist. "Well, even a Commie can be a good worker, a good citizen of the United States of America."

Nancy let him speak, frowning, her face closed. Later, she didn't come to bed but went to sleep downstairs. She was silent for days, until the middle of the month, when she usually left for Boston. And then she departed, without special preparations, saying good-bye to her father, her brothers, and tossing him a "so long." Ferranini had no illusions, he knew he was losing her, but he had determined to be brave, and he was. Two months went by. She didn't return. Thanksgiving Day came and went. She didn't show up. (He had clung to the hope that she would come back for Thanksgiving.) She phoned her father once a week (and also her mother at Vanport), with vague news of herself, never speaking of her intentions. She just said she was moving from Boston to New York. She'd gotten a job as the editorial secretary at the *National Review*.

Demarr and Ferranini, both suddenly widowers, studied each other; the old man stunned and confused, the other mute and embittered. Ferranini's father-in-law began to lecture him in a way that seemed silly, to put it mildly. It must be another man who had taken her away, you had better go find out, if you care about your honor. It's not right to leave a girl alone at her age. "Oh stop it," he once shot back. "Honor. I couldn't care less about it. I couldn't care less about living. Understand?"

He was still going to work, punctual and patient, his head elsewhere, the accounts bouncing around inside like marbles. He was terribly restless, in perpetual motion from office to warehouse to office, and there were evenings when it took him an hour at the calculator to draw up an invoice. He'd find himself with the telephone in hand unable to remember who or why he was calling. As for Old Laurel, where the crocuses lay under deep snow, he went back (for the fourth year and this time without anyone waiting for him and without being sent). He knew so little about himself and these things that he had no idea what drove him to return, to count those trees one by one and name them, and the bushes, and the stones. Pale he'd always been, but now his skin turned yellowish and he neglected himself, his clothing, and all the rest, until Demarr had to remind him that in America you shaved every morning, at the very least. And ever fatherly, handed him a jar of Saint Andrews iodized salt, good for the liver, he said.

He had been living the life of an animal, without looking ahead or back; he had drawn no conclusions, sought no justification. The war's end, a great breach closing for him too, brought him no relief.

He preferred not to register it, to ignore it. All those years, the announcements, the bulletins, the propaganda (the devastation of that poor country of his he'd left behind), the whole gigantic hue and cry had passed him by without moving him from his stolid tranquillity. From time to time he would think to himself that he was utterly rotten, that he stank. He lacked conviction, though; it was a weary litany.

He didn't bother to cross-examine himself, now that he had abundant evidence. He didn't try to imagine or put together a future, or accept the past, now filled up with rubble. It was years since he'd read a book, or debated, or tried to make sense of a problem. "My mind's scattered" was enough of an excuse. Honing a definition to the point of paradox, grating away at an idea to expose the nerve, things once so compelling (at the age of twenty, twenty-two), things that drove him to confront even more difficult ideas, an impulse to react (for example, against the anarchism widespread among his comrades in Spain): all that was finished and forgotten. The impulse he'd once had to assert himself, to impose a thought process, a discipline around him—gone.

He did not look back, however; he didn't confront himself. Self-examination, taking stock of one's life, those were worth doing when a man still cared, still had personal hopes. Days dragged by, hours spun around on the kitchen clock; he shuffled along, eyes shut. As far as he was concerned the world was irrelevant, he had no purpose, no interests. Old Joe Sorrentino, one of the company's suppliers, told him he was leaving the business, that he had bought a little house in Florida. Did Demarr intend to keep on working; who was he going to leave the firm to? Ferranini gaped at him, stunned by such an absurd question, as if he'd been asked for news from the great hereafter.

Yet someone was making decisions, and for the both of them. Just after that sad Thanksgiving, Ferranini got the news. The letter was under the door to his apartment when he returned, dazed, after he was treated to a long tirade from Demarr, who was worrying about the business. No more war, goodbye windfall, the days when people bought without weighing price and quality were gone. The army was demobilizing, industries were laying off, it was tough to sell. Nothing new, thought Ferranini as he listened, no big deal: Are you capitalists or not? You aren't the ones who really suffer, and so you accept the downturns, the unemployment, as part of the system. Demarr didn't see it that way. His company depended a lot on working-class customers, and when people were out of work, profits fell. To stay afloat, they must cut costs. The war is over, get it? Time to tighten our belts, at home and on the job. Ferranini had to do his part too. Could they keep Old Laurel, for instance?

Fair enough, Demarr was right. And he was right to involve Ferranini. Wasn't he a capitalist himself by now? He'd enjoyed all the fat years without a word; how honest was it to stand in judgment now, to condemn "you capitalists" just because the last years had turned lean? He couldn't find fault with Nancy either. He had to admit she was right in one respect, unless he was a hypocritical lout. Socialism meant both men and women enjoyed liberty; when he was young he'd been critical of bourgeois matrimonial servitude, was he going to cling to it as a husband? It made no difference that her letter was shabby and pompous, its false courtesy meant to hide her indifference, her contempt. America (the letter went on) demanded the active participation of its women, as it had in frontier days, to defend itself against internal enemies, and Nancy Demarr was certainly not one to hold back. She would thank him "with all her heart" for restoring her liberty. Standing as they did on opposite sides, there was no future for them. No man loyal to the Communist Party could be true to the United States. His silence during these last weeks "encouraged" her to believe that he shared her judgment, therefore (here was the point Ferranini had sought, with an icy attention he hoped was indifference, among all the pointless words) she asked that he deliver his written consent to their mutual liberation to Lavy and Blumenstein, attorneys at law, New York, NY. Thanking him in advance, and her thanks also for the "good times" that would remain "indelible" in her memory. Et cetera.

The next morning Demarr was waiting for him at the office, in shirtsleeves in front of an open window. His face was apoplectic, the old man sweated and panted all the time, even in winter.

"Are you aware, Walter, that we have dozens of gallons of solvents in the storeroom? You'd better get them out of there! If an inspector comes around, not even the Blessed Virgin of Carmine can save us."

From time to time, the inflammables were supposed to be moved to a warehouse out of town. Ferranini hadn't given the order for a month. He'd simply forgotten about it.

"I'm an idiot," he said, but his tone was truculent, he didn't try to justify himself.

"You're no idiot, you're just going crazy. Make her come back, I tell you. Bring her home. She's okay, believe me, good as gold, but you've got to understand her. Listen, here's something I just remembered. She was nine years old; we wanted to put braces on to straighten her front teeth. There was no persuading her, and so I said, 'Look, Papà isn't going to smoke until you go to the dentist.' And I threw my pipe in the stove. There I was, after dinner, all silent, with a toothpick in my mouth. She was watching me. Then she got up and grabbed my arm and said, 'Papà, take me to the dentist.' What's the matter, Walter? You think that's funny?"

"Don't mind me, Demarr. Forget about me."

"What is it, Walter? You don't believe me?"

The doors to the old twin-engine Dakota that would take him across the Atlantic, listing badly, closed for departure a few minutes past midnight on December 30, 1945, as his thirty-first year drew to an end. During the long, restless night journey he was struck by the coincidence. His youth was gone. America was slipping away in the night behind him, its darkness and its lights, and with it, irremediably but also without any residuum, his past, the good and the bad that had been his.

Naturally, he was wrong about that too. They were late to land at Shannon, and in the half hour he waited, he eagerly took in the Irish accents of the airport workers and the girl at the newspaper stand, reminiscent of the way his mother-in-law and Nancy spoke when they first met. Their documents were inspected; American nationals were invited to step to one side. Without thinking, Ferranini joined the group of Americans. The customs officer came over.

"Sir, to the other side."

He felt like cursing.

5

ITALIAN rail workers know the Provvida well, the commissary in all the big stations where they and their women shop. Ferranini, ex-rail worker, had his reasons to remember it too. While they waited for the 8:34 to Rome, he pointed out the place to Nuccia.

"I spent six of the most wretched months of my life there." A lot of places and things in Reggio still brought his rotten American adventure to mind. Too many.

"I worked there as the manager, just after I got back from Camden. It was one big room with nothing in it but a few crates of dried pea flour, condensed milk, and cans of mackerel. Made in the USA. From New Jersey to Reggio, just like that."

They were walking up and down under the platform roof in a thick fog, which isolated them. He was telling her about his return, how everything in those days was alien to him ("Tell me that's not unpleasant"), how everything was alien, as if it were a crime to speak Italian, or live in Italian-built houses. It took a while for him to feel cleansed, to regain his old sensibility. An American army rifle company from the East Coast, half of them Chinese, was stationed in Parma. He didn't go there, didn't want to hear them speaking or smell the Virginia tobacco. If people asked where he had been all those years, he didn't reply. He changed the subject.

"You do go in for self-criticism," said Nuccia. "Such a dedicated Communist. Can't you just say you were in love?"

"The people from State Rail, from the State Rail cell, came to ask me to join in January '46. Them, understand? With open arms. They had been here starving, getting shot at from every side, while I was living it up. And understand, I was ashamed to be seen getting a party card. But about the rest, all my fool Americanitis, I wasn't ashamed, you see."

He was talking quite loudly. Someone under the platform roof turned to look. "Watch it." Nuccia smiled. "You're an authority in Reggio Emilia."

But Nuccia wasn't one to give up. Now she was citing the example of Karl Marx.

"Your wife didn't deserve it, but when a man's in love, there's nothing to be ashamed of. Marx was in love with Jenny, and one time he didn't show up at a congress in Belgium, just because Jenny asked him not to leave her."

"Marx, the saints: what do they have to do with it? My problem was that I pulled the wool over my own eyes, if you see what I mean. I knew what my wife and America stood for. I just pretended not to. A man like me is subject to constant temptation so long as he lives in a world that's not socialist. He has to struggle. That world got inside me; that's what was disgusting! I defended it. I longed for it."

As if to confirm that Ferranini really was an authority, a bald, bent man in a gray jacket, his face radiating hope, emerged from the door of the Provvida.

"I recognized your voice. You don't know me, but I am, believe it or not, your successor. At the Provvida. My name's Zamboni. Sorry to bother you, but I wanted to ask a favor, for my son."

"Walter, the train's arriving," warned Nuccia.

"We'll take the next one. Tell me, Zamboni."

"Well, briefly, my boy was the switchman here in the station. Now he's at home with psychasthenia due to exhaustion, and they've acknowledged he's sick but won't pay the compensation he should get because it was work-related. Ivan Zamboni. Should I write it down?"

"Don't bother. I'll talk to the station chief right now."

"That would be a great help. Ferranini, my son is in bad shape. You're a socialist, tell them that the days of the exploiters of labor are numbered. But when are we going to be liberated from labor itself?"

The train had pulled in and was already departing. Ferranini left Nuccia in the café and went to look for the stationmaster.

He was out, but there was a deputy. A young fellow from the hamlet of San Donato near Vimondino.

"Remember Don Marx?"

"Sure thing."

"I'm his brother's son."

The old man, who'd been dead for a while, was the priest of Vimondino, Massimo Panciroli, "Don Max" or "Don Marx," as some of his parishioners liked to call him. It seemed that one day at the pulpit he'd disclosed that the evil Karl Marx was not in fact the devil but more like Jesus Christ, since both preached against Mammon and the worship of material goods.

Village news finished, the young Panciroli spoke of his party affiliation. He was proud of his position.

"I head up the rail-workers union here in Reggio, we're affiliated with the CGIL. Officially—in practice I'm in charge of other things, too. You must know the Keller plan."

"I know of it."

Keller was one of Lenin's assistants, and when the provisional government fell he served the Revolution by reorganizing Russia's railroads. Keller was the name used by insiders for a plan prepared by the party to run the railroads in central Italy in the event of an emergency.

"You must know, comrade," young Panciroli went on, getting up to close the door, "that under our plan the Piacenza–Arezzo and Ferrara–Ancona lines are divided up into many segments, each one assigned to a group, in addition to the three commands for Bologna, Florence, and Ancona. I'm the leader of a group, which is in turn divided into several teams with different functions. There are two types of action to be undertaken: Operation T, meaning transport, and Operation S, sabotage and interruption of service. I have one team at the engine house, one that's responsible for the track, one that takes care of the power lines, and another in charge of signals and switches."

Ferranini thought of the great party headquarters on via delle Botteghe Oscure, where the Keller plan lay in one file among thousands, hidden and probably forgotten in a locked safe covered by an inch of dust.

"Let's hope that the zero hour doesn't come too late," the young man said.

"The plan is good," Ferranini replied.

"Although the human element leaves a lot to be desired. In certain ways, if you know what I mean. There's plenty of initiative—too much, even. What's lacking is discipline. And you, who are outside the railroad environment, it would great if the next time you came back to Reggio you could look into a matter between me and my subgroup leader. My immediate subordinate in the structure of the plan. He's only a switchman in the company, but he's destroying what I've accomplished in two years of hard work. With his presumption. He stirs the men up against me. He wants my job, he doesn't want to be under me. It's not right; the position is mine, I earned it and I have the right to hold on to it."

"Oh Christ, they're all the same," Ferranini blurted out.

"What was that, comrade?"

"Nothing. And who is this subgroup leader? He wouldn't be a certain Ivan Zamboni?"

"Yes, Ivan Zamboni. He's on sick leave now. A slacker. Do you know him?"

"I've been told about him."

"You see? He's got people talking about him, when even the names of the individuals involved and everything else is supposed to be top secret! You see what I mean?"

"Yes, yes, I see," said Ferranini, getting up. "And I can't wait to get out of here. What time is the train for Rome?"

"At nine forty-five," said Paciroli, surprised. "But tell me, comrade, was there something you needed when you came over here?"

"Yes there was. I wanted to know when the next train for Rome left. Goodbye."

They departed, finally, and Ferranini sat in silence until the train, shooting through the fog, reached the great Apennine tunnel and passed through. When they emerged into the sun on the other side, Ferranini, too, brightened up, and he put the window down to let in some fresh air.

"Well," he said to Nuccia, summing up his private thoughts, "it was worth it in the end to meet Zamboni, the father. You know what he had to say, Zamboni? 'You promise to free us from capital, and that's a good thing, but it would be even better if you could free us from labor.'"

"From labor? And how would you do that? Isn't that just rubbish?"

"No, it's not rubbish; as a matter of fact the classics say labor will be reduced to a minimum once communism is established. But the way I see it, labor cannot be reduced, and certainly not abolished. There's a law, not a law of economics but a biological law, or perhaps simply a physical one."

There was a universal law, he told her, an eternal law known as evolution. To speak of evolution was to speak of the struggle for life, which manifested itself in two ways: in war (with one's fellow human beings) and in labor. Labor was also a war, against the world around us, against nature. Men might abolish war. Labor, no: they would never be able to abolish it.

"You're a politician," said Nuccia.

"Me? No, PCI activist, nothing more. And I'm proud of it."

"All the more reason: why not leave theory to the theorists? Forgive me if I say this, but what I mean is, isn't it better not to go beyond faith in God the Father, the catechism they teach at the Federation? Which you're supposed to teach your base."

She thought his tendency to take big questions to heart, questions that were bigger than he was (and he did, he did), was not at all good for his equilibrium. No peace would come of the autodidact's somewhat tedious enthusiasms (and his surly prickliness, easy enough for her to glimpse under the autodidact's intransigence). Nuccia had studied philology at university to a highly specialized level, but she liked to dismiss it all, she gave it no importance in her life. The main benefit of knowledge, she believed, was to instill a certain skeptical detachment, especially from worship of knowledge. Here, she and Ferranini were in opposite camps. She found herself thinking that there were two things that stood between Walter and herself: his wife and night school.

But she had set out their lunch on the tray before them (he'd turned down her proposal they go to the restaurant car), and Walter tucked into his food. Only the plentiful noise of his satisfied chewing was to be heard. Serious. From time to time he looked around as if someone might be out to grab his meal. Meanwhile he ate and his mood changed, for the better. When he'd finished he even pulled her close to him, as they were alone in the carriage, and put his arm around her hips, pressing his elbow where he knew she liked it.

"Tell me you're happy to return to Rome."

She wished that Walter were attached to Rome, the birthplace of their love, as she had once or twice dared to call it.

"I certainly don't spend time in Reggio willingly. Whether that means I like Rome, that's something else."

"America, then? *Your* America?"

Their conversations, evening and morning, should have granted her more than that modest irony, and Nuccia was not a little jealous. She took care to conceal it, and it helped that she knew how capricious masculine affection could be, and she wasn't entirely wrong about that. The beautiful Nancy was far away, and not just in time.

"So, would you go back to America?"

"You must be kidding. Comrade Ferranini has but one ideal."

"Paradise, on earth," she said.

He laughed. "The USSR, obviously."

"And yet," Nuccia observed, "America made you forget the news I came with. One of the chiefs wants to meet with you."

"Maybe I didn't forget. I've got compartments, like this railroad car."

"Some of those compartments are pitch dark, eh? A Communist MP can't hide behind the unconscious, you know. The classics don't permit it."

The conversation was veering unusually close to the profane. Ferranini needed to get control.

"The truth is this," he said, putting Nuccia in her place, "socialism is a difficult thing. In some ways, it's better that many people don't know that."

When they got down from the train in Rome, Nuccia pointed out that there was time to go by Botteghe Oscure. To the head office of the party.

He was reluctant. That door, those hallways and offices seemed both too narrow and too grand. They disappointed, and they intimidated. Inside, Italian Communism was all too Roman. A chance meeting with Comrade Togliatti was the one thing that might tempt him to go in, but that morning he had read in *l'Unità* that Togliatti was away from Rome.

"It's late," he said.

"Here things are just waking up, you know that." She pushed him into a taxi. "Good luck, Walter."

"What good luck? I'm getting my marching orders, that's all."

If only there had been marching orders. Nobody had any. Nobody noticed him or even recognized him.

His prickliness was roused. "I'm not known here," he thought, "I'm just a gate-crasher." He went into three or four brightly lit offices. No one looked up. In the halls he wandered past hurried underlings (the party leadership was meeting with Deputy Secretary Longo). The place rebuffed him as usual, and he said to himself: "It's normal, it's the typical relationship with the base. I'm just the base in here."

The one friendly face he saw was the smooth, austere countenance of D'Aiuto. A functionary—just a few days ago he'd been working at the Federation here in Rome—a man of the base like himself.

"No one was looking for you as far as I know," said D'Aiuto. "In case it was Amoruso, let's just call him."

Right, call Amoruso. They called his hotel, they called the chamber. No trace of Amoruso.

"Damn Neapolitan, he's always out and about, probably at Caffè Rosati," Ferranini decided. He turned away from D'Aiuto and made to leave. In the entry hall he saw a guard. He had the bad idea of stopping him.

"Tell me, is it true that Comrade Togliatti is abroad?"

The man raised one corner of his mouth and glared severely at the tips of Ferranini's shoes.

"I'm sorry, I'm not authorized to tell you that."

"Hey," said Ferranini, "I'm not a spy or something. I'm Ferranini, from Reggio."

Later, ruefully going over that moment, there were two things that didn't make sense: he'd snapped back in dialect, which he never spoke; and somehow, just as he grabbed the fellow, a button had flown off the man's jacket.

Deputy Boatta now appeared. He saw his colleague shaking the guard, both hands gripping his lapels. Boatta grabbed him by the arm and dragged him into the elevator. He understood everything right away, and since he was fond of Ferranini, he softened his tone.

"What do you expect? You never come here, so of course they don't know you. You must show up more often. What was it you wanted to know? Where Togliatti is? Well, he was in Prague, and right now do you know where he is and what he's doing? He's down in Mondragone, where his niece lives, the married one. He's probably playing puppet theater with his niece's kids. He adores them. His niece's husband is a devout Catholic and the kids are preparing to take Communion. The priest comes by to instruct them, and they say Togliatti has friendly conversations with the man."

"You know what, Boatta? This sort of chitchat annoys me; I'm not interested in Togliatti as a private person. In fact, I refuse to let him to be a private person. I don't know if you get my drift."

Intransigent.

Freeing himself from Boatta he headed along Palazzo Bolognetti toward Piazza del Gesù. Behind him, a taxi stopped. Nuccia got out.

"I've finished, I went to the store and now I'm back, tell me."

She listened, disapproved, and decided he must next go to the chamber.

"There's no session tomorrow."

"Go there anyway. You may find Amoruso."

Next morning he went. None of his colleagues were there; altogether, he saw no more than a dozen deputies. Empty, the room reserved for his party; half empty, the corridors and even the bar. His committee would resume work only on Monday. After an hour spent reading the newspapers, he walked around again, downed two coffees, looked enviously at the smokers. A deputy without a crew of hangers-on, with scarcely any ties to his colleagues, he'd been bored since the day he began to haunt these halls. "Money spent badly" was his succinct judgment on the bombastic spaces, the superfluous consumption of beverages, the time wasted in chatter, and the overpowering smell of floor wax (it stuck in the nose, annoying and emblematic). He finally decided to leave. But first he had to pass by the internal post office. Before the window, a gray, bent, heavy back, and a rotund voice that was saying to the clerk, "Printed matter, *sotto fazia*." Bulk rate. *Fazia*, meaning *fascia*: category, bracket.

Ferranini could think of just two politicians from Romagna who had never overcome the region's incapacity to pronounce the *sc*. As in fascist. There was Mussolini himself, who personally invented the doctrine yet was never able to call it anything but *fazismo*. And there was the distinguished member of parliament who was mailing the parcel. The man nodded at him in return, and then noting the copy of *Izvestia* sticking out of his pocket, said, "Am I indiscreet if I ask to look at your paper for a moment?"

It was a week old and carried an article (great pomp, little substance) about the prevention of industrial accidents in capitalist Europe. Now, as the other man scanned the paper, Ferranini decided he had not wasted the morning. He had been wanting to introduce himself for months.

"Ferranini," replied Nenni, so warmly that Walter blushed with gratitude. "But I know you. You are from Emilia, from the PCI." Nenni invited him to sit beside him.

"We've met, I mean, eighteen years ago," said Ferranini.

"Where, in Spain?"

No, they'd met in Paris, at an old restaurant on the rue des Petites

Écuries near boulevard Poissonnière. Brighenti, the Passy wine mer-
chant who would later get Ferranini his ill-fated passage to America,
was not cut out for political exile but he had been a Socialist, a
backer of Serrati and the hard-line wing of the party. He didn't like
to risk having close ties with the Italian exiles but he kept an eye on
them, and he knew where to find people without endangering anyone. One evening Ferranini had walked all the way to the center of
Paris. At the restaurant, along with other compatriots, was Nenni,
the man who would be the leader of the Socialists after the war, then
in his forties, myopic and slightly leaden-faced. Moderate in speech
and appearance, lively in action, a sharp and cautious planner, he
brought to his party (Ferranini sensed this even in those days) a persistent realism it had always been short of. The small main room,
badly heated, gave onto a courtyard wreathed in fog. Nenni was finishing his meal, seated beside Albini from Ferrara, who helped him
put out the party sheet in France, and Casiraghi from Lombardy,
also a veteran of Spain, where he'd commanded a Lister Brigade, and
who would be killed by the Germans five years later in Cuneo. Nenni
ate very frugally; he said less. Under the navy blue beret he never took
off, his brow was smooth and clear. Casiraghi and Albini began to
argue about the different—opposite—prospects of the two Italian
parties, Socialist and Communist. Nenni let them go on. Then he
modestly observed, "Have you ever talked to a priest? A priest will
tell you he's Catholic, but if he thinks for a moment he'll say he's
Christian above all. Well, we may be Serrati-followers or Stalinists
or Trotskyists, but above all we are Marxists. Pirèin, what say?"

Pirèin, that was Piero Albini. Nenni had an inclination (so rare
and so human, it must be said) for tolerance, or so it seemed to Ferranini. But in those days he was immature, too young to understand
that tolerance does not mean accommodation, he didn't really appreciate it. Those were the days in which rumors of an accord between Moscow and Berlin had just begun to float around. Casiraghi
turned to him to ask, polemically, "You, as a Communist, how
would you explain such a shift?"

Ferranini had a ready defense: "Stalin is pulling back so the

Westerners will tear each other to pieces. Why should he pit himself against the Germans? Aren't the French and the English and the Polish also capitalists?"

"Right," said Nenni, peaceably, and Casiraghi did not persist.

But there was something else behind that broad face on which a pair of spectacles glinted, something well beyond easy bonhomie. Nenni had invited him to eat something with them (Ferranini was deeply, wretchedly hungry). He questioned the young man sympathetically, uncondescendingly, and when he left, Nenni was the only one to get up and shake his hand.

"A catastrophe is on the way," he had told him. "After the war, socialism will prevail, and definitively. We will all be able to go back home, and yet what is coming is so terrible that I would rather continue this, this bitter life, if by doing so the worst could be avoided."

Nenni didn't recall the episode (why should he?) but he was interested.

"And what are you doing now, Ferranini, what's your specialty? Seeing as we all have to be specialists now, they say!"

After Ferranini explained, Nenni observed, "The rightists accuse us of being profiteers, because those cooperatives of yours are so efficient. I mean, economically as well."

Ferranini smiled. "When I was involved, up until less than a year ago, the rightists used to accuse us of putting PCI politics ahead of our members' interests. Now it seems they consider us profiteers, 'apes of capitalism.' A good sign. It's fine with me."

"And how do you reply to the charges?"

"You know how our adversaries judge the way things are going in Russia? By the economy. If things are going badly, Communism is to blame. If they're going well, they say Communism is contradictory, that it imitates capitalistic methods, and therefore it is the methods that make the difference. The same goes for the cooperatives of Emilia. Now that they're prospering, the bourgeoisie complains we're money-grubbers. My translation: We're productivity-grubbers. To my comrades in Reggio Emilia I say, pursue productivity. We shouldn't shun productivity but particularism, that is, interest construed not as collective benefit, organism, but as individual profit and recognition. Enemy number one, in cooperativism as in every aspect of socialism, is this: particularism, personalism."

"Agreed, Ferranini. I preach the same thing."

He rose. Unconsciously, Ferranini held him back, carried away.

"But comrade, as I'm sure you know, it's not always easy to distinguish in practice. The same behavior that's good when it aims to enhance the collectivity, is bad when it's not aimed at the collectivity. The 'I, individually, must make money, must distinguish myself, enrich myself, surpass the others.' It's not easy to distinguish, it's a question of intention, state of mind. Isn't that right, comrade?"

"You are right, Ferranini. These imponderables become highly ponderable in the long run, in their effects. We'll meet again, no? Continue the discussion."

A minute later Ferranini was on the phone. He had to let it out, tell the whole story right away.

"Where are you?" said Nuccia. "Still at the chamber? Is everything all right?"

"Yes, I'm fine, better. I feel like another man." His friend Amoruso the doctor, his diagnostic skills honed, understood that in a glance. They'd run into each other in the doorway as Ferranini was leaving parliament.

"Just coming in at this hour? But it's midday!" Ferranini said to his colleague.

"What, I'm supposed to get in at nine? I have more important things to do."

Here Walter got the explanation he'd been looking for. Amoruso was the personal physician of Luigi Longo, the deputy secretary of the party, and he'd gone to examine him at Botteghe Oscure. The last time Longo had said to him, "We're going to need Ferranini one of these days. Tell him to stay in Rome."

"But is Longo ill?" Ferranini's concern was genuine. He was the only one among the party leaders who had approached him, and he liked him for his dry, sober manner. He liked his reputation, too: a tough, severe Piedmontese from Cuneo.

"Well, I guess I can tell you. He makes no mystery of it, he couldn't care less. He's got a gastric ulcer big as a dog's dug, too large, really, and he only survives by living a monk's life."

At Piazza Colonna they turned onto the Corso. Amoruso took him by the arm and continued, confidentially: "It's the ailment of leaders, especially political leaders, and of our party above all. Because at the base we are 'compact,' as the song goes (and as we should be) but at the top we're anything but, dear friend. Longo and Della Vecchia. Especially Longo. They're pulling left, they want to take action, they're *Battleship Potemkin* types, not possibilists. And let me say that as a Communist, a militant Communist, by no means do I approve of them."

"No, I don't suppose you do."

"Anyway, for the last thirteen years Longo and Della Vecchia have been gnawing at the brakes, but in Filippo Turati's case it's the lining of his stomach he's gnawing at, which is worse. Understand: we're not talking about actual conflict here, Don Filippo is discipline incarnate, he's a born lieutenant. He obeys, goes along, conforms. A man of perfect loyalty (if there's a second attack let's hope they shoot at me, he told me) but certainly another condottiero, someone more bellicose, less cold, less methodical, less wise, might have been a good thing. As for the big man himself, he's happy to have a Longo at his side. Togliatti is a man of two natures: one is his own, the extremely able temporizer, and the other is the combativeness of Longo and Della Vecchia. And who is to say the PCI has not profited from this dual consciousness; we're still the strongest in the world after the Russian and the Chinese. There's nothing new in this; it's no great discovery."

"It's all much ado," said Ferranini, who was thinking longingly of his talk with Comrade Nenni.

"Now," said Amoruso who hadn't taken offense, "I'm coming with you to via dei Corornari, I'll have a bite with you. Because I worry about you too, my boy, and I need to see how you eat. Show me how you eat, and I'll tell you how you're doing." He waited in Piazza del Popolo for Amoruso's mud-spattered Appia to appear, and after a quick foray into Caffè Rosati for an *aperitivo*, they got in the car. When they arrived at the trattoria, he saw that the gate next door was draped in black. And inside the courtyard at the printshop there was more black. What had happened? Ferranini rang the bell and the delivery boy came out.

"They just took Gennaro away. He lived upstairs. Died yesterday in the shop."

"Oh Jesus. What was it?"

Gennaro, the returned American, master typesetter in the shop, had been felled by a heart attack, he had simply fallen forward onto the counter without saying a word.

"The doctor said he worked too hard," said the boy.

"Did you hear that?" said Ferranini. "And he wasn't even thirty years old."

He thought of what Zamboni had said to him at the station in Reggio: "When will we abolish labor?" He no longer felt like eating.

"I'm working on legislation for occupational safety," he told Amoruso. "The truth is, labor is always, in and of itself, an attempt on life. Despite the rhetoric we continue to hear, on all sides."

"Hard labor is depraved," said Amoruso, "you're telling that to me, a Neapolitan?"

"Be serious, come on."

"You think I'm joking? It's a medical fact that hard labor is pathological."

"Look," said Ferranini, "it's difficult to contest the notion that labor is a human necessity: I can't do it myself. For a while now, however, I've been asking myself whether it's possible to have socialism without deconsecrating labor."

Amoruso's reasoning followed its own path. "Nature"—now he was being quite serious—"teaches us that labor is by definition fatigue. Labor begins when a task becomes pain and fatigue because it is forcibly prolonged. Leave a horse free in the yard and you'll see he will gravitate spontaneously to the post. But harness the horse and make him circle the post for an hour, and the horse will grow tired and try to resist. In a human being there are various psychic factors that resist having to repeat a series of gestures, even when they do not demand excessive effort. If instead, as usually happens, excessive effort is needed, and also attention, the threshold of the fatigue index is rather quickly reached."

"You admit, then, that Gennaro, the printer, died of exhaustion from overwork."

"That's quite possible, and there is no reason to look for weaknesses in his constitution or general state of health. Among the ideological superstructures of capitalism, its lies, are theories (including medical theories) that work is health-promoting. It is false that work is salubrious, healthful. A doctor who knows his stuff and doesn't conform to capitalist doctrine will come to the opposite conclusion."

Amoruso, the easy-going Amoruso, was a more orthodox socialist than he was, Ferranini had to admit. He framed the matter in class terms. He found an argument against the bourgeois mystification adulterating reality. Ferranini merely felt uncertain. He wondered if the problem was not much larger. Was it the bourgeoisie alone?

Still in her dripping raincoat, Nuccia, as soon as she got home, put half a liter of milk on to heat—her supper. She sat at the kitchen table and took out her football betting card. She was in a hurry; it was 10:00 p.m. and the shop downstairs would be closing soon. Once a rigorous systems player, she'd now returned to hopeful empiricism, that is, chance and gut feeling. SPAL against Palermo: who knew which team might win? Okay, tie. Pro Patria against Genoa?

Playing the football pools was a way into popular fantasy for her, and she wasn't blind to that. There was the pleasure of standing in line with the maid who worked for the lady across the hall, the cashier in the grocery shop where she'd bought the biscuits and Cirio sour-cherry jam. It was how she convinced herself that those four pages of comment on Jean-Paul Sartre's theory of social objects (or collective structures) that she'd just delivered to *Paese Sera* would not separate her, the intellectual, from the good people who worked (and daydreamed) close by her personal and "practico-inert" life, in Sartre's cumbersome phrase. Big ideas and so forth could still be forgiven, Nuccia said to herself resolutely, so long as they were free of privilege and claptrap. No posing, no inane stances. Bucking platitudes, both figurative and concrete, was something she did even too diligently, if not actually charmingly. She risked the noted perils of anti-conformism, being formalistic in reverse. In the bookstore when friends and clients asked "And what are you reading?," she had a copy of Carnacina's huge gastronomy tome on her desk, she whose supper consisted of a caffè latte.

She hadn't even told Walter she was toiling away at an introductory essay to a collection of works by Blanchot, Rousset, and Barthes (from *Writing Degree Zero*), commissioned by her editor, who thought she was (and had said so) one of the few in Italy critically competent to approach that bristly tribe.

It was here that a less estimable side of her character appeared, for as we know pride/modesty employs a subtle semiotics that fools the very victim, to his/her detriment, and not only his/hers. For example there was the episode (it turned out well, as it happened) she had become involved in while she was a partisan in Val d'Ossola, among the young volunteers who had followed Alfredo Di Dio and his men that fabled September of 1944.

She had distinguished herself by her courage and her perfect knowledge of the territory, and thus one day she was chosen to go down the valley, south, to stockpile medicines. One young woman (herself), two young men, and three mules: they had to skirt the ridge of the mountain, staying as high up as possible. On their return, Nuccia, leaving the others in a secure spot with the supplies, crept down toward the track to inspect a column of Germans with their tanks and trucks who had stopped to take a swimming break by the river (a lot of them were already in the water). The reconnaissance mission was her idea, and the Germans might have shot her for it, but in her weakness (her mistaken pride) she didn't want to mention it, even to the chiefs, though the information might have been useful. She got it in her head that they would praise her, and she didn't think she deserved that and didn't want to look like she was chasing rewards.

But then the Germans went back on the march. Vague, alarmed reports came through, and Nuccia, sorry now that she hadn't spoken, decided she must put herself to the test again and do better this time. She had been writing up, with very little help, one of the newssheets they printed up there to keep alive a sense of orderly civilian life (not to keep spirits up—no need of that), and she suddenly abandoned her comrades on a pretext, donned a pair of white tennis shoes, and with a racket under her arm hurried down steep paths to meet the German column on the main road. She met them that evening well ahead of Cuzzago, as they were lighting their campfires. Her courage was of the clearheaded, ironic variety, not very common in a woman. She let herself be captured and questioned, maintaining, in French, that she was a foreigner on holiday.

Naturally they didn't believe her, nor did she expect them to; she had a plan. That night they put her in the back of a car with a man sitting in the front seat keeping watch on her. She kept her eyes open and noticed that while the tanks stayed behind there was a great coming and going of Alpenjäger troops on a mule track that most likely went up to Monte Zeda or Monte Tògano. They were trying to get around the Val d'Ossola front from the east by sending men and light artillery up on the heights. That was good to know; now all she had to do was get out of there. That is, if she was lucky, because the guard did not sleep, did not talk, would not even take a cigarette. She was lucky. Drawn by the scent of young flesh, a predator was circling her cage. It was the Oberstleutnant who had questioned her the evening before. She gave him a signal. It was night, raining. She continued sending him signals, doubly tenacious (she recalled cheerfully) because even at twenty-four she hadn't been beautiful, although she prided herself on having an intriguing face. Until finally he appeared. The guard was sent away and the large, short-legged, heavy-breathing Oberstleutnant—half satyr, half paternal, Nuccia recalled—carried her off, tossing a coat over her, to the woods at the edge of the road. There would be no Judith in Val d'Ossola; as soon as they lay down on the sopping-wet moss at a safe distance from the camp, Nuccia leapt up again. She was urchin-thin at that age. Her escape was not all that thrilling; she had guessed right that the man would not shoot or raise the alarm; it wasn't in his interest.

Now, tonight, those old tales of Val d'Ossola so distant they were next to unbelievable, she had the football pools, the betting card. The faint promise of a Saturday night. Simple, superficial things, these were vital too, in their way, and nothing was at stake beyond two hundred lire.

Nuccia was convinced she needed to win, and win a lot, urgently. The count in her head was very simple: she needed two million to keep Giulia with her, expenses, school, clothing, the things the grandparents were now taking care of. Another million to get herself an old Seicento to drive and to pay for that lightning trip to America.

A four-day, round-trip visit to America was foremost among her immediate plans. Nuccia wasn't one to waste time investigating her own psyche. Why did she have to go and see Nancy? To try to reconcile the two of them. That was how she spared herself remorse, pain, doubts. But I want my heart to be hot, scorching (she said to herself), not at peace, I couldn't care less about having a clear conscience. Which meant she was really going to hear that woman say: I don't want your Walter, you keep him (and maybe she'd shoot back: You are a fool, you have no idea what kind of a man Walter is, and in any case, have no fear, I'll certainly keep him). But more than that, and above all, she wanted to see Nancy with her own eyes. She was burning with curiosity to see her. And finally to be able to say, "And so? That's it?"

Walter. A rapid burst from the doorbell, it was Walter. She was befuddled, hastily hiding the betting card.

"How nice, you've never surprised me like this before. Stay here, sleep here."

Ferranini never visited her there in the evening. All those magistrates living upstairs, downstairs, next door. He was ready to make the socialist revolution, but still a man of order.

"I came to tell you that I'm leaving at six tomorrow morning. They're sending me out. With Comrade Reparatore."

"So you saw Longo, did he call you?"

Ferranini had seen no one. He'd gotten his instructions by letter at home, and that was it. He was not in a good mood.

"Where are you going?"

"I don't know."

"And what are you going to do?"

"None of your business."

"Oh, the great conspirator!" said Nuccia, but without hard feelings. "Don't worry, I won't snatch your secret."

He sat down on the table to remove his shoes, which were full of water; it was pouring outside.

"I'm only going away for a day, I don't see why I have to sound off about it. Come on, tell me: why should I squeal?" He turned sour, tossed his shoes on the floor. "Really. Why squeal? Okay, you're my woman. And so? You make me sound off and what do you get out of it? Tell me!"

He had an obsessive temperament, Nuccia supposed. She'd seen him unable to back away from an (unhealthy) thought at a certain point, unable to wrestle that thought back to its real dimension. It was pointless to try to distract him. You had to plant a different thought in place of his doubt, his suspicion, a thought with some connection to the other, one that seemed no less significant.

"Walter, as of noon yesterday I'm a Communist too, I want you to know. I finally got my card. Yesterday at the Ludovisi section."

Ferranini stopped rubbing his feet and stared at her. "Why was that?"

"Why? Well the idea came to me when I was talking to Amoruso the other day. He didn't trust my political convictions."

"Oh, wonderful."

"Not just because of that, damn it! It's perfectly reasonable that I should want to line myself up with my man, have another bond with you."

"Oh, wonderful. It's not your duty but your man that inspires you to join the party. Any idea what the party means to the Russians, how you join the party in the USSR?"

Here Nuccia came out with the wrong answer. "But this is Italy!"

"So we do things the way we please, *all'italiana*?"

"Hey, they took me. And I thought it would please you. Oh, Walter!"

"I'm not saying you don't have the credentials, you have a history that many might envy. If they'd gotten their hands on you in '44, you would have ended up in some torture chamber. But that's another question."

"I'd say it's the same question."

He was walking up and down in agitation. In his socks.

"You signed up the way you might go to the shop to buy a bottle of cologne. And you went to the Ludovisi, where the rich people live."

Nuccia searched for another tack, another tone. She took off her suit jacket; there was nothing underneath but her slip and brassiere.

"I'm going to be a lousy Communist, I'm not much interested in politics. I'm interested in you. So, private life doesn't count? Longo is always the deputy secretary of the PCI even in bed with his wife?"

"Listen, drop it now, it's better."

"You like private life too. Who was it that coined the verb *nucciare*? To nuzzle. Come on, warm up, be a good fellow, who invented the term?"

He wasn't quite an obsessive, but Ferranini was utterly devoid of any sense of humor, that was for sure. Accustomed as he was to taking everything seriously, he blamed his origins: people from Emilia were like that.

"That has nothing to do with it. It's your fault that you brought it to mind."

Her snort of laughter met an uncompromising frown.

6

THAT SUNDAY the monthly order sheet had Comrade Deputy Ferranini down for a meeting to discuss "The USSR Under the Guide of Comrade Khrushchev." It was no great prospect, forcing three hundred workers to forego a morning of leisure while he served up that threadbare topic inside the Traiano Cinema of Civitavecchia. But this other matter they'd palmed off on him, to take Comrade Mazzola by the ear because he was suspected of, or accused of, deviationism (easy to say, but it was a serious charge, something that could sink a man), that one he didn't like at all. Mazzola. Roberto Mazzola of Turin. He didn't know him. Remembered reading somewhere articles under that name, knew that he was an important figure in the Young Communist Federation, although he had no role in the party nationally, at least at present, and that he had been a partisan in Piedmont. Or in Lombardy. That was it, and he had never met the man.

"What can I say," Reparatore was lumbering into the seat to his right, "I don't know him either but maybe that's why they sent us. What did they write to you?"

"That Comrade Bordino would give us more details when we got there. It seems the man's disorganized, muddleheaded. There's nothing solid against him, but they say there's an 'atmosphere of indiscipline.' He says he doesn't believe in de-Stalinization, and these days, you know—"

"An atmosphere. Okay, so we come because of the atmosphere, alight from the atmosphere, to correct the atmosphere. It's crap, Walter, crap! Anyway, why didn't Longo speak to us about it directly?"

"Hush, you're too loud. Don't shout like that, Giobatta."

Big Giobatta Reparatore, *u' notaro*—the notary, as they called him down in Cerignola—represented old-school trade unionism in the chamber and in the party: he was the rebel, the *frondeur*. Schooled by Verganini and Del Buono, an associate of Di Vittorio and from the same Puglia town, he'd done two years of jail time at Santa Maria Capua Vetere, two years of *confino*, internal exile, in the far north at Baselga di Piné, and had been shot during the uprising against the Nazis in Naples. He'd been one of the first leaders of the CGIL. In his three sessions in parliament he'd become quite a figure because of his thundering oratory and refusal to mince words (reprimanded innumerable times by the president), and because of his fierce, unsociable habits. He shaved twice a week, saw no one, recognized no one. He was fond of Walter Ferranini, of whom he'd once said, in his absence, "He's one of the few here who never lifted a finger to get here." And he himself was also certainly among those few. The party electoral archive held a singular document, the doctor's statement he had sent in '48 in support of his refusal to be named a candidate (the fact was, he was close to stone-deaf). But Togliatti, urged by Della Vecchia, had forced him to accept.

Reparatore was still talking in the same loud voice. Fortunately they would soon be taking off, the plane engines had begun to roar.

"Wait and see if I'm not right that this Mazzola is a kid. In Rome our beards are gray, we like the quiet life. The young prefer to protest in the streets."

Ferranini let him go on.

"You'll see, this Mazzola is a leftist. Deviating left is just being consistent, or at the very most, intransigent. Deviating the other way, that would be bad. I can't stand this making us play the Dominicans of the Inquisition. What do you say? Say something," he was shouting in his ear. "What's the matter? You won't answer?"

Ferranini lost his patience. "Oh, leave me alone. You want me to start yelling too? They give us instructions, we carry them out. Or at least I do."

"Between us," Reparatore started up again, quieter now, "is there a single one of us who doesn't deviate? The undersigned? Well, the undersigned, too, deviates, potentially. They treat me with respect, treat us with respect, because as Di Vittorio used to say we are one of the two wheels of the cart, and you can't do politics without the unions, the CGIL. Are you aware of that?"

"Who says I'm not?"

"Let me talk. Suppose that tomorrow the interests of the unions are no longer in accord with the party line, something that is by no means impossible, because let us not forget that labor has needs, both immediate and not, that are not identical to those of the politicians. Well then, what happens: they accuse us of trade-unionist heresy (at the least). That is, of doing what we're put on earth to do. The leader of the unions after the October Revolution, the great Mikhail Yefremov, better known as Tomsky, veteran of the Putilov steelworks, was in constant conflict with Lenin and Trotsky. Is that true, or not?"

"I guess it is."

"Furthermore, leaving aside the matter of trade unionists and myself, who can swear to understand everything, to approve of everything, for example, why Khrushchev drew back after going into Hungary; why all this zeal, this bluster against the Cold War as if it were strange that there's a war between existing socialism become state and power, world power, and the capitalists? I speak of those of us who live in direct contact with the base, the masses, the worker who wants to know and judge. I'm not talking about bureaucrats. I'm not talking about the theorists in their paper tower, *Critica Marxista*. Tell me, are you happy with all this, do you approve of everything? If not, say so. We're just two friends here. Eh? Read Marx's letters. If someone had an objection and spoke to him about it, he'd thank him: 'You are helping me make progress, to improve myself.' Eh?"

Under this hail of verbiage, Ferranini had long since unfolded his newspaper to read, or try to. (Italians live on blather, consume themselves in blather. Everything ends in blather, what a fool country.) Then his mind began to wander. He remembered a trip from

Philadelphia to New York. It must have been in '41. Because of the war certain imported goods were hard to find and the old man had sent him to look for them. Just before he left there was an imploring phone call from the school in Meadville. "I need tulip bulbs, you can find them in New York. Mind you, only the Fulgens cultivar, from Holland, nothing else." As if the war were just a dream, and nothing existed but Nancy Demarr and her love of tulips. And yet her certainty that she mattered a great deal in this world was a powerful force, and he had to struggle with that force, and continued to struggle with it in some way.

Comrade Reparatore had decided to stop talking and was getting ready to fall asleep. Fine thoughts, Reparatore's, great discoveries: who didn't share his objections? Who didn't know all that? He, Ferranini, envied the comrades whose only objections had to do with the conflict between politics and trade unions.

His doubts went quite a bit deeper; they were a bit more serious. These last few days "his" problem had taken definition with sudden clarity. Socialism was an optimistic program, and that was nothing unheard of, nothing new. And nothing to object to, except for one point. Ignored by the others (or considered negligible) that point expanded in his mind and became overriding, fundamental.

Abolition of the existing conditions (in Italy for example). Substantialization of freedoms, which would cease to be mere formal rights. Excellent. All power to workers and, finally, the withering away of the socialist state itself. Good. To each according to his need, without having to endure a pinchpenny calculation of his abilities. Victory over privilege and selfishness, and even, apparently, victory over nature. But here was the point. The victory over nature was only apparent. The servitude of labor remained, it was a physical necessity, even when the species did not exploit it. And the fatigue, the ordeal of labor remained as well. Biology certifies that there is no escaping the struggle for life, which is the struggle against surrounding reality, and there's no getting away from it, and in fact no one does.

When they got to Caselle, it turned out that a colleague from the

chamber, Comrade Montobbio, had traveled with them. The pleasant, smiling Montobbio said, "Oh, I didn't want to disturb you, you
were discussing serious matters. I listened with pleasure and I'm almost entirely in agreement with you." At the airport exit they
watched him drive off at the wheel of a convertible, a powerfully
built man, some fifty-five years old, and though the morning was
clear and very cold, Ferranini saw that he wore no more than a suede
jacket and nothing on his head. Reparatore had been with Montobbio in internal exile in '38 and '39, under police custody in Trentino,
and knew him well. A good comrade, a good Communist; his
thinking might be limited but he had tremendous courage. An excellent element, with a tendency to take charge, not a man to obey
someone else's directives. He'd been a partisan outside the command structure, alone and a bit of a ruffian. In the car that was taking them into town, Reparatore told him, "After he'd done away
with quite a few Fascists (never consulting anyone else), he nearly
finished off Mussolini, Il Duce himself, in December '43. It was an
equal match, when Il Duce was still strong, not like when they
strung him up like a side of beef in Piazzale Loreto at the end of the
party. It was a story that didn't end well, and Montobbio had confided it only to a few close friends. You see, one fine day he and a lady
friend every bit his equal moved into a place near Salò, pretending to
be a couple on their honeymoon. They were there for a month, waiting for the right moment. Christmas arrived, and the priest came by
to bless the house, as they do in Lombardy. The girl leaned out the
window.

"Father, my husband is ill, please come up." The priest came upstairs, they gagged and bound him, and Montobbio put on his cassock and took his pass (because in those days the priests and friars
used to associate with Mussolini) and went to Il Duce's villa. They
let him in and he got to the anteroom with the loaded 7.65 in his
pocket. Nobody knew that Il Duce was out, he had left by a secret
gate. Montobbio waited; half an hour went by, an hour, and finally
he had to leave empty-handed. He arrived back just in time. The
priest, a big, strong fellow himself, had gotten free, and the lady

friend, to keep him from running out and reporting them, had gone to bed with him, but now even that was finished and the priest wanted some fresh air. "Montobbio told me these details himself, laughing about it. In short, they tied up the priest once again, and gagged him, and off they went by motorbike to hide in Brescia."

"A shame," said Ferranini.

"A shame?"

He thought for a moment. "When a man is faithful to his ideas, he shouldn't mix courage with certain other things."

Corso Francia. Headquarters of the Federation.

Bordino, the Federation secretary, was waiting for them. He hadn't requested their intervention but he felt it was a good thing. The Mazzola case was somewhat special; there were as yet no reasons to refer him to the Disciplinary Committee, and anyway Mazzola held no high position: he'd been the secretary of a town PCI youth circle, then a local party secretary. But he had a certain following in Piedmont and even beyond, and a certain prestige, and the dissident stance he was taking had begun to be a problem. Longo had done well to send people from Rome, people outside the local organization, so that there would be a guarantee of impartiality. Mazzola must listen and let himself be convinced. Bordino seemed a man of few words and quite frank, and yet there was a hint of embarrassment in his voice as he went on.

"Comrade Senator Pisani has been here in Turin for quite a few days now. He'll be coming with you. Longo telephoned me from Rome about it."

"Goddamn," Reparatore blurted out, "this Mazzola moves mountains."

"Okay, so we're in agreement? Mazzola has been informed and he's ready, and Comrade Pisani will be here any minute."

Reparatore shook his head. "Not so fast, my friend. You have Ferranini, you have Pisani, who's an authority, not to mention a big intellect. So tell me what I'm doing here? I'm going back." He took out the train schedule.

"You people here, you yokels, make an excellent dish, fonduta.

And I have time to walk around town, eat some fonduta, and make the rapido back to Rome."

"Longo gave orders," said the Federation secretary.

"He gave *you* orders. And in case you don't know"—now Reparatore was talking to Ferranini—"Comrade Bordino was a warehouseman at Fiat Grandi Motori ten years ago, did I get that right? And today they call him the anti-Fiat, Agnelli's great antagonist. Every day the big man Valletta reads *l'Unità* to find out what Bordino's up to. You think Bordino's afraid of some bureaucrats in Rome?"

At 10:00 a.m. precisely Ferranini, followed by Senator Paolo Pisani, rang the bell at the building on via Savarino a Rivoli where the young Mazzola couple lived on the second floor, their windows shaded by the branches of a cedar.

Signora Mazzola received them shyly. "My husband is very pleased you have come to see him."

Ferranini had heard Mazzola was in bed with a broken leg.

"They put on a plaster cast, and now I'm keeping him in bed because he has the flu. This morning he had a fever over a hundred."

"Take us to him," said Pisani. "We won't trouble him for long."

Ferranini was surprised to find that Mazzola appeared genuinely content to see them. From his slender face, you'd guess he was no more than thirty. His skin was delicate, fair, and reddened by the fever.

"I'm afraid I must receive you here," he said smiling. "Broke my tibia skiing. Twenty days off work. It's a bourgeois sport, I'm aware," he said, once again excusing himself with a smile.

"I've read that the Soviet ski team is winning some races at Chamonix," said Pisani, who lowered himself carefully (old, thin, arthritic as he was) into a cretonne-covered chair between the sickbed and the window. Ferranini took his place on a chair beside the door.

"There are other things that may be more bourgeois in your mode of acting and thinking," Pisani resumed. "Your lack of self-critical knowledge. You don't mind if I get right to the point?"

"Go ahead," said Mazzola, with just a tiny tremor in his voice.

"All right. That and the exhibitionist satisfaction of showing off what we all too easily take to be our own ideas, and which are instead timeworn errors. What, in a fashionable expression that you, too, have helped to disseminate, is called the impatience of the base—very often no more than the presumption of young people reluctant to bow to the experience of their elders. Recently you spoke at a debate on the question 'Is there a crisis in the youth movements of the parties?' At Novara, if I'm not mistaken."

"No, comrade, it was at Vercelli. And not recently. Three months ago."

"The details are irrelevant, I think. You spoke in the presence of Liberals, Social Democrats, and Republicans. You said there was a crisis in the Young Communist Federation. A symptom, in your view, of a lack of communication, both practical and ideological, between the new grass-roots generation—buzzing with intransigence, eager for concrete action—and the hierarchy. And here you mentioned the Central Committee, for what reason it was unclear. Implicitly or not, you accuse the hierarchy of being paralyzed by *attendismo*, by fence-sitting. And even by *trasformismo*, by political opportunism. In any event, of being obsolete, laggards, defeatists. Disappointing, in short. A scenario both callous and unwarranted."

While he spoke, Comrade Pisani observed with evident interest the motions of a great cedar bough that the stiff northern wind was whipping back and forth until it nearly struck the windowpanes. Pisani, the most cultivated and incisive speaker in the party, if not the most stirring or persuasive, expressed himself in a cool, quiet monotone. Ferranini had heard him speak many times but never so close at hand, in such a small space. The pleasant Pugliese inflections of Giobatta Reparatore were still in his ear, and what struck him most about Pisani was an indefinable something that both drew and repelled him. In a country where such a thing was practically unheard of, Pisani's diction was lucid, coldly precise. There was no accent or any trace of a provincial or regional origin (he'd been born and raised in a Tuscan city). It made his words sound neutral, inconsequential. Like a Sangiovese (thought Ferranini), that might even be fourteen percent alcohol but had no zest, no distinction.

"The Novara episode was just the first that comes to mind. I'm told you've held dozens of meetings and written dozens of articles. Three, recently, in a publication of the metalworkers' union. One of your favorite theses is that socialism contains a 'Christian' tendency and also a 'Catholic,' that is to say a lax, negligent tendency, and the PCI, in your view, is 'Catholicizing.' This distinction between the two tendencies is not your own, Mazzola."

"That's true, I read it in a book. I don't remember which book."

"I'll tell you. It comes from a 1919 issue (if I'm not mistaken) of Gramsci's *L'Ordine Nuovo*, in which Tasca wrote of that distinction for entirely different purposes. I advise you to read it, Mazzola, to refresh this argument of yours, which smells of rancid anti-Catholicism. Not just in honor of our open-door policy toward the Christian Democratic masses but for an even better reason. Have we ever asked ourselves" (here Pisani fixed his eyes on Ferranini for a moment; the matter was addressed to him, then) "why the Communist movement has spread so widely in Catholic countries, in Latin America, for example? I would say that even the most timid interpretation of the phenomenon urges feelings of solidarity, and let me say in all seriousness, gratitude toward the Church of Rome. That clarified, let us now turn once more to ourselves. Comrade Mazzola, the leitmotif that I pointed to in your public expression, the oft-repeated theme, is that those who wish to obtain a reform of the party's inner life must join with you and those who think like you. To restore intransigence. And more, to restore morality. Do I quote you accurately?"

"Yes."

"The 'purists' like yourself must prevail over the bourgeoisified, that is, the rest of us. And afterwards, wage war on external enemies, realize programs without compromise, refuse all temporizing tactics, align with Stalinism that's understood as extremism."

Mazzola listened, his fine hair glued to his head with sweat. He didn't move a muscle. He said, "It was far too great an honor for you to have come to see me, comrade. But I was pleased. Now I understand why you came." He smiled, a smile apparently neither bitter nor ironic, and then said, "The honor you do me stands, nevertheless."

He didn't bother with his other visitor; it was clear that so far as Mazzola was concerned only Pisani mattered. And yet Ferranini felt sympathy for the man.

"Don't be upset, Mazzola. Comrade Pisani came to"—he stopped for a moment to search for a word and found nothing better—"to help you."

Pisani looked around, sent him a glance that did not express agreement but neither did it show dissent or surprise. If anything it meant: What you may have to say is of no account, it is nothing. He saw young Signora Mazzola come into the room. She carried a tray with three steaming cups of coffee.

"Roberto, I'm going out before the shops close. I'll leave you with your friends. I'll just leave the front door ajar."

She left, and Ferranini was the only one of them to take a coffee. While he drank it, he noticed that the room was not a bedroom but a very plain sort of sitting room, and Mazzola lay on a sofa made over into a bed. Ferranini thought: His wife transferred him here so that we would not have to enter their marital bedroom, out of delicacy, then, out of modesty. Then he thought: They love each other. And then he thought: Nancy. Would Nancy have ever done such a thing? Meanwhile the other man resumed speaking. The words with which he began ("Now it's time for me to classify your attitude, except that it amply speaks for itself") made it clear that Pisani felt the mission he was carrying out was beneath him, tedious. His tone was cold and patient, annoyed.

Reparatore had not exaggerated. Pisani was a big intellect, and the party colleagues who called him the Italian Suslov after the Soviet hard-liner were not wrong, nor were the bourgeois papers that dubbed him Doctor Subtilis, the hairsplitter. Not that he hadn't played an active political role in the PCI; when still quite young, he had been one of the founders at the Livorno Congress of 1921. But by education and temperament he was destined to occupy himself with doctrine, and he was a strenuous and honest defender of rigorous orthodoxy. Yes, he had a good mind, and in party circles it was said that Joe Stalin (another doctrinal highbrow) had once observed: "With Togliatti we have the poet, with Pisani the philosopher. Fortunately there's no need yet of the revolutionary." That revolutionaries were superfluous in the present moment, or rather, harmful, was exactly the objection that Pisani, annoyed, was now repeating to that young man in his little room.

"Your attitude speaks for itself, Comrade Mazzola, and there is no need here to mention the great man who diagnosed extremism as the infantile disorder of socialism. I'd like to think you were able to recognize your errors on your own. But the fact they are so elementary and so evident makes your conduct harder to justify. By seeking to spread them by means of your naive but persistent proselytizing you have assumed a great responsibility. Are you aware of this? I'm told that in just a few months some two to three hundred letters from your sympathizers have arrived in your office in the Turin Federation. That is a not a negligible number, Comrade Mazzola."

"My sympathizers, as you call them, are many more than that. Each letter is signed by three or four persons."

"May I ask where they come from?"

"The work I've done, I've done between Milan, Genoa, and Turin. The industrial triangle, and that's not by accident. My method—you will call it elementary, like all my errors—is this: every time I'm off work I go to wait for the workers as they exit the factory gates, and call about twenty or thirty of them over to me. And then we sing 'Bandiera Rossa.' Yes, don't be surprised, I begin by singing 'Bandiera Rossa' with them, and the older ones teach it to those who are my age or younger. Because 'Bandiera Rossa' is outlawed and nobody sings it anymore. Then afterward I say a few words, and the substance is this: Are you Bolsheviks? Do you want the party to be Bolshevik? And I explain the meaning of the term, because it too has been outlawed and nobody knows it. Here, I'd really like it if you could explain, even if it bores you. Why has the term Bolshevik been out of fashion among Communists for so many years?"

Once again there was no trace of irony in his manner of speaking, thought Ferranini, a silent witness to the exchange. The young man's question was serious, intent, respectful. Pisani stuck his thumbs in his vest and stretched out his legs. His eyes were fixed on the wall above the bed where a promotional calendar in color showed a mountain landscape covered with snow. He began to explain.

"The term 'Bolshevik,' in parentheses, was regularly printed on Soviet government official documents after the words 'Pan-Russian Communist Party.' Up until 1922. After that it was discontinued, and for good reason. You, Mazzola, would know that if instead of engaging in dilettantish, itinerant propaganda, you bothered to learn some history. The reason, in any case, is this: at a certain point it was no longer necessary for Bolshevik Communists to distinguish themselves from the so-called revolutionary socialists of the left and right, or from the Mensheviks. Do you see? Those groups had ceased to be politically relevant. They disappeared."

Roberto Mazzola was silent for a moment. And then he said, calmly, almost sweetly, "Here among us, the Mensheviks have not disappeared. These days they are the majority inside the party."

The distant wail of a violin could be heard. A radio, downstairs. For several minutes, to Ferranini it seemed quite a long interval, the two men did not speak or move. To Ferranini's relief, finally one of them spoke. The even, accentless voice of Comrade Pisani.

"Would you please clarify your thinking?"

Mazzola reached for the coffee cup, Ferranini pushed it toward him, and Mazzola downed a swallow. Then, addressing Pisani, he said, "We're in a phase of de-Stalinization, are we not, comrade?"

"And so?"

"And so, forgive me, but if Stalin was not the whole of communism, he was much of it. He was, he personified, all that was rigorous, uncompromising, I want to say tragic, in a revolutionary phase that is not yet over. Not even in the Soviet Union. And I won't mention, comrade, his dedication to plans for world revolution, plans for active intervention—"

"But," Pisani interrupted with a smile on his face, "are you speaking to me of Stalin or of Trotsky?"

"Stalin!"

"Are you certain you're not confusing the two? At any rate, continue. Speak."

Mazzola pulled himself to a seated position and his eyes lit up. "I say, the PCI is de-Stalinizing and this exacerbates, speeds up its transformation. There's a tendency to compromise, to back down. In my view, de-Stalinization in a context such as ours can have no other consequence. I feel that too many comrades are effectively becoming social democrats in their thinking and their political action."

Pisani raised his shoulders slightly. "You used the term Mensheviks before. Now you speak of social democrats. Shall I deduce that the two things mean the same to you?"

The other thought for a moment. "Yes, in practical terms, yes."

"Well then, I must once again explain something. Long before the October Revolution, Lenin and his comrades chose to call themselves Bolsheviks, in opposition to the Mensheviks (the 'minority'). However, up until March 1918, that is several months after the Revolution, Lenin and his colleagues kept their official title of social democrats. And thus 'Bolshevik' and 'social democrat' meant something quite different to them from 'Menshevik.' While according to you, 'social democrat' is the same as 'Menshevik' and can equally be used to vilify. Do you see, Comrade Mazzola?"

"I think so."

"In Italy the party of the Social Democrats is our adversary for the simple reason that they are not social democrats. They are reformists, mere reformists. To use a phrase from Lenin, they are not red but yellow. Comrade Mazzola, have I been able to resolve your misunderstanding?"

"Yes."

"Spend less time propagandizing and pay more attention to your terminological baggage and you'll be spared the need for second thoughts. Note, also, that I am not concerned with the substance of your accusations against party leaders. There are organs dedicated to making discipline respected, to bringing to heel those who violate it even if only in rash judgment, and the task of reporting on your case to those organs falls to Comrade Ferranini, I think. My job relative to you is to identify the criteria (let us call them that) that direct your, shall we say 'factionalist' approach. As for the practical manifestations, as for the consequences of that approach, it is Comrade Ferranini's job to look into that. Ferranini, do you have a clear picture of what Mazzola has been saying? Speak up, please. Have you no questions to pose?"

Comrade Ferranini in turn considered the matter before he replied, "No."

A shadow of disapproval passed across Pisani's eyes as he turned his gaze on him. "You wish no further clarification?"

"I think things are already clear."

"As for myself," Pisani continued, "I need a bit more information. From what I understand, one of the preferred targets of your attacks has been Comrade Deputy Gildo Montobbio. Just a few days ago at the Turin Federation offices, Bordino and other leaders present, you accused Montobbio of deviationism. Once again, it isn't the substance of the matter that interests me. I ask you: In what way does this deviationism express itself, in your view? First off, what does deviationism mean to you?"

While Pisani spoke, Ferranini studied the young man's leg in plaster, awkward and immobile, so evident under the bedclothes. He saw that when the name Montobbio was pronounced, all that was alive in that body shuddered. He looked at his face, that gentle and determined smile he had liked. He no longer looked the same; the face was drawn, frantic.

"Montobbio? Montobbio is pitiful; a poor, puny man corrupted by the bourgeois leprosy. That's what I have to say to you."

Pisani frowned, raised his eyes to the ceiling. "Be careful now. I'm not interested in the personal, as I said."

"The personal, in this case, is a human matter, a serious, very serious matter that concerns me, that concerns the party that this individual pretends to represent in the chamber and elsewhere!"

"Mazzola, calm down," Pisani advised him. He took his hand.

"Let me say it, let me say it! You ask: In what way does Montobbio deviate? Here's how! He's rotten with particularism, that man, he's rotten with personalism. What drives him—and he'll use any means to get it—is his triumph as an individual, is winning, pushing others aside, undermining this person or that, replacing them, and you people in Rome, how can you not know that? The party counts for nothing, what counts is that he's talked about, that he stands out, that he gains a lot of space, that finally he, a man who has suffered (he even said as much!), has the good life. You want proof? You will find it, the most recent proof, in the newspapers of Rome and Turin (not in ours, not in *l'Unità*, mind you) of October 10, 11, and 12, and November 1 and 2, under the headlines 'Flora Construction Co-op' or 'Tyrrhenian Real Estate' or 'Tyrrhenian Bus Lines,' et cetera. You propose I study the history of Russian communism; I propose, forgive me, that you read what the press has to say about Roman communism!"

"Is the comrade very sure he is not committing the same sin he so vehemently berates others for?" said Pisani, calm, superior, indulgent. "I mean particularism, personalism. Are there not strictly personal motives, or rather familial motives, behind this attack? Can you guarantee that?"

Mazzola thrust his elbows down, as if he meant to get out of bed. He was shaking all over. He raised a hand to brush away the hair in his face, and came down on one hip facing Ferranini, his back to the other man. Without trying to change position, without looking at him, he spoke.

"I can guess (oh, can I guess!) what you refer to, comrade. And I guarantee you that I do have reasons, not to detest him, no, but to *know* him. I know Montobbio better than anyone. He was a soldier in Croatia and after the armistice in '43 he came back to Italy and went in a military hospital to be treated for otitis. My mother, a Red

Cross nurse, worked in that hospital. Afterward Gildo joined the partisans and was active in Lombardy, around Brescia; I used to see him often. He would come to see my mother, who was living with me and my grandparents in a villa on Lake Garda. He became friends with my mother, and with me. I was fifteen, he was a grown man; he intimidated me but I admired him, wanted to be like him. He was a sincere Communist, a good fighter; he won both of us over, he converted us. I say 'converted us' intentionally, because he came from the working class, while we were of the masters; my maternal grandfather had owned a wool mill in the Veneto. We felt we had discovered a new world in him, and we entered that new world with all our enthusiasm. Gildo went to Rome after the war, and we followed him. My mother had been widowed for twelve years; she was still young, free. I studied engineering in Rome, while he began his climb up the party hierarchy, was named a deputy, changed. He changed in the way I told you. He renounced his past, and it was logical that he would renounce his ties with my mother and me. We finally came back up north. He had mistresses; there was one in Turin who had a child by him and he'd invite her to Rome—"

"Enough!" Comrade Pisani interrupted him. "Such particulars are not necessary. Your story amply confirms one fact, the only one that interests us. Your political judgment about the person of whom you speak cannot in any way be considered objective. Be good enough to admit that!"

"May I?" came an energetic voice from the hallway.

It was the doctor. He came into the room, a man about the same age as his patient; he didn't look around and paid no attention to the two visitors. He sat unceremoniously on the edge of the bed.

Ferranini got up and left; Comrade Pisani followed.

Not a word was said between them. Standing, smoking a cigarette, Pisani looked around inquisitively at the three rooms, one after the other (one was the kitchen), that could be seen from the small dark hallway. The doctor remained with his patient for no less than twenty minutes. Coming out, he said, "Mazzola's case is atypical, and quite severe. He needs rest. He must be left in peace."

Pisani shrugged his shoulders. "No one's threatening his peace."

The other man opened the door to leave. "When I was coming up the stairs," he replied dryly, "I heard the sounds of an argument."

"You mean to say, of a conversation," Pisani corrected him.

They went back in.

Mazzola picked up immediately, continuing to speak without turning toward Pisani.

"You were saying, comrade, that I'm unable to be objective. But I was speaking of facts—facts in the public domain. The bourgeois press has been able to exploit these. No denials have been issued."

"Permit me to insist that your objectivity is deficient," replied Pisani with great didactic patience. "A deficiency that is evident and I would add excusable, if we consider the peculiar character, the peculiarly private character, of your relationship with the person who is the object of your attacks. But now, before terminating this conversation so far as I am concerned, let me restate what has emerged. Your ideas suggest a certain confusion, or imprecision, and so I shall try to reorder them in terms of what I've understood. In the first place, you are opposed to the political line vulgarly known as de-Stalinization. Which line amounts, in your opinion, to a form of revisionist backsliding (defeatism, fence-sitting) already today manifest among the PCI leadership. Furthermore, generalizing from a single case that you claim to know and be competent to judge, you speak of moral laxity. What's more, you don't rule out a broad, overall tendency toward deviationism. A rightward 'drift,' shall we say, of the entire movement. Am I right?"

"Yes."

"The cadres, at the top, and also in the middle ranks are here and there (did I get that right?) guilty of Menshevism, of social democracy, in your opinion. Both of those terms to mean a propensity toward reformism. Correct? The remedy you suggest is obviously a shift to the left, both in organization and objectives. Incidentally, I wouldn't say you show much originality. Shift to the left and return to the Stalinist line: this is 'your' hard line, your maximalism? Among other things you suggest that the anthem 'Bandiera Rossa' be reinstated. And this, perhaps, is your most concrete proposal. I invite Comrade Ferranini to present it in the appropriate forums."

Mazzola looked calmer now.

"'My' maximalism is quite different from what you imagine," Mazzola said. "It's not reckless or illusory. It's a call for cohesion, for discipline. I believe that to build communism we need men willing to sacrifice, to become 'masses' in the real sense. Not men who see in communism a way to stand out. The bourgeois accuses us of negating the personal, that is, accuses us of just what we're proud of, what ought to be our merit. He gets his back by exciting that domineering instinct of personalism, the individual, in us, too. And so he breaks us apart. The nations in the Communist bloc must exalt their nationalism (see, Yugoslavia detaches itself, Hungary revolts), and the men who make up the communist masses must exalt their individualism: this is what the bourgeois wants, because he knows that is the way to liquidate his enemy. And Montobbio and his like are the liquidation of communism. I say 'and his like' because individualism (or personalism, or careerism, et cetera) is a widespread phenomenon among us."

Ferranini put a hand on the bed to shake Mazzola's. Widespread, he thought: Yep, do I ever know about that!

"We must submerge ourselves in the mass, and repudiate ourselves as individuals."

"I see there is also a mystical component in you," Comrade Pisani observed, half smiling. "Don't forget that reality (including that of the Turin PCI Federation) lies in praxis."

"I am being fully practical! I say, if we add together even as many as five million individuals, men who perceive themselves above all as individuals, that doesn't add up to a communist movement. Are you going to tell me otherwise? There are two tendencies that favor individualism and discourage cohesion with the collectivity, and one of these is the pursuit of affluence, which means the motorbike, the cheap car, the TV for the worker, and for Montobbio, as we know, a great deal more. The other tendency is attachment to hierarchy. I don't want to rely on others, I want to stand out, take command over others. Note that this second tendency has nothing to do with interest in politics. It's the death of that interest. Those of us who work with the base know that today the base is all too often apolitical. Largely apolitical."

Ferranini could not help but think: Is he right! He's right.

"This *hierarchism* doesn't represent a desire for responsibility; it's the wish to gain *position* even inside the party organization. Against hierarchism, I preach comradeship. Be very wary of positions! When they offer you a position on the internal committee, in the cell, in the section? You turn it down. Don't worry, there will always be plenty of people, too many, who want that position and will take it."

Standing in the embrasure before the window, Comrade Pisani was drumming his fingers lightly on the glass. He turned around, smiling.

"Yours is an old anarchist error. Please take note. An error that leads us a long way from socialism. Nevertheless, if your words imply that you profess humility, personal subordination, and discipline, that will be taken into account quite willingly. We shall see how disciplined you are in your own particular case. If, and in what spirit, you obey the instructions the party may deliver."

"Instructions and perhaps measures," said Mazzola. "I've thought about that. I don't have many responsibilities, and those I have are modest. Will you divest me of those too? Very well, I'm happy to go back to being one hundred percent a follower. Certainly I won't have another opportunity to speak to someone as influential as you, comrade, so allow me to take advantage of the situation and make a suggestion, however presumptuous. Bureaucracy, even in the USSR, is fought on a technical level. We must fight it at the moral level. We must make it so that in the party, people would prefer to work, rather than to command."

The other man didn't bother to reply. He cast a last gaze out the window, at the mighty cedar bough whipping in the wind.

"Get well, Comrade Mazzola. I hope you'll get well! You'll need to."

There were no farewells. Ferranini alone shook the young man's hand, without saying anything. He would have liked to, but couldn't find the words.

Outside, Comrade Pisani said he'd like to walk for a bit. They did—some two hundred paces from the gate of the house to the main street—the Federation automobile trailing behind them. As they were about to get in the car, Mazzola's wife caught up with them. She was out of breath, she had run, with two long loaves of bread and a bottle of milk poking out of the string bag on her arm.

"Roberto will be on sick leave for a while. If you gentlemen are staying in Turin, please come back to see him. Come back. And thank you, sirs!"

She shut the car door.

7

On the 1:00 p.m. rapido back to Rome, Ferranini looked around in vain for company.

He wanted to talk to someone. He marched past all the compartments on the train, hoping to find Giobatta. He wasn't there, the pursuit of fonduta had taken time. Ferranini was left alone with his thoughts all the way back; the hours were not pleasant.

When he arrived that evening at Termini station, he found someone he wasn't expecting.

"How did you know to be here?"

"Didn't you say you were coming back with Reparatore? I telephoned his wife, she told me where you were and that you'd probably be back now. Your colleagues aren't as secretive with their women as you are."

"Who did you say you were?"

"I said I was your secretary. Do I get scolded?"

"I'm not saying anything. We'll have to see how this thing plays out."

They ate in a little place on via Firenze.

Scowling, ignoring her warnings ("Don't stuff yourself like that before going to bed, you'll pay for it tonight!"), Ferranini was silent for a long time. Then he said, "In '44. Did you by any chance know a partisan chief named Montobbio?"

"He was Captain Bianco back then. And now he's in parliament with you, in your group. Yes, I knew him."

"What kind of guy was he?"

"A tough guy. And women liked him. If you want the truth, I liked him too, you know, from afar. Later he got involved with a woman who looked like Ingrid Bergman and they lived together, not only up north but in Rome, too."

"Do you remember her name?"

"No. They said she was a widow, with a grown son. The son lived up north, but he came down to Rome and took her away by force. She was attached to both of them, to her lover and her son. A great drama."

"Did you ever meet the son?"

"No."

Ferranini went back to his food. He was thinking, and she meanwhile pursued the matter, giving it a peculiar slant.

"I haven't had reason to speak to Montobbio since, but I've seen him, and he has the reputation of being, even today, the handsomest Communist deputy in the chamber. Along with Magrò."

"What?" Ferranini was distracted.

"Yes, well you're not the most attractive bunch in the chamber, in general. You had Antonio Giolitti, but he went over to the Socialists. Three or four of the Christian Democrats are not too bad to look at: Alessandrini, Moro, Colombo. The neo-Fascists are better."

"The neo-Fascists?"

"Help, I'm not saying another word, or you'll take away my party card."

After they finished eating, they walked down via XX Settembre and via delle Quattro Fontane.

"What if I meet a colleague at this time of night, with you on my arm? They all know we're married, you to another man, me to another woman, and here we are walking along together in the center of town. And we're not even young. What are they going to think? Behaving like sweethearts!"

"I am your sweetheart," said Nuccia. "Hey. Why are you always so frightened?" All evening she'd been excited, happy. She'd met someone that morning. The encounter seemed like a good omen for the future. "Walter, you can't imagine what happened this morning, such good luck. I hope. This morning I went to the bookstore even though it was Sunday, because I wanted to work in peace while the store was closed. It paid off: about one o'clock I went out and there on the corner of via Frattina I heard someone calling me. It was a girl from Milan I hadn't seen in years, a classmate from school, Bianca, who's a teacher and who's married to a Swiss fellow named Weiss, who owns and runs a school in Frascati. We had lunch at a *tavola calda*. She told me her story and I told her mine. She says they can take Giulia as a boarding student in their school."

"A boarding school, with nuns?"

"No nuns. Not a Catholic school. They have sixty little girls and bigger ones, rooming together in groups of three. Nice gardens, playing fields, greenhouses. They teach foreign languages, economics, typing."

"And the cost?"

"Well, Bianca is offering me a special discount. I did some calculations and I think I can swing it. The publishing house will have to give me a ten percent raise and help me out with some articles. In these last months I've been able to publish a few things, and now I'll have to write more. But through the bookstore I know people who can help, you know. I'll do anything, even knock out stuff for the women's magazines, or better, comic books."

"Journalistic prostitution."

"If it means I can have Giulia with me, I'll even do the other kind, if anyone will have me," she said laughing. "No, don't worry, there's no need. Think about it. You in Rome with me, and Giulia close by in Frascati. You're happy too, aren't you?"

"Yes."

"If I go to Frascati on Sundays, you'll come with me, won't you?"

"Well...."

A simple man and woman, and such was the life they led.

But Ferranini didn't feel easy, he needed another sort of warmth. It was 11:30. Reparatore might be back by now. On his way home he stopped by the bar on via della Scrofa to phone. Giobatta himself answered. He'd taken the 7:00 p.m. plane from Turin.

"I went to the stadium this afternoon. Juventus was playing Fiorentina, you know...."

Ferranini was actually happy to have found him. Reparatore's physical appearance and even his voice reminded him of his father. He was the man who could understand him. Or at least hear him out.

"When are you going to stop being a football fan, Giobatta, aren't you ashamed? At your age."

Giobatta was crisp, to the point. "At the stadium I feel I'm an individual, that's what it is, and along with me, sixty thousand human beings! I'll bet my day was better than yours. So, how young was the 'young man'?"

"About thirty."

"Mm-hmm. And tell me, did our man correct him?"

"Well, no, not to my eyes. And the young fellow—he made some concrete observations. The pursuit of affluence, careerism. These really are our limits."

To Ferranini, Mazzola's critique had seemed neither naive nor confused. He had taken it on himself to put together and express ideas that Ferranini shared, and with a degree of precision and concentration Walter knew that he himself did not possess. He felt Mazzola's courage surging into him.

"That poor guy with the broken leg made sense, we need to take steps, okay our numbers may increase, but what about quality? We need to practice some self-criticism here!"

"Hey, lay off the self-criticism," said Reparatore.

"Sure. If a party card is just a lottery ticket, folks, let's be sincere, let's be honest. We're turning bourgeois, turning bourgeois all over again. Am I right? And then, everything we do for our own dirty selfish reasons we can do, if nothing else, without a bad conscience. Today the rallying cry is: To hell with you, Stalinists of Prague, Stalinists of Warsaw. But Stalinism (it must have had some defects, I don't know), what did it consist of? Intransigence. Which is a duty."

"Get out of here, Walter, since when do we talk like this on the phone? You're not yourself!"

"Let me speak. I'm telling you there's something better than de-Stalinizing. What we need to do is de-Bukharinize, you know what I mean? We have to sweep the rubbish—*il rusco*, as we say in Emilia, the garbage of compromise, of accommodationism, of the 'quiet life'—out of the corners (and we should hope it's just the corners). Am I right or not? What was it you were saying this morning on the plane? Speak up. Speak!"

Tonight it was his turn to be emphatic.

Once he'd said (to the same Reparatore, the old wolf, who listened indulgently), "If what happens to all of us in the chamber had happened to me two years ago, or last year—this having to sit here all day long like an empty chair listening to empty speeches—I swear I wouldn't have gone through with it. Now it seems normal. Is it that I've smartened up, or am I just another moron?"

He ended up convincing himself that there were good reasons for his inertia. Parliamentary rule, such as it was, could only be a phase in the upward arc of socialism, or better yet, a moment of anticipation. They were there to oppose the institution itself, not what it decided or how it functioned. They were waiting for the moment when the state of affairs that institution represented and proposed to advance would be consigned to the museum of the past. Lenin had said to Amedeo Bordiga: Participate in parliamentarism to eliminate parliamentarism. Their role was not to propose, advise, or criticize, for even criticism is a contribution. Accordingly, there was no place where a Communist could repose so peacefully and so responsibly as in the bourgeois Chamber of Deputies.

Ferranini had told himself these things and told them quite seriously to others (absolute positions were made for him) but that did not prevent him from treating the institution with a certain formal deference. As Voltaire observed, the atheist is one of the very few not to take out his snuffbox in church.

He'd been in parliament for five months, but he still crept in and reached his bench on tiptoe. It astonished him when colleagues shouted down the halls to one another, as if that august building were a public meeting place or a private address. He had never permitted himself to attend to his correspondence inside the chamber, and every day he took home piles of official papers and read through everything scrupulously. He was always prepared when he went to the sessions of his committee. And still there was plenty of time to take it easy. The minute he became a deputy he had relaxed, comforted by the knowledge he was not in any way responsible. He listened, he watched, with a detachment that wasn't at all presumptuous, just happy indolence. Nor did those hours seem too long to him. Now that he was the eyes and the ears, the performance was almost always interesting.

In five months he had not opened his mouth. He felt no need to. In Rome he had learned that his nature and vocation was to be a follower: he, once so combative in Reggio, so inclined to take responsibility. "When I worked with the base, I wasn't the base; here, next to the leadership, I'm on my way. For a lot of people the opposite happens; this is better." It was painless for him to observe group discipline in the chamber, and what Reparatore called platitude assignment—the fine-tuned apportioning of speeches and intervention times—seemed reasonable enough. Anyway, as he knew, discipline was not less rigorous in other parties, nor less respected. The incoherent bourgeois attack on party rule was just beginning.

If only he'd continued to keep his mouth shut. One day he finally spoke, tossing in two brief quips, and it was a disaster.

The middle of December. Comrade Pigato was questioning the minister of the interior on whether he was aware of the regulations governing the American troops stationed in the Veneto. Did he not find it indecorous that the Americans, as if it were not enough that they kept military bases on Italian soil to protect their own interests, also treated our people with the contempt reserved for natives in the colonies?

Pigato read out some of the regulations in question. Military personnel were "advised" to avoid contact with the inhabitants of the country (and not merely those of the female sex); to stay away from their homes and places where they gathered, including cafés, clubs, playing fields, educational institutions, churches, and public transport. They were forbidden to take on familial duties; to sign contracts or contract debts; to join firms, companies, or other commercial enterprises; to join any sort of association, even if for athletic, cultural, or religious purposes or simple entertainment. They were forbidden to purchase foodstuffs of any kind from local merchants, including, sweets, beverages, beer, cocktails, and other liquids, and in particular milk and ice cream. They were forbidden to buy or use medicines and drugs of Italian make. Et cetera.

The longish list was heard by the assembly with unusual attention, and a hint or two of embarrassment on the part of the center benches (no efforts were made to interrupt). In the minister's absence, Undersecretary Mazza spoke. It would be useful to determine whether the information supplied by Deputy Pigato was authentic. Many of the details seemed to him unlikely.

"In any case," Mazza went on, "further clarifications with regard to the matter can be supplied by the foreign minister. Or the defense minister."

"In any case," came Pigato's retort, his voice strained because he didn't have much of one, being one of the oldest PCI deputies, "you will tell us as a member of the government, or if you prefer, in your personal status as an Italian, if what I just read out seems compatible to you with the dignity of our people? Are Italians plague-ridden, are they inferior beings? As for whether the regulations are authentic, let me simply say that I received them firsthand."

"You, a Communist, have firsthand relations with the U.S. command?" The undersecretary's observation was ironic.

The center and the right welcomed Mazza's remark, and there was a "hear, hear" and a few laughs. From the Christian Democratic benches someone shouted, "Hey, old man, tell us about your Red Army friends and how sweetly they fraternize with the Hungarians in Budapest."

But Pigato didn't budge. The veins of his neck swelled with effort as he barked, "I'm proud to say I have no relations with the Americans.

None of any kind! The orders to U.S. troops that I read aloud are in the public domain in my parts, in the Veneto."

It was at this point that Ferranini, who was sitting nearby, felt he must intervene to support his comrade.

"What is more," he rose to speak, "what you have heard is perfectly in accord with the American mentality. They are racists."

He couldn't see and was never able to determine which colleague from the center benches shouted out, "Ferranini? But isn't he the one who spent ten years in America?"

Ferranini rose again and replied, "I was there but I'd never go back."

Hours later that evening, he felt he could hear his own voice echoing off the walls: "I was there but I'd never go back." Thank heavens, thank heavens! What if Togliatti had been present to witness his debut? To have spoken, his first time, and revealed himself guilty of personalism. Pretending to take a political position while underneath there was nothing but his miserable private life. And supposing that guy, that unknown colleague, had added, "Ferranini is here on the far-left benches only because a woman dumped him, otherwise he'd be an American citizen," what would he have said?

He had said he'd never go back to America, and that was true. Materially, literally true. But it was also true that they'd never take him back.

That bitter conclusion stymied him, and all he could do was try to distract himself. Block his thoughts. Later that afternoon, thinking about it—still in the chamber, the session was dragging on—he decided he was being unfair to himself.

He wasn't ignoble. Even if they would take him, he wouldn't go back. When he arrived in Boston in '39 he'd sworn he would be America's enemy, America the nerve center of world capitalism, executioner of Sacco and Vanzetti. Now that he was older he saw, less ingenuously but deeply, what was intrinsically lacking in a system that socialism had outreached. Love too was behind him. A falsifying love, making him confuse America and happiness, America and youth. He would never go back. Yes, his conscience was clear.

Or was there more?

A few days earlier ("I don't know why but I don't like saying I have a mistress; it's the term I don't like") Nuccia had announced that Walter was not an introvert, nor, for that matter, introspective. A characteristic defect and a commendable one (in a world where not only the educated but grocers called themselves introverts). So long as he didn't exaggerate, although in her opinion, Walter did exaggerate sometimes, yes. Nuccia was quite right, yet this once Walter proved her wrong. This once he looked within himself, so attentively and with such determination that Nuccia, poor thing, would have been astonished. Here was the point: he had managed to lower the tone of the debate in the chamber by introducing an emotional note, his reaction to something that had once injured his petty ego. Were Americans racist? They discriminated. Physically. They didn't like dark-skinned people, they didn't like *five-footers*, short people. They admired the tall, the blond, the Germans, English, and Scandinavians. But this was no "fact"; it was an old injury to his amour propre (or to his love itself). Ferranini had not spoken as a critic of capitalist America, he had spoken as a man rebuffed. America, the sweetness and the rage, was still in his blood.

As a boy in Vimondino, eight or nine year old, he'd had a crush on a girl his own age (red-haired like Nancy, and called Nellina, or Nella). To hide his feelings, almost as if to revenge himself on this Nellina, or Nella, who hadn't noticed a thing, he shoved her and scowled at her, and if anyone mentioned her he'd say, "She's ugly, she's stupid." And that was what had happened here too. Pigato was merely the occasion. Pigato didn't need his help. He'd jumped at the opportunity to castigate a country he'd been unable to forget, to revenge himself *because* he'd been unable to forget.

(I'll never say another word unless the group obliges me to, and only when the budget is being discussed. Some technical point, about public instruction or labor, when the budgets come through next year. They won't catch me again, mother of G . . . !)

The following morning he was due in Reggio for a meeting of the provincial council of cooperatives. As soon as he boarded the train he sat down to pore over the newspapers column by column. Both *Avanti!* and *l'Unità* had brief mentions of Pigato's questioning, and neither wasted even a line on the "American," Ferranini. He exhaled.

One of the good things about parliamentary sessions was that they gave him an opportunity to meet his comrades (and his friends, at least that). Reparatore, Amoruso, and Boatta. The first two he never saw outside the chamber. Reparatore was always traveling around Italy in his role as a CGIL inspector. Amoruso had recently become department chief at the hospital in Formia and only appeared in Rome when it was strictly necessary to attend the sessions. Devoid, and unenvious, of the professional political experience of Ferranini and the other two, Amoruso belonged to the educated bourgeoisie (if somewhat in the manner of the old, rhetorical Italian humanism) and had cultivated and would go on cultivating a role as a good Marxist dilettante.

He owed his seat to the cardinal decision Togliatti had made to move away from the strict working-class mobilization of the post-war years and open the party to intellectuals and technicians, an opening that had its critics, among them Luigi Boatta. A onetime teacher at the Oenological Training Institute of Alba, he liked to say that by watering down the proletarian wine, the PCI is going to end up like that Barolo made of seven parts Squinzano and three parts Verona, with only the label from Piedmont. Amoruso had come to the party without going through any intermediary reformist stages, a point worth noting because in 1950 he had married the slim, blond Socialist senator, Adele Cariboni. It was a successful marriage, not in the least political, but the husband had been known to tell close friends that the Popular Front didn't work in bed either. A joke that masked his one torment: he and Adele had no children.

First in Naples, now closer to Rome in Formia, Amoruso had gracefully, his classy bourgeois pride tempered with irony, showed off his "little library" of some ten thousand volumes divided into three sections: biology, Marxist sciences, and the theater. The theater critic Silvio D'Amico had pronounced it one of the best private collections in Italy. A real Neapolitan, Amoruso's taste in cultural matters was ample and eclectic. One Sunday he would read the works of Chekhov in the original (he'd taught himself Russian), on another he'd read Stalin and Lenin, or Claude Bernard, J. B. Haldane, or Huxley. The books in the first two sections passed, half a dozen at a time, from Amoruso's library to the table in Ferranini's room, and when he brought them back he would put them in place himself, his hand lingering on their spines. That wealth lined up on those walnut shelves, and the picture of marital serenity that Amoruso and Adele made: he admired them both humbly and without rancor, amazed that such good things existed in this world and could be enjoyed so unselfconsciously.

Antonino Amoruso had an unflagging curiosity characteristic of some doctors. He had not forgotten about Ferranini's friend, the printer in his thirties who had died suddenly in his workshop, and wanting to get to the bottom of the case, he contacted the physician who had seen the man just after he died. His brief investigation confirmed that Gennaro had been the victim of an aneurysm due to overexertion.

He spoke to Ferranini about it during a break in committee.

"We go to enormous trouble to change the bedsheets of the sick," he said. "But we need to be able to cure them as well. And there we don't succeed, I'm afraid."

Ferranini could see where those curious words were going. "And then what?"

"Then what? That is precisely the problem! The concept of the labor-harm index has remained an economic abstraction, without any practical remedies. The socialist classics describe the dehumanization of labor, but this dehumanization is seen as a negative consequence of exploitation. Take the first man on earth, though, didn't he wear himself out working too?"

This was what they habitually discussed on meeting in the chamber or in the trattoria on via dei Coronari. Once in a while Reparatore or Boatta also took part. But the discussions brought no new insights. Once Reparatore observed, "In southern Italy we don't say *lavorare* to mean 'to labor, to work,' we say *faticare*, as in 'to slave, to slog.' Labor implies undergoing violence; it is travail, a toiling through brute matter, digging it out, transporting it, transforming it. Where there's no effort, there is no work."

Amoruso explained that indeed labor was a dispersal of energy, energy drawn from that physical and mental reserve that helps keep the organism above pure survival. The wage laborer pays "in person," spending his vital substance, the stuff of his organic functioning. Ferranini observed that years before, he had seen workers leaving the job after a day at the cooperative (where their labor was not exploited by the ruling class), and they looked weary, depressed, even sad. He had tried to explain the situation to himself by saying that in any case they were living in a capitalist environment. Hounded by the competition, by the enmity of the capitalist firms.

"If that is the case," said Reparatore, "workers in the USSR must come out of their factories cheerful and energetic. But that I'm not inclined to believe."

"As I see it, the division of labor is at fault," said Boatta. "It's the division of labor that makes work hateful. And capitalism is responsible for the division of labor."

"Or technology," said Reparatore. "And as a matter of fact, you find the division of labor in industrialized socialist society. Or perhaps nature is at fault; perhaps it's an objective, natural, and inevitable thing. But still, leaving aside the division of labor, labor is harmful all the same. Take Robinson Crusoe, he did everything on his own, but it was still exhausting. And mechanization—that doesn't help much either. It transforms work but doesn't improve it. The machine brings greater fatigue. It transfers the wear and tear from the arms and back to other organs."

When Amoruso came up from Formia he parked his automobile in a courtyard on via delle Carrozze near the Corso, and that evening he continued the conversation with Ferranini in the car, measuring

Walter's blood pressure and perfunctorily applying his stethoscope. He had done this sort of checkup before, given that his friend was averse to a more thorough examination.

"You see," said Ferranini as Amoruso was putting the cuff away in his bag, "I may be a pessimist, but for me work and its ills are merely trials that living creatures have no choice but to endure. To end that, you'd have to put an end to the antagonism that exists between living beings and the inorganic world. The 'class struggle' of life against the physical surroundings in which it affirms itself (or in spite of which it affirms itself) never ceases. The fact that labor is inescapable is an expression, I believe, of the active or inert hostility of the environment. Earthquakes, drought, illness, the cholesterol that clogs up arteries."

"You can add the hidden injury, the viral aggression, of violence and injustice," said Amoruso. "On the part of other human beings, who, let me say, aren't really wrongdoers because they are driven by nature's same hostile impulses. As you can see, I, too, am a pessimist."

"What about machines? Machines are often blamed for our disorders and ills. But aren't they nature too? A casing that we make to hold the forces of nature. We think we are the masters, but that's an illusion."

Amoruso was fiddling with the car's interior light, which had gone out. They sat in the dark, the courtyard intermittently lit by a flashing neon light.

"This idea of a conflict, a 'class war' as you call it, between life and external reality is an old idea and it's not easy to refute. At heart, it's the grim and unassailable basis of evolution: the struggle to survive, the endless battling if you aren't to succumb, and the only organisms that do survive are those with enough resources not to give up the fight."

"I know," replied Ferranini, "and it's also the basis of evolutionism, which argues that evolution never ceases. That is, it finally overwhelms every creature, even us humans, in the perpetual struggle of one creature against the other and the environment. Now I ask: We socialists believe in a process that comes not only to a conclusion but to a fine and happy conclusion, the triumph of man over injustice. We look forward to a society without privileges and above all without conflict. Now, how do we reconcile these two views? Because the doctrine of evolution is also science, not just poetry, and Marx praised Darwin and his great discovery. Lenin says, 'Progress is the result of the struggle between opposites.' But Lenin thought that the October Revolution was the beginning of the end of that struggle, and that at a certain point, let's say after a hundred years, there would be peace and perfect well-being for the workers."

Amoruso made sure to have the last word. "We are socialists, and therefore believers, and we look forward to a transformation without expecting life itself to change much. But to do away with a certain kind of egotism is already a lot. This is why we must be socialists. With no illusions."

For many days his professional obligations kept Amoruso from leaving Formia. Ferranini got a long and earnest letter from him "about your problem."

"The just war is not always the fortunate one; for us it is enough to know that ours is a just war," wrote Amoruso, as always so ready to comfort and console himself. "Certainly, as a doctor I'm aware that a laborer cannot avoid suffering. Feeling depressed, defeated, demeaned by the product of our labor or by the materials we handle and the tools we work with adds up to a permanent and inescapable industrial injury that every worker faces. Whatever the 'system,' regime, et cetera employing him.

"The other evening we were saying something like: If labor always diminishes your liberty and the healthy expression of your personality, aren't you inevitably going to fall ill? And when we speak of hostile physical elements, even those superficially domesticated, like water, fire—and tomorrow, uranium—don't we also implicitly refer to our lives in a human world where there is no benevolence except in appearance (and that intermittently)? Competition, envy, jealousy of other men (and women) or instead their indifference, estrangement, their stubborn spurning or misunderstanding. Marx, in *The German Ideology*, mentions the elimination of labor, but neither Marx nor Engels nor Lenin ever pretended to free us from all these innumerable and serious ills. Now let me add: If we don't mean to treat the fathers of socialism the way the women of Naples treat Saint Anthony of Padua, we must recognize that Marx's program, and all the rest, was modest and limited. There won't be happiness after the advent of world socialism. Nothing will be rosier and more pleasant (beyond substantial economic progress) than today. The actual abolition of work is merely hinted at, a promise that no one could ever dream would be met. But—also—there will be no more exploitation. And that is what makes our war 'just.' We must be content to change the sick man's bed, but at least we'll remove the leeches that are feeding on him."

It was Saturday, and the next day Ferranini was supposed to lead a meeting at Borgo Isonzo near Latina, a meeting of farmers. He telephoned the hospital in Formia but was told that the *professore* was on his rounds and couldn't come to the phone. Ferranini didn't pursue the matter. But what he wanted to say to him was this: Do you authorize me to inform the comrades of Borgo Isonzo that the real program of Communism, as you put it in your letter, is "modest and limited"?

The chamber would soon be adjourning for Christmas. Ferranini came out of the party headquarters with his usual friends and they headed back toward parliament.

"I'm here to inform you," said Amoruso, "that a committee to study the pathology of labor in the light of Communist principles is *not* going to be convened."

The others studied him, eyes questioning.

"It's not happening. I've just spoken to Nicolussi at the Research Department. I said to him: 'Let's put together a little committee to study the matter. We Communists have a pathologist and a physiologist of some standing in the Senate, and we have some very good doctors in the chamber. It's not a new question, but it needs to be studied in relation to Marxist tenets.' Nicolussi heard me out, then shrugged his shoulders. 'Pathology of labor? Okay, let's start with ourselves. You know we're being driven crazy by the work weighing on us? And you come here to talk about a "little committee"! We're completely overloaded with work. And what does it consist of? De-sta-lin-i-za-tion,'" said Amoruso in comic emphasis. "I de-Stalinize, you de-Stalinize, proletarians of the world don't unite, don't advance, just de-Sta-lin-ize."

"Even with that committee of yours," said Reparatore, "the good thing is that you'd never have achieved anything. Talk is not enough to resolve the problem."

Now Boatta spoke: "I think you're all exaggerating. Marx will certainly have resolved the problem, he resolved others even more difficult. Our job is to put his teachings into practice."

They had arrived at Piazza Venezia, right under the famous balcony of Mussolinian memory. Ferranini grabbed Amoruso and Boatta by the forearm. They were standing on either side of him.

"Marxism is as solid a truth as the walls of this palace. There's no turning back, but to go forward we may have to discard some illusions. When the exploitation of workers has disappeared, will the burden of labor also disappear? Today people discuss alienation far more than they discuss Marx. In a nutshell, the worker, exploiting his own life substance, creates the world of things. We may have some doubts about that characterization, but never mind. Will alienation disappear in the socialist state?"

Ferranini looked around. He went on: "Let's leave alienation aside. If you ask those girls stepping off the sidewalk who are probably typists returning to their offices 'Do you feel alienated?,' they'll say, 'We feel tired.' Ask the same question of the man over there at the wheel of the bus, and you'll get the same answer, and maybe he'll even add, 'If they paid me ten times more it would still be a beastly life.' The real problem is that work is a burden, an ordeal, a sentence of indefinite term. Suppose they square the circle and find some kind of work that doesn't eat people up, won't it be just a sort of living death, a contradiction in terms?"

"Technology can do a lot," said Boatta.

"Sure, technology, the miracle worker, the saint. But wasn't it supposed to be socialism that worked miracles, not technology, which belongs to the capitalists as much as it does to us? And yet, there are miracles even saints can't perform. The need to work is only going to increase, along with the population, while the available assets remain the same."

"We'll colonize the planets. Russia already has Sputniks."

"We'll colonize the bottom of the sea as well, although it will be an immense effort causing great pain and suffering. Admit it, there are things that technology cannot achieve. There is a law that can't be breached, a physical and biological law that says life can't arise and survive without sweat and struggle. And especially not without struggling against the environment, the surrounding material reality. And labor is part of this."

"Come, my friend," said Boatta as they began to walk again, "humanity has always labored. Worked and worked, without thinking about it so much."

"True, true. But Marx taught us to look at the hard reality of labor, and to see what a plague it is."

Amoruso addressed Boatta: "If you think about it, Ferranini's argument is in a certain sense Marxist. Marx would never have conceded just because the conclusion was negative, or not very heartening."

"Our Ferranini, eh?" Reparatore was teasing. "Who would believe it? All those wheels of Parmigiano-Reggiano producing a speculative mind."

It was almost true. When he was expounding his ideas, Ferranini spoke clearly and precisely. But when it came to those images, vague yet substantial images that precede and occasion ideas, he'd never been able to articulate them. As a kid, after he'd been fired from the railway, he'd become a driver for the shoe factory at San Donato di

Vimondino. For seven years he worked himself to death, driving around in the van loading and unloading, up to sixteen, eighteen hours a day. He imagined the world, the world of his companions who worked in the shoe factory, and the world of everyone who labored, as a face of solid rock. A rock face. There was just one reality, a solid, heavy reality of machines, of asphalt, of soil and cement, and it bore down on the human beings destined to hold it up, the struts and beams made of living flesh. Hundreds of millions of human beings with their feet nailed to the ground, shoulders and heads bent under the load of one heavy plate. That huge gray, hostile, malign mass that would crush them otherwise, crush everything and everyone. He could see them vividly before his eyes. There was a sphere of pain and effort, and thanks to it, there were men and women free to move about and enjoy life, enjoy their repose.

Later, after much reading and listening he had matured politically, and that image was replaced by a more logical design of the relationship between the classes, between labor and the parasite classes. The disparity between the two had seemed fatal and inescapable, but it was actually nothing more than injustice, man-made and eradicable. What always struck him when he read socialist texts was the sarcasm with which they treated that falsifying ideology extolling the *benefit* of labor, considered a gratifying and elevating activity (and so man was called *homo faber*). When this was all just ruling-class rhetoric defending the status quo by sanctifying toil and fatigue. As if a man could elevate himself when machines and matter bore down on him, squeezed out all his energy, leaving him just about able to eat, sleep, and reproduce, manufacturing more human material. This all seemed clear and obvious. And yet the rock face remained. Maybe it was part of the superstructure? Part of the capitalist contrivance the proletariat would sweep away?

Ferranini sank into this familiar meditation. In the meantime they arrived at the entrance of parliament.

"Nattering, nattering," said the irreverent Amoruso, "here we reach the gates of the natter-mill."

"Have some respect," said Boatta.

"You're giving me history lessons? In 1917 the Bolsheviks called the Duma the chatter-shop. I'm merely saying we've arrived at the natter-mill."

I, who come from the shoe factory, should not complain, thought Ferranini. Why go and get so worked up? The people inside, every one of them, would call me a fool.

It was 11:00 p.m. when Nuccia got back from Frascati. December 17. She'd gone there for the third time, to arrange every last detail with her friend Bianca. Her daughter would enter boarding school (as Bianca called it) after Epiphany in January. Her room, already occupied by a girl of her age, the daughter of a man with the Swiss legation, was as nice as could be, with furniture painted sky blue and a window looking onto the pines of Villa Aldobrandini. After a series of phone calls that had tested Nuccia's patience as well as her finances, the grandparents had agreed. (Her mother had always found it incomprehensible that Nuccia didn't keep the child with her but left them to look after her, and she did have some objections.) At New Year's Nuccia would go to Monticello and get Giulia. Things were going well, so well she had trouble believing it herself. Her life was falling into place, and she was finding peace. At last, at age thirty-eight. She had been struggling and it hadn't been pleasant: her soul split in two, the remorse (the child sometimes asked total strangers for news of her mother), the instability, the secrecy. ("What do you do in Rome?" her father would close his letters. "Tell us the truth, you're involved with someone.")

Now she could fling the windows open and relax a bit. When Giulia was in Rome staying with her, maybe she'd be able to confide in her father, to tell him the truth (nothing she wanted more!) and get him to accept it. What luck, her running into Bianca Weiss; the world was not such a bad place after all, if you could meet a helpful person who could resolve all your problems there on some street corner. That morning (the 17th and a Friday to boot, and she believed in such bad omens) she got a reply from her publishing house at the bookstore. They agreed to pay her ten percent more. It wasn't much but still reassuring. There was money to send the girl to Frascati; she'd be able to look after her.

In the mail was also a summons to appear in the party section, on via Alessandria. Signed by one Enrichetta Pignatti, never heard of her, who had scribbled a note, "Ask for me personally." She was about to toss it in the wastepaper basket but then she thought, I haven't been back since I became a member. Better go. She would do it the next day, Saturday, in the afternoon.

And so at five on Saturday she left work. The shop was full of people, and to be as quick as possible she didn't even take her bag, just stuffed her cigarettes in her pocket. She ran all the way to via Alessandria, where she was told that Pignatti would be in any minute. She showed up after five thirty, blond, just married, with a shiny new wedding ring displayed on her finger. Very polite, all smiles.

"Come join me in here; I'm so sorry I'm late."

She showed her into a small empty office and carefully closed the door behind her. Nuccia realized that she would have to defend herself.

"I'm not much of a regular, in fact, to be precise, this is only the second time I've come to the section. The thing is, even when all goes well, I don't get out of work until nine."

"Ah no, Comrade Lonati, it's not about that."

Comrade Lonati? Her face darkened. "My name is Anna Corsi."

"You are married to Comrade Commendatore Cesare Lonati," the blonde insisted.

"I was. But so far as the section is concerned, I am Anna Corsi, which is the name written on my card. Excuse me, who are you?"

The smile she received was not quite affectionate.

"I'm in charge of the women's committee; I teach at the Antonietti trade school. I think you've understood what the matter at hand is. I've been charged with a confidential mission. Comrade Lonati, your husband, is now in Rome."

Nuccia felt herself shiver. Making an effort, she said, "He's often here."

"No, now he's living here. And he wishes, he aspires, to reunite with you and put an unhappy time behind him, wishes to have his child, his wife, in short, his family back. His health, it seems, is not what it could be. It's natural for him to want to resolve what must be a painful situation for both of you."

"And so he talks to *you* about it. And not to me. If Comrade Commendatore Lonati knows that I'm signed up in this section, he must know where to find me at work."

"Your husband has been concerned about you for some time. With understandable devotion. He turned to us to employ our good offices, which is our job."

Nuccia delved mechanically into her pocket for her cigarettes and was unable to find them. She tried to control herself. Her voice dull, she said, "And what business is it of yours? Tell me that. The section is not a parish."

"And yet it can play a similar role. The section is a great family, you'll see."

"*Oh Mamma mia!*" said Nuccia loudly. She closed her eyes, feeling icy and numb, her fists rigid in the pockets of her overcoat. She had forgotten where she was, and the other woman's presence.

"Comrade, are you ill?" the other said, standing up.

"No, I'm fine. Allow me to go now. I believe I've understood."

"Please be aware, I didn't mean to offend you. The party is not simply a political association like other parties, it has the responsibility to keep an eye on and assist comrades, both men and women, with all their needs."

"Even in this."

"You can count on our complete discretion. But do allow me to hope that our intervention will prove beneficial to the welfare of your family. That's the only reason we summoned you. Please think it over, and we'll expect an answer from you after you have."

"I'll give you my answer right away," Nuccia said, rising from her own seat. "I find your lack of respect for a person's private life incredible. For the private life of a party member. And if I don't follow your directives, well, that's the way it is. Draw whatever conclusions you like."

Out on the street a driving rain wet her face and the wind stung; she felt liberated, cleansed. Physically she was better, but inside there was a furious, crushing avalanche of thoughts. At the first bar she drank a cognac and smoked half a cigarette, tasting nothing. Then back in the "shop," which felt as irritating and alien as books, work, everything now, she shut herself up in her little office, and there, finally, the clock on the wall struck six, reminding her of Walter. At eight, Walter would be there with her, as he was every Saturday, at least there was that certainty, and she understood it had been holding her together. Walter was there, her man was close by, she would see him soon. They would eat dinner together. And the rest? All gone, Frascati, her serenity, the order she'd put in her life, her pitiful happiness. Gone.

The only reason she didn't cry was because she couldn't. I weep dry tears, I don't cry, I don't let it out, she once said. I'm destined for a gastric ulcer. Once again, her insides turned icy, and she sat for an hour by the radiator, sending Holzener, the chief salesman, away. The bookstore was buzzing with people and he would come and knock on the door of her office.

But she pulled herself together again. She had some vital instinct that kept her balanced and functioning; at times she'd even reproached herself for it. She began by ripping up the brief telegram she'd jotted down to send to her parents: "Plans off. Giulia stays with you." Her mistaken haste to destroy, to do herself more harm. Better to talk to Walter first, that would help. And accept that she would have to see a lawyer. What rights could Lonati claim when in four years he hadn't bothered even to ask about the girl, hadn't sent his greetings once or a box of sweets? And why should she give up like that without first trying to defend herself? Walter would help. She tried to think about immediate, practical ways he could help. Lonati was mobilizing the party to get his way, but she was connected to a man who counted in the party, who really should count

more. Cesare, with all his money, was a parasite on Italian Communism; Walter was one of its strengths. Self-effacing, reserved as much
as you like, but he had a name and qualifications, even official ones.
He'd been sent to Rome by his people in Reggio with several thousand preference votes. He was fully capable of neutralizing Lonati.
And if Lonati wanted to make legal trouble, she had some arguments of her own. She could be stubborn too. Yes, she would have to
fight. But there she had no inhibitions. She would fight.

Her heart was bitterly calm and her pale, drawn face composed
when she arrived (a quarter of an hour early) at their meeting place
on the corner of via Firenze in front of the trattoria.

"On Epiphany," Ferranini announced as soon as they were seated,
"we're going to see *La Bohème*. I went by the opera house and they're
doing *Bohème* with a tenor I know. Gianni Raimondi."

"Two bohemians in the gallery," she tried to joke.

"Okay! But at the same time we're going, and we'll go again."

In honor of opera, one of the few things he was receptive to in the
world of culture (and other than socialism in the world at large), Ferranini spoke while he dined, for once. He was not short of ideas on
the matter, even if none of them were revolutionary.

"Italian opera comes to an end in 1896 with *La Bohème*. There's
nothing after that. The score of *La Bohème*, meanwhile, is beautiful
and presents no special difficulties for the singers, and so it's fine
even for voices of our times."

"Walter."

"It's music that sings. Today, Menotti writes operas without mel-
odies. It's like saying we make cheese without the milk."

"Walter."

"Have some cheese, by the way. You haven't eaten a thing."

She had scarcely eaten a thing. She'd drunk her couple of glasses
of Valpolicella, and the alcohol gave her strength to begin to tell him
what was going on. She needed strength; listening to him and
watching him eat had made her feel how far away he was.

Ferranini didn't interrupt her or ask for details.

When Nuccia had finished, he said, "You didn't expect this?"

"Should I have? I haven't heard from him for five years. I saw him last month on the train, you remember the circumstances. The company he was in. I was supposed to think he would turn up again just like that? To destroy me?"

Ferranini pushed aside his plate and sat with his arms folded on the table, his gaze trained above her head.

"We let ourselves be seen, Nuccia. We were visible. Something had to happen. Now he's come to live in Rome, he's found a way to make money in Rome as well, and not only that but he's gotten himself a role in the party."

"So you knew. And said nothing to me."

"Look, the less I have to talk about him, the better off I am. He got himself appointed to some kind of high position in the Press Office."

"Oh yes, they feel an affinity with his ink supplies. But Walter, it's of no concern to us what he does in Rome. Our concern is to defend ourselves. If I may say 'us'?"

"Why, aren't you sure?"

"If I weren't sure I'd be crazy. Lonati playing the bully is no surprise; he's always been a bully. But where did this Pignatti woman come from? Why did the party get involved?"

"Because we're out of line."

Nuccia was incensed; she flushed. "Togliatti's also out of line. In the very same way. Your dear Togliatti. You know it, too; and everyone knows it."

"He has merits that I don't."

She banged her fists on the table. "Merit has nothing to do with it! I'm telling you. And in any case, I don't think he's doing anything wrong. These are problems that bother the bourgeoisie. My sister, for example. My sister would denounce me for the life I'm living. She's married to a colonel, she's bourgeois. Are Communists bourgeois?"

"Maybe."

The two of them were silent. Ferranini saw before him that little room in Turin, poor Mazzola feverish and shouting.

"However," he said, "if Comrade Pisani were here he'd tell you that revolutions always finish in moralism. Robespierre said that every attack on morality (sexual morality, that is) is an attack on the Republic."

"That was a revolution made by mill owners; I was talking about communism. About the communist revolution."

"Okay, so here is Lenin: 'Free love does not coincide with our principles.'"

"So I'm opposing Lenin? Walter, don't you see? You say: You're just a woman in love. Not true! I'm a thinking being. And I maintain that there's no point in battling for a revolution if it's going to preserve bourgeois morals. It's said that when Russian youth dance, the Komsomol prescribes a gap of at least twenty centimeters between the guy and the girl."

"Stories."

"I'm beginning to think it's the truth. Once upon a time communists thought differently. In 1919 in Russia they used to say that a husband's ownership of his wife had to be abolished along with other sorts of ownership. The lawful husband's powers over his wife. Don't you remember Alexandra Kollontai?"

Ferranini closed his eyes.

"It was 1919. We were in the subversive phase, after which came the constructive phase, the revolution became consolidated, and there was a return to morality. Is there anybody who doesn't know these things?"

He thought of Comrade Pisani and changed his tone. He had to be patient.

"That's how it was, Nuccia. Think of Soviet films, of the night-clubs that don't exist there, of the propaganda to increase the population. Of the families that win prizes for being prolific."

"And I tell you that the degree of liberty and progress in a society corresponds to the degree of evolution in the sexual domain. You can turn everything upside down, even destroy everything and rebuild it from the ground up. But so long as your morality requires a government stamp to legalize love, Walter, you have changed nothing. Not a thing, I tell you. Sorry. My voice is too loud. People are staring."

Ferranini shook his head without looking up.

"I'm beginning to think," said Nuccia, lowering her voice, "that no other human instinct is as powerful as order. We start out intending to make a revolution, and maybe we even do, and then we decide that order is absolutely necessary. Order, rules, tranquillity. Not that I don't appreciate order as much as anyone—although I couldn't give a damn about the government stamp. But I'm no revolutionary, while you want to change the face of the world. And you harden into formalism."

"One becomes pigheaded," Ferranini admitted glumly.

"Yes. But I can be pigheaded too. I joined the party at the beginning of the month, now I've had my experience, and we'll see what happens between me and my husband. You'll help me find a lawyer, and I'll see what he says. As for my party card, I'm taking it back to Signora Pignatti. She can keep it."

"Nuccia, you're forgetting something." At last he turned his head to look her in the face. "There are two of us in this situation. Renounce your membership; no one can stop you. You'll only have your conscience to come to terms with. But you'll be renouncing me, too. I remain inside, in the place where I've been put."

Nuccia said nothing. Her arms hanging limp, hands in her lap, she stared at the chop and peas on her plate, now quite cold. She thought of what she'd said to Pignatti. The section is not a parish. Perhaps not, but the party was a church. For once, you had to give credit to the bourgeois newspapers that always said so. And I, she thought, am having an affair with a bishop.

The grotesque thought did not make her smile.

And yet as they walked back home under his umbrella, close to each other and silent, she was already trying to buck up. She was a courageous lady, after all. Literary references. Well, better than nothing. To love politics you must be able to take advantage of its game, and women are too jealous of politics to be able to do so. Where had she read those words? In Sainte-Beuve, most likely.

8

THE LETTER came in a yellow envelope marked "Strictly Personal." It was mimeographed, nothing more than a form letter; okay, so not something unusual. The letterhead read: "The Direzione" (the Central Committee) "Confidential."

> With regards to the Rivoli visit and interview with Engineer Roberto Mazzola, member of Section G. Bravin, Turin. Comrade Deputy Ferranini is hereby invited to formulate his opinions as to:
>> a) the above-mentioned Roberto Mazzola's political conduct [several blank lines followed]
>> b) the opinions expressed by the same [more blank lines]
> The recipient is further invited to indicate the appropriate sanction in his view: Reprimand/Admonition. Formal Admonition. Condemnation with Injunction. Suspension from All Responsibilities. Expulsion. (Indicate the applicable measure by underlining.)
> Please return this communication, properly completed and signed, to the Direzione, headquarters, within two (2) days of receipt, in person or by registered mail.

Giordano, the cabinetmaker who doubled as the building's doorman and to whom the party messenger must have handed the letter, hadn't bothered to leave his workshop for this, as usual. The next morning his little girl handed the envelope to Ferranini as he was going out. He couldn't bring himself to open a letter from the

Direzione marked "Strictly Personal" and read it on the street, so he climbed back up the stairs and shut himself in his room. He was ready to get the message and ready to reply to it. Without giving it a moment of thought, he leaned over his chest of drawers and began to write, he who was always so unsure whenever he found himself with pen in hand. It took just a few minutes. "Conduct: honest and sincere, a Communist of integrity." On the opinions expressed: "A certain practical intransigence." He took out the word "practical" and added "maximalism and." Sanctions to apply: "None. In my view there are no substantive grounds to punish Mazzola."

He signed his name and stuck the sheet back into the envelope. He would take it over today.

Now he was free to go out again. He had to pass by the Ministry of Public Instruction. Comrade Fubini had written from Reggio asking him to find someone at the ministry to deal with the case of his brother, a middle-school teacher in Parma who had been the victim of an error (a genuine error) when the results of a job competition were posted. Professor Amleto Fubini had already been down to Rome to protest, to no avail. The ministry, in its wisdom, was in no hurry to repair an error at the expense of a Communist, the brother of a Communist. Ferranini had never before performed this office, the one that kept most of his colleagues in parliament so busy. He didn't want to be someone's political patron. And to tell the truth, up until that moment no voters had called on him for help, at least not on the personal level. Fubini was the first to ask him a favor, and Fubini deserved help. A true friend, serious, intelligent, one of his few remaining friends.

He was just turning the key in the lock of his room. A cold, sour stench rose up the stairway from the cellar. He inhaled it uneasily: a whiff of dead air that seemed to drive away all his composure. He opened the door again and went back in.

He took out the letter. So, he was criticizing a decision of the party. Because suddenly now, the evidence was staring him in the face. The Direzione had sent him the letter because they considered Mazzola punishable. That is, guilty.

He leaned over the table, his chest hard against it, hands pressed to his face. Fifteen years of consistency, of loyalty, and today a rebel. A deviationist. Aligned, allied with a man that the party considered guilty of deviationism. Pointless to recall Comrade Pisani's opinion (of Mazzola) or the even clearer words of the local party secretary. Pointless for him to re-try the man; there was the Direzione, and the Direzione had made the decision for him, and for everyone. The Direzione had said: "That fellow is deficient, he has to pay, let's hear what measures you would apply. We already know he deserves punishment, but we will do you the courtesy of hearing you out."

And Ferranini's reply was going to be: You are mistaken. I stand with Mazzola.

He sat for some five minutes, immobile, the mimeographed sheet open before him, like a fool.

Rectify. And then gouge it out of his memory.

He took another sheet of paper, wrote: "Reply to communication [number, date, et cetera]. (Original conserved for my records.) With regards to interview conducted by Comrade Senator Pisani and the undersigned in Turin with Comrade Roberto Mazzola. Political conduct of aforementioned Mazzola. In my opinion, rebelliousness." He crossed that out and wrote, "indiscipline." He corrected, adding before "indiscipline" the words "aspirations of."

"Aspirations": a word he liked. He'd often used it to describe himself to Nuccia: "I had various aspirations; for many years I fed on bread and dreams." While "indiscipline" seemed vague, generic. Mazzola was something more than undisciplined. He crossed the word out and wrote "insubordination." So: "aspirations of insubordination." Mazzola's opinions? Okay, he had listened while Mazzola expressed his ideas, but as a silent witness. Pisani had been the judge and the letter from the Direzione was a consequence of the report filed by Pisani, and therefore all he had to do was repeat what Pisani had said that day. He wrote: "Mazzola states he opposes de-Stalinization. He would like to push the base toward a type of naive extremism." Yes. Naive was the right word. He added: "His views reflect a factionalist tendency due to moralizing attitudes, if in good faith." He canceled "moralizing" and replaced it with "moralistic and rigoristic."

Sanctions. Better not to exaggerate. Mazzola was a good kid, fully salvageable. Formal Admonition? No, it was wrong to make too much of it. He wrote: "I propose that Mazzola receive an Admonition."

He signed the letter, put it in the envelope, and hid it in the top drawer of his chest. Then he opened the folder containing his proposal for the reform of industrial safety legislation. He had finally remembered (how had he been so distracted?) that he could not go to the ministry for the simple reason that it was Sunday.

So he sat down to work. He still had to write the longest and most important section, the accompanying report. This part (it now struck him that he might present it directly to Longo in his role as deputy party leader in the chamber) demanded above all a certain diligence in the writing, and when it came to style, Ferranini was hopeless, as he himself knew; the first few pages had been a great struggle. When he finished, he'd decided, he would get Nuccia to do a thorough edit; she had a degree in letters, was a writer, et cetera. But first he had to finish it. Before the new year if possible.

Half an hour later he hadn't been able to knock out half a page. The law dated January 7, 1956, was outdated already. No one respected it and no one enforced it. "What we observe on construction sites is typical: the only law being observed, as the saying goes, is the law of gravity." Having written that, he was unable to proceed. His head was elsewhere. At 10:00 a.m., he gave up (rare for him; he was always loath to stop working even when his heart wasn't in it). He gathered the pages and put on his raincoat. As he descended the eight flights of stairs, pausing at the landings to look out on the courtyard deep in fog (a rare event in Rome), he'd already found an excuse. He liked it when his ideas were clear, and now he had come up against something that was anything but clear. There were aspects to the business (the Mazzola business) that didn't add up. Didn't convince. Among other things, why hadn't Mazzola been made to come to Rome? His leg was broken—well, they could have given him time to recover. But no, suddenly there was a great rush;

they had to go and question him at his home in Turin, while he was in bed with a high fever. And furthermore, how to explain the tribute (you honor a man by condemning him, too) paid to a modest local secretary of the Party Youth Federation? They send old Reparatore, they send Ferranini, and at the last moment they ring Comrade Senator Pisani. Pisani, a big wheel. Somebody who can walk into the Kremlin any time he wants.

In the soupy morning air, the street empty on a Sunday, Ferranini walked and thought, gray and vexed; he walked and interrogated himself, a chill light rain soaking his hair. Be honest, Ferranini, that's not the point. You don't care whether it was Reparatore or Pisani they sent. Since the trip to Turin, you haven't once thought of Mazzola, the whole thing slipped your mind. You knew they had condemned him, and it annoyed you that you would have to sign off on it too. (No, that's not it. I stand behind the party; I was behind the party.) Yes, that *is* it. Sooner or later they were going to say to you: You must ratify. Pro forma, of course. Just to dot the i's and cross the t's. However, ratify. And now the moment has arrived and you don't want to ratify. You like Mazzola. Okay, you only spent a couple of hours with him the other morning; you don't know much more about him. They're throwing him out. So? You've seen a lot of people ousted from politics (and elsewhere), and you didn't go all teary. No, tell the truth: it's that Mazzola's ideas are a lot like your own ideas. Very. And so, one of two things: Either you acknowledge that and join him and say, "Sorry but you have to punish Ferranini too." Or you send the letter, that letter which is by no means the formality you'd like to think it is; you sign it and you send it, and you do the dirty deed. It's up to you.

He stood in front of a window. It was a small place lit by neon lights, empty except for a man busy polishing the countertop. It was the fellow who filled up his thermos when he stayed in his room to work. The man saw him and came to the door.

"Morning, Deputy. Caffè or cappuccino?"

The deputy hardly heard him. Let's see, are Ferranini and Mazzola alone in thinking this way? A few days earlier in Reggio, he had seen

Oscar Fubini at the Federation. Fubini hadn't minced words: "Careerism rules here." The Bignami cousins were of the same opinion. And what had Reparatore said that morning on the plane? That revolutionaries were becoming functionaries, and as functionaries, they wanted peace and quiet. If it was a crime to discover that Communism had become bourgeois, well then many of us are guilty. Even Nuccia. She too had asked whether their comrades were turning bourgeois.

Togliatti was no bourgeois, Longo was no bourgeois; there were some fifty, maybe a hundred men like them, who had the right to lead the party and who set an example. But the rest of them? How many leaders were not infected with personalism, with the individualism of a Montobbio? People who enjoyed the easy life, the good life, who used the party to command, to stand out, distinguish themselves, gain a position. (And people who used it to cover their backsides, like Cesare Lonati.) And the party line won't be affected by this? The base has been silenced, those who want to interpret the base's aspirations are called exhibitionists, "pizza-spinners," those who still hope to realize socialism are credulous hard-liners. It's all parliamentary maneuvering; they polemicize against the reformists and the Christian Democrats, then offer themselves as allies. In the meantime an individual like Viscardi is the nominee to run Reggio. Italy's Kiev. You go up to Reggio and find a struggle raging. What struggle? To advance the masses to power? No, the struggle between Viscardi and Caprari. Between Panciroli and Zamboni.

He'd reached Piazza Colonna. He looked for a phone booth to call Reparatore. Someone who didn't give a damn about orthodoxy, who was familiar with the Mazzola affair, someone who could give him advice. He called, and Signora Francesca answered. No, Giobatta wasn't home. (Right, when was he ever home, he was a southerner!)

"Ferranini, now listen. Don't forget, now."

"What?"

"You're invited on Wednesday. You *must* be here. A friend of the family, get it? There will be hell to pay if you don't show up."

Yes. The wedding. Their daughter was getting married.

"On Wednesday I'm in Reggio Emilia. I've got obligations."

"Get out of them. Giobatta will be offended if you don't come."

"I'll see."

He walked homeward, very slowly. What was the point of calling, anyway? Reparatore had made his position clear right from the beginning. He hadn't wanted to take part in the Mazzola trial.

No, there was no denying it, Mazzola was a good Communist. That was the truth, even if Comrade Pisani had reasons for teaching him a lesson. And so Ferranini could not send that letter to the Direzione without lying, at the very least. And since that letter was ready and waiting, and the words "naive extremism" were written in his own hand, of his own free will, he already counted as a liar. Hadn't it been Reparatore himself, on the plane to Turin, who said that a man who disagrees and keeps his mouth shut is a hypocrite? Again he walked past the coffee bar where the man had come out to say "Caffè or cappuccino?," and the alternatives—deviationist or hypocrite—began to hammer in his head absurdly, in the tone and voice of the barman, as if the two phrases were connected. After turning the corner of via della Scrofa he changed his mind; he didn't want to shut himself up in his room. At 4:00 p.m. he had to speak in Frosinone, the usual Sunday thing. Nuccia was away in Frascati with her friend again. He decided to go to the station and take the first rapido. He would have lunch at the Hotel Cesari in Frosinone, the food was good. But he was scatterbrained and when he got to the bus stop he realized he'd forgotten his notes for the meeting. He had to go back. For the fourth time he passed in front of the place. "Caffè or cappuccino?"

A small downpour was drenching the hilly part of southern Lazio with gloom. Ciociaria, home to the city of Frosinone. At the last minute the rally called for Piazza Libertà in town was moved to the union hall, large enough to hold no more than a hundred people, tightly pressed. For Ferranini it was two hours of torture; everyone was smoking cigars and pipes, and the smoke, however proletarian, was more than he could bear, hard as he tried. The hall was dim and overheated, his eyes were itching and he began to cough; every five minutes he had to stop for a glass of water.

After a brief nod at current affairs he quickly moved on to one of his favorite topics: the political futility of any intermediate formation (third force) between the capitalist bloc and the USSR. Reaction or socialism, that was the choice, and it had to be made domestically as well as on the international chessboard. Anyone who hesitated, looking for balance or neutrality, ended up a reformist, assuming he was in good faith. And reformism only served reaction. This wasn't quite what he'd come to talk about, though, and now he needed to make some sort of reference to doctrine. Human history had originated—Ferranini launched into his lesson—when humanity succeeded in producing its means of subsistence. And so history was written in part by human social organization. An elderly man in the first row got up to interrupt him.

"Comrade, explain please, we don't understand."

"In two words: for the Marxist, men are created by their mode of production, that is, they *are* what they produce and how they produce. Where production has been organized and shared, there you have men."

The old man didn't ponder that long. He stood up again.

"Okay, but then bees, and I have ten hives at home, are men like us."

Ferranini replied that in the biological world there were hierarchies, and although bees also collectively produced their means of subsistence, they were not at our level. He resumed his remarks unwillingly, thinking all the while: How *can* we account, in Marxist terms, for hierarchy in the biological world? Marx accused Hegel of having an animalist conception of the state. Hegel argues the monarch's claim to sovereignty depends on "natural selection," on his belonging to a *species* (in the zoological sense) held to be elect. And Marx was right; those criteria are silly, and must be abandoned. But how can I show that bee society is inferior to that of human beings? Damn it, nothing was coming out right today.

They took him back to Rome by car and before 7:00 p.m. he was downtown in Piazza Colonna once again. A Sunday evening alone in the city without Nuccia: that too was an unpleasant novelty. While he was glancing at the paper to see what was playing at the cinemas, a distinguished-looking young man wearing glasses came up.

"Deputy Reparatore is waiting for you."

"And where is he?"

"We're over there in that café. I'm Assuntina's fiancé."

In the café Giobatta sat towering over his womenfolk, nursing his Toscano cigar with conviction. He didn't give Walter a chance to speak.

"You called? Were you looking for me? Well here I am. Let me introduce my son-in-law, he comes from your parts, Vicenza, that is. State Rail inspector. Fine young man. As for the rest of the family, here they are, my bosses, you know them. Sit down, Walter!"

Ferranini knew them well, the two daughters Nina and Assuntina, and their mother. At the start of the parliamentary session, he had spent the better part of his first month in Rome at his friend's home. The fiancée Assuntina appealed to him: plump and soft as an olive, shy as her father was bristly, expansive, dark eyes, smiling and demure. Assuntina ventured to speak over her father's thundering, "You're coming on Wednesday, aren't you?"

"Hey, careful," warned her father, "if you don't come you are no longer my friend. Boatta is traveling. Amoruso is ill. Woe to you if you don't show up. And," said Giobatta without waiting to hear his reply, "Comrade Togliatti is likely to be there."

Ferranini's expression changed. "No, are you serious?"

"I invited Togliatti and he accepted. We were close friends in other days. If he's at all able, I think he'll come."

Ferranini was feeling relaxed when he left the café. The meeting with Giobatta and his family, good, warmhearted people, had been invigorating. Waking the next morning, he thought again about the Mazzola business. He no longer felt any hesitation. "Naive extremism, moralistic revisionism" and as the sanction to apply, "Admonition." At the very least. A balanced judgment. It was true that

Mazzola had expressed views and opinions that coincided with his personal views and opinions, but there were times when you had to set aside personal opinions. Otherwise we're finished. Otherwise we fall back into an anarchic atomism that Communism has long surpassed. Precisely because it has succeeded in becoming a great and unified mass movement.

Suddenly the matter was luminous, clear. Come, Comrade Mazzola, you speak of discipline and you oppose discipline? Some consistency, please. You, Mazzola, have become personalist in your anti-personalism, individualist in order to combat individualism. It is precisely in the name of your principles that you must be judged wrong. Just as I would be wrong (because I share your opinions on various matters) to play party reformer instead of going down to Frosinone to proselytize.

The party has a great leader—and he'll take care of getting it back on track, if needed. We stand behind him. Our job is to implement. To obey, and to pursue the struggle, if necessary.

He was astonished that he had felt any uncertainty at all. No, he would go there in person. He took the letter to party headquarters and by 10:00 a.m. the matter was closed. That evening when he came by the bookstore to meet Nuccia, she found him in good humor.

"Walter, I'm pleased to see you smile. What's going on with you?"

"Nothing."

"But something's up, no?"

"Tomorrow I'm going down to Formia to see Amoruso who has the flu. The day after, there's Reparatore's daughter's wedding. The chamber's on holiday, isn't it? Holiday for me too."

Nuccia, though, was down. She hadn't been able to grab on to anything to lift herself out of her despondency. She'd spent Sunday afternoon at Frascati with her friend, who suggested she look for a lawyer among Walter's colleagues. She must find out about her rights (and responsibilities). The only way was to talk to a lawyer. She tried to raise the question with Walter.

"Yes, there are lawyers in my group, too many of them in fact. But face it, yours is no ordinary matrimonial tale. To some extent, it involves discipline. And they are bound by party discipline too."

The party, that machine bearing down on her. It had been foolish to think she would find someone in it to help her.

"But Walter, I'm alone. Like this, you leave me alone."

They went out shopping, which provided a little distraction. He'd asked her to help him choose a present for Assuntina Reparatore.

"First of all, you need a blue suit. And you don't have one, am I right?"

He didn't.

"I'm going dressed like this. I'm not the elegant type, some Montobbio wearing a suede jacket. A Communist doesn't need to be elegant."

"Come on, Khrushchev has beautiful blue suits, and wait and see, your man Togliatti will show up in blue with a pearl gray tie."

"You think?"

"Of course."

"That may be but I cannot permit you to say 'your man Togliatti.' Respect where respect is due."

Still, her observation had struck him. He had already resigned himself to going to Zingone for the suit when he hit on the ideal solution: tomorrow in Formia he'd ask Amoruso to lend him a suit. They were the same size.

For Assuntina's present, Ferranini proposed a rosoliera.

"What's that?" asked Nuccia.

"A service for rosolio: a decanter and glasses."

"Good heavens, of course. In a Pirandello comedy they'll come in with a rosoliera full of some cordial. But that was forty years ago. Today people drink large glasses of vodka. You spent fifteen days at Reparatore's; be good and return the favor. Send a refrigerator, or, I don't know, a television set."

"A record player."

Nuccia suggested consulting Reparatore's wife to make sure

someone else hadn't already sent one. "I'll call her; this is woman's business."

But everything she touched stung back; it was her fate. They'd gone inside a household appliances shop on via dei Due Macelli and she had already lifted the receiver of the phone. Walter stopped her.

"Better you don't call."

"Why?"

"You told me you already called her once. Now you're calling again on my behalf. We're just making things worse. We'll get what I said and that's the end of it."

She put down the phone and said nothing. Walter was right. They went back and got the record player.

Amoruso hadn't recovered from the flu but he got up all the same to receive his guests. Besides Ferranini there was Pieraccini, a Socialist, with his wife, and a student who was getting a degree in the history of theater at the University of Naples and who had come to borrow some books from Amoruso's collection. (This made Ferranini a bit uncomfortable, since he'd also come to borrow from Amoruso, the blue suit.)

Amoruso the bourgeois convert, "one of the hircocervuses," he called himself, the fanciful "goat stags" of medieval legend, was born of the effort to mate the class struggle with a multi-class system. The house where he and his wife had been living for some years was by no means a convert, however. Elegant without being ostentatious (on the ground floor a single large space served as entryway, sitting room, study, and library), it was very much a bourgeois home in its nonchalant elegance, its rustic-country style, not in keeping with the canons of *House & Garden* but reflecting instead the charming experimentalism of the lady of the house. Adele Cariboni Amoruso, who came down from Rome every night even at the cost of missing a vote in the Senate where for two terms she'd sat with the Socialists, liked to say that furniture and books, carpets and pictures were like shoes, beautiful when comfortable to their user. Ferranini had already been there a number of times. Each time he went, he was surprised and somewhat intimidated by the odd arrangements, the fireplace with Delft tiles and the frame of books around it, the polished andirons on which, benignly and smokelessly, an oak fire burned, the ceremonious serving of coffee that "Comrade" Adele performed so gracefully. Coffee accompanied by large servings of torte with whipped cream (she made it herself; her origins in Trentino led her to Germanize in the kitchen), her guests serving themselves from the cart rolled between one armchair and another.

The dour cooperativist (and activist) was forced to confront a new world, perhaps too foreign to really interest him, except for the vague memories that floated up from his past, from the capitalist quagmire into which he'd risked sinking fifteen years ago. But he didn't mind going down to Formia. He appreciated Amoruso's eclectic hospitality and his library, he admired his wife: Adele had battled fearlessly against the dishonest *legge-truffa* in its day. She knew the errors of a Blanqui and didn't want to repeat them. Who said you had to live in a hovel to help the people free themselves? A hundred meters away from Amoruso's, Comrade Nenni's house was no hovel either. And didn't Deputy Secretary Longo own a villa in Grottaferrata?

The afternoon passed pleasantly, gusts of *libeccio* hurling waves of rain against the windows, while friends talked in the nice, warm sitting room under soft lights. In his dressing gown and slippers Antonino Amoruso battled the flu with glasses of slivovitz and soda and reviewed, from his armchair, the political scene with occasional assistance from Ferranini, who was feeling lazy, and from Comrade Pieraccini. Signora Pieraccini, jealous in that pathetic, banal way that often annoys the man whose fault it is, complained that her husband had too many commitments and never made time for the family. "He even works on the First of May." Her husband observed that a Christmas holiday might be permissible, but labor day had to be celebrated by working.

A threadbare quip he instantly looked sorry for having said, wanting to apologize. But Amoruso got there ahead of him.

"Oh no, my friend. The First of May is not a celebration of labor but a celebration *against* it, and in fact it's observed everywhere by abstaining from work, even in the USSR. It's like the Day of the Dead, the way I see it: it honors the dead but neither acclaims nor honors the fact we must die. The First of May serves to remind us that labor is a deadly fate. Everyone sees it that way at heart (without saying so), and that explains why the rite is universal. I mean laborers, of course. Your work and mine is research, invention, deliberation. Without the curse of repetition, it's not labor."

The other man was taken aback. A plainspoken Tuscan, Pieraccini hadn't expected to elicit such a reaction. He turned to Adele, smiling.

"Everyone's a speech-maker in Naples, eh? Everyone's a sophist. Even hospital department heads."

"Being department head has nothing to do with it," said Amoruso. "But hospitals, medicine, yes. Am I right Ferranini?"

Ferranini just nodded.

"The fact remains," said Pieraccini, "that it's a problem Marxist doctrine isn't all that clear about. We're supposed to think that one day we won't have to work anymore, but it's said—Marx said—that labor is natural and immutable, part of the metabolism between man and nature."

"And you?" Amoruso asked. "You have to take a position too. Otherwise you're no socialist."

Imperious. But Pieraccini was too clever to take the bait; absolute positions were not to his liking.

"You know, for us Socialists, Marxism is like Gregorian chant for a priest."

"Meaning?"

"Meaning that it's not obligatory. Oh, and speaking of priests, we've got to get back to Rome."

He got up. Ferranini was happy to stay a bit longer, and he hadn't yet found the moment to mention the blue suit. Pleased by the invitation to stay for supper, he sat back down while the blond Adele went out to drive the Pieraccini couple and the student to the station. At Amoruso's, however, new guests arrived when people left.

At 6:00 p.m., the others just gone, a car came through the gate, headlights flashing across the windows, and pulled in. A broad-shouldered man with a lively, bitter, expressive face appeared, his jacket collar turned up and dripping, dowsed by the rain in the ten paces from garden to door. He tossed aside his gloves and hat and a moment later was sitting by the fireplace, warming his feet before the flames. Amoruso poured him a drink.

"Alberto, the much esteemed. Where do you rain down from? As it were."

"My God, eight hundred kilometers in this downpour. From Taormina. You know the Taormina Prize. When I got to Naples I had an idea: Formia, Amoruso, medicine, and politics. Fruit torte *mit Sahne*. Adele's not here, though."

Ferranini was busy trying to identify that bony face, the prominent jaw and brow. Where had he seen the man? Amoruso made introductions. "Comrade Ferranini, and if it has to be said, Alberto Moravia. What were you doing in Taormina? Adele will be back in a minute. Don't you already have enough prizes?"

"I do. I was a member of the jury."

"They must call you regularly."

"Naturally. How many writers are there in Italy who read other writers' books? Three, four? Maybe only me. Ah, so the fruit torte is guaranteed."

Adele had come in and she joined them by the fire. The conversation that followed gave Ferranini even more room to rest—and rest was in good supply these days. He was always grateful to be ignored, to remain silent. When not disturbed, he could brood much better in company than alone.

It was a way of a being present without having to think or listen, justified by what he called "fatigue." He didn't so much keep his distance, as shrink physically. He turned off. In someone usually so attentive and responsive—sometimes too much so—it was strange.

The discussion between Amoruso and his friend (Adele had gone to the kitchen to make spaghetti) turned to the inexhaustible question of socialist realism, and Ferranini was asked his opinion.

"I can't say; I know nothing about the question." The truth was, he hadn't been listening.

With unexpected patience, Moravia summarized the problem. He cited Engels's famous dictum: "Realism is the truthful reproduction of typical characters under typical circumstances."

"Now, tell us what you think."

"Well, I would say that realism is not confined to socialists. Everyone, socialist or not, has relations with reality. It can't be eliminated from life. Whether it can be eliminated in literature, I don't know, but it doesn't seem to me a requirement for literature."

Adele, who had left the door to the kitchen open, now intervened. She quoted Marcel Jouhandeau: The most profound purpose of literature, the only one that gives it value, is to comprehend the realm of the human.

"Evidently Jouhandeau thought comprehension not only possible but communicable," said Moravia. "Lucky him."

"My wife," said a serious Amoruso, "is right as usual. Here you are, Alberto, a writer, or more precisely a storyteller, and so let us limit ourselves to literature. Now I would say that the most important thing we need to know before deciding whether a writer or narrator is worth reading is: has he extended the realm of consciousness in our experience of life or not? Including my own personal, individual experience. Do you see? We who don't give much of a damn about orthodoxy believe it doesn't really matter whether the result is achieved through socialist realism or by other means."

He was ready to go on. But his guest had moved on to another subject. The reticent Ferranini had somehow captured his interest, and he said, "Now that I'm here and seeing there's also a PCI colleague of yours, I'm reminded that in the next number of *Nuovi Argomenti*, we're going to begin a series of comments by politicians, one for each party, about how they interpret their political role in relation to their lives, convention, today's complex society. What I heard Ferranini say just now made me think we could begin with him. I'd need something lively and nimble, not more than three or four pages."

Amoruso instantly approved. Enthusiastically, even.

"Perfect. Ferranini is a Communist of the first order, I guarantee you. A thoroughbred proletarian."

"Now you, Antonio, are certainly a pillar of the PCI, but you're a cultivated man first and a political animal second. You have, besides the hospital, your books—politics is your *violon d'Ingres*. Your hobby. Here I want to turn to people who are typical politicians, and probably exclusively. The *politique d'abord* types. Like your colleague, I'd say."

Walter sat listening.

"We're singing your praises," said Moravia, "and what's more, you should know that a few years ago we had the honor of publishing the views of your commander in chief. What do you say? I'll need the piece in ten days or so."

"I'll think about it."

He would think about it very soon.

The following morning at eleven, wearing Amoruso's blue suit, he went to Assuntina's nuptials. Only Assuntina and her husband-to-be had awakened with so much trepidation that morning.

Reparatore lived on the fifth floor of one of those ugly yellowish apartment blocks once called ministerial (they looked like graceless public buildings). No elevator. Ferranini hadn't considered that detail. How could they expect him go all that way up on foot, he said to himself as he slowly climbed the stairs. He found a cluster of guests, some thirty, almost all relatives, spilling out of the dining room into the entryway and even into the hall, and his hopes dimmed further.

The groom (from the Catholic Veneto) was very religious. Reparatore explained they'd had a service in church.

"What can you do, this is the practice in Italy—I was about to say, praxis. I'm going to end up a sacristy socialist, I can't help it. The boss in this household has never been me."

Ferranini mechanically scoured the crowd while he listened, leaning against the doorframe in the corridor. He felt like he wasn't there. In front of him the door to Nina's bedroom was partly open. Nina, older sister of the bride. A high iron bed frame, a blue cotton bedspread, a headboard fit to hang a rosary on. The chest of drawers and walnut table were polished to a mirror shine, and there was a tidy pile of books on the table.

"Nice furniture," he said, to distract himself.

"We Pugliesi," said Reparatore, "are the only southerners who care about tradition. Every feast day has its own food and drink. Nina, bring Walter some taralli and wine. Now try a glass of this Zagarese. Made from special varieties our forebears brought from Zagarise in Calabria. Our dear departed Di Vittorio loved it."

"Who?" said Ferranini. (Where was his head?)

"Who? The great Giuseppe Di Vittorio! I had hoped to get Comrade Togliatti to try it."

"He's not coming, is he."

"Well, at this point, no. I spoke to him on the phone Monday and he promised he'd come. He asked who would be here and I said, 'Ferranini, Walter Ferranini. The man from Reggio Emilia!'"

Walter wasn't in a joking mood. He waited until half past noon, said his goodbyes, and left. His train departed at two and he'd have to hurry if he wanted to change and get his valise. One consolation: he and Comrade Togliatti had been of the same mind when it came to choosing the couple's wedding present. Now they could hear music on *two* record players.

He tried to call his friend Nuccia at the bookstore. She was out. This too annoyed him. Didn't she know he was leaving? He went into the station restaurant.

At one table Comrade Deputy Filippetto was finishing her meal. Fanny Filippetto, a longtime MP for the PCI. The only woman to have been in the chamber since '46, the year women got the vote. She called him over, smiling, and practically whispering in his ear, inquired, "Arriving or departing?"

"Departing, on the Milan train."

"That's my train; I get off at Arezzo, you can keep me company. Now go eat. I'll wait for you here."

As soon as they boarded the train and occupied the compartment she had chosen, she told the conductor who she was and had a "Reserved" sign put up on the door. She lowered the shades on the side of the corridor. She smiled again.

"What's that face? Yes, I want to talk with you, but I don't have anything dreadful to say. Relax, my dear." Then, looking involuntarily pitiful, "It's hot in here. Suffocating."

"But you closed the door."

"I'd rather it was closed. Care for a cigarette, Ferranini?"

"I don't smoke."

"Better for your lungs. So, you are off to cultivate your constituency. That's what they used to call it. Oh, the belle epoque, when the voters knew their representative personally."

She spoke of this and that, amiably and somewhat erratically. An attractive woman in her fifties (he scarcely knew her except by sight), Filippetto liked to show off her smile and the elegance she was known for. A dark suit, very well cut, on whose lapel discreetly glittered a gold badge, the Soviet peace prize. Beyond that tiny hammer and sickle on her ever so slightly matronly bosom, the rest was (once again) distinctly bourgeois. A soft hat of buckskin, worthy of a fashion house, that she tossed negligently onto the luggage rack. Looking at her, Ferranini was reminded of "Comrade" Amoruso. That whole tribe of worthies who represented the proletariat in Rome.

She told him how she'd begun her political career in Rovigo where she'd been a school principal. Oh, those were the days. Now, widowed and alone, she had no one but her married daughter and two grandchildren. "Grandmother of two little kids, I am. I'm off to visit them in Arezzo." It was her one great satisfaction.

All this beating around the bush, thought Ferranini. He was flagellating his leg with a newspaper. Ever since that morning he'd been depressed, yet also (though he was far from being aware of it) elated. He'd hoped to sleep a little on the train.

But not before the train departed. Filippetto stretched out in her corner seat. She lit a cigarette.

"Well then Ferranini—please, relax!—I would have come to see you anyway if we hadn't met up by accident. We need to talk about the situation you know about. One you're in. One in which you haven't weighed the consequences against your responsibilities. Now let me begin by saying this. The window."

"Begin by saying what?"

"The window, there. Lower it, it's stifling in here, don't you feel it? Let me begin by saying that within the party, I direct the Schools Department and the Cultural Secretariat. I imagine you know that."

"No!"

"Take it easy. The comments I'm about to make are not made on my own initiative. I've been commissioned, I've been asked. Unofficially. And those who assigned me this mission are counting (quite rightly) on my womanly capacities."

"But *who* assigned you?"

"I'll let you guess that; I've already told you the positions I occupy, haven't I? I can't be any more specific. Listen, instead, to what I have to say. I'm speaking to you as a woman, I was chosen because I'm a woman, in order to facilitate our interchange."

"But you haven't explained anything!"

"I'm coming to the point. You have to get it through your head that this is not a personal matter. There is little that is personal in the lives of any of us at the head of the party. Do you disagree?"

"No."

"Here's the point, which I will gloss over slightly. A certain signora has vaunted her extramarital relationship with you. She travels with you, she stays in the same hotel, she receives you in her home. I won't go into details. Need I observe that this is a classic, well-known, and inexcusable case of adultery? You think I'm being severe? I don't wish to take a hard line with you; there's somebody else much guiltier. The signora is married and she refuses to return to her husband. In short, a disgraceful ménage where there should be a marriage. Am I making myself clear, Ferranini?"

9

THE TIBER valley was already white, but snow continued to come down sideways, thickly, and the train slowed. Ferranini closed the window again. He was half frozen. He could feel the cold in his bones as if he'd been tossed out there in the middle of the snowy countryside.

The heel of one of those suede shoes was tapping against the seat.

"You understand, Ferranini?"

"Ah, yes. Now, yes."

"You asked who's dealing with your case. You were thinking of some committee, perhaps. Maybe even the Disciplinary Committee. We're not at that point, have no fear. Your case is in a fluid state, but care must be taken that it does not change form, if you see what I mean. I believe that's another reason I was asked to intervene, to avoid the appearance of a disciplinary proceeding. Don't you think?"

Ferranini nodded, passive.

"Now let's hear your reply. Speak."

The door opened and someone cautiously placed a bag on the seat.

"Sorry. Not here," Fanny said promptly.

"There's not a seat in the entire train!"

"I'm sorry," she said and tried to close the door.

The man, small and bearded, resisted. "I'm a rail-company engineer on leave."

"This compartment is reserved for members of parliament. Read the sign."

Bag and beard disappeared. Fanny smiled again.

"You say nothing, Ferranini, and I respect your silence. In any case, through my humble intervention, you're being sent an invitation. To reflect. And if I may, I will add some advice of my own: reflect. Now I'm done," she said, resting her hand lightly on his knee for a moment. "I'm done. My unofficial role ends here. But listen to me further, because now I'll speak to you in another fashion. As a friend. May I?"

"Go ahead."

"You live alone, I'm told. Lord, what misery!"

"What?"

"That blast of heat from the radiator, can't you feel it? You have no family, no relatives, no friends. You're alone. Unattached, one of the few in parliament. Do you know how many unmarried deputies there are in all the parties?"

There were seventeen. Less than four percent.

She aimed him a maternal, admonitory look.

"Be strong, Ferranini, protect yourself from certain disreputable temptations. Choose the purer path of the sentiments. You are still young, and life can offer you affection that is peaceful, gratifying, reassuring. Bountiful."

Et cetera. She went on talking although Ferranini hadn't been listening for some time. And when she got off the train at Arezzo, he didn't move or change position. He stayed in his corner, hands crossed behind his neck. Not a thought in his head.

Then someone came in and sat where Filippetto had been sitting, took out sandwiches and a thermos, and began to eat and drink. It was the man with the beard. There were some people, Ferranini thought, for whom freedom came as naturally as that.

It was his first conscious thought.

He was numb. He got up, stretched, and pulled a book out of his briefcase. He started to read where the book fell open: "The communist organization of society will transform the relations between the sexes into a purely private matter which concerns only the persons involved and in which society will have no occasion to intervene." That little volume, which never left his side, contained the

Communist Manifesto along with comments, notes, and variants mostly provided by Engels. The definitive critical edition that he had himself reviewed in its time in the magazine published by the Reggio Federation. The passage he was reading came in fact from Engels.

He knew that humane and liberating declaration, of course. But he had never stopped to think about it. Now its importance expanded and illuminated the entire praxis of communism, directly and by reflection. *Society will have no occasion to intervene.* It seemed to have been written for them. Shouldn't he defend himself? It was an abuse, the party could not allow it. Filippetto or whoever had sent her had committed an abuse. He had the right to hold on to the woman who loved him. There was no need to sacrifice Nuccia; she'd done nothing wrong. And he had done nothing wrong. The only one damaged was that bully Cesare Lonati. A man who richly deserved a woman who strayed.

He was paging through the book, his "bible." All of a sudden he stopped.

Comrade Togliatti's absence. At the Reparatore wedding. After promising to come, he didn't show up. Why? It was obvious. Because he'd been told that *he* would be there. The "man of Reggio." Ferranini.

Obvious.

But that Comrade Togliatti had asked Filippetto to intervene, no, that was unthinkable. Togliatti didn't deal with this sort of thing. However, he knew of it, and hadn't wished to run into him. And poor Reparatore had never suspected. He hadn't had a clue.

And then there was sense of isolation he'd been feeling in the party, the chamber—what other explanation could there be for that? Was Lonati, the husband, behind all this? On the one hand, it didn't seem impossible; Lonati was in the Press Office, Filippetto in Schools and Culture, they might have had dealings. And yet. She had been rather specific about this thing, this reprimand, having come from someone rather high up, which was to say not Lonati, at least not directly.

Anyway. It was pointless to imagine interferences, intrigue. His conduct had been open to question and the party had looked into it. Nothing more. The facts spoke for themselves. And Engels? No, the passage from Engels didn't apply. Not given the present state of society, and not even, perhaps, in Soviet society. How had he failed to see that before? Engels wrote in the future tense. Logical.

Hot and flushed as she had been, Filippetto made sense. Nothing in the lives of anyone in the party is "personal."

Just think if Mazzola had known about him and Nuccia. What would a man like that have said? You, too, are becoming bourgeois. It's convenient for you to take the wife of a comrade, and you take all you can get. My dear Ferranini, our purpose is to build socialism and you're frittering it away in adultery. The truth is, you have sinned and you have enjoyed sinning—proudly and stubbornly.

And what was more, the party had treated him with consideration, it had been indulgent. In its knowledge of men's failings. A word was put in his ear, he was invited to mend his ways: You're behaving selfishly (like an individual who hasn't been socialized, like a bourgeois, they were all synonyms). For now we forgive you, because to err is human. That the go-between had been the curvaceous, flirtatious Filippetto mattered very little. A man may be inadequate, what matters is the message he transmits. The spring, the well he draws upon.

Fine. Good. Nothing could be more true. Okay, but do I have to be as solitary as a dog? That was also true.

He tossed aside his "bible" and tried to cover up. He was cold.

When it came down to it, why was it he who had to make the sacrifice? They say: socialism. But can't we build socialism all the same, even if Walter Ferranini has a human being to look after him? How are you feeling; you're not entirely well, go see the doctor. Come over here and let me give you what you need. For God's sake.

In the white dusk the train compartment lights came on, and Ferranini, eyes closed, continued to examine his conscience, contrite but stubborn. With his raincoat thrown over him right up to his mouth, under the curious gaze of the little man in the corner who went on chewing.

At Reggio he skipped his supper and went straight from the station to meet Fubini at the Federation. Two hours later, now past nine o'clock, after a long conversation with his friend, he still wasn't hungry. He asked him to drive him straight to the hotel.

Not hungry, not able to sleep. At midnight he was still tossing about in the bed, turning from one hip to the other: when he thought about it, it could only be a bad omen.

Now the problem was Nuccia. The hotel entrance, the lobby with its rattan chairs and the gray carpet in the hall, all this forcefully brought back Nuccia. In that bunch of magazines on the table in the entryway there might still be the one she was paging through that morning when they returned to Rome. Nuccia. His thoughts of her were neither amorous nor sentimental; he just felt the hurt, the meanness of that shabby life, his life. He tossed in the bed and repeated to himself: "Solitary as a man on the moon, a man on the moon."

It was *Lunik*, the Soviet spaceship, deep in the empty, lunar solitude of its cosmic voyages, sailing straight into the heavy heart of a poor devil unable to sleep. But Walter always perceived misery as physical, not emotional. This evening, the ache from his neck to his shoulder, then precordial pain in his chest. Pain and constriction that were familiar and localized; nothing psychological there. He got out of bed and put on his suit jacket. Down under his window there was something going on, a noise, like metal clattering, a lamppost or a street sign. He needed to see what it was.

Without turning on the light, he left the room and found himself in the hallway. It was dark. He took a few steps. "I'll go find someone."

Then he thought about going downstairs and calling her. At her home on via Ovidio. I'll tell her: they can't force me to do without you. They know very well they don't have the right. Anyway, let them do what they will. He had stopped in the dim hallway, a few steps from his door, and he stood there for five or ten minutes immobile. Wide-eyed, one arm hard against the wall for support.

He went back to the room. He was having trouble breathing and he rang the bell, hoping to get a coffee. In the meantime he sat at the table waiting (no one came) and instinctively, without being aware of it, drew pen and paper from his briefcase. He lay them in front of him, spellbound by the graph-patterned pages of the notebook. He was still shivering from the cold, and that mournful noise of clattering metal kept up outside. Finally he began to write. "In the pretechnological world. . . ." He went on. Slowly, but with a peculiar ease, as if he were writing a lesson he'd memorized. The mechanical activity of writing relieved him. After a little while he felt better. He threw himself on the bed, jacket and all.

"I've reconsidered," said Fubini. "We must get Ancillotti to come along. He's the one who's up on things now."

Ferranini didn't object. In the end, his antipathy for the man was also a case of personalism.

"Let's go get him. Provided he doesn't talk too much."

They planned to drive around the province; there were several things they had to deal with, the most serious of them being the perennial fierce struggle (beyond rivalry or competition) between entities of similar origins and scope that should have been able to coexist peacefully—and even cooperate to some degree or at least provide mutual assistance. There was a case in Olmeda, toward the hills, and Ferranini suggested they begin there, at La Vittoria, a factory cooperative that he'd played a large part in founding in '49, during the time he'd worked so hard to expand the cooperative movement from its traditional base (consumer, agricultural, artisanal, and mutual insurance societies) into the industrial sphere. La Vittoria had a labor force of some seventy men and women, and was the economic backbone of the town. But it was administered by two men, both paid-up members of the PCI, who were as greedy and shortsighted as any monopolistic entrepreneur, ambitious and not very scrupulous. Last summer, selling children's leather sandals on street stalls across Emilia at a price of two or three hundred lire per pair, they had decimated the local market. Other producers, among them some small cooperatives, had suffered badly, and the complaints had made it all the way to Rome. One of the worst hit was the shoe factory in San Donato di Vimondino where, when it was still privately owned, he had once worked. The section rep at La Vittoria, a warehouseman, had tried to stop them from underselling and the management had fired him. Just like the classic factory owner facing insubordinate labor delegates.

Comrade Guidotti, the ex-warehouseman, had mysteriously been informed of Ferranini's arrival and was waiting for them as they drove into town. The car stopped and he nearly forced himself in, his face purple from the cold north wind and from bottled-up rage. The gist of what he had to say was: the time has come, get rid of those two and put me back in or I'll take my party card and rip it up before your eyes. Such were the problems Ferranini had to resolve during his pastoral visits, often right then and there, improvising. It wasn't pure politics, no; politics was only tangentially involved, but this was the life of the base—petty, combative, concrete issues—and it was his life.

Pastoral visits. The term was not inappropriate when it came to Villa, half a kilometer outside Olmeda. The little hamlet of Villa owed its modest prosperity to the Garagnani family, for whom a hundred of the hundred and fifty inhabitants, including kids, worked at home or in the factory. They made rosaries. The factory was the largest producer of its kind in Italy and exported to all five continents. The Garagnani family were among other things convinced socialists, and eight percent of the population of Villa belonged to the PCI, a decent percentage even in the province of Reggio.

All went smoothly, and Ferranini the Marxist only had to conceal some annoyance once, when he spoke to Garagnani and his workers and this guy Ancillotti urged they "pray to the Blessed Virgin" that devotion (rosary sales) would flourish. Ferranini was nicely prepared when the problems and questions did come out. He was all patience, very much against his own grain. When possible he chose the route of persuasion, and proved astute, at times even subtle. In his favor, his prestige was known to all up and down the province, though he was quite unaware of his glory, only enhanced by his modesty and by the reputation he had for being not just fair and impartial but severely, even austerely honest. He'd be the first to be astonished if someone told him that, sure, Reggio province was happy that it was quite impossible to slip a pair of shoes or a couple of kilos of cheese into his car—but that he earned their deepest respect when, after a lunch in his honor, it was never said that he'd drunk a glass too many or left a bruise pinching some girl at the rally.

On this tour, since Ancillotti had come along, Ferranini held back somewhat, curious to see how the Red Hunchback (whose own prestige was on the rise, said Fubini) would handle things. Quite often, though, he'd had to intervene. Around noon they'd arrived on the plain to visit the Workers' Furniture Factory in Fratta Po. According to Ancillotti this was a party stronghold, managed in an exemplary way. Ferranini, dubious, asked some questions and it became clear that the factory wasn't making full pension contributions or keeping proper records, and that out of the thirty-four employees, four workers, immigrants from southern Italy, didn't even have labor books recording their job titles and periods of service.

Confronted with these facts, Bolognesi, the manager, came out with the excuse that "we're a family" and that people preferred it that way, without the withholding and the formalities. Ferranini then pointed out that in the older of the three shops the circular saws lacked the legally required safety devices, even though the law was not all that exacting. He told him quite calmly, "I intend to inform the appropriate authorities. You can provide your explanations to them. If you intend to put things in order, fine, if not, I will make it my business to suspend your production." Bolognesi grumbled something about "nice solidarity" and hinted that someone in the Federation would defend him (meaning Viscardi). Ferranini added, "I can assure you that your party membership for '59 is at risk. To be a Communist means to be willing to make sacrifices, not play the gangster. Do you understand? This comes to you from Comrade Ferranini, someone who still makes sacrifices himself." Fubini was staring at him.

Back in the car, Ancillotti took it upon himself to defend Bolognesi. Ultimately, they were all owners at the furniture factory. Economize on the contributions and the gain still went into the worker's pocket. Later Ferranini would learn from Fubini that Bolognesi was in the Hunchback's good graces because, being a huge football fan, he financed the Reggio team, of which Ancillotti was the president.

Ferranini knew Fratta Po well, he'd lived for a few months, from August to December of '46, in the nearby village of Càsole as the manager (in practice, clerk and teller) of the Family Circle, a consumer cooperative. Cooperative: in other words, a tavern with a grocery shop attached. Between Càsole and Vimondino there were fifteen kilometers of paved road, but back then it had been just gravel, with tall poplars on one side and fields, usually deserted, near the river. Every day at 1:00 p.m. when his work at the Family Circle was finished, he would wear out the gravel riding his bicycle back to Vimondino, where his afternoons were dedicated to the PCI, to a little section that had just been founded in a barn at the edge of town. Instead of staying in Càsole to eat at the tavern and to save those few lire he had on him, he'd pick up lunch at the shop, a hundred grams of mortadella and a quarter loaf of bread. He always stopped to eat at the same place, where beyond the line of poplars was a hedgerow of robinia, and in between the two ran an irrigation ditch. A *riale*, as they called it there.

He looked for the place, and when the car came close, made up a reason to stop and get out. The trees were bare in winter, but otherwise nothing had changed, not the stones at the bottom of the *riale*, not the elasticity of his legs as he jumped over it toward the robinia and the fields. A crooked wall of mossy stone ran along the meadow's edge, and far away you could see the bell tower of Vimondino, red with its small metal cross, it too a bit crooked. Some days when it was hot he'd cooled his feet in the water before eating his lunch, and once, just as he was splashing in the ditch he heard a woman's voice call him. It was his cousin Alda, more or less his same age, on her way back to San Donato on her motorbike. They hadn't seen each other for months.

"Hey, come and work with us," she shouted. "Forget about Communism, come work with us. I've got a dozen Dubied machines in my shop and a dozen girls, and it's going great, you know. I need a man! Why not you?"

It was true, she had a knitting factory. She'd earned it the year before with the Allies. An American battalion had planted their tents between Reggio and Parma, and Alda had gone with a few others to offer her services. She earned canisters of gasoline, to barter for sugar, oil, and pasta. Between bed and the black market she'd made herself a pretty penny, and though she had no wish for a husband to order her about, she could sure use a man, if only to guard the factory and drive her finished products to Reggio in the van.

"Come on, Walter. What do you care about politics, you're eating sliced hunger and bread and drinking water from the millrace! Come work for me!"

Yes, well. There was much to be said for Comrade Fanny Filippetto's objections to his love life; nevertheless, Communism was something he had earned. Temptations, large and small, had presented themselves, but he'd resisted. He could look straight into the eyes of someone like Bolognesi and say, "You are a traitor."

They'd last seen each other Monday night. In front of Germini's shopwindow on via dei Due Macelli after the business about the record player; since then, they'd been apart. On Tuesday, Walter had invited Nuccia to Formia; Wednesday afternoon he took the train to Reggio. It wasn't the first time she'd felt abruptly forgotten, but this time it was worse. He must have known very well how she was feeling. That calm of hers that Walter said he admired, the strength and loyalty he was so proud to count on, where were they? It had been two days of feeling barely alive and very tense, with a rabid desire to weep or scream. When she thought of Frascati and Bianca

Weiss, of Giulia at Frascati, of the future she'd dreamed about, she felt nothing but poisonous resentment. Bianca telephoned. She had them say she was busy. When Bianca insisted, she said to her, "You know, maybe Giulia is too young to stay with you. I've reconsidered."

That resistance inside her, the thing that set her apart from others (or so she'd always thought), her determination to put things back together, her instinctive control of her nerves: it was all shattering bit by bit. She was just a common female, like all the others. She had better put the phone on silent, stay away from customers in the store. Thursday morning, just before Christmas, she began to revive. She made herself undergo what she called the purification, a sort of ascetic remedy she had used since she was a girl when she wasn't happy with herself (infractions of the sixth commandment, that is, impure acts committed by introspective girls). All day long she went without smoking, without coffee, without any nourishment apart from a glass of milk. By evening she was worn out, but her mind was cold and clear. Reason had returned and her first decision was that tomorrow she would leave Rome. She must go and spend the holidays (such as they were) with Giulia and her parents at Monticello.

She left on Friday morning, knowing full well that her publishing house would not be happy that she'd left on Christmas Eve, the prime day of the year for selling books. But she had to get to Milan in time to see the lawyer. For a few minutes at Orte she and Walter were almost reunited, their trains passing on parallel tracks. Nuccia had no idea that Walter had left Reggio at 2:00 a.m. in his hurry to see her.

The lawyer she'd decided to consult was Vigezzi in Piazza della Repubblica, near the Stazione Centrale. Enrico Vigezzi was a young man she'd known since September 1944, in those valiant days when she and a few other partisans had put out a little paper called *Ossla da Fer* ("Ironclad") at Domodossola, a title that wasn't pure rhetoric since three of the five journalists, among them Enrico, who'd been tortured, fell injured in a shootout at Vogogna. Now Enrico was a successful professional; he came in late, and she had to sit two hours in the glass-walled waiting room on the twenty-second floor, full of the sky and silent as the bunk room in a lighthouse. She spent the two hours in a disheartening review of the years gone by. From her youth in Val d'Ossola, in fourteen years (or perhaps, worse, in just a few days) she'd plunged into drab, worn-out, irrevocable maturity. On the train, the mirror in her handbag had revealed a small, weary face with strands of gray swirling around.

As she went in, Vigezzi studied her.

"So you're in Rome. Sirocco doesn't suit you. See what a nice northerly wind we have here, from our beautiful Alps."

After he listened to her story, he was optimistic.

"There's no way Lonati can harm you. Although you're not legally separated, for more than four full years he never objected in any way to your de facto separation. Which is to say, he endorsed it."

"Now he regrets it. Now he wants his wife and daughter back."

"This late it makes no difference that he's changed his mind. But I will give you one piece of advice. If your husband has taken up residence in Rome and put down roots, so that it would be difficult for him to move away, leave him there. Come back to Milan. In these cases distance makes all the difference."

Nuccia was groggy from the train ride, hoarse. She opened a second pack of cigarettes, lit one. Leave Rome? So Enrico had not understood.

"There's the child," she said.

"Is she Lonati's child?" he asked, looking out the window. "Sorry, you know."

"Yes. Just as I'm my father's daughter. Unfortunately. But he has ignored her for five years. Never even sent her a postcard. And obviously, not even five lire. He knows her grandparents are well-off, and that the child is with them."

"And what is it that the good man expects now? To get her back because it's convenient? Have no fear, *patria potestas* is both a right and a duty, and when you neglect it, you lose it. At the same time, look: I deal with patents, and that's pretty far away from matrimonial law. But I know a specialist; I'll write you a line of introduction."

Half an hour later, while paying for the doll she'd stopped to buy for Giulia on her way to the other station to get the train to Monticello, she fished out the card Vigezzi had given her. "Atty. Commendatore So and So, Counsel, Cassation Court." She tore it into pieces. To go to some hotshot lawyer, unpack all her woes, her personal life, and this time in front of a stranger. To what end? Even with Vigezzi she hadn't had the courage to mention Walter. Their relationship. And that was the point. The point Lonati could appeal to. And not merely because of the ongoing adultery. She knew very well that the law was accommodating when it came to male sins, just like popular morality and the church. But there was one church that was severe, one set of morality that sinners could not escape, and she had joined that church, and even worse, her lover was part of it. Very much part of it. Did he have a position, was he loyal!

Ferranini, too, had begun to pay for his sins. What a hateful day it was, Christmas Eve, the whole city now frantic with acquisitive furor like a rowdy market fair. He'd arrived at Termini at 7:00 a.m. He wanted to run straight to Nuccia, to her apartment on via Ovidio, but he held back. He had a stubble of a beard and hadn't slept for forty-eight hours; on the bus someone turned around to look.

He got back to his room, and while he was shaving, Giordano, who hadn't seen him come in, apologized and gave him Nuccia's letter informing him she was off to Milan. "I don't know what to do, Walter, what to decide. I was thinking I'd spend the holiday with you and then go to Monticello at the New Year and bring Giulia down. But now? It seems unwise to leave the child in Frascati when Cesare is quite capable of going there and taking her away, and then blackmailing me. As for your help, Walter, I know I mustn't rely on it. I'm having a hard time these days, Walter; forgive me if I'm not selfless enough to keep that to myself. Tomorrow night I'll be in Monticello; back, I expect, on the 31st. In time to mark the end of 1958 with you (if you'll have me)."

He hadn't been expecting this sudden turn of events. For a moment he felt he'd been betrayed.

He threw himself on the bed, swearing. Among other things, he wasn't used to missing his sleep; he had a manual worker's habits, early to bed, a sound sleep. His head was so painful and prickly it felt like it was putrefying. In theory he had things to do; an "invitation" from the Rome Federation had assigned him no less than three sections to visit (the usual administrative inspections), all in the outskirts, the projects: difficult to reach for someone without an automobile. He'd have to be out every afternoon. He sat down at his table, took his papers out of his briefcase distractedly, and saw the five or six pages he'd written in Reggio, that bad night. It was (in a first draft barely legible) the "piece" Moravia had asked him for. He reread it and was amazed to find it worked. It was consistent, complete, clear. Even read well. How strange: he was never able to write even the most ordinary report with facility. He read it again. Yes, why not? Well then, I'll get it off my back; I'll copy it right out. Oh, the typewriter. He didn't own a typewriter and usually Nuccia loaned him her portable. "What a fool beggar I am"—the words came to him in Reggio dialect—and then, in a better humor, he began to recopy the pages by hand.

He really was a beggar, or nearly. Parsimonious, completely unattached to money. For six months he'd donated half of his pay as a deputy to the party, keeping just enough to live on. In Reggio, he'd been every bit as spartan. Once, after his friend Oscar Fubini affectionately accused him of being a fanatic, he decided to give him the lie and try speculation. Food interested him, so he invested some money saved from his salary in a cooperative restaurant, a very nice one that had just opened on Corso Garibaldi, and he began to frequent the place at lunch and dinner. After three months it closed down. Ferranini lost his little wad and gained a case of gastritis thanks to the high-quality butter and lard that the manager (from Vimondino and a relative to boot) had acquired for the kitchen. Fubini laughed. Walter said, "Yeah? I got what I deserved."

It took him less than an hour to recopy his article. He read it again. No two ways about it: it flowed. He thought it was good, and even felt rested. Now he would take the piece to be reviewed by the Press Office. To get the imprimatur. He decided to go immediately.

Via delle Botteghe Oscure. It was Christmas Eve at party command, too. Fewer people than usual, fewer bells ringing and buzzers buzzing, doors slamming. He even felt less the dog in church than he usually did. The people in charge at the Press Office were out, so he left his piece in a sealed envelope with a clerk, giving him the necessary instructions. On his way out he exchanged a few unsatisfying words with Comrade Della Vecchia, who was on his way in, his big head of hair sticking out of his scant beret, his large belly prominent, in contrast to his small, thin, hesitant voice.

"Comrade Ferranini, it's been while since you've been back to Ferrara, hasn't it?"

"Excuse me, comrade, I'm from Reggio. I was there just yesterday."

"Yes, you're from Reggio. And what fine things are you accomplishing in Reggio?"

And he was off with an evasive wave of the hand. Della Vecchia was one of the party grandees—not obliged to know much about Ferranini. But it was odd that he addressed him with the formal *you*. Usually he was friendly. Did it have to do with Filippetto and her mission?

Back on the street, he tried to distract himself by looking up at Comrade Togliatti's windows. From the layout of the floors, he knew that Togliatti's office sat directly above the Press Office he'd just passed though. The lights were on; the room was probably occupied. He was there. The famous office, not very large, with the green blinds and the desk to the left as you entered and long shelves loaded with books to the right. And what had particularly impressed him: next to the desk was a table with a telephone and above it, a buzzer panel. And on a shelf below, a cat, a plain tabby cat, sleeping. A live cat.

For Ferranini had been there. At the beginning of the term, Togliatti had received the newly elected deputies and senators in groups of fifteen or twenty, welcoming and inspiring them. Antonio Amoruso was in Ferranini's group. Togliatti spoke, the new parliamentarians rapt with attention.

"During the first thirty years of our century, which began with

Sarajevo, Italy was extraneous to the concrete and urgent process of History. It shall be our job to make it a permanent part—"

"Excuse me, comrade," Amoruso had jumped up to say, "I would suggest pushing the beginning of the century back further—to the Russian Revolution of 1905, say. The march, Father Gapon."

Who could shut him up, that incorrigible Neapolitan?

He turned toward the Forum. Father Gapon. Gapon. That was it: *capitone*. The stewed eel they ate in Rome on Christmas Eve. A peculiar train of association had led him to the word. He realized he was very hungry, thanks to not having slept. When he got to the trattoria they were just setting the tables.

"*Porca matina*, I'm going to stuff myself," he said in a loud voice as he was being seated. At that moment, the best thing he could think of to do was to fill his stomach.

He ate vigorously, bent over his plate, a napkin protecting his front. Oblivious.

When he got to the cheese, he looked up. The owner of the place had been staring at him briefly.

"Deputy Ferranini, sir. I know you don't wish to be disturbed. But there's someone who wants to see you."

"Who's that? I come here for my food poisoning and to be left alone, and you want to bust . . . . Who is it?"

"Don't know him. He didn't come for dinner."

No, Roberto Mazzola had not come to dine, he looked like a man who never ate—who never even thought about it. He was thin, his eyes fanatical in their bony sockets. And tall; he filled the space of the doorway where he was standing.

"Come over here, Mazzola. We need to talk."

Strangely, the visit was not unexpected. But who did Mazzola remind him of? He must have seen someone similar somewhere. He pulled out a chair.

"I'm bothering you," Mazzola said, limping forward. "I know

that and I'm not apologizing. I'd only offend you if I asked your pardon."

"And in fact you don't have to. Sit down."

"I left Turin last night. Just like that, suddenly. I was so agitated. I think you can imagine."

Ferranini had to lean toward him to hear: he spoke very quietly and stared at his hands, joined tightly at the table's edge. They shook.

"How did you find me?" said Ferranini.

"They gave me your address in parliament; the doorman told me to look for you here. You know, they gave me the sanction. Formal Admonition with Injunction."

"Injunction," Ferranini repeated. "Damn, they hit you hard. They laid it on."

He was unhappy, he really was. And then he thought: that sanction, so much more severe, wasn't his doing. He had proposed a simple Admonition, and only after a morning of thinking it over. He had not signed that sentence, and so he could offer some comforting words.

"Don't lose heart, Mazzola. It happens."

"To traitors."

"Not always. In the early days of the NEP they detested Lenin."

Who did Mazzola remind him of? Father Gapon? What did Gapon have to do with it? The name, however, got him on the right track, Russia. At the Zlatoversky monastery in Kiev in '54, he'd seen someone like Mazzola, a tall saint with glazed eyes, painted in the apse of a church.

"It happened to the greats; it can happen to us."

Mazzola shook his head in desolation. "You speak of the NEP. That was a war maneuver, because even a retreat is a maneuver. Today's de-Stalinization is in no way a retreat in the battle against the bourgeoisie. We're being infiltrated by a bourgeois mentality. It's not an armistice, it's peace, peaceful coexistence while the enemy takes advantage of us. Our social environment is contaminated, and each of us would need permanently active antibodies to resist. Look what a spectacle Christmas is. So corrupt. We've been infected by consumerist reification."

"Yes," said Ferranini, who was more concrete, "it's the quest for the Christmas bonus."

"It's obvious that we've let ourselves in for being infected. I meant to explain, not justify. I was trying to make other people more vigilant, to build up their antibodies. In my own little range of action, speaking and writing for young people. They accuse me of engaging in politics. Politics is what you do here in Rome. Comrade Pisani, you."

Ferranini scowled. "Oh, bravo! You make me laugh."

"I'm treating you as my equal, Ferranini. I have no right, it's only because I remember how good you were to me in Turin. What a day that was, and what came after. The ground opened under my feet. Just before you arrived I got a letter from the company where I was working, a tire factory, and they fired me. The owners tolerate workers of the socialist creed (if they do nothing, if they aren't activists), but the managers and the technicians don't want socialists. I come from a wealthy family, but I have nothing to do with them apart from my mother, and I depend on my wages. I was married in August and we're expecting a child. I'll find another job. But there was nothing selfish about my speaking out. I swear! And I'm a sincere man. Mine was a crisis of conscience. It was disappointment and despair at finding that no one would listen."

Ferranini pursed his lips and exhaled; such considerations put him off. Unmanly confessions, too effusive, too personal.

Both were silent for a few moments. Ferranini felt aggrieved, his encounter with Filippetto came back to mind. In that case, he had been the accused. And just after that meeting, hadn't it been Mazzola (or his ghost) scolding him? All that rigorism. That presumption.

"Now listen, I don't understand crises of conscience. And I don't approve of them. First comes unity, then comes conscience. We are socialists. Resisting factionalist tendencies is our first obligation."

Mazzola folded his arms on the tablecloth and put his head

down. In that state of humiliation and surrender, he spoke again. A doleful voice that came up from the soul, a fine, firm vibrato. "Listen to me, Ferranini. You, at least. Teresita and I love each other, and we're united, but I've said nothing (not a word!) so as not to upset her. And out of a kind of embarrassment too. I'd feel ashamed if I needed to involve a woman."

"Who are you talking about?"

"Teresita, my wife. Let me say this, though. Ferranini, I've been close to going down. Giving up. Even last night on the train I argued with myself for eight long hours. Because it's the individual, the rebel in each of us who *refuses*, pushes the chalice away. You don't know these trials, the weakness of needing to say yes. Temptations to conform, understand? Because only a few of us appreciate the danger. The threat hanging over the workers' movement, over our comrades! Forgive me, Ferranini."

The owner appeared briefly in the doorway, to see whether the deputy was ready for his coffee, or perhaps to observe this unusual encounter.

"You should have thought of that some months ago," Ferranini objected. "The Turin Federation did well to warn Comrade Mazzola, but Mazzola paid no heed. He didn't give a damn."

"But a man can't oppose his inner convictions. He must not."

"Lies. 'I've repented, weakness, inner convictions.' And meanwhile you were doing what you pleased."

What the devil, he thought, I'm just telling him in turn what he told me, or what I think he told me. He was too honest not to feel it was unfair to retaliate against the kid.

"Okay," he went on, "enough of that. Let's get you a coffee."

"You see," Mazzola sounded as dismal as before, his head still sunk on his arms, "you see, there was a way out with integrity, and I took it. With difficulty. Sorrowfully. At the end of November I did not renew my membership, and when they called me up, I said: Yes, I'm a communist—because I am that to my marrow—but not one of you. At your side if you wish, but one of you, no. I believe, I hope you'll see my point. I know you will."

"One moment," Ferranini interrupted him, moving his chair. "Did I misunderstand, or what?"

"My group's been in existence for two weeks now," Mazzola went on as if he hadn't heard, "and it's made up of people who've followed me, or preceded me out. Our headquarters is my home in Rivoli. We're going to call ourselves the Leninist-Stalinist Fidelity Group."

Damnation.

And he'd been ironizing about repentance. This was anything but repentance. Or factionalism. This kid was a man. Without intending to, he pulled back and observed the bent figure of Mazzola anew, more seriously now, almost with respect.

"We met," the other said, "twenty-eight of us in all, including twelve workers from the plant where I was employed. We read Gramsci, articles from *Pravda* and *People's Daily*, the works of Stalin and Lenin. This is Turin, where even workers want to learn, to consult the sources. There is nothing special about our project, we prepare workers, through close contact and with lessons, to keep alive the anti-revisionist consciousness. And make it clear, if we have to, that the party, not us, is guilty of deviationism."

"So you're leaving," said Ferranini. It was his turn to listen, to ask questions. He was the subordinate now, the younger. That's how he felt in front of this kid who'd summoned up the courage.

Mazzola, though, was not thinking about what the other man was feeling; he was making a confession, in all seriousness, and he wasn't finished.

"You don't know how these decisions work. They seem so resolute, so sure, so *decided*, yet they don't do away with the discord inside. They don't root out the reasons. However, if they had agreed to see me this morning—"

"See you where?"

"At the Direzione. I would have said: Look, here I am. Not as a rebel, not as an adversary. As a friend. There are many paths to socialism, allow me to proceed with my comrades outside your way. So far as I can without betraying Marx and Lenin, I'll walk beside you."

Ferranini was listening now, absolutely intent and stunned, not in a bad way. He stared at the man's head (there were a few gray hairs on it), at those shoulders and the slightly threadbare fabric of his suit.

"Since I couldn't speak to Longo, I'm speaking to you. So I won't have come to Rome for nothing (I'm off in an hour, can't leave my wife alone on Christmas). The man I'm speaking to, here front of me, represents the party, the way a priest embodies the Church. I still have mixed feelings; dissent, but also regret. I wonder if I can get this across to you."

"Lift up your head, Mazzola," said Ferranini. "Please, lift up your head."

Very slowly he reached out a hand. At any moment he was going to touch him.

10

WHENEVER Nuccia was invited to visit Walter in his room on vicolo del Leonetto, once they'd done what they meant to do, she
would begin to poke around in his chest of drawers. It needed
straightening up, she said. Once, she pulled out a photograph.

"This poor old picture. The other day it was hanging over the bed,
now it's here in the middle of your dirty linen. What's going on?"

It was an old photo of Ferranini's mother, maybe the only picture
ever taken of her. Ferranini always had it with him, and although he
was not a man to curse (just enough to keep his blood pressure
down, as Amoruso put it), sometimes when he was in a foul mood,
he would take it out on the photo. It really was a sad old thing, and
sometimes ended up on the top of the wardrobe or in the pile of old
newspapers. He wasn't interested enough in himself to analyze or
criticize that curious habit.

"You're an intelligent man," Nuccia went on, "and all things considered, you don't entirely lack genuine feelings."

For Nuccia, as for other women, scolding her friend was one of
the affectionate aftereffects of intimacy.

"Here you are in this freezing room, previously occupied by a
priest," she observed. "To take a bath you have to ask the landlady's
permission, and go down to her apartment. Is that any way to live?
At least get a room with a bath."

"There are more bathtubs in New York City than in the entire
USSR. But the USSR remains the most advanced country on earth."

"Come on, socialism with a bathroom would be even more advanced."

These were Nuccia's usual remarks, regularly repeated, and, Walter had noted, a mere hint of polemical heat turned her face hard and her voice shrill. She immediately looked ugly. He had thought about it that morning, as he was taking a few bills from the drawer to replenish his wallet. (His money was kept in a little notebook between his socks and his shirts.) He was doing it mechanically, and all of a sudden he'd seen Nuccia, right in front of him. Saw her face, heard her voice.

Hey, he thought, this woman, this Nuccia: it's only five or six months that we've been together. Or rather (to be precise) that we've been in the same city. Before that I knew her, yes, but at a distance. Here in Rome we began to make love. But that, if anything, would be a reason to get bored. Why do I think of her and miss her? It means I love her, no way around it. As much as I like to call it friendship.

In truth he had never really thought about the nature of his feelings for Nuccia, and the uncertain dawn of love (at age forty-five!) seemed no more reason for cheer than the Christmas morning shuddering with rain and sleet now breaking on Rome. He had gotten up late and was dressing slowly, meditatively, between the window that didn't close and the warmth of the electric heater. There was no great advantage in just being *attached* to her with a disinterested, unselfish affection, that was for sure, and he'd known it for a while. It was not passion; if they were thoroughly honest, they had to see that (*she* had to see it). The time for passion was past, this wasn't the sentimental thing young people had. He didn't want to lose Nuccia. But he didn't want to leave her hanging, with all that might entail. Yes, she was an intellectual and no longer young, but like all women, she preferred to rose-color the daily gray, or apply Modugno's blue. And Filippetto?

Reflux rose from his stomach to his throat, the acid taste of a badly digested meal. And something else: bitter, physical heaves. Gagging on the circumstances. Filippetto. Cesare Lonati.

Idiot that he was, here he was worrying about it—while those two were already at work resolving the problem. Already he and Nuccia were as good as separated. Hopelessly far apart.

That evening on his way home he had stopped at the landlady's on the first floor to pay the rent. The doorman and his daughter were at the dinner table with her. He was a widower, the landlady separated from her husband, and they made no secret of any of it. Giordano took his meals with her and he probably shared her bed. Who was to stop him? There was nothing wrong with it. It was a crime only for Ferranini and Nuccia. For them, no. He sat down on his bed and looked around.

"What a mess. What a mess."

Reggio, just a year ago, Christmas Eve. At a conference before a hundred leaders of local party sections, he had given an address entitled "The Coming National Elections and Us." It was one of the few speeches he'd made that he recalled happily. A speech he liked. Between any one of us and the party there can be no middle ground. It would not only be wrong; it was illogical. He who sacrifices himself for socialism realizes himself, he's coherent, he's not giving something up the way he would be if he were sacrificing himself to a religion or a state.

Keep this in mind: the party is not outside of us, *it is us*, everything from the animal on up. From the belly on up. Does the party rule us? It's our conscience that rules.

He wouldn't change a word. Perfect. All the more so because the man who said that and thought that believed it one hundred percent. He still did.

One moment, though. In front of him, among the section leaders, had sat a man he'd never seen before. A man in his sixties, with a beard, who every so often applauded approvingly. And Ferranini, as he spoke, had seen himself reflected in the ardent, honest, sweaty face of that good comrade. When the meeting was over, he pointed him out to Oscar Fubini. "That guy? He was a Fascist of the first hour. Friend of Dino Grandi, used to write for *L'Assalto*. Today, sure, he's a good element, head of the PCI organization in such and such." (A large town in the province.) What, then, was this abstraction, the party? These men and their missions, the mass plus the cadres. There were the Fubinis and the Ferraninis (the Mazzolas—no, no longer), and then there were the Fascists of the first hour. There were the profiteers, like Montobbio. And the gangsters. Like Bolognesi. But how could a party represent our conscience if it was not uniform, not consistent but only a jumble? A jumble.

And so our conscience really is *ours*, Ferranini, in a fit of naive black nominalism, went on thinking. A man's personal conscience, if he had one. And that was that. Anything more was drivel, even if in good faith. Especially when elections approached and above all when we were running for office.

Sitting in the bay of the window where he could see without having to turn on the light, he began to look over the notes for the bill he intended to propose. He wanted to add something. An article that seemed pertinent. It wasn't difficult to get down, he had it clear in his head, sentence by sentence, and he scribbled it on the back of a receipt from the trattoria. "A worker who over a period of two years suffers two or more serious industrial accidents, where it can be determined that these are not due to objective causes, shall undergo, at the employer's expense, a period of no less than ten days of observation in an authorized medical institute specializing in psychiatric and behavioral examinations. Treatment, if deemed necessary, shall be equivalent to that enjoyed by the permanently disabled."

"Enjoyed by"? Better say "prescribed to."

The thermos of hot coffee, ordered last night at the coffee bar, sat on his chest of drawers, but he couldn't make up his mind to drink it. It was his sole pleasure of the morning, and he was hoarding it.

It was his fate that 1958 should end this way. In Reggio, pushed aside. All but discarded for the benefit of Viscardi-Ancellotti. In Rome, unknown. Unappreciated. (Priceless that encounter with Della Vecchia who had no idea who he was; so gratifying!) Fate had made just one little concession, his work. Because it looked like sooner or later, probably sooner rather than later, Nuccia would resign herself to giving him up. So there was only that dream (contained in those thirty pages, including the introduction), that one day the Ferranini plan might become known, debated, law. Hopes he could save some worker's skin. And meanwhile, admit it, save himself. Keep afloat as best he could.

More? No more.

Or yes, books. Humanity's bible, Marx, his guide, and a guide for all mankind.

He shut himself up with his books all morning. There was a passage in some work by Marx that had given him the idea for last year's speech in Reggio. After a couple of hours of research (and some brushing up in the meantime), he found it in one of the texts in his room. It was Marx's critique of human dichotomy in today's society, capitalist society. Modern man is split; there's the citizen—political man—and there's the private individual with all his inherent characteristics and inclinations (what Marx, with the power and economy of a sculptor, designated as *forces propres*). Only revolution could unite a man's halves. Communist man does not submit to the state but identifies his whole self, even what is most personal and heartfelt, with the community. There is no conflict, only full and spontaneous harmony. The Communist shall be the complete, unbroken human being.

Let's hope so, he thought bravely as he put on his raincoat and went out to eat.

The next morning as he was just waking up, Giordano arrived with two telegrams. One came from Monticello: "I wish you a happier Christmas than my own. Nuccia." The other was from Formia, from Amoruso: "Telephone immediately. Good news."

The second was amusing more than curiosity-provoking. What did you want to bet that the lovely Senator Adele Cariboni was expecting? First the wedding at Reparatore's and now a happy event in casa Amoruso. These friends of mine are not exactly stray dogs.

He went out to phone, but quickly found himself at the train station. By one that afternoon he was in Formia, arriving at Amoruso's house in a freezing rain, panettone in hand. Remarkably, there were no guests. Adele was in bed, with a cold. Ferranini, unworldly though he was, had the good sense not to mention what he'd thought when he read the telegram. Amoruso, responding to the unexpected visit with his usual sociable expansiveness, led him to a chair and pushed the drinks cart toward him.

"Now let me tell you. You'll be thrilled. Hey, did you see the northern Christmas we've got down here? There's snow over there on the Aurunci hills."

The two of them ate by themselves at a table by the fire, and Amoruso told him the news. The Soviet Academy of Sciences in Leningrad was celebrating its second centenary, and Amoruso had been chosen to represent the party. The elderly Di Costanzo, a professor of chemistry in Naples and one of the patriarchs of southern Italian Communism, was supposed to go with him. But Di Costanzo didn't feel up to the trip and had asked Amoruso to help him be exonerated. Amoruso had then called Longo in Rome.

"Were you able to speak to him?" Ferranini interrupted. Poor Mazzola was on his mind.

"Now listen, this is the good part! Sure, naturally Longo took my call."

"Because you're his physician."

"Because I am—I won't say a PCI deputy, but a PCI member. You amaze me. Damn it, Communism abolishes the state, and party hierarchies will remain? We'll still be cooling our heels in a waiting room? So. Longo knew nothing about the matter. He asked me to call back in half an hour, and he would look into it. I call back. I say, 'In place of Di Costanzo we'll name Ferranini.'"

He said no.

"'Now just a minute,' Longo says, 'he's not a scientist!' I say, 'What do you care? The party is not a scholarly academy, and its delegation can include politicians.' And I say, 'I'm not a scientist either. And Ferranini knows Russian, he's already been to Russia.' 'Okay,' says Longo, 'call me back in half an hour. I'll look into it.' I call him back the third time. Approved."

"Me? You mean I'm approved?"

"You're approved. In three days, Ferranini and Amoruso are off to Leningrad. Say you're grateful, and that you're pleased. As soon as you get back to Rome, confirm your consent with them."

He was much more than pleased, he was moved, and he was having trouble not showing it. They'd conferred this honor on him, setting aside the fact that he'd been admonished for his private conduct. He had been feeling alone, a pariah, and now this comfort arrived from on high. With a rush of gratitude he thought: once again, the party shows—to one of its least-worthy sons—its generosity and foresight, its readiness to forgive and console. And the news came just as he was succumbing to a further doubt, criticizing the way party leaders behaved toward the troops.

"I don't know what to say," he said to Amoruso. "I don't deserve this."

When he arrived in Formia, he'd been tempted to speak to his friend about the meeting with Filippetto. Luckily, he'd kept silent. That thing was finished, no need to mention it again. Now he must return the favor, obey his leaders, and put his affairs in order. No point in digging things up again.

Amoruso asked, "And Moravia? The piece for Moravia. You have to write it, you know."

"It's done," he said with new enthusiasm. "It came out a lot better than I expected."

"Send it to him. You'll see, Amoruso's going to launch you, put you in the picture! Damn it, you're a fellow of merit, but you're also a shrinking violet. It's no good hiding yourself in this world, my friend."

The next day his "piece" for *Nuovi Argomenti* came back from the Press Office in the mail. Someone had attached a slip with the following word scrawled sideways in red pencil: "Unreadable"—followed by some initials, MC or NC, and the date.

He was on his way out of his room. "Unreadable." He didn't understand the word right off. He began to walk and think. The mystery resolved itself quickly and his good humor returned. Confound it, with that handwriting of his. He had copied out the article by hand, and the folks at the Press Office had given up trying to decipher it.

Let's see if the people at Moravia's review were any better. No, they're going to send it back to me, them too. He bought an envelope at a tobacco shop, addressed it to via degli Orsini, and sent it off. He also mailed two lines to Nuccia at via Ovidio. Two dignified lines radiant with seriousness and modesty. "Leaving with a party delegation for the USSR. I can't say exactly when we'll return. Regards from yours truly."

Comrade Cariboni Amoruso came along with them to Ciampino Airport on the morning of December 29. Feverish and stuffy-nosed, Adele had risen from her bed to accompany her husband to the gate. In the car was a heavy overcoat with a fur collar that Amoruso was lending to his friend. "You want to fly to Hyperborea in a raincoat? By now we have a wardrobe in common, so try this on!" The coat fit perfectly. Ferranini's embarrassment amused Adele.

"You'll say I should have thought of it," he said.

"Don't excuse yourself, Walter," said Adele, serious once again. "Unfortunately we're no longer used to men like you. You are a socialist of the old school."

They flew into Leningrad after a night in Warsaw. Tired, they had shared a room. Amoruso had made an odd remark: "Now that it's too late, I'm having qualms. I hope the shock won't be too great for you."

Ferranini's face clouded. "What do you mean."

"Well. The plane trip, the climate."

Ferranini, uncharacteristically, had eaten very little. Amoruso hadn't eaten either. Fatigue.

"Forget about your qualms," he said. "I needed a change of scene badly."

As soon as they landed in Leningrad, he suggested they send a telegram of deferential regards to Comrade Togliatti.

A second telegram went to Comrade Longo. Finally he felt he was getting possession of himself again. His relationship with the party: this was the true measure of his life force.

The past few days had deeply shaken his composure. With the

Mazzola episode, in his relationship with Nuccia Corsi, he had, without willing it, without even understanding it, allowed himself be put in a state of potential conflict. It was impossible to feel that all was well. Writing those telegrams had made him think of his father. Strange, he wasn't susceptible to family memories. But there had been a reason. His father had once said of the Italian Socialists of his day, that they had "too many heads." Even then, the party was infected by personalism.

To call someone a socialist of the old school was no compliment if you knew (and Adele Cariboni Amoruso evidently didn't know) what socialism looked like in Italy today. Millions of workers and one leader, a man who defended their rights with a firm hand, who embodied their ideals. And what a privilege.

No sooner they arrived at the hotel than Ferranini wanted to go out again. He wanted to see the Academy of Sciences, which wasn't far away. (They'd been taken to the Hotel Evropeiskaya.) Amoruso protested.

"Now, at the worst time of day? Who do you think you'll find at one in the afternoon? The celebrations start tomorrow morning. Time for a nap, my friend. We deserve it!"

Amoruso awoke at 5:00 p.m., well rested, and came to check up on Ferranini in his room. He found him huddled in a chair next to the radiator. His eyes were swollen and his face greenish. He was shivering.

"Don't know, must be a bit of a fever."

Amoruso took his temperature. One hundred and something.

"Clothes off and let me have a look at you. It will be the first time I get to give you a proper examination."

He listened to his heart. He put on the blood-pressure cuff.

"Well then," he finally said, "the fever is nothing much, a rheumatological thing. As for the 'pump,' the organ itself, I'd say there isn't anything structurally wrong with it at the moment, but there is a notable malfunction. Your extrasystoles are right out of a textbook. The heart compensates but has never returned to normal. In this context hypertension is significant, as is cardiomegaly."

He tried to laugh. "It's been ten years since I learned my heart was too big and my blood pressure too high. Do you give me another ten?"

"My lad, I order you to hold out for another half century. However, we need to figure out how far along things are. I'll need an electrocardiogram when we're back in Rome."

"I don't believe in that stuff."

"I don't believe in it much myself, but it factors into the decision. These febrile rheumatological fibrillations need to be controlled or they can weaken your heart permanently, and then it will be my fault that I made you come here at such a nasty time of year."

"I've been just fine recently."

"Recently means?"

"I don't know. For three, four weeks."

Amoruso, his pipe, cold, clenched between his teeth, stared out the window, deep in thought.

"Want to know my opinion?" He turned around. "About your health: you tried to cheat yourself out of it when you were young. I don't know how; don't know you well enough. But you must have done something; yours isn't a congenital problem. And I'd rule out vices."

Ferranini laughed. "Vices? Mine are poverty and worries."

"You must have worked yourself close to death. Sometimes a person won't look after himself for a year, maybe even two, three. And then he'll think, Now I'll be more careful. But certain errors exact a penalty. You're the kind who says, Let time do what it will. What happens, happens; if I kick the bucket, so be it. And sometimes that's a perfectly respectable way to operate. As a doctor, I disapprove; I think a man has a duty to live and if he's ill, to get treatment."

"For whose sake?"

"Yours, to begin with. And none of us is alone. Not even you, sorry. There's someone waiting for you back in Rome. Your friend Corsi."

No response.

"Oh by the way," Amoruso went on, "I see you've remained true to your organizer ways. Nuccia Corsi told me she intended to join the party."

Ferranini rose from the bed where he had been examined, and sat down again in his armchair.

"Ferranini? I'm speaking to you. You aren't going to reply?"

He didn't insist. Walter's silence seemed telling enough.

The conversation was livelier the following day when Amoruso returned to the hotel from the ceremony at the academy. Ferranini was waiting for him, his curiosity as feverish as he was. He leapt off the bed to welcome him.

"Out with it, Amoruso. Tell me."

"First thing: it's perfectly organized. Simultaneous translation on headphones in three languages, right off the bat. Remarkably serious, no rhetoric, no long official speeches. There were six hundred people present, divided into groups housed in various halls, and work began immediately, discussion of the different topics. This is not just a commemoration; it's a real conference, with notes and reports being read. With debate."

Ferranini lit up with the other man's enthusiasm. "And who's here?"

"People from England, India, Mexico. And not only delegates from our parties but bourgeois types, scholars, men of science (and women!). Mikoyan representing Khrushchev. Obviously the academy with all its members, hundreds from Moscow. Because these are the historic premises but the Academy of Sciences was transferred to Moscow back in '32. I didn't know that. Did you?"

Ferranini didn't mind boasting a little. "Hmm, yes I did know. Makes sense, Moscow is the brain of the Union. It's logical. But keep going. What did you listen to?"

"I found a group and listened to a presentation by a colleague, a doctor, who teaches pathology in Kiev. He said, 'We must combat the theologizing of science. Scientific research must not become a surrogate of divine providence. The miracle-working capacity that some politicians attribute to researchers damages us. . . .' This professor, name of Vinicenko, was somewhat polemical. He also said, 'Science knows that nature places insuperable limits not only on humans today but on all future living human beings. Technology may seem to perform miracles, but we must remember that technology too acts within the sphere of scientific possibility, and it is ridiculous to believe it can do more.'"

"The talks will be published, I imagine," Ferranini interrupted. "Maybe right away. In that case, please make sure to bring them to me."

"Vinicenko says, 'Communism knocks down the pillars of bourgeois society but the revolution only takes place in the social sphere. The founding works of socialism, ardent and fundamental as they are, never mention revolutionary struggles in other spheres. But there are other limits, other pressures, other hostile forces that are not social but alien to life. These counterforces limit all volition (including communist volition) and they cannot be pushed aside.'"

"A reasonable line of argument," said Ferranini.

"But listen. Some Americans were sitting near me. They were smiling ironically, and one of them whispered, 'The men of science are watering down the Communist wine.' Which is pretty stupid, given that the limits Vinicenko was talking about are limits to capitalism as much as to revolution."

"Of course. And meanwhile, capitalism produces nothing in the social sphere."

"At the end of the session, there was a comment, too brief, by a Bulgarian named Arkanov. He took up Vinicenko's points. I wrote down some of his remarks. He spoke of a 'contradiction for which no simple dialectic solution exists: the confrontation between a living creature and the natural world, between the individual organism and its physical environment.' He also said, 'Life resembles a bubble of air in a liquid, it's something unstable and improbable suspended in hostile conditions.' Here's something else: 'If we're optimists, we can say that the inorganic world and the physical world *tolerate* life. But often they seem to battle it.'"

"This Arkanov, he's a biologist?"

"He teaches biology in Sofia. A young man, as small and dark as a Neapolitan."

"Was there any disagreement when he spoke?"

"Not that I heard."

"And the other side says there's no freedom of opinion in the Soviet Union."

In front of the mirror, Amoruso was trying on an Astrakhan that he seemed very pleased with. He'd just bought it.

"You have to admit," he replied, "there's been a thaw. These are no longer the days when Comrade Stalin was an infallible pontiff, even in matters of physics and biology. But enough! Let me tend to your flu. Felled by the evil eye, weren't you, my poor friend!"

The fever hadn't subsided, and Ferranini, very subdued, had stayed in bed. It was exhausting to speak, even to think. Much as he regretted missing the occasion—even more interesting than he'd expected—he was resigned to it now. His organism accepted the chance to rest without impatience; there seemed to be a bottomless well of fatigue in him.

However, his friend's sympathy annoyed him.

"Poor Walter. The pilgrimage to the Holy Land has gone sour."

"What do you care?"

He didn't like to admit that, in truth, Amoruso was being very kind. He'd offered to keep him company and proposed they have their meals brought up. Ferranini had to stop him.

That evening, Amoruso called Formia from Ferranini's room. It was San Silvestro, New Year's Eve, and he wanted to wish Adele a happy New Year. After twenty minutes, the call went through and Senator Adele answered in her small, high-pitched voice.

"Antonino, take care. With the cold they have there...."

"Are you kidding? Everything is perfect in the socialist fatherland; the hotel is as warm as a greenhouse. We flew in on a giant Tupolev! And the congress is a real congress, a high-level one. So, you've recovered, brava. Okay, you were at Comrade Nenni's house, with Comrade Pieraccini, Comrade Giolitti, good. A sort of select central committee, *en amitié*, excellent! Nothing new? Eh? Have no fear of the Circassian beauties, of the Georgians, I'm here with the austere Ferranini, who's ever more austere; I'm in no danger. Off to a good night's sleep. See what a rascal I am? Happy New Year, my dear."

Ferranini listened, scowling. Scratch a bourgeois and you find a bourgeois, he thought uncharitably.

Having talked to his wife (some socialists, both of them!), Amoruso was in good spirits. He rang the bell to order champagne.

"They used to say you drank the best French champagne in Petersburg. Let's see about Leningrad."

"Technology and Labor" was the theme of the scientific discussion the following day.

Kudirka, a Lithuanian and an engineer, was presiding. A few people spoke up to criticize the "industrial atomism" under way in the Soviet Union, which was disadvantageous for the workers. Soviet shoe manufacture, Kudirka observed, was normally divided between five or six large plants. The uppers came from specialized factories where they put together the vamps, quarters, et cetera that in turn came from other specialized factories, possibly situated hundreds of *versts* distant. Then the assembled uppers traveled for hundreds of kilometers to other yet other plants, and there finally the uppers met the soles.

Disjointed like this in the name of productivity, labor became perverse. It lost its inbuilt efficiency, and the coarseness of the products confirmed this. We don't notice this because today few of us remember the products made in the old way. Still, industry's "objective degradation" would not be very important, if it weren't connected to the worker's estrangement from his labor, which depersonalizes labor and turns it into a subhuman activity.

"Thus the Lithuanian. I didn't agree with that point," said Amoruso. The division or subdivision of labor is an integral part of the industrialization process that men are so proud of. An American from the Massachusetts Institute of Technology then spoke. My friends, he said, what you complain about in Soviet industry is just what we complain about in American industry.

"Yes," said Ferranini, "however, given that America is capitalist, it's only logical that the workers are dehumanized."

"But not here, you mean? In this world, you can't have everything. When industry develops so magnificently, you have to put up with the odd inconvenience. I'd like engineer Kudirka to come to the back streets of Naples to see our poor shoemakers at work."

Ferranini paid no attention. "And if you then consider," he said in the abstracted tone of someone talking to himself, "that the workers are extraneous to the management of the enterprise for which they work—concretely extraneous, I mean. It's not a pretty picture. The hardship typical of labor in all its forms is in no way compensated in industrial society. Whether or not it has been expropriated by capital."

"You don't want the collectivity to be broken up into many tiny Central Committees?" said Amoruso. "As many as there are factories?"

"I don't want anything. What I say is: Either economic activity is managed by the workers, factory soviets, or internal committees, or the centralized bureaucracy takes care of it, which means we're back to state capitalism. Or call it bureaucratic collectivism if you like."

"We are Marxists," said Amoruso in unusually grave tones, "and therefore we trust in Marxism, we're content to know it exists. What are we trying to say here, that society—contemporary society of whatever stripe, collectivist or capitalist—is sick, as our sociologists maintain? A fine discovery. What do we want to do, abolish industry? It's not like we can go back to preindustrial days. The days of Dante and the guilds."

"There are those who speak of a postindustrial society," Ferranini observed.

"And what does that mean, 'postindustrial'? They make me laugh. A meaningless word that suggests overcoming reality. Reality cannot be overcome."

Ferranini was silent for quite some time, thinking about things, deliberating. His second visit to the Soviet Union (no less than the first) was truly a pilgrimage to the Holy Land. He wished it could be free of any doubts at all. He could not share Antonino Amoruso's facile touristic zeal: everything is great, everything is wonderful.

That night, at least, his fever declined. In a couple of hours, just the way it had first spiked. The following afternoon, overcoming his unease at the mere thought of the open air, he made himself go out.

They arrived at the Academy of Sciences in a taxi that wove among the black ministerial Chaikas to set them down right at the door, under the columned portico of the grand building designed by Giacomo Quarenghi. Ferranini quickly inquired about comrades Vinicenko and Arkanov. They had already left. And Aleksandr Oparin and Bosciàn? They hadn't come. That was a disappointment.

However, before they returned to their hotel he did manage to persuade Amoruso to come with him to the Finland station. Comrade Lenin had arrived there in '17, returning from Zurich across Germany aboard the legendary "sealed train," and the small Bolshevik general staff, which was soon in violent conflict with Kerensky's provisional government, had been there briefly. Lenin gave one of his decisive speeches standing atop an armored car parked right in front of the Finland station. On the way back the taxi driver drove down Liteiny Prospekt and stopped in front of the prison where Lenin had been held for three years before going into exile.

Ferranini stepped out of the car, teeth chattering in the cold. For a few minutes he stood there in contemplation, his eyes trained on the aged, reddish building as the snow began to come down heavily. Amoruso the Communist stood by him, but Amoruso the medical man protested.

"You're convalescing! Can't we perform our devotions without getting out of the car?"

"Don't worry."

"Tomorrow," said Amoruso as the taxi started up again, "we must go to the Hermitage."

"Which is what?"

"The most famous picture gallery in the universe! It's no more than half a kilometer from our hotel."

"I'm not here on a pleasure trip myself," said Ferranini. "I'm here to learn. You go."

This was Leningrad, which had witnessed the great Revolution, it seemed to Ferranini he could do nothing worthier than study and learn. The question that plagued him resurfaced—labor today, labor eternal, as he would have put it—a question that coincided with life itself. And chance led to some interesting encounters.

Chance—and the fact that after more than six months inside an artificial (hence abstract) environment, he had stepped out of it, an environment where everyone acted in the name of the workers while none of them were workers. That this was Leningrad made these encounters stand out all the more, strengthening a belief that was already quite strong in him. Borders did not exist as far as labor in its hard fatality was concerned. Not even borders between systems.

In the Hotel Evropeiskaya's crowded lobby the Intourist guides were a fixture, there to escort foreign visitors. But with their PCI passes, Amoruso and Ferranini could circulate without guides. They were their own masters. They had spotted an inexpensive restaurant on Jouskovo and Ferranini decided to go in. The menu offered some Italian dishes, and later they found out that the head cook was an Italian from Foggia, who had been in Russia since '42 when he arrived with the infamous ARMIR, the Italian army sent to the eastern front.

Not only a restaurant; the place, all three stories of it, was also a workers' canteen, or rather there were two canteens: one for technicians, functionaries, and clerical staff on the second floor, and a more modest one for workers on the ground floor. They decided to eat at this second one and had no problems finding a place at a long table where eight or nine young men, a group of workmates, were already seated. As soon as it became clear that the two new arrivals were foreigners, they got up one by one to introduce themselves: surname, name, and patronymic, as well as job title.

Ferranini was struck by this last detail, because in Reggio he used to tell his friends, "Don't say, 'I'm so-and-so the lathe man, or the millwright,' we mustn't honor specialization! Say, 'I'm a worker' and leave it at that." Otherwise the Russians were quite polite, almost formal, with a hint of deference that in no way diminished their dignity as builders of socialism.

The conversation quickly departed from the commonplace, the generic. They were construction workers at a nearby building site (the Italians had seen it while coming in) where they operated steam shovels, bulldozers, and jackhammers. They were laying the foundations of a building that would house a branch of the government department store GUM. Workers who had just come from the job, fully aware of its importance and blessed with a high level of general education. Their persons, their overalls, had none of that humble, resigned untidiness that immediately marked workers in a capitalist country such as Italy.

One of the younger ones, the dark, curly-haired Andrey Carlovich, had a volume of Chebutykin's *History of Scientific Thought* tucked under his arm while he ate.

"We have seventeen hundred libraries in Leningrad," said Andrey Carlovich. "Is it true that in Europe workers are not admitted to libraries?"

"It certainly is true in Italy. The hours are such that workers can never use them."

"And so only the rich frequent them?"

"The rich are far too uncultivated to want to educate themselves in a library."

"Well then, who uses them?"

"Professors, the educated, those who write articles and books."

"But if the workers aren't able to read books, what use are writers?"

Amoruso turned toward Ferranini, looking chastened, and somewhat amused. "Right. What good are Italian writers?"

Andrey Sergheyevich was strong, blond, with pale blue, watery eyes. He might have been German, but he had the Slav's intense, slightly ecstatic expression. He said, "I read in the newspaper that Italians detest nature."

Andrey Sergheyevich, too, was right.

"Your government does not plant any trees, and so Italy is a country without trees."

"The city of Leningrad probably plants more trees than our government does in the whole of Italy," Amoruso admitted.

"But the people, how do they enjoy themselves when they are not working, if they do not love nature?"

"Italians," said Amoruso, "have three ways of enjoying themselves. They sit in bars and taverns, they go to football matches, or they race up and down the roads on motorbikes and in cars, making a tremendous racket."

"And have they no other desires?" said Andrey Carlovich, somewhat dismayed.

"No other desires nor any more noble needs."

They were curious about Amoruso's literary Russian, and they didn't always understand him. Ferranini, for his part, asked about how their labor was compensated: wages and social insurance. Wages turned out to be good, something he already knew. Andrey Sergheyevich, twenty-six years old, a steam-shovel operator, earned a net wage equivalent to 130,000 Italian lire. But his real wage was higher, considering what prices were in Leningrad. The cost of housing was impressively modest. With a wife and two children, Andrey Sergheyevich paid the equivalent of just 10,000 lire a month for lodgings that included two bedrooms and a toilet, and he lived less than five kilometers from the Nevsky Prospekt.

"You live well, therefore you are pleased to be in this world," Amoruso concluded.

"Life is a house; we merely furnish it." Andrey Sergheyevich fell back on the wisdom of an old Russian proverb.

"The government of the Soviet Union," said Ferranini, "promises that by 1975 all housing will be free. Are you satisfied with that?"

Andrey Sergheyevich nodded, looking serious.

Ferranini ate with appetite, making up for the three days in which he'd scarcely taken any food. The others ate much less, and Amoruso noticed that of their eight young fellow diners, three were on a special diet. Boiled fish, boiled vegetables, and a few slices of toasted bread. They sent their meal down with milk.

"It looks to me as if there are tastier choices for dinner," he said, "so why is this, young fellows?"

Andrey Sergheyevich reddened and began to laugh. "I've got nervous gastritis," he said, "and so do my comrades. It's the machines. It's the vibration of the machines, the noise they make."

11

"WHAT A coincidence," said Amoruso in Italian, turning to Ferranini. "A few days before I left Italy four or five young working men came to the hospital, employees of a company that is leveling the ground for a new plant at Trivio di Formia. They complained of stomach problems. Since when had they had the problem? 'We were hired this summer and put to work operating backhoes—and we haven't been well since.' What do you eat, what do you drink? Do you smoke? 'No changes in any of that.' Simple indigestion was my diagnosis, and we prescribed the usual Pepto-Bismol, the usual sedatives. But now I've changed my mind. We're looking at a specific etiology. A collective one."

"And you can speak about it just like that, so cheerfully?" said Ferranini, pushing away his plate.

"But it's nothing alarming! It's an illness that can be treated."

"It's not the illness. It's the fact that we find it in Leningrad, in the Soviet Union."

"And why are you so surprised?" Amoruso snapped back, this time losing his patience. "Good Lord, people have stomachs in Leningrad just as they do in Formia. If anything, I'm sorry I didn't take the machinery into account when I saw those men in the hospital in Formia—"

"And that's it, eh?" Ferranini cut him short.

After many hours at the Academy of Sciences they returned to the restaurant that evening, but they didn't find their worker friends. The canteen on the ground floor was closed. They had their supper on the upper floor with a very different group of diners sitting at smaller tables. They recognized the French delegation and also the Yugoslavs, who had come out of the meeting hall at the State University on the Neva embankment along with them, but Ferranini chose not to sit near them. If he had to talk while he ate, he'd rather do it with the Russians.

It was a white-collar population—administrators, office workers, teachers—most of them regular clients who knew the waiters and didn't have to consult the menu. Each of them, even those who then went on to chat with their tablemates, unfolded the newspaper resting by the water carafe and put it on the table in front of him. These were bureaucrats, Ferranini guessed; a broad ethnic variety to judge by their different features and body types. A good many of the Soviet republics seemed to be represented, but they all spoke the same Russian, thick with administrative and technical jargon.

"Look at those terrible old things," said Amoruso, pointing to the fans suspended from the ceiling, spinning over their heads. "They look like the ones in the movies thirty years ago. But, what the devil, aren't we in January?"

Such were the things Amoruso thought about.

As they were finishing their meal a well-dressed man in his fifties sat down at their table and apologized for his companion, a huge dog with a slate-colored pelt, as gentle as could be. The beast curled up on Amoruso's feet under the table and didn't move a muscle.

The elderly man with the dog was an engineer, Leonid Victorovic Schmidt, professor of metallurgical chemistry, doing research at the Kirov plants. A bachelor, he told them right off. With a decent literary culture, among other things. He didn't speak Italian but immediately understood they were Italians, and quoted (without mangling them) some of Ungaretti's verses. *Appiè dei passi della sera / Va un'acqua chiara / Colore dell'uliva....*

Schmidt put them through a clipped and courteous series of questions. At a certain point he said, very solemnly, "Comrades. You belong to the PCI. Why has the party not yet taken power? The Italians are tired of waiting."

"Inevitable question," said Amoruso with a wink at Ferranini.

"Russia is an immense octopus in its geographical dimension," added Leonid Victorovic. "It's difficult to know where to grab it. Italy is a charming young lady with a tiny waist. The PCI has the girl by the waist, controls Tuscany and Emilia, the roads and the railways. Grab her. She's yours."

"It's a pointless observation," replied Ferranini, bitterly if less imaginatively.

"Why?" Leonid Victorovic shot back. "Don't you have plans? Do you lack the will?"

"You must understand that not only is it not discussed; it is forbidden to discuss it. The PCI doesn't speak of it. The left doesn't speak of it, inside or outside the party."

"There is a left outside the party?"

"There are several," Ferranini replied. "Anarchist and Trotskyist groups, and one called the Communist Internationalist Party."

He thought of Mazzola and was about to say: And now there's even a group of loyal Stalinists.

Amoruso spoke up. "My friend Leonid Victorovic, my friend Ferranini, let's not accuse anyone of fence-sitting. The PCI policy is based on sound logic, it seems to me. I'm optimistic. In Italy we hold general elections about every two and a half years. At each election, our party gets five percent more votes. And so within fifteen years we'll be in power (we'll win the girl) with the greatest of ease. By means of formal democracy, thus providing an example to the other countries in the Western Bloc and creating precedent. I'm fifty-five years old. There's still time for me to be elected the commissar for health and hygiene in Italy. I'm a doctor and I'm counting on it."

"*PazhAlusta, ya ni panimAju,*" Leonid Victorovic replied. *I don't understand.* Perhaps thinking he hadn't heard correctly.

"I was saying I expect to end up as the health minister in the Italian Communist government. I'm a doctor."

"The doctor," said Leonid Victorovic, "likes to joke."

Maybe, but Ferranini thought Amoruso might be serious.

Comrade Schmidt then spoke of himself. A member of the party (none of the young men they'd met at lunch were), Leonid Victoro-

vic had an important position in the management of the Kirov industries, was able to study as much as he liked, and had an excellent
salary. One of his younger brothers was a worker in Arkhangelsk.

"Matvej's not as fortunate as I am. He works as a varnisher in a
factory making electric engines. One of the lighter jobs, apparently.
This summer I went to see him. One of his arms, his right arm, is
swollen. It worries me."

"Don't worry," said Amoruso. "It's probably arthritis. Send him
to Crimea."

"No, it's not; I was told hypertrophy of the limb. He spends ten
hours a day in front of a conveyor belt, every day repeating the same
movement thousands of times. When he gets off in the evening he's
groggy, and doesn't want to read, listen to music, or even talk to a
friend. He's not as fortunate as I am. Maybe not even as fortunate as
Ghipki, my wolfhound."

"Typical laborer," said Ferranini.

He was thinking of the mute fatigue of the Ukrainian farmers
he'd met in August '54. Unable to respond to the questions the interpreter asked. Like the farmers and field hands of Emilia.

There were still the Andrey Carlovics and the Andrey Sergheyev-
ichs, however. Those who had the time and desire to read, those at
least. Right, and their reward was a job that gave them nervous gastritis.

"In the end, though," Leonid Victorovic went on, "what are we
talking about? I belong to another world, that of the clean hands.
Every intellectual ought to be made to work with his hands half a
day out of every two. That's not unimaginable."

Those obsolete class distinctions return to reproduce themselves
within labor, Ferranini thought to himself. Still, it wasn't so strange.
Labor gave birth to hierarchy, above all. You couldn't do without
hierarchy. Even without an army, a clergy, or whatever other stratify-
ing order, men would have been stratified by labor. Organized labor
was divided labor.

Leonid Victorovic must have sensed the Italian's doubts, and he
confirmed them.

"There are social groups here too; the bourgeois might even speak of 'classes.' In any case we have them and they are not challenged."

"And will they be?" asked Ferranini.

"You may know," Leonid Victorovic replied, "that from the Seventeenth Congress it's been officially established that demanding equal treatment for individuals is petit bourgeois nonsense, it's not socialism. Also, Marxism is opposed to egalitarianism. Further, if labor is fatiguing, it is also true that we managers are overburdened. We intellectuals. For example, if I want to follow the technical literature, domestic and foreign, I must lock myself in the library every weekend, and even then I can't keep up with all the publications."

"I know what you mean," boasted Amoruso. "The same happens to me."

"It all derives from progress," said Leonid Victorovic. "Today specialist knowledge proliferates like the cells of a tumor. You find the same phenomenon in America."

Amoruso didn't appear to be taking Schmidt's confidences too seriously, just as that morning he hadn't asked many questions of the workers they had met. But Ferranini's head was pounding. Was it just an obsession of his (therefore wrong) or was this really the reality?

The next day, the day before they were due to depart, presented another important encounter, a new aspect of the problem.

The celebratory session of the Academy of Sciences was finished. Amoruso had gone off to explore the great labyrinth of the Hermitage. Ferranini went on his own to see the cruiser *Aurora*, the Industrial Cooperative's Cultural Center, and the Kirov plant that had taken the place of the old (renowned, glorious) Putilov works. He didn't look up Comrade Schmidt, who had invited them to visit him at work. Exhausted, he sat in one of the recreational clubs inside the plant, and while drinking a coffee jotted down notes for an article about Leningrad that he intended to publish in the Reggio Federation newsletter. He took the subway back to the hotel because the boulevards and immense squares made him feel slightly gloomy. They reminded him of Turin.

Earlier, leaving the hotel that morning, they had asked to be taken to the Warsaw station. They wanted to reserve sleepers for the night, so that they could depart in the evening. Amoruso was keen to make the trip by train.

So familiar with the din and the chaos of the Reggio Emilia station, Ferranini had been astonished by the silence (and cleanliness) of the old station, one of many in the city, at 9:00 a.m.

"It's like being in a church," Amoruso had said, raising his eyes to the glass of the arcade over the rails. "It makes me think of Anna Karenina, ready to throw herself under the wheels, poor thing."

An elderly attendant with a white apron over her dark uniform stood near them on the wooden platform, a great brass samovar before her emitting a wisp of steam. There was a passenger car at the head of the train, and on the stairs sat a bearded fellow with a grave expression, polishing the door handles.

A moment later, the express train from Poland burst in and cut through the silence, bearing sleeper cars from Vienna, Berlin, and Paris. The locomotive (and the detail didn't escape Ferranini) was a very modern electro-diesel model as tall and long as a house. It made an interesting contrast with the environment, including the people, of the station. While they were admiring this machine, one of the engine drivers got down.

They were in the station buffet, warming up with a drop of slivovitz. As they were getting ready to leave, the driver came in.

"I'd like to talk to you for a moment," said Amoruso.

And so, while the man was drinking a steaming glass of green tea, he joined him. The driver was handsome, in his thirties, short, stocky, his gaze slightly inert in a rather expressive face. His brow, under blond hair, was what you'd call pensive. To Amoruso he looked more like a violinist than an engine driver.

"I'm a comrade from Italy," Amoruso said to him. "Can we exchange a few words? First off, I admire your locomotive. It's powerful! How fast does it go?"

"When the line permits, more than a hundred forty kilometers per hour. Two thousand horsepower."

"And have you been using it for a long time?"

"Several years now. Our electro-diesel engines are the same model used in the United States."

He said it quite coolly, without a hint of professional pride. In the meantime, Ferranini had come forward, and Amoruso introduced him.

"He's Italian too. Son of an engine driver, a colleague. Now tell me. Why did you make that comparison with the United States?"

"The Soviet Union and the United States are two of the greatest industrial nations."

"Yet socially and politically they are two opposite poles."

The man thought for a moment. "Whether in Russia or in America, if you drive the same engine, you live the same life."

"And what life is that?" Amoruso went on.

"Well, in the cab we have drivers' seats of foam rubber and air-conditioning. There's no more hot or cold for us. And if I want to stretch my muscles, I do gymnastics at home."

"Progress, in short."

"But when I'm driving, it's like the train's seven hundred tons are all sitting on my chest."

"Nervous tension. How many hours were you on this morning?"

"Four."

"Are you tired?"

"I feel slightly drunk. I don't quite understand what you're saying to me." His mouth twisted into a frown.

Ferranini took Amoruso by the arm. "Let's leave him in peace."

When he was a kid, he'd heard the same words from his father when he came off his shift: "I'm drunk."

Amoruso had a further question. Was there snow on the route? The driver replied that there was snow and it was still snowing. His train had in fact been delayed.

"How much?"

"Eleven minutes."

"Did you hear that?" exclaimed Amoruso. "God bless the Soviet Union. Eleven minutes and they call it a delay!"

The conversation had been extremely useful, thought Amoruso. He gave up the idea of traveling by train, and right there from the station they telephoned the Aeroflot office to reserve seats on the plane.

The effect on Ferranini was different. He reflected that he had discussed these questions with Amoruso back in Rome and the doctor had seemed to take them seriously. Now he'd completely forgotten. As if nothing had happened. What kind of man was this? One who amused himself, a tourist. A bourgeois.

The trip back was long and fairly turbulent. Terrible atmospheric conditions. They arrived the evening of the 5th and Ferranini did not get home and settled until midnight. In the morning, the trouble began.

In the stack of mail was a notice from the Reggio Federation of a meeting of the provincial membership on the 7th at 2:00 p.m., and also, separately, a letter from Viscardi. It said: "On the 7th we have a meeting in Reggio of great importance to me, where I hope the situation will finally be resolved. I urge you to be there, because I believe I'm entitled to your support. If you leave Rome on the 8:00 a.m. rapido, I will pick you up by car in Bologna, and bring you up to date on the way. Please telegram, your presence will be extremely useful to me."

So there it is, he thought, just what I need to feel right at home. That conceited Bolognese egotist! The day after tomorrow I'm supposed to go to Reggio, not to offer my advice on how to advance socialism in my home district but to "support" *him*. Because he wants the job. Well, he can wait. A bunch of selfish pigs, all of you.

The mail also included the notice of another meeting on the 7th, that too in Reggio. This was a recently convened interprovincial committee to promote a new bridge across the Po between Emilia and the province of Mantua, a committee over which Ferranini presided. A memo had been prepared for the Ministry of Public Works. The project itself had been submitted to the ministry a number of months ago but had met with the usual inertia (or stupidity), and so before he left, he had written directly to the minister using strong words: "The Po, alone among all the great European rivers, cannot be used for navigation. And it can barely be used for irrigation. It is absurd and shameful that this river's exclusive purposes are 1) to flood low-lying areas, and 2) to serve as a barrier between the inhabitants of the two banks."

He had gone at the matter with all his determination, as if it were personal (whatever small amount of prestige he had left was tied up in it, he felt), and used the occasion to unleash all his ideological and personal ire on the central bureaucracy. He decided he would go to Reggio to the interprovincial committee without showing up at the other one. He'd go just to show them the letter he'd sent to the minister and assure them that at least this once, the bureaucrats of the bourgeois state would not prevail.

He began to look for the copy, rummaging in drawers and on shelves, in the bag that was still on the floor to be emptied. He shook out his briefcase with his papers; he even looked under the bed. Everything was in scrupulous order; each evening he would go through his papers, catalogue them, and file them. Without that meticulous ceremony his day did not come to an end. So he began searching again, starting with the chest of drawers, but meanwhile his hands had begun to tremble. His rage (not out of proportion, but where did it come from? he wasn't sure) had begun to boil, it clouded his eyes, and when he bent over to search the wastepaper basket he lost his balance and hit his temple hard against the corner of the table. Swearing brought no relief. He kept on opening and closing things; obsessively, mechanically, moving things about. Almost frantically.

His valise was underfoot, and he gave it a kick that sent it flying through the doorway and left it upturned on the landing. A patient hand gathered up the dirty socks and handkerchiefs and lightly returned them to the bag. Nuccia, on her way up.

"So?" he shouted. Enraged now.

Nuccia was bent over the bag.

"What are you doing here?"

But she was intelligent, she loved him. Walter's rages were never without reason, no matter how trivial the pretext. This she had grasped in their few months together. The rage was a sign of disappointment, of misery. This time it was the trip.

"This is the third day I've come, Walter. I didn't think you'd be away so long."

"I mean, at this hour! Why are you not at the store. At nine in the morning."

"Come on, calm down, you look like a ghost. It's Epiphany, that's why I'm off. Tell me what happened."

She was standing with the bag by the door; he was blocking it.

"You know you mustn't come up here any more. Wait for me down on the street."

"I won't come again. But for now let me in, be a good man."

She could come in.

"I warn you, though, I'm leaving. I'm off to Reggio."

"Are you kidding? Giordano told me you got back at midnight. Anyway there are no trains now. You can leave at two."

"I'll leave when I like." And he went to sit on the bed.

"Tell me what happened, Walter. On the trip."

"We were delayed coming back. Because of the snow, they didn't want to let the planes take off."

"No, I mean over there. Your impressions."

"Impressions don't count. Facts count."

Things must not have gone so well. But it was pointless to insist. After a while she dared to say, "I came back on New Year's Eve."

"Why?" he said distractedly, and already calm.

"Why? What choice do I have? Giulia remains with her grandparents. By now I've long given up the hope of bringing her to Rome with me, but I wish her health were better, she's so thin. A serious little girl, her eyes are too big. Who doesn't want to do her homework. And what is worse, doesn't want to play."

He had reclined on the bed and was staring at the ceiling, not even listening.

"The news when I got back was not very pleasant. Cesare, my

husband. He came by the bookstore and asked for me; luckily I was out at the time. Then he wrote to me."

"Ah."

"He says he's set up house in Rome, and that business is excellent, but he is sick. I can't remember what illness it is. 'Let's meet again; let's put things back together.' 'Let's get Giulia to come and live with us; we're not all that old.' And finally, 'On Wednesdays and Saturdays I eat my supper at Tre Scalini in Piazza Navona. I'm there from eight to eight thirty and will wait for you before starting to eat.'"

Ferranini snickered. "He's better to you than I am. What are you waiting for; make him happy."

"I'm waiting to be sure you don't love me anymore. No, that's not true. I'd find Cesare odious in any case. However, I really don't know whether you do love me. Couldn't you just tell me?"

He glanced at her. That thin face, nose, neck, that dark knot of hair with the copper streaks. Her long, fine nose with those strange delicate nostrils that quivered. She was tiny and so alive. So much life inside. What's more, he liked her. He liked to watch her get excited, respond to him.

"Come over here."

"And where is that?"

"To bed."

She was a woman, she thought she was pretty shrewd, and didn't obey.

"No, Walter. I'm staying put here."

He didn't invite her again, but adjusted the pillows under his head on the unmade bed. (Some nights one pillow was not enough.)

"So, you won't tell me? Not much room in Walter's life for his woman friend, eh? There's room for memories. Room for ideas."

"You'd better say facts, not just ideas. The province of Reggio would not be what it is without Ferranini."

"I agree. Let's say Reggio. Let's say Il Migliore. Let's not say parliament, because parliament doesn't stir up a lot of ideas." She was trying to make a joke of it.

"I'm not one for gallantries. I guess I was rude just now. I was trying to find an important letter that has disappeared."

She looked around and saw the open drawers and the mess of papers. She went straight to the wardrobe and searched the pockets of his clothes. Turning, she tossed a pair of carbon copies, rumpled and half torn, on the bed.

"Damn," said Ferranini, astonished, "there they are."

"So, you do need me?"

"Yes, I was just saying so. I won't pay you compliments, I'm not like Cesare. But I can say this, and I don't know how many men could say the same: I have nothing besides you. Not only no other women—no other human beings. There's Oscar Fubini. He's a political friend."

"Don't treat me so badly again. Oh Walter."

"I don't treat you badly," he said, for he had already forgiven himself. "Look, a minute ago, I wanted to fool around with you. I tell you, that's the truth."

"My dear, you must be able to come up with something better than that."

"Something better than that?" he said all too frankly.

"Okay." Now Nuccia's laugh, too, was frank. "You wanted to fool around and then you changed your mind seeing that I resisted and didn't join you in bed."

"No, I changed my mind when it occurred to me: she'll think I only need her for that. And I don't want to give you that impression."

"And I believe you." She moved to his side and wrapped her arm around his head. "It's easy for a woman to know a man, and with you, it's very easy. You don't pay compliments, no—but since you're pretty rugged, when you come out with a sensitive thought, it's quite convincing."

"Really?" he said, without having understood much.

"Oh, my man. You."

Ferranini pulled himself up to sit on the bed. "Careful. I mustn't lead you on."

He would have liked to say, Careful, I'm not in love with you in the way you want. But Nuccia understood differently, and still stroking his head, she said, "So it's over, fast. Who are you pledged to, let's hear. Yourself, or the party?"

He didn't deny it. "It should be one and the same."

"But are you sure it's worth it?"

Right. That was the point. Ferranini rose and began to walk up and down the room. The space was tiny, but Nuccia guessed he had already forgotten she was there.

So she pointed out to him that the carbon copies were in shreds. Unusable.

"Tomorrow morning I have to take them with me to Reggio," said Ferranini. "I need to find the time to recopy them."

"I'll copy them out for you. Give them to me and I'll bring them to you tomorrow morning at the train."

At 7:30 a.m. she boarded the bus in order to be on time for the train.

On the platform she saw Walter talking to someone, a small, gesticulating man. No way they would have even a moment together. She guessed the man was some political figure; how was she going to deliver the letter? She walked up to Walter and said, "Here are those papers, Deputy Ferranini. Will there be anything else?"

She left, consoled by that smile he'd beamed at her.

The political figure was the Red Hunchback. Asvero Ancillotti, also departing for Reggio. A nuisance, thought Ferranini; he was looking for a way to get free of him. (And what could he have come to Rome to stick his nose into?)

"Dear Ferranini," said Ancillotti with that ventriloquist's voice of his, "so we're all on our way to the plenum. An important meeting today!"

Ferranini had just scanned the party paper *l'Unità* where the meeting, under the heading "Party Life," was mentioned in a scant four lines of small type. Go screw yourself, he longed to say to him. You and your "plenum." Fool.

The paper also reported that Roberto Mazzola of Turin had been expelled. "An individual who has amply demonstrated his faulty Communist preparation and persistent lack of discipline."

This piece of news was given nine lines on page six.

Parliament reopened (resumed its "work") after a twenty-day break. Ferranini returned to the chamber, which smelled once again of cleaner's turpentine and felt even more verbose, bourgeois, and superfluous.

A brief, very brief encounter with Comrade Longo was the only event of note in those days. One afternoon, around the middle of the month, in a hallway: Longo was talking to Reparatore, and Reparatore signaled to him to come over. It had been some time since Ferranini had spoken to the man, esteemed and admired by him with hushed intensity from afar, because Longo had been the head of the early partisan command and then one of the leaders of European Communism. He went up to him, timidly studying that broad face with bushy eyebrows tumbling over a pair of keen, glacier-blue eyes. A gaze renowned (and feared) for its ironic edge.

Ferranini saw that edge sharpen as Longo said, "I received your telegram. Thank you. Did Leningrad do you good?"

Reparatore, consulted that same evening, interpreted Longo's comment this way: "There's no reason not to take it positively. He meant: Did you feel at home? The climate there is not that of Rome, did it trouble you? Good things, dear Walter. I trust my instincts on this."

"Oh, sure! He asks me whether the climate troubled me. He's not exactly my uncle. He meant: Ferranini is an ailing socialist, from the ideological point of view, and in terms of habits, way of life. And therefore, I hope and presume that the trip to Leningrad served to . . . et cetera."

"Are you kidding?" said the other. "You're here, a deputy in the chamber. Which means that one year ago the names of the deputables from Reggio Emilia appeared on Longo's desk and yours was among them and he wrote to one side of it, 'Approved.' Dear friend, if one of us doubts himself, doesn't that mean he doubts the whole apparatus?"

It was the kind of dialectic that just might sway Ferranini's conjecturing mind. Had Reparatore not continued: "And anyway, my permanent recommendation is to try not to give such a damn, or you'll lose your mind. Or get a hang-up."

"Listen, when I don't give a damn, I don't give a damn about anything. Understand? Nothing!"

He was often at Reparatore's house these days, in the evenings and on Sunday. Instinctively (he hadn't yet really thought about it) he was in search of a friendship that could become real, concrete. For someone like him, it wasn't easy to make friends. His affections, except for one perhaps, were mired in the fog of habit.

He had returned to Reparatore's one Sunday afternoon, the last day of January. In the morning he'd been to speak at the Federated Chamber of Labor in Tivoli. He had gone to Tivoli with Reparatore and Boatta, but when they got back to Rome the other two went off to the stadium for the Roma–Lazio game.

One from Puglia in the south, one from Asti in the north, very different temperaments and mind-sets, the two, both nearing old age, were bonded not by shared, heartfelt political faith but by their passion for football.

"But if it pours rain," he had objected.

"Let it rain, with our side heated up to a hundred and five degrees, we won't even notice."

Ferranini knew nothing about sports; he didn't even experience a small itch, let alone a big fever. And then there was a question of principle.

"Sports," he warned, "are a bourgeois distraction. The class struggle is a boiler under pressure. The bourgeoisie opens a crack in the boiler to let the pressure subside. Not by chance it is the big monopolists who finance football."

"Lenin didn't denounce sports. And the USSR walks away with the Olympics."

"I guarantee you," Ferranini went on, "no opium of the people is more powerful than sports."

Reparatore was teasing. Ferranini spoke with all seriousness.

"And this, what's this? Does it take the place of the party?" He had his finger on the team badge his friend wore in the buttonhole of his jacket.

"That's a Lazio badge. Aren't you aware that the Federation here in Rome advises us not to wear our party badges? And it's not the only group."

"In Reggio, I always recommended they be kept in evidence."

"And you were mistaken. We must not let the Christian Democrats count us, know how many we are."

He stopped smiling.

"Walter, my friend, you are a smart fellow, but I don't see you as a politician! You confuse ideas with reality, past with present. If we're not careful, people will choose between the game and the party. You're antiquated, Walter, and that's coming from someone twenty years older than you."

Walter backed down and (to tell the truth) not out of respect for those twenty years. The words came as no surprise to him. Nuccia (they saw each other rarely these days, communicating by telephone) had said pretty much the same thing: You take things too hard, if you were a real politician you'd stomach it better. And anyway, weren't Nuccia's and Reparatore's efforts to push him away from politics at least implicitly the advice he needed to return to himself and his best days? He came from the "peripheral cadres" in the technical and literal sense of the words. He wasn't someone from the center, the head. He had begun to see the importance of that. He must now fight back against this phony role in Rome, where he'd been sent by just the people who meant to replace him (promotion = elimination). He could fight back. On the interprovincial committee for the Po there was Comrade Bonvicini, the mayor of Guastalla. Bonvicini was stepping down because his arthritis was torturing him, and he had said to Ferranini, "If you want, they'd be happy to have you in my place in Guastalla at the next local elections." The idea didn't displease him.

Better to be first in Guastalla, than last in Rome? No, that wasn't it. There was his vocation as an organizer. The need he had to build things, he who had an almost erotic passion for ideas. A bridge over the Po or the elementary schools of a town of some twenty thousand souls. Leave his mark on things, on people. And rediscover things, and people, above all. In Rome, he was a parliamentarian for a party that didn't believe in parliament, a representative without representing anything in any way. Walter Ferranini, what was he doing. Every couple of days someone was telling him, "You are no politician."

That Sunday would be momentous. Ferranini had nothing to do, and was waiting for Boatta and Reparatore to return to casa Reparatore. There was no one there to let him in but the eldest daughter.

Much more attractive and lively than her married sister, Nina, for some undisclosed reason, hadn't married. She had a degree in Russian literature, and now at twenty-nine was about to apply for a university job. Meanwhile she taught courses with the PCI Federation in Rome and worked as a translator for a publishing house. She flooded him with questions about his trip.

"And this encounter with Soviet life and society," she said at a certain point, "didn't change the ideas you express in your article?"

"What article?"

"How modest of you! The article in Moravia's review."

Ferranini had received it, yes, but he hadn't yet taken the trouble to tear off the wrapper. It didn't seem possible that those four pages of his had been published.

"And how did you see it?" he asked the young lady.

"By chance. When I found out you had contributed, I decided to get hold of a copy. So now you can read what you wrote."

"Me, no. I don't care."

He didn't care. Later, he would be amazed to think that those four printed pages destined to weigh so much on him had not aroused his curiosity at all. They felt remote, impersonal—like some youthful episode recalled by a now mature man. It didn't occur to him that the visit to Leningrad had come in between, and while it might have confirmed some of his ideas, in fact it had brought about a breach. He didn't stop to ask himself why Nina made him feel uneasy talking about the article. The flutters, a sense of inhibition not without reason, not indecipherable; he saw them, but he was listless. Listless, wanting to remain at his own margins, to escape himself by resorting to banal platitudes. When they left, walking down the stairs, Boatta couldn't stop babbling about how beautiful Nina was. She didn't appeal to him, Ferranini remarked.

"What? She's gorgeous!"

"I couldn't wait for you two to get back. Maybe I'm just too serious. It's like the question of sports. You're right, age is weighing on me. I'm too old."

Boatta thought he was not quite being honest, and said so.

Nina read the article to him, her voice tense in an effort to liven up the text, which needed it. The article that Ferranini had "knocked out" in order not to waste a sleepless night, was as follows:

LABOR, THE PHYSICAL WORLD, AND ALIENATION

In the pretechnological era, geographers speculated on the shape of the earth in the same way that Aristotelians (to whom they were closely related) speculated on the soul. Sitting at their desks, they postulated that the southern hemisphere of our globe must contain lands to maintain its balance, counterweights to Asia and Europe. And so, reasoning on purely cerebral grounds, they drew a continent they called Terra Australis Ignota on their maps. The philosopher Hegel, when he speaks of the *objective* world (that is, the one that must act as a counterweight to consciousness), behaves like one of those geographers. But the young Marx behaved quite differently.

He repudiated abstraction, ventured out into the southern seas, set foot on continents still unexplored. He brought the extra-subjective world, that is the world of action (labor), into the realm of the concrete, he explored it. He demonstrated that the world must be made habitable, human. This is the revolution that Marx introduces even in his earliest works, in contrast with Hegel's speculative lucubrations. This is why we say Marx ended the era of philosophy; philosophy, that is, only concerned with knowing rather than with changing things.

It is pointless to dwell on the ties between Marx and Hegel (dozens of volumes on the question have been produced by rigorous specialists). Let us remember that the relationship between the two men was a complex one of opposition, despite certain similarities of method more apparent than real, and despite certain concepts they shared, such as the all-too-renowned "alienation," which has unfortunately become a bourgeois cliché. It has been argued that Marx's life story is in large part the story of his liberation from Hegel.

Broadly speaking then, it is a relationship of opposition. It must be acknowledged however, that there is also significant accord between the two, an outlook we see in the early Marx that leads him to understand the world following, yes, Hegel, but also (via Hegel) all post-Renaissance European thought. An orientation we can describe as humanistic, anthropocentric, optimistic. Culminating in idealism and then in historicism.

European speculative thought is in fact typically backward compared with science (science not in the Marxist sense but as investigation of the physical world). European modern thought has been slow to learn (or ignores altogether) the lesson deriving from Copernicus about the limits to human ambitions, and is not disposed to profit from the equally valuable lessons offered by science today, from the general theory of relativity to the uncertainty principle of Heisenberg. Speculative thought remains, as I suggested, anthropocentric.

Returning to Marx, the axis of reality is History, meaning, of course, our history. Man. No longer reason, consciousness, the idea, the subject, or the self—as for the philosophers and in particular the post-Kantians—but production and praxis. Yet always centered on man's action, man as the core of and rationale for nature. The thinking subject is replaced by the productive subject in the economic sense, but reality is always at the service of man, and never vice versa. *Things* have no activity nor really any autonomy. Production, the engine of the world, is the sole true activity, and all things are open to and subject to it. A humanist in other lofty meanings of that term, Marx is also a humanist in this sense, which makes him kin (despite the noted fundamental divergences) to the family of Western speculative thought, a body of thought that is deeply anthropocentrist and inclined to measure every quality, every energy, every living existence in relation to man. Man as the end, if not the beginning, of the universe. In Marx's collaborator Engels, this tendency is particularly strong; I refer to Engels's efforts to subordinate the physical world not merely to production and labor but to *ideas*. According to Engels, molecules and cells, chemistry and biology must all fall under the realm of the dialectic (derived from human history, not from physical fact).

But in Marx's vision, too, nature is derived from and dependent on human sovereignty. Marxist thought admits, it is true, that the environment influences us in various ways, but only insofar as the environment is the (passive) object of human productive activity (and therefore of transformative and even generative activity). According to Marx a man who feels reified (= no different from an object) is especially debased because man is a priori called upon to dominate the world, given that without his presence and action that world would not exist. As we know, "alienation" means for Marx the way man, in present society, finds himself bound to things (which he had set out to conquer with that expansive activity that is labor), and is unable to return to the human sphere but can only understand himself through things. In short, man must not let himself be dispossessed, he stands "above things" and under certain social conditions will return to that sovereign role, as is appropriate to his position as the pivot of reality, to which every other being is subject.

Now this view, later modified and played down in Marx's classical works—when his attention turns to far more concrete matters—raises in my opinion some questions, because daily experience teaches us that the external, physical world does not depend on us but quite the contrary: we depend on it at every instant and in every action of our existence. It further teaches us that our dependence is not confined to the activity of labor or to any particular regime of production. If for a moment we deceive ourselves into thinking we are independent, reality and above all that reality we call physical nature will quickly make us understand we are part of it, mere elements in a natural system. It will make us aware of nature within our very bodies, via cold, hunger, illness, weakness, and fear.

We have no choice. Labor, production, is never a spontaneous act, an affirmation of our personalities, it is simply a necessity that never ceases. It is in fact the necessity to survive, to forge a space and catch our breath among those external forces bearing down from all sides that slowly close in on us. Life shows us daily that to labor (and therefore suffer) is a law imposed upon us from outside. "Alienation"? I would say that there is no way to alienate ourselves (that is, to lose ourselves) outside of ourselves. The danger that threatens us is quite the opposite: to be suffocated inside the self by the physical reality surrounding us and besieging us. The danger is to be unable to emerge from that kernel of living, conscious substance that is crushed on all sides by the hostility (whether inert or active) that weighs on it and opposes its expansion.

In the end, the destiny of all forms of life is to be compressed until life is dissolved and reabsorbed, and so this danger is far from just metaphorical. If we wish, we can use the term alienation for the semi-life (and here the author has direct and personal experience) of the worker who consumes himself day by day on the assembly line, at the lathe, or in the mill. But alienation presupposes that man and his activity preexist in an *expansive* state, and this seems to me optimistic, unrealistic. Mortification, I would call the condition of the worker. And in my view, we must recognize that his is merely one example of a more general human condition. The constant struggle the elements force upon us is no different: the freezing cold, the storm, fire, the seas and rivers, the atom unchained weigh heavily on us and all our works. The misery of having to resist illness and aging, organic breakdown is no different, ultimately. I mean resisting the hostile will of nature, which permits life, then reclaims it, destroys it.

We might say that these situations in which we are obliged to defend ourselves are also, in a broader sense, "labor." And thus labor, and the harm it causes, is a universal and ineradicable condition. Unredeemed.

12

NINA STOPPED reading and came closer. In the apartment next door a baby had been crying for at least half an hour, alternately wailing and sobbing loudly. The noise had gone on during the entire reading, as if the baby were in the room.

"Are you pleased with your article?" Nina asked.

"They didn't send me galleys to check, but the text is fine. They didn't skip anything."

"I won't venture to judge," said Nina, "my Marxism is too scholastic. But I see one mistake right off, and you ought to see it too. You attack a theory. But today Marxism is no longer a theory; it's an idea fully embodied in action, a series of guiding ideas. An ideological lever that moves the world (thank goodness!) and transforms it."

"So therefore, in your view, there's no more need to discuss it."

In truth Ferranini had no desire to discuss anything. Nor was he particularly interested in Nina's hand, which had positioned itself on his forearm and slowly descended to squeeze his wrist. He had never before noticed Nina taking any special interest in him. Her intimate gesture made him feel curious but not flattered. He thought about how strange this conversation was in this house full of southerners, where he had been a guest for a month and where, despite the familiarity of his hosts and the small spaces, he had never found himself alone with one of the young women who lived there.

"You're wasting your energy and intelligence, Ferranini. Now that you've begun to show up here again from time to time, allow me to assist you, let me give you some advice. Don't you think a woman might be useful to you in some way or other, even if you are the far more well-informed?"

On the other side of the wall, the baby began to sob and wail.

Ferranini looked at his watch. He would not be unhappy if Boatta and Reparatore were to return; this unexpected tête-à-tête was going on too long. Marxism combined with the polite approaches of a young woman while sitting on the sofa in his friend's front room was not particularly pleasurable.

"Why don't we finish reading? There are only a few more lines."

The physical world may at times appear man's kingdom, a realm merely temporarily in revolt against its sovereign, who must stir himself and reestablish his rights. But such optimism is disproved by the facts. This supposed "kingdom of man" reveals itself to be a dense, opaque, omnipresent thing that oppresses us, does not recognize us, has no place for us. We must effortfully remove it, to permit access to life and the conservation of life. In labor (and not only in labor) we feel the weight of things that we must *move aside* in order to live. Liberation is not (contrary to what the theory of alienation asserts) the recovery of that part of ourselves dispersed in things. Anything but. Liberation, if it were at all possible, and *it is not* possible, would mean distancing things from us, enlarging the space we need to breathe and to move about.

Today, it is true, each of us dedicates a face and a name to the cause of his own servitude; we work at the orders *of*, we work *for*, for the benefit *of*, a person, a group, a class. But even were all these to disappear, our fate would remain unchanged. We would still go on suffering, submitting. At the mines of Marcinelle, when the alarm was sounded, the order to cease work came from above. And work ceased. But those hundreds of men trapped underground continued to dig with their picks and their hands in hopes of opening a way out. And we are all like them, we are all miners of Marcinelle. The bosses, up above, can be replaced, they can even disappear. One day, we too may receive the order to cease work. Yet we will be forced to continue.

The door was heard to open loudly. Nina was almost finished reading. Giobatta came in and threw himself heavily into his armchair. Behind him, his wife and Comrade Boatta, all equally exhausted and triumphant. Their favorite team must have won.

"An argument?" said Reparatore, eyeing his daughter. "Wherever my Nina is, there's always an argument."

The young woman had hidden the review with the article. "Ferranini was telling me about some of his ideas—"

"In other word, that *work fatigues*," Boatta interrupted, his voice hoarse from shouting at the stadium.

This time Ferranini snapped back. "I've several other ideas. If you don't mind!"

"Let's hear."

"Well, for example, I, Ferranini, am the only one of you, and maybe the only one in Italy, to have posed the problem of the so-called third forces. Against any collaboration with third-forcers of any kind, in ideological or practical terms. If you don't know what I'm talking about, go to Reggio and learn about it."

"Yeah, to Reggio," said Boatta.

Reparatore jumped in ahead of Ferranini's reply. "On the subject of ideologies. I heard this one in Zagreb, at the union congress. What's the definition of capitalism? Short and sweet, I mean. So, capitalism is that system wherein a man exploits another man. While with socialism, it's vice versa. Get it? Let's change the subject, because Boatta here is going to have his fill of ideology tomorrow."

The following day a meeting of the Central Committee was taking place, Boatta attending.

"Are you kidding?" said Boatta. "If there's one place where theory never comes up, it's in the CC. Togliatti says that facts produce politics, not theories."

The four of them sat down at the table to drink a glass of wine and play a hand of *scopa*. Boatta was telling them about the meetings of the CC and the man in charge, Palmiro Togliatti. His style.

"He's all calm, tranquillity. When he's there you always know where things are heading. One time, the disagreements were a little stormy, and he was listening with a slight smile, and Schiassi was heard to say, and not in a low voice, 'When you're in Togliatti's position, it's easy to be superior.' There was a five-minute break and they served coffee, and Togliatti as usual had them bring a hot chocolate. He then went over to Schiassi, and in that chilly melodious voice (which has its charm, as you know) said, 'Cacao does not contain caffeine; it has theobromine, a mild sedative. The secret of my superiority is simple; you can share it.'

"Everyone says he has a weakness for art, literature. Poor Marchesi used to say his speeches were models of the use of the language. But his real passion (and the thing in which he outstrips everyone, from the days of the Comintern) is international politics. Big strategy. There's no one with his broad-scale vision, either in Italy or outside. Here's something he said recently: 'We must be grateful to Eisenhower for not recognizing Communist China. In his place I would have recognized China and invested a billion dollars, and in return I'd have demanded neutrality of Southeast Asia. The Chinese have and have always had an interest in conflict with the USSR. And vice versa. The Americans are too obtuse to understand that, and we must thank them.'"

Ferranini listened, transfixed by various emotions. He never drew the right card. Giobatta, his partner, was chewing him out. But then it was Giobatta's turn to be chewed out, by his wife, for smoking too much. The packet of Toscani was sequestered and disappeared into Signora Reparatore's immense bosom. Boatta then handed over his packet of Nazionali. "Stick this in there too; I'm smoking too much myself."

"Hey listen, you dolt," Giobatta leapt up, "you think you can get away with that? We Pugliesi are jealous men, don't try it." Reparatore's laugh was contagious, and even spread to Ferranini. The game then resumed in silence; on the radio they were giving the football scores. Nina got up and, beaming a pointless look at one of the card players, left the room. The atmosphere was smoky and friendly, deeply petit bourgeois, and it wasn't as if Ferranini could pretend he didn't know Lenin's observation. That the petit bourgeois was simply the expression of the bourgeoisie.

Yet as much as one pretended to consider them absolute, there were certain precepts that hovered stubbornly in midair, remained relative—and to hell with the theory. In this case, to Ferranini's relief. He lacked a point of comparison; for him this was just a house and a family, a colleague; good people he willingly spent time with and who made him feel less alone. The petit bourgeois qualm, at least, he spared himself.

In the following days he gave not a thought to that article the pretty girl had reminded him of, until a telegram from Amoruso arrived. The doctor was in Naples and he wrote: "Have read your work; most sincere compliments."

He stuffed the telegram in his pocket with a shrug. (What had got into him?) It was the afternoon of February 6. That evening, on his way into the trattoria after the session in the chamber, it was nearly 10:00 p.m., he was approached by an individual who identified himself as a reporter for a popular Rome weekly. He wanted "a statement or two" on the piece that had come out in Moravia and Carocci's review.

He was surprised, not pleasantly. Still, his reply was fairly polite. "If you're interested, I'll get them to send you a copy."

"No, no need for that," the other man said. "Tell me, what was the political intent of the article?"

"Political intent? None. Mine was just a point of view."

"A theory?"

"Call it a theory." Ferranini sat down. But the fellow hadn't finished.

"You deal with Marxism?"

"Yes indeed."

"And what do you think of Marxism?"

"I think it's the greatest thing that has happened in the modern era."

The fuzzy, incompetent air of the reporter nearly made Ferranini laugh.

"Give me a break," said the young man, annoyed. "The managing editor sent me to squeeze something out of this famous article."

"So return to your boss and ask for instructions. Then come back and squeeze."

But the following day, in one corner of page three, *Il Tempo* wrote (under a blandly questioning headline "In Odor of Heresy?") the following: "There's no denying Moravia has exceptional instincts. In an obscure Communist MP brought to Rome by the recent elections from his native province in the north, our man has found a very unorthodox interpreter of Marx's gospel, it seems. In the most recent edition of *Nuovi Argomenti* the deputy in question, Walter Ferranini, expresses a decided critique of the messianic optimism underlying the Marxist and Communist doctrine. At present, the experts in the field don't seem to have replied, and what reception the article has had in official PCI circles is unknown. However, it's easy to imagine it will be widely read and elicit reactions."

Two days later, the *Corriere della Sera* took up the story. "We know just how cautiously," said the journalist, "Communist militants and leaders are granted the party imprimatur when they express their views to press outlets not those of the party. And therefore it is all the more significant that a PCI deputy, Ferranini, dared to publish in *Nuovi Argomenti* a piece of Marxist exegesis that is novel, to say the least. In substance, the article affirms that the enervation that comes with labor is not merely the consequence of alienation and exploitation but an intrinsic quality of work, part of a process that is not historical but physical, natural. At present, it should be noted, the PCI daily has made no comment." One of the popular weeklies, along with a photo of Ferranini (a Polaroid, taken by someone—a paparazzo?—in Largo Chigi standing next to Luigi Boatta), offered some clever speculations. "The man is not important enough to merit a proper excommunication. We predict he will be sent to atone for his ideological sins by doing pious works (organizing) in the provinces. Or perhaps to meditate on the holy texts (Marxist) in some Red convent."

In one week, Ferranini's article had been quoted from and summarized, more or less arbitrarily and in bits and pieces, by many other bourgeois newspapers of the north and center.

"You might as well get a subscription to *Eco della Stampa*, the press service," said Nuccia in an attempt at humor.

They met in the bookstore, on Tuesday, a day that Ferranini had noticed was less busy than others. He joined Nuccia in her tiny office; the only concession he granted her. He stayed at the most half an hour.

"The press likes a scandal," he said, "but journalists have a short memory. Next week they'll have forgotten about me."

"But in the meantime, they will speculate."

"They don't know where to turn. The Italian bourgeoisie has no arguments, and cannot have any."

"And how is the party reacting?"

"I have no idea. What will be, will be."

He spoke calmly, he seemed certain. Nuccia didn't believe it; she was afraid of what Walter was hiding, and at the same time, it hurt her to feel she was no longer in his confidence. She tried to inquire: "It strikes me as odd, on your part."

"What?"

"That you didn't ask you superiors for permission. To write that article."

"I did ask them. But then I was out of sorts for a number of days. All those things, including the ones you know about."

That is, the meeting with Filippetto, which he'd told her about. And the Mazzola business, which he hadn't.

"In any case," he said, "that same review published Comrade Togliatti's views some years back."

"My dear," she said, genuinely touched by his ingenuity, "don't you know there are different standards? Look at this article. There's a column about the Ferranini affair. It ends up like this: '... the party leadership in Reggio Emilia has already caused the PCI serious headaches in the past.' What are they getting at, in your opinion?"

"I don't care."

"Excuse me, but you might get an idea of how your case will play out by looking at the precedents."

He was sitting at Nuccia's desk; she was standing near him with a hand on his shoulder. He rose, pushing the hand aside.

"The precedents? As if this were some case in the law! I laid out a thesis. Thoughts that have been in my head for years, not something I imagined. Based on my own experience and that of many other workers."

"And what does Reparatore say? And Boatta?"

"Boatta's up in his home territory, Piedmont. Reparatore's on the road, in Busto Arsizio and Monza, for the textile strike. The chamber's on leave; there are local elections in various provinces. We're on call at home. And so, I'm on my own. It doesn't matter. I laid out a thesis, a truth. The experience of the workers."

He was repeating himself. But that conviction kept him afloat.

"And Amoruso?" she insisted.

"Amoruso's gone home, too. For all that I can expect from Amoruso! I mean, he's as much of a Communist as you are. Or rather, you are much more of one, you come from the Resistance."

That he didn't have to attend parliament in those days seemed undeserved good luck. Not only did he not mind the isolation; he sought it. For the first time in six months he decided to change trattoria.

In the morning he waited for l'*Unità* to arrive with the mail and for Giordano's little girl to bring it up. He didn't want to read the other papers, and kept clear of the newsstands so as not to be tempted. For an entire week, apart from his meals, he stayed in his room to study, to work. He completed his proposal to reform the industrial safety laws, having taken it apart and begun afresh. One afternoon when Nuccia ventured to approach vicolo del Leonetto, she found him unshaved, lying on the bed with his feet at the head (to catch the light from the window), taking notes from three huge volumes of Nordenskiöld's *History of Biology*, one of which lay face-down on his chest, so that he appeared to be standing at a lectern.

"Walter, you mustn't let yourself go like this!"

"Well, I'm purging myself of my sins. And my ignorance."

He seemed somewhat cheered to see her, and didn't scold her for not warning him of the visit.

"I suggest you go to Reggio until the chamber reopens. In any case we won't be seeing each other, and in Reggio you have Fubini. And the Bignamis."

He said nothing. But you could see the thoughts passing through him, and Nuccia regretted having spoken.

"Come with me tonight. No, not to the restaurant; we'll have a caffè latte at my place. Nobody knows you there."

"So what I wouldn't permit myself a week ago, I should now permit?"

The words, if laconic, were clear. Nuccia shouldn't have insisted.

"And why not? If anything, now's the time."

"From now on," he said, scratching his beard noisily with both hands, "I'm obliged to be pure. I don't like the word much, but that is the truth."

"Ah, what fun it is to be your woman!" she let slip.

"Drop me then, if you want to have fun. You're free. I know what I'm doing; I don't want them to be able to attack me for my private life as well. Yes, it is a sacrifice, but I'm the first to make it."

Those friends in Reggio were on Ferranini's mind, yes. Too much. He thought of them, of his city, even of Vimondino. With nostalgia (as if it had all been suddenly taken from him), self-reproach, bitterness at having been unworthy, having disappointed.

He regretted thinking that Ancillotti was a fool. After all, he was a good element, someone who made an effort, courageous. When it occurred to him that maybe the Red Hunchback was gloating and telling people at the Boiardo "I knew it!," he suppressed the thought.

Fubini didn't get in touch. He wasn't the type to put a good face on things. Viscardi, out of spite, bothered to. "Sorry to see the absurd campaign that the right has mounted using the pretext of your text. I believe you are wrongly accused and as such I trust you will count on my friendship."

Amoruso's solidarity was also something he could have done without. One evening, on his way down the stairs to go out to eat, he heard him coming up, out of breath and speaking in dialect with his fellow Neapolitan Giordano. He got right to the point, there on the landing.

"My friend, it's an unpleasant thing, this. Threatening to turn bad. Then again. We discussed those three or four concepts in your article so many times. Profoundly. They're watertight. I say: We reason, and to reasoning, one must respond with reason. Let's just see if they're able to prove us wrong."

Meanwhile it was clear to Ferranini that Amoruso, glib as ever, had hijacked the whole discussion. "No longer my thing," thought Ferranini. "Joint paternity and many thanks if he even recognizes I had something to do with it."

But the other, wheezing and ranting, said, "The party, discipline, they say. But I'm a doctor, my good friend, and before discipline, for me, comes knowledge. True, or not?"

"Do me a favor and let me out. Come down. Let's go eat."

"I'll take you down to Formia, we'll eat at home. Now tell me: is it true, or not? How does this get in our way? These are not the days of Stalin. Debate is permitted. And I repeat: I'm a doctor, not just a deputy for the PCI. Truth matters!"

"Got it. You are a doctor, the party doesn't count for you, it's just a club. Between you and me, that is the difference."

There was no more talk of dinner in Formia.

On the afternoon of February 21, Ferranini interrupted his self-imposed quarantine and went out, to the movies. He'd seen in the paper that they were showing a Western at the Metropolitan. At his front door, he was stopped by a big kid who'd just gotten out of a van.

"Is there a Walter Ferranini here?"

"Who sent you?"

"Pasticceria Ribaudengo. There's a letter."

The truck, full of parcels, smelled of fresh pastries. The letter was from Boatta, who, he now remembered, lodged with a cousin, the owner of a confectionery shop somewhere near Termini station. "I'm expecting you this evening for communications that concern you."

Nothing else. But it was enough.

He thought of his meeting with Filippetto, right there at Termini station. Those seemed like good times, long ago.

He began to walk mechanically down via della Scrofa, unaware of the driving rain. In Piazza Colonna the traffic was blocked by a hundred or so men and women with flags and placards: textile workers on strike from Tiburtina Tessile, on their way to demonstrate under the windows of the Industrialists Association and the Ministry of the Interior. He stood for a while watching them. He was about to join them when it occurred to him that he might stand out. He looked at them enviously, tenderly. He'd have stopped the march just to go and touch one of their red flags, looking black in the rain.

Three weeks ago those same people had been listening to him at the union hall in Tivoli.

He trudged through the streets of the center waiting for 6:00 p.m. to arrive; he walked by the window of Nuccia's bookstore. At 5:30 he reached the little place on via Varese that served as the cousin-pasticciere's office and as Boatta's office and pied-à-terre when he was in Rome. Boatta was out and only appeared an hour later. The cousin was typing up invoices and so Boatta took Ferranini to the fourth floor, where his bedroom was. The conversation was brief. When he'd returned to Rome two days ago, Boatta had learned the Direzione was about to consider the Ferranini case. He'd asked for any decision to be postponed, and for authorization to speak to Walter.

"Rectification is impossible; some action will have to be taken. However, if you don't make a fuss, and you align yourself right away, the situation may improve. But first of all: how did you get into this mess? Look, this thing is huge. Did you see the press, how they exploited it?"

He clutched his face between his hands.

"If you wanted to tackle a theoretical matter (whatever *you* may have to do with theory!) you could have sent it to *Rinascita*, or, I don't know, *Critica Marxista*. They would have shot it down, bang, party's over."

Old Boatta had taken the only chair in the dimly lit room, and Ferranini was perched on a trunk. He was sweating.

"*Critica Marxista*," he said. "Above all, a review I've been reading for years. Yes, that was the place. And as for shooting me down, maybe they wouldn't have. So I shot myself down. What can I say: I lack a brain, or mine is upside down."

"What got into you, wretch? This is no joke. Sure, I've heard you go on about those questions. Was I supposed to know you'd go and put them in print?"

"I hadn't ever thought about it. But apparently I was waiting for the occasion without being aware of it. They said to me: Send us an article—"

"Oh, fine. There you are, one of the two or three hundred of us who have Italian Communism in hand, and this was how you were thinking. I have to say, I just can't fathom what you're made of."

"Now look, Boatta. I'm at the party's disposition. I'll stay in Rome; I won't move from here. I'll wait. In the meantime, thanks. Thanks for speaking to me."

He left. And he was telling the truth, he was grateful to him. Now he knew, he was certain, that he could consider himself guilty. He needed that. Until that moment, he hadn't been able to. He had been minimizing, as if the grave, inexcusable deed he had done had been unconnected to him, merely formal. He had continued to mull over the article and its content; he hadn't even touched the wrapper on the review, but he remembered what he had written word for word. Honestly, as much as he had racked his brain with self-criticism, he had found no transgressive intent, no deviationist tendencies. Not even "substantial error." It was the opening to a discussion, in the expectation that the others were more right than he and would demonstrate it. Finally, he recognized that.

After the meeting with Luigi Boatta, his error stood out, obvious, capital. It was to have chosen (chosen?) a bourgeois platform for the debate. About a problem that touched the core of Marxist teaching. A problem that might be one of the delicate points, maybe even one of the deep weaknesses of the system.

Now, convinced of his error, it was a comfort to feel indebted and ready to pay. He had no doubts: he had not responded to Moravia's invitation out of calculation or vanity. Yet it was still unforgivably careless, the behavior of an individual who had acted utterly on impulse. They would accuse him: You are irresponsible. And he would admit: I'm irresponsible. Take all my duties away. I don't deserve even to lead a party cell.

It was not yet 7:00 p.m. He was on his way home.

As he always did, he went by the tobacco shop on via della Scrofa where he had bought the envelope and stamp before posting the article. The mailbox stood outside. The shop had been crowded that morning and he'd joined the queue waiting to be served. He remembered every detail. He'd been excited, impatient; the prospect of a trip to Leningrad that seemed to him a recognition, a distinction, had made him euphoric. He'd tossed the envelope into the box, pleased to be free of an obligation. One thing less he had to do. A kid going on holiday. Then Formia. In Formia, Amoruso had asked, "Is the piece ready? What are you waiting for, send it." Amoruso, always going on about something. All he had to say was: No, I'm not sending it.

No excuses, it was his fault. The relief he'd felt at the clarity following his meeting with Comrade Boatta was short-lived. The evening was long and terrible. He went to have a coffee after dinner in a place on via della Stelletta. He'd been going there for several nights now, certain he wouldn't meet anyone he knew. He sat in a little passageway between the bar and the billiards room, from time to time glancing at the television on the wall in front of him. He sat there for an hour, maybe a little more, not moving, not opening his mouth.

But feeling observed: a guy making a phone call two steps away, cue in hand, was staring at him. It seemed to be—it was—a certain Bosi, an accountant and head of the Quarticciolo section where he had been for the usual inspection chores for a couple of days in October or November. Things at the section were in perfect order administratively, and Bosi had seemed a bit annoyed at the meticulous check "alla Ferranini." "As you can see we're honest folk, all in order; no need to come and nitpick." And he had replied: But a good Communist is above all one who submits to discipline. Words that cost nothing to say when they concerned others.

Otherwise he and Comrade Bosi (Tuscan, from Pistoia) were practically colleagues: between '49 and '50 the man had worked in the Reggio Federation under Caprari, at a time when Caprari had taken it on himself to defend those party comrades "threatened" (in their personal interests) by the cooperative movement. Those tradesmen, shopkeepers, and farmers hostile to the constraints of being part of a collective. A category that saw Ferranini the cooperativist as a hardheaded fanatic and in any case a terrible job-buster. There had been daily clashes with Caprari, sometimes quite harsh.

Bosi put down the phone. He pointed a finger toward Ferranini, not very respectful, or anyway not friendly. His words confirmed it: "Oh look, it's Ferranini, hiding." And as he passed him on the way back to the billiards room, he added: "What're you doing here? Don't look so scared, there's no Caprari around."

He didn't react, just let the other man go by, and then left. Head down, he walked for several minutes, quickly, as if he were being followed.

The following morning the chamber resumed session, but he had decided not to show up. He wrote a note to Nuccia, which he neither mailed nor delivered, and it remained among his papers, where she would find it months later. "I have no one but you to listen to me. I've lost my way and don't know where I am headed, I only know this is an ugly moment for me. The party, when it wants to punish someone, has no need of sanctions." As he wrote that line, Mazzola reappeared in his imagination as he had done so often in these days. "Nuccia, I've never written you love letters, and you wanted that, but I'm no longer able to write them. Forgive me if I speak of these other things that interest you less. In terms of love, I'm long past it. Maybe you'll appreciate my sincerity, if nothing else." And he ended with a literary phrase (where had he gotten it?): "It is a sad, and perhaps fatal hour for your Walter."

He didn't suspect that with those words he was bidding farewell, if not to Nuccia, to her hopes. Nor did it occur to him that his sincerity came a bit too late to be appreciated. From the same tablet of scratch paper he'd used for that message, he began to write another. At the top of the page he wrote: "Due Clarification to the PCI Direzione, Headquarters." Below this, he wrote, "Today February 22, 1959, in full self-possession and serenity, I herewith supply the following justification for my recent behavior. Although I am honestly convinced my party loyalty has never faltered, I am nevertheless aware of the obligation that every party member...." And here he stopped. In full self-possession, if not very serenely, he had no idea what offense he intended to provide justification for. Was it to endure what he was enduring?

As he passed by Giordano's workshop on his way out, he looked so distraught that the carpenter nearly asked him what was wrong. He did not go to the trattoria. He'd eaten nothing since the night before, and when he arrived at Villa Borghese and sat down on a bench near two soldiers, he hadn't the strength to walk another twenty paces. There, with a cold, hard wind blowing and the mountains of the Sabina in the distance white with snow, he sat all afternoon. He heard one of the soldiers say, "I was assistant paymaster, and they found me with *Avanti!* in hand, reading it, and they threw me in artillery." The two of them were sitting close together, arm in arm like kids. The other one, who had said he was from Montelibretti outside Rome, observed: "Jackass, what got into your head to make you take up politics?"

But the premonition isolated him, left him senseless to the voices, even the cold. The premonition. The thought that throbbed in his temples, sharp and insistent, was: tonight. Now, when I return. He got up at about 5:00 p.m., the sun low in the sky, and seeking to keep control of himself, slowly walked down, step after step, to Piazza del Popolo, where he hailed a taxi. He thought of Nuccia, who said he was an obsessive. (I'd like to see how someone else acts in my place.)

Nothing. There was nothing at home yet. He went down to the street again, and walked to the printshop behind the restaurant where he used to eat. It was a pleasure to listen to his old friends talk, the fellow workers of poor Gennaro. They told him that the dead man's younger brother had applied to work as an errand boy for the CGIL on Corso d'Italia. If he could put in a word, that would be good. He promised. And went back home again. Almost running.

This time the letter was there. On the floor, set on top of the newspaper at the end of the landing along with an ad inviting him to "Fly to New York (USA), fly TWA."

He opened the letter, read it, folded it carefully, and put it in his wallet. Okay. Now he felt calm. But he had no wish to lock himself up in his room. Once again he took a long walk down the streets of the city center, aiming nowhere, in an utterly passive state. Almost insensible to his surroundings, he found himself in the middle of the street halfway up via del Tritone, hard between two buses, and got out of it alive only because one of the drivers stopped sharply as his bumper grazed him. I'm at the end of the line, he thought: the asphalt of Rome. He stopped to eat somewhere, and ate with transport and the starving man's unwitting gratitude, and meanwhile he asked himself whatever was the name of that review that had printed his article. He had forgotten.

With two fingers in the pocket of his jacket, he felt the letter inside his wallet. It was a certainty and, therefore, a strength. During the film (he'd entered a movie house), he took it out and reread it by the light of a match. They "invited" him to appear "as soon as possible" at party headquarters "to supply information." It was positive, then; within twenty-four hours he would know. That was fine. The wait was almost over; then there would be another, but that was something else, and it wouldn't be worse. After midnight on his way out of the movie, instinct drew him toward the station. He realized he was at Termini when he found himself at the bar in front of a glass of white, and was astonished by his ingenuous attempt to escape. Now he was here, and here he stayed, loitering, comforted by all the life that circulated under the roof as if it were day. He ended up in a lounge, napping on a chair, around him the comings and goings of a company of women laden with parcels and rosaries getting ready to leave on a pilgrimage to the Virgin of Pompeii. But they didn't disturb him; he fell asleep just sitting there. The room was warm and in a drowsy state he saw and heard Roberto Mazzola, who spoke to him at length. Fanatical, insistent as he was in life, standing tall in front of him. Later there was a buzz of activity among the women; they changed places and moved their parcels and somewhat rudely jostled him, while he, only half awake, continued to reason with Mazzola. (Yes, resigned, chastened. It's true, but dear man, I got thrashed. One has to go on living. A crisis, you say; and you were able to handle your crisis. You decided; I didn't. But I couldn't, I'm different; I'm a modest activist with a dilettante theorist inside. An autodidact. The truth is, I'm no politician. You say I was born for self-criticism, and you are right. Quote me four lines from some text and my revolt is good and quashed. Okay. I'm no politician; even Reparatore noticed that.)

He fell back asleep, and then the women unwrapped their food supplies and began to eat. He woke again and felt very cold. (It's true, there's nothing I like better than letting myself be persuaded. I'd rather be in the wrong, it's true. I'm a member, a joiner. I'm no politician, I'm just a poor guy. I got thrashed! I read the classics, I study them, take notes; I can do no more. What do you want?) Once again he fell asleep and heard nothing more. He was now alone, lying down, his head resting on a paper bag full of scamorza rinds. Dawn had already come when a guard woke him by rapping a broom handle against his seat.

In all, he'd slept maybe six hours. He thought he might have regained his balance a bit. He had a shave at the barber there in the station. Drank two caffè ristretti, one after the other. But he couldn't shake off the chill inside him, although he forced himself to walk all the way. His teeth chattered unless he paid attention. He had to stop twice to urinate.

When he got to via delle Botteghe Oscure he raised his eyes to the window with the green blinds: still dark in that gray morning. A simple soul, he went in repeating to himself a phrase he'd heard the night before at the movies: Okay, the moment of decision has arrived.

"Historical Department and Archive," said the porter to whom he showed the letter. "Dottor D'Aiuto is already here."

D'Aiuto? He was just a functionary.

He went upstairs. D'Aiuto rose to receive him.

"Thanks, you're good to come. You can help me out of a fix."

Ferranini collapsed into a chair. He couldn't take any more of this.

"Let me explain. On November 1 and 2 you carried out an inspection at the Tor Pignattara section. The rules say you then sent a report. The other day they were asking me for it, and it just couldn't be found. Therefore, either we lost it, or you never sent it."

Ferranini could only stammer, "How strange, so strange."

From the other side of his desk D'Aiuto, Calabrian, intent, smoothing his red hair with his left hand, studied him.

"What's the matter, Ferranini? No cause for concern. Just take a look at home among your papers."

"Yes."

"You know, things are in a shambles here, files, documents. As for the summons you got, I didn't compile it myself, it may have been a bit peremptory. You'll forgive me."

"I forgive you."

"Oh, and be a good fellow, pop by with that report tonight or tomorrow morning. Or anyway send it to me quickly."

"Yes."

He was still ashen-faced that afternoon when he went by the bookstore to see Nuccia. But he didn't tell her. He couldn't face ironic comments.

"You haven't been well."

"It's the cold; I'm feeling the cold. Nothing special."

She, however, had something special to report. "Guess who came in here this morning?"

"Your husband."

"No, thank heavens. Someone far more important. Dear to your heart. Comrade Togliatti."

"Doing what?"

"Oh, he was looking for Stendhal's *Lucien Leuwen* in French. I wasn't in yet; he spoke to Holzener. The clerk. Holzener told him, 'We don't have it, try at Rizzoli or Hoepli.' He replied, 'I'll try, but I'm not hopeful. Rome is no city of *bouquineurs.*'"

"Meaning?"

"Meaning, book-lovers. But he was extremely nice. Now, supposing you met him coming in, what would you say?"

"Nothing."

"Come on. If I saw him, I'd talk about us two. You can be sure of it."

Ferranini didn't move or say a word.

"Walter, you're strange, you know. Your chief, your hero. You'd be indifferent?"

"No."

He left soon after. He thought he might go see Reparatore and began to walk. He hadn't considered the distance. Reparatore was at least three kilometers from the bookstore. He was totally worn out when he got there, then realized he couldn't see his friend without repeating the usual explanations, hearing the usual arguments. He stood staring at the huge yellowish building, the window on the fifth floor where in summer he'd often come for a breath of air, and then he walked back toward the bus stop.

"What's more I've become apathetic, a neurotic," he said aloud. And turned to see if anyone had noticed.

A few steps behind him, a pretty young woman waved to him. Nina Reparatore, with a satchel of books in hand, like a schoolgirl.

She joined him.

"What were you doing? Looking at my window?" She was vivacious.

"I wanted to see your father."

"At this time, Walter?" she said, incredulous, stepping up to get him under her umbrella. "My dad's never here at this hour. He was looking for you at the chamber. Concerned not to see you."

"What does he think of my situation, your father?"

"Because of the article, you mean? He sees a distinction. Politics and theory are two different things. Politically, discipline is required. As for theory, one can also have ideas. My advice, on the other hand, Walter, is: Careful with the ideas. Don't get too involved, don't squander yourself. Hey, why are you walking so fast? Are you in a hurry?"

"I'm in a hurry."

13

HE SAID goodbye. In a hurry. To go where? No one was expecting him, he had nothing to do.

He was jobless among the many, he could certainly permit himself to be apathetic. And he hadn't stopped to chat with the girl. Why.

The report on his inspection at Tor Pignattara had turned up at home, or rather he had found the notes he had forgotten to transcribe (he hadn't been there with his head for a while, he thought). He had them in his pocket now, he only had to type them up.

The following morning he went back to the bookstore, and Nuccia sat down in her office and typed them up, just two pages.

"I'm leaving tonight," she said when she was done.

"For where."

"I have my troubles too. Business here at the store is still not thriving, and they've called me to Milan again. I hate leaving you in a moment like this."

"Don't worry about me!"

"I do worry. On the other hand, though, I'm happy to get out of here. My husband's bugging me. Things are going well for him, he's bought into a real estate company here in Rome; he's going to find a way to make money in the building trade too. He writes to me, sends me flowers. See the roses?"

"Ah."

"There was a note, where he said he'd been to visit my parents and Giulia in Monticello."

"You'll get back together."

"Are you crazy? However, I bet my mother received him with honors. She would."

"It makes sense."

"No. My father could never stand him. And anyway there's me. They'll have to deal with me too."

He was putting on his raincoat, the lining coming unstitched and already soaked with rain.

"Anyway, I'm ready. Nothing means anything to me. Let the world do what it will."

The bookstore opened directly onto via delle Botteghe Oscure. It was noon and he didn't want to be late for D'Aiuto. Who in turn was grateful for his consideration.

"If you need anything. For what little I can do, count on me."

Mere words, but a relief all the same.

Going down the stairs he made way for three personages, comrades Magrò, Cagnotta, and Guglielmo Schiassi, who were coming up. All of them in the Direzione. As he passed, Cagnotta recognized him and stopped.

"Comrade Ferranini. Why haven't you been coming to the chamber? Are you ill? You must let the group know."

He couldn't bring himself to lie and was silent. Meanwhile Cagnotta called the other two, who were up ahead.

"Here's our man. Do we want him to come in now?" He turned to Ferranini. "You've got some time now, right?" He signaled him to follow. His signal gave the lie to that superficial tone, admitting only one reply. Ferranini followed without opening his mouth.

The room they entered was new to him, a small room with a few chairs, a table, and a telephone. On one side of the table sat the three authorities, who hadn't even taken off their overcoats; they pointed to a chair on the other side, and he sat down. Of the three, Cagnotta, the chief of the party's Central Economic Committee, was the highest ranking. It was he who spoke first.

"Well then, comrade, we haven't seen you at the chamber. But you're not avoiding people, as we can see from the fact you are here. A sign your conscience is untroubled. Am I right?" Abruptly he said to Schiassi, "Let them know upstairs, please."

Schiassi called an inside line and said to someone, "We're here with Comrade Ferranini," then sat down again.

The panel of judges had been assembled. For that was what it was, and he knew it. He unbuckled the belt of his raincoat to get some air. He must try to remain calm. He raised his eyes toward his judges, who didn't look at him. Schiassi was loudly tapping himself on the forehead with a rolled-up copy of *l'Unità*. Walter was surprised to find he was not anxious. He was only sorry he didn't have his little edition of the *Communist Manifesto*. His codex, his magic charm.

"We know," Cagnotta began again, "that recently you have taken up journalism. I would in fact like to ask you some particulars. About this activity of yours. These comrades and I have been so charged." His gaze went around the room in circular fashion as if his eyes were underlining the words, uttered in a flat voice like a notary.

"A review," he went on, "has published an article signed by Ferranini, expressing a negative opinion of the Marxist concept of alienation. If I have that right. I'm not personally familiar with the argumentation laid out in that illustrious document. Comrade Magrò, having thoroughly studied the text, can fill us in."

Among his colleagues in the group at the chamber, Aniello Magrò, a professor of history of the law at Naples, was also known as Nasser, to whom he bore a resemblance. Togliatti had once praised him as the "most elegant Marxist" (after Labriola) born south of the River Garigliano.

"Ferranini affirms," Magrò began, "that in the early Marx the worker is still, in Hegelian style, a sort of evoker or creator of external reality, even though in certain circumstances this creative function has regressive consequences for the worker. According to the article, pardon me if I go into detail in the interests of clarity, in Marx's vision the worker with respect to his world continues to have the expectations typical of the Subject, in the idealistic sense. The world is seen to be at his disposition, or rather it owes to the worker, to man, its very existence. In short, as presented, Marx is steeped in idealistic illusions."

"One moment," Ferranini spoke impulsively, almost interrupting, "I wrote that the mature Marx goes beyond this perspective, and that seems to me an important point."

Cagnotta silenced him with a wave of his hand. "Slowly. Slowly. There's no hurry."

He bit his tongue. He could have avoided that reprimand.

"In any event, if you will," now Ferranini's words and tone were measured, "if you will, in my view the concept of alienation is somewhat too abstract to hold the position it does in a reality like Communism, which is concrete, popular. The favor that word has had with the bourgeoisie makes it suspect to me. When I speak of work with my friends in Reggio—manual laborers, farmers, not intellectuals—I speak of fatigue and not alienation. Otherwise they wouldn't understand me. I speak of so many *biolche* plowed by a tractor in a day, and the fatigue it costs."

Beret on his head and belly protruding, Della Vecchia was now entering the room. He was breathing heavily, and greeted the group in his disproportionately reedy voice as he took his place to Cagnotta's right. The fourth commissar was thus Della Vecchia, a real honor. He thought of Amoruso's ironic remarks about "the Inquisition," as he called it.

But he wasn't inclined to irony, not even privately, just as he felt no overwhelming awe. Nor fear. This was not a rebuke for an act of indiscipline. They were criticizing an opinion, and he had the right to defend himself.

Della Vecchia authorized him to continue. The floor was his again.

"If I am speaking to workers, I was saying, I speak of the fatigue produced by labor, a fatigue that should not serve to enrich an owner. And that is a language they understand. We cannot have one Marxism for the educated and another for the people. The people know nothing of alienation, which is a concept. They know that labor means fatigue, which isn't a concept but denotes concrete wear and tear. Labor costs flesh and blood."

Magrò-Nasser turned to look at Della Vecchia, a faint expression of pity on his face. He moved a hand as if to say: As you see, that's all there is to it.

"We'll pass over that," conceded Cagnotta, who apparently was leading the discussion. "Let's go on. Schiassi, what did you want to say?"

Schiassi had been flailing around in his seat for some time. "I detect a far worse error," he burst out. "Ferranini has not merely mounted a criticism of alienation. He has mounted a criticism of socialism! He has criticized the Marxist promise to give human beings a better life under socialism. Is that true or not?"

Cagnotta and Schiassi, seated alongside one another, were like brothers, with the same piggish eyes, the same hairless round face, the same eyeglasses, but Cagnotta was placid and easy-spoken, Schiassi full of tics and jerks, scowling and taciturn; from time to time he'd cuff an ear with his right hand. Together, in their affinities and contrasts, they were like a stage act, and for a moment Ferranini stared at them, mesmerized.

Schiassi stamped both feet on the floor. He was prompting him to reply. Ferranini thought: My mind is wandering, which means I am relaxed.

And in fact he replied quite calmly, "It's not true. Socialism promises to free labor. It offers huge progress, and that justifies our struggle: I've always believed this and I always will. What I wrote in the article is different: that even when socialism is achieved, we will still have labor. And it will still be harmful, injurious. There's a text of Marx's that I consider fundamental, in which he writes: 'Men make their own history, but not under circumstances of their own making.' And that is true. The circumstances matter more than the men and history."

He heard a snort of laughter. Magrò cleared his throat and said, "You've forgotten Marx's great prediction. That is, with the real and universal victory of socialism, the effort connected with work shall be reduced to a minimum."

His elbows sliding over the table, Della Vecchia leaned forward and pointed his open hands toward Ferranini.

"You," he said, and it would be his only comment, "you know very well that before publishing a piece of writing of this kind, making such claims, that you should have had it examined, and that there are appropriate organs right in this very building. Why didn't you?"

"The Press Office took care of it. I thought that was sufficient."

"In what way 'took care of it'? Explain."

"I took the article to the Press Office. On December 24, in the morning. It was still in script, it hadn't been typed up yet."

"And are you sure of this?" Della Vecchia insisted, a hint of surprise in his thin voice.

He was sure. It was the truth. "Yes, comrade. And all the details can be checked. I went to the Press Office in the morning, you and I met each other here, and you asked me whether it had been a while since I was back in Ferrara. And I told you I come from Reggio."

Della Vecchia drew back, making it clear Ferranini should be silent. Later, it seemed to him that Della Vecchia had paid less attention to the rest of the questioning. Ferranini turned toward Magrò and continued his self-defense.

"And so a promise in the sense Comrade Magrò refers to can be inferred from certain passages in Marx, although I believe there has never been a wish to linger over that point, and I think with good reason. Because in truth, labor cannot be abolished. Nor can its onerous nature be suppressed, the fact that it is irremediably fatiguing. Often labor is illness, almost always mortification. In this sense, if you will, 'alienation.' The duration of labor can be reduced, but the intensity increases and it becomes more harmful. Let us ask workers on the short week if that is not the case. And if labor is transformed so that it no longer exploits manual skills, it then weighs on different bodily organs. In general, these are even more susceptible to fatigue than the muscles are."

He had spoken with an ease and precision that were unusual for him. He himself was astonished.

Schiassi pinched his own cheek between two fingers, ferociously. "My dear man, but this is the age of technology! This is what you overlook. Technology, even capitalist technology, is on the verge of miracles. Automation!"

"You know," said Ferranini, "in my opinion the massive propaganda we hear about automation making workers unnecessary is a new, powerful weapon of the ruling class. What's new about neo-capitalism is not its notions of co-management and worker-shareholders, or its progressive paternalism. What's new is this new classist mystification. They want to sap and destroy the workers' movement using the specter of total unemployment."

"Automation is a fact," Schiassi thundered.

"It's not a fact," Ferranini replied, tenacious. "It's a phantom. It takes twice as much labor to build (and maintain) a halfway intelligent robot as it does to make the products it could supply. I tell you, technology cannot do the impossible. It cannot change the order of things. Labor's inescapable, along with the wear and tear it brings, and this is an objective consequence of the battle for life, and not only human life, in nature."

"Come on," Schiassi sputtered, "everyone knows work is rewarding, that it's good for a man's health."

Now it was Ferranini's turn to smile. "Sure, the bosses, the capitalists, have always said so. And also that it is ennobling."

"And so?" said Schiassi.

"I say the reality is somewhat different," said Ferranini. "The labor of the workers, of the laborers, is not beneficial. Sometimes it is lethal. Nearly always, in one way or another, it hurts. Diminishes, debilitates, dulls."

"Under a capitalist system."

He would have liked to say: Any system that puts out the lie "work has its rewards" is a capitalist system. But he held his tongue: Schiassi didn't seem capable of understanding. It was the others he had to deal with.

Comrade Magrò now intervened on a different point. "You referred to your theory that nature is hostile to life. Remember that the founders of scientific socialism have shown that the same law that governs human and economic affairs and all the rest applies to nature too. You forget that that law, the dialectic, admits no contradiction except insofar as it overcomes contradiction. Further, your thesis is gratuitous. Nature can't be hostile to life. For the simple fact that nature produces life, which then develops in the successive phases of a process that is the law of dialectics in action."

Ferranini thought of Comrade Pisani's elegant style of expression that morning in Turin. Pisani, Magrò: Communists for whom communism was a kind of privileged cultivation. A caste.

Then he saw that Comrade Della Vecchia had written down a few lines on slip of paper, which he now passed to Cagnotta. He understood what the gesture meant: in those penciled lines was their decision. He felt himself stiffen. He thought, I'm going to panic.

Magrò persisted. "Do you know Engels's contribution to the interpretation of nature? Do you know Stalin's theories? You do know, at least, that they have given a new orientation to scientific research."

"Comrade Magrò," he replied, aware that he was losing his voice, "Comrade Magrò, may I say what I think?"

"Fair enough. This is not a trial, you must speak freely."

"I would say that Comrade Khrushchev is correct here, that science must be left to the experts. Engels should have done that; it would have been better. At a certain point, Engels decides to philosophize about the reality of the physical world—that is, to do metaphysics. Then again he also argued that as science expanded it would restrict the domain of philosophy. Those precepts seem to me contradictory."

He slid a hand beneath his jacket to massage his stomach. He had the bad habit of swallowing air when he spoke, and he could feel the pressure on his diaphragm. But panic, no. He spoke smoothly without having to search for words (a problem that sometimes troubled

him even with Nuccia), but not too fast, even pausing slightly between one sentence and another. No, it wasn't panic. He shifted on
the chair. Went on.

"Engels considered the natural sciences crucial to the study of
natural phenomena. In physics, biology, et cetera. And that is a recognition that in all these fields there is no room for concepts or in-
terpretations, but only for the data that emerge from research. He
praised the enormous progress in knowledge due to Darwin and the
discovery of evolution. What need is there to pit competing ideas
against them? Ideas that are not scientific?"

Facing him on the wall in front, the clock marked 1:20 p.m. A
guard opened the door, and from the hall a grave, well-tempered
voice with a hint of an accent could be heard approaching, a voice
well-known to Ferranini.

The short, stocky figure appeared in the doorway. Behind the
clear lenses, those eyes, you could swear, didn't even register the five
men inside the room, all of whom had risen to their feet.

"Della Vecchia," the voice said, "let's go."

Della Vecchia reached the door at a trot, and it was closed.

"So therefore," said Magrò, "the dialectic is to be junked, in your
view?" And he turned to look at the clock. A professor in a hurry to
finish the exam. Like Comrade Pisani in Turin: professors irritated
by the foolish exam-takers, priests in a hurry to lock up the chapel.
The caste of the enlightened, faced with presumptuous amateurs
like himself, like Mazzola.

But he was not going to give up.

"No, pardon me, comrade, I never said that. The dialectic explains perfectly the history of production and related phenomena—
that is, the history of man. But the history of man is not the history
of nature, and trying to explain nature using our criteria is anthro-
pomorphism. We human beings are newcomers, our 'history' began
only yesterday, while this little Earth on which we're guests has existed for billions of years, and mature life appeared hundreds of
thousands of years before us. If we want to believe Engels, we must
assert that from the origins of the celestial nebulae to Comrade

Khrushchev's speeches in Red Square, it has been all one, identical process. I say we can be good Communists without believing that—"

"Ferranini!" Cagnotta interrupted. "Make it short! It's late."

"Yes, I'm about to finish. I am not a scientist but I have formed an idea, that the inanimate world around us is different from life, different from us, knows nothing of us, is extraneous and hostile. I'm finished now! Let me just say that so long as we live, we will be obliged to struggle to live. Struggle, and therefore be under constant stress. Labor is only one aspect of that stress. The appearance may change, but the substance will always be this."

Schiassi was thrashing around on the floor in search of his gloves, or his glasses, which had fallen off. He got up, red-faced.

"Leave it alone, Ferranini! And the class struggle? Do you think it's all pointless?"

"Socialism is essential. If all human beings, all living beings, must struggle, there must be no small minority that sits by and earns a profit from the labor of the others."

"And you call yourself a Marxist," an enraged Schiassi snapped back, "with ideas like this?"

"You know what Marx had to say, Schiassi. He said he was not a Marxist. If you prefer, I can say the same. However, six thousand preference votes show that as a Communist organizer back home, somebody trusted in me."

Cagnotta brought down a chairman's fist on the table.

"Enough! We've said what has to be said. We must now issue a communication. To Comrade Ferranini. As follows. You will submit to us the draft of a statement to appear in *l'Unità*. You will say this: 'The article published in a well-known review is the result of a slanted misinterpretation of my thinking. Therefore, I do not recognize it as mine.' Then, next Sunday you will speak at a rally. In Frascati, I believe. You will expand on the same concept, using particulars that will be communicated to you and which you will insert verbatim into your speech. Are we agreed?"

Cagnotta held up the note that Comrade Della Vecchia had passed to him not long before.

"The sanction that the Direzione applies in your case is Reprimand. I repeat: Reprimand. On the following grounds. 'Rash and inconsistent theoretical position expressed.' The meeting is over."

On the street, walking toward where he would have lunch, Ferranini had a thought. An incongruous, sudden thought that came unprepared by internal argumentation. No, he was not going to leave the party and join the Gruppo Misto, the MPs not attached to any of the main parties. No, he would rather resign from parliament on health grounds.

So. It had come to this? What next?

Next, to begin with, something to eat. Hunger, a nervous hunger, sapped his legs. He hailed a taxi. All the same, when he got out at the trattoria, his old trattoria on via dei Coronari, he decided it was best immediately to get down on paper what they had asked him, sentence by sentence, and what he had replied. He took a few sheets of paper from his briefcase and pushed the plate away. Two copies, he thought, and one I'll send to Fubini. In any event.

He tried to reconstruct the encounter, but he was unable. His mind would not obey him. He'd gone in there, in that place he hadn't been for a while (because of his need to isolate himself for all those days, to hide), and he'd had the sense that another individual, every bit as alive and real, had emerged in his head. Yes, there was the timid and resigned Ferranini, who could not be happier than when someone showed him where he'd gone wrong. But under fire, another individual took charge. Or another instinct.

The white sheet lay before him. "Dear Fubini," he wrote, "I'm sure you're aware of the Ferranini affair. But you haven't written. I write to you after undergoing a one and a half hour examination at headquarters. To inform you of the following."

What? That what had most offended him was the indulgent attitude of the examiners? Yes. That was it. What had happened to self-criticism, his vocation for self-criticism? He had fought for his ideas, he hadn't given an inch. In the end, he understood that he had expected, he deserved, more serious adversaries—intransigent adversaries—and a final sentence. He felt he was a heretic. In a certain sense, yes, he had expected thunderbolts and excommunication. Two days ago, today's outcome would have been the one he hoped for; now he rebelled against it. His contrition, the angst of those last days, his intention to submit, utterly, today suddenly became a cast-off suit.

"Maybe it was because they wore me out," he wrote. "But I guarantee you, Fubini, that I can't believe the business ended up this way. They treated me as if I were half a windbag, half a bonehead student. Why? My objections were quite substantial. (Theoretically, I mean; ideology had nothing to do with it.) The fact is, Fubini, that people here don't stick to their guns. They wear themselves down in routine. They defend that cuckold Lonati, rich, bourgeois, a profiteer, and throw out Mazzola, poor and honest, an extremist because he's unable to compromise. The 'Curia' (as Togliatti calls it) is full of good people all busy keeping the train on track, signing up as many members as possible, and making the organization, the press, the inspections, the archive, and parliamentary policy run. It's the continuation of the state of things, dear Fubini, a profitable, secure, restful, pleasant state of things. And meanwhile some isolated voice appears to say: Watch out, it's not all perfect! Mazzola denounces things blocking progress: bourgeoisification, paralysis, and so on; a reformist-style line of moderation that's classified as anti-Stalinist. He's a rebel, a potential danger, get him out of the way. Okay, at least they took him seriously. I, Ferranini, bring up some theoretical contradictions, point out where reality gives the lie to the theory and makes it unrealizable, absurd. But I'm just a dilettante wise guy, a pain in the neck. Not dangerous at all; I simply have to promise to shut up, and if I agree, they'll pardon me. There you have my impressions, Fubini, and you can decide whether you can or cannot remain my friend. Best, and regards to the Bignami boys and the others."

He'd needed to get that off his chest, after so many days. To make sure he didn't change his mind, he gave the letter to the kid in the trattoria. "Now run and post it." A minute later he was already thinking that the letter wasn't clear, that Oscar Fubini knew nothing of that cuckold Lonati nor of the honest Mazzola either. No problem, I'll tell him when I see him, I'll explain. On Sunday I'll see him. I'm going to Reggio. To Reggio? But on Sunday there was the rally in Frascati, Cagnotta had said so. Simple: he wouldn't go. He'd hold a rally at home, with the comrades of Reggio, *his* base. Whether Cagnotta liked it or not. Now he felt calmer. To the man who brought him his lunch, he said, startling him, "Lent is over." His penitence, he thought to himself, had been hypocrisy. But that was to malign himself: his approach had been sincere and tentative, provisory. With relief he enjoyed the taste of the rice with sausage, alla Monzese, his Friday meal, which they had brought without waiting for him to order.

Up in his room, he found a parcel Nuccia had sent. A vial of tranquilizers and a book, just published.

The book was titled *Comparative Study of Industrial Safety Legislation*. Then he noticed that it was published by the Common Market Interparliamentary Assembly. After the advent of de Gaulle, no one among the PCI deputies had a less flattering opinion of the newborn European Common Market than Ferranini. The acronym MEC, as Italians called it, stood for Militarists and Capitalists, Ferranini had quipped, and his remark had spread across the left benches and even into the public domain.

He immediately stopped reading, thought about this business of the tranquilizers, and swallowed two. He'd never taken any in his life before. He threw himself on the bed, just as he was, and fell asleep.

Later, Giordano's little girl came in, as usual without knocking. In her hand was a letter. She sat down in a chair near the bed and stayed there, serious, looking at him. Ferranini woke for an instant and saw her. He woke again after a while and the little girl was still there. He fell back to sleep again.

It was 9:00 p.m. when he got out of bed; he was rested and feeling well. He had an appetite, and went out again. The express mail letter the little girl had brought came from the Federation of Reggio. He didn't open it; he had no desire to. He wasn't ready to resume the weight of occupations, interests. His political life, his entire life, depended on what he would decide in the next few hours. But he didn't feel any hurry. Tomorrow. Tomorrow I'll see. He was astonished and pleased by his capacity to dismiss thoughts that had once been the very foundation of his beliefs. Eat, sleep: apparently this was what mattered. He ate once again in his trattoria, ravenous, silent; as the man selling the evening newspapers moved among the tables, he yanked his eyes away so as not to read the headlines.

At home, getting undressed just before 11:00 p.m., his gaze fell on the letter, and this time he opened it.

There was nothing but a telegram inside. A day and half old, from New York. It informed him that Nancy was ill, gravely ill, and would have liked to see him. "If possible."

Dawn was just breaking, the streetlights were still lit, and Ferranini was waiting on the street below Reparatore's. He had sent him a telegram. Reparatore came down with his bag, he was leaving at 8:30 for Foggia. A car took them to Palazzo Margherita. Signora Francesca's brother, Reparatore's brother-in-law, was head doorkeeper there at the American embassy.

They had to wait; he wasn't awake yet.

"A weeklong visa. Sir, they won't even give you one for a day."

"Well, try!"

"Impossible, and you know why."

Ferranini, the Communist, knew all too well why. Exasperation's illogical lucidity came to his aid.

"I'm married to an American citizen! Here, look at this. All the details are in this memo. Show it to them."

The other man shrugged, doubtful, but he took the memo.

"And what's more, you want to leave tonight. It's going to be difficult in any case. Okay, I'll get on it, let me try. Call me back at noon."

Having accompanied Reparatore to Termini station, Ferranini inquired about air tickets. But there wasn't a single seat available.

He could, of course, at his own risk, try at Ciampino Airport a few hours before the flight departed. Sometimes a seat turned up. After he left the agency it occurred to him that even if there were a seat, he didn't have the money to pay for the ticket. He didn't have it with him, and he didn't have it at home. The cheapest ticket he could buy would cost him 400,000 lire. He thought of Amoruso. Too far away in Formia. Anyway, it bothered him to think of borrowing money from Amoruso.

He went to sit in a lounge. The same lounge where he had spent the night between Wednesday and Thursday. He was alert, though; his head responded. A solution soon came to mind. Go to the chamber and try to get an advance on his pay. He leapt onto the running board of a bus.

To the office of the presidency of the chamber. He asked for the deputy president, but without much hope: at that hour, 9:15 a.m., he wouldn't be there. And he wasn't. Instead the president himself was in, a man noted for his singular early-morning habits, as it happened. A few minutes of waiting, and Leone had him let into his office. Scowling, very polite but severe, a penetrating gaze.

"I've been following your case, I know why you have come."

"If I may. I'm here to request—"

"Believe me, Ferranini. I know! And I say this to you: Parliament's integrity is above any and all groups. Whatever measures the group intends to apply. Or better, presumes it can apply."

"No, no. If I may speak, Signor President."

Leone removed his spectacles and polished them at length on his handkerchief. It was the third time he performed this maneuver. Another one who's always fiddling with his eyeglasses, thought Ferranini annoyed. Not one of them who can see with his own eyes.

"Very well, speak. Well, what it is you want to say? Your mandate comes from a part of the electorate. It is irrevocable."

"Look, forgive me, I'm here for a strictly private reason. Allow me to speak!" The annoyance, the irritation, were fraying his nerves.

"Speak, speak! Who's stopping you?"

He explained in a few words. The other made a face and took off his eyeglasses. His booming Neapolitan voice turned mother-hennish.

"I see, I see. Sorry about your wife. Inform your group that you must absent yourself. The rest of it is beyond my sphere, it's a matter for the general secretary. Go, you may go now."

He was lucky. The end of the month was near. He got the approval, his MP's allowance was paid in advance, before noon he was finished and out. He hadn't wanted to call from the chamber and looked for a public phone instead. Caputo, head doorkeeper at the embassy, told him he hadn't been able to accomplish anything. He should call back later, not before 3:00 or 4:00 p.m.

Nuccia's bookstore was only a few steps away. He appeared.

"Where is Signora Corsi? Is she out?"

"She's in Milan. Didn't she tell you?" said Holzener. Indiscreet.

"That woman's never here," he shouted. "Never."

She had told him, of course. But who had the brains to remember? The fact was, he needed her, and she wasn't there.

"To Milan to do what? To do what, I say. Always in Milan, always away! Never here."

He was shouting. Holzener, the former seminarist at the Collegium Germanicum, was tall, cross-eyed, and tended toward melancholy. He kept him at a distance with an amused, contrite expression.

Ferranini gave a kick to the door and went into Nuccia's office, sat down heavily in her chair. In front of him was a packet of Turmac, her cigarettes, just opened, and, like a bullet aimed at the ceiling, the little golden warhead of her lipstick. He looked to see if there was a sheet of paper and an envelope to leave a message. He opened a leather file and then a drawer. With difficulty. He was quivering with rage.

"Holzener, get me an envelope! There isn't a sheet of paper in this effing store!"

This time the clerk appeared. All shyness. "The envelopes are there, sir. There, inside. There they are."

But now he didn't feel like writing.

"You tell her," he said to the girl in the shop, looking her up and down without lowering his voice, "I have to go away, and I don't know when I'll be back. Say this to Signora Corsi: that now I have a better picture of things, and all the rest is hog shit. Those exact words. Hog shit!

The girl, surprised and dismayed, looked at him and shook her head.

"I'm saying that to you, and I can say it to anyone, I'm not ashamed!"

He took out the telegram, the telegram from New York, and opened it on the desk, slamming a paperweight on top. He left. When he got to the corner, he turned around. He walked back through the bookstore, arrived at Nuccia's desk, and put the telegram in his pocket. He saw the golden lipstick case. He put that in his jacket pocket, too, and left.

Back at home, he packed. As he struggled to fasten a belt around his old valise, he understood that this was not a departure but a return.

Those thirteen years that had passed compressed themselves more easily than the contents of his overstuffed bag. Despite all the life they held, they were only an interruption. All that life, all those things that had mattered so much for thirteen years.

Dragging his bag behind him, he arrived at Palazzo Margherita. The good Caputo spread his arms wide. Still nothing.

Yet Ferranini had no doubts he would depart. Two hours later, when his passport was returned with a visa for a week's stay as, irony, a "tourist," Caputo proudly claimed a miracle while for Ferranini it seemed no more than he'd expected. Nor was he surprised when at Ciampino they gave him a seat for the 8:45 p.m. flight. He *had* to leave. The cycle was finished; Nancy's call had come at the right moment. As always Nancy was the designing woman, like the title of that film he'd seen at the cinema. She had marked the hour of his departure, and now she marked that of his return.

At the airport, another lounge, and some two hours to wait. He wrote to Amoruso. Putting the Formia address on the postcard, he added, "Many thanks to you and Adele for everything." It was a farewell.

To who else could he send his farewell, keeping himself busy while he waited? A name came to mind, but for that, a phone call would do. That morning, from the taxi, he had recognized Reparatore's daughter across the street in the doorway behind her father.

He called. She came to the phone.

"If you only knew how happy I am to hear from you," she said before he could even say who he was. "I had a bad night. Tell me, tell me what's happening with you!"

He told her: he was leaving. He explained, briefly.

"What? But aren't you divorced? Forgive me, Walter!"

"I am. Divorced."

"And you," she regained her voice after a pause, "you hope not to get there too late."

He didn't reply. Why he didn't know, but he was sure he would not get there too late. The end hadn't come for him yet, he still had a life to live, and for that Nancy was needed, Nancy and all the rest. She would be there; as soon as he'd read the telegram last night, he'd known that's what would happen.

"And for the article, forgive me again, was there any unpleasantness?"

The question led him back in time, disagreeably.

"Nothing. They soft-pedaled it. Though did I ever speak out!"

"What did you say? Soft-pedaled in what sense?"

"We undertook to make a complete change of life, a positive change—"

"Don't talk so loud, we're on the phone!"

"What difference does it make? It's a false promise, I said, because the final sum is always the same, even if the terms change, or the signs. There will be less injustice, not less total suffering! That's what I said yesterday. They didn't touch a hair on my head, everything as before, we're all the best of friends."

"And isn't that better? What did you want them to say? Walter, please, tell me when you'll be back. You must come back!"

"Come back? I've been away thirteen years and though I didn't notice it, I missed America. There's more space there. You can't imagine. The countryside is immense there. Like huge estates. There's more room. In every sense! It's a different way of life."

"Think about it, please, think," the voice was stunned and indignant. "You don't mean to say you prefer America for that. Impossible."

"It's another world," he went on, "and I am tired, I want a change. I want to live, to be free, understand?"

"Impossible, you'll be back, this is an impulsive reaction, and you'll be back soon, back to yourself—"

"You don't know. It's easy for you to say. It's been months, years that I've been debating this."

"No," the voice begged, "change your mind, Walter, you won't get what you're looking for in America. That can't be your country. It will disappoint you."

"But at least I'll have a change. You don't believe me, but I guarantee you there's nothing to be done. I thought of myself as a follower, a peaceful type. Docile. I kidded myself, and probably also others. Enough! The time for clarity has arrived. You understand now, yes?"

He felt ridiculously sordid and shabby. Had just finished the call and was closing the door of the phone cabinet. What was he doing? Telling that girl his private business, his deepest secrets, his weariness, his doubts, his battles.

Letting himself be scolded, letting himself be commiserated with. Because he hadn't found Nuccia, here he was grabbing on to this other one, confessing to this other. And he was supposed to like women, phony Communist Ferranini! Like Mazzola, who when the most dramatic moment of his life arrived, didn't tell his wife a thing.

He headed for the exit and went outside. He needed to move, to get some air. A nervous system with a brain as accessory: so Lenin had defined people like him. Ex-proletariat, yes, with a bourgeois nervous system.

14

THE MAN behind the counter who served him coffee pointed to another man at the far end of the bar, sitting deep in thought over his glass.

"See that young fellow, the Negro? He's flying with you and he just arrived from New York this morning. American. He comes in three or four times a month, doesn't leave the airport, returns in the evening. He's got money to throw away. He leaves these fliers in here or on the seats in the plane."

There was one on the table. It had a few lines printed on it. *Life's but a walking shadow, a poor player. It is a tale told by an idiot, full of sound and fury, signifying nothing.* While Ferranini was reading it, the American, athletically built, tall, elegant, about thirty-five, came over.

"Those are lines from Shakespeare. Do you know Shakespeare?"

"No."

"Would you rather speak Italian? I fought in Italy during the war, I speak the language."

"Better English. I need to practice."

They sat together at the table. After 8:00 p.m., it was the dead hour at Ciampino, and they were almost alone.

"You hand out these sheets. *Life's but a walking shadow, a tale told by an idiot.* What on earth do you mean? Not a very cheerful message for someone going on a trip."

Lamoureux (the man had introduced himself as "John Lamoureux from New York and New Orleans") laughed. "Not cheerful but salutary. People who travel delude themselves they are keeping busy, or getting away, they delude themselves all the time. Their travel is supremely pointless, like that pinnacle of pointlessness, their lives. I've taken it upon myself to warn them. They should know they are going for no reason but to go. Would you like a drink? A cigarette?"

"This moral, did you gather it from personal experience?"

"Yes, from my experience as an American, and America is a world, it is *the* world. And so it pertains to everyone. I hand out my fliers in Rome, Frankfurt, Paris. I land in those cities twice a week on average, alternating among them. But I alone don't delude myself. Only I know I'm going with the sole purpose of going."

Ferranini asked no more questions. The Negro, who was lighter-skinned than many Italians, was too friendly, too histrionic for his taste. They separated and Ferranini went to the restaurant to eat. But fate would bring them together again. On the plane, they had adjacent seats. And after taking off in a whirlwind of rain, when the roar of the engines had quieted, Lamoureux turned to speak to him.

"You look at me and find I'm not Negro enough. I don't have that typical smell. In fact, I am half white. But my soul is black, and I'm black on the outside too for all intents and purposes. Your Sicilians are often darker than I am and have hair less straight than mine. But there's the cornea, the damned cornea. In whites, including Sicilians, it's white, or blue-white. Look carefully. Mine is pink. That's enough. That marks me."

He laughed, and went on: "I don't complain about what I am. In my family it's a tradition, I dare say a destiny, that we Lamoureuxs should get something positive out of negritude. My grandfather, in New Orleans several years after the Civil War, caught the eye of a French lady because he was a handsome, tall, strong Negro, and she left him her surname and some money, along with a son. My father made that money grow during a lifetime running a pawnshop for black people in New Orleans. He married a white, a Mexican. I hope I'm not boring you with these tales."

He had them bring him a drink, cigarettes. He drank, lit up, and then said, "And as for myself, I'm no slouch either. I've earned a lot of money since the war in the honest profession of broker. Allow me to explain. There's a little part of New York, some thirty blocks, where successful black people try to infiltrate the whites. Or to share the neighborhood. A black family that has been fortunate or has accumulated means would like at a certain point to leave Harlem and 'make it.' I find them the lodgings they aspire to, on the edges of the forbidden city. They rent, or buy, and pay me well. After six months they realize that for them, for us, life is impossible there, life is made impossible. I help them get out of their obligations, and they pay me well. The following day, new candidates turn up. Such has been my profession for the last twelve years. Little effort, a great deal of money."

He leaned over graciously to look at his traveling companion, and said, laughing, "Am I putting you to sleep? Quite often my tale has that effect: the airline companies ought to pay me a stipend. So, for twelve years, the good life. But suddenly the wind changed. A rotten illness. Which reduced happy Lamoureux to a miserable worm, lacking the strength and desire to wiggle forward. Anxiety neurosis. Three months in a clinic, watched day and night, forced to remain alive despite myself by those guarding me—for this is a disease with a certain outcome, and one only. You know what I mean, don't you? I survived and was cured because I contracted a disease that was slightly less serious, depressive asthenia with dissociation, a condition that permits me to breathe, eat, and deambulate. Not to work, not to sleep. I haven't slept since October 25."

He rested an enormous hand on Ferranini's knee.

"Shakespeare wrote no tragedy about insomnia, and that's a pity, he failed to address the noblest subject. And so my friend, I spend three or four nights each week three miles above the Atlantic. This consoles me. Sometimes near dawn I'm able to close my eyes. And now, let me tell you how I fell ill. My fault, friend! My fault. I used to like to go south, to New Orleans, city of my forebears. I would buy stuff, old stuff, I liked cheap paintings and assorted junk. I used to drive down in comfortable stages, stopping in a small city to sleep at an elegant hotel with a ballroom where Duke Ellington played at one time. I would stop there without needing to, out of defiance because that hotel was forbidden to my race. I was passing as white, I knew it was a risk. That small city was Auburn, Alabama, a place where they don't take it lightly when segregation is violated. In the summer there, the mood turns ugly, it's the hot humid weather. That night pandemonium broke loose down below, and then there was a raid, a 'cleanup' of the rooms. They came in, I was sleeping, and they recognized me by my smell; they have a sixth sense. They tied me up and hung me outside the windowsill on the seventh floor. Three women, and two of them were older, wearing eyeglasses, maybe schoolteachers. They left me hanging out there for a couple of hours. But all's well that ends well. Except for this damned insomnia.

"I'll leave you now, my friend, I'm going to stretch my legs. I've become a philosopher; I understand men and men's fates. Want to know what my doctrine is? Causes are infinite, all is necessary, and nothing has a purpose. I repeat: There's not a single purpose, not one, in anything, whether outside or inside us. This perspective allows me to feel empathy with others and understand them. Even while they sleep, I am awake. I wish them a good sleep with all my heart."

He stood up on his long legs and walked off into the depth of the plane, already darkened for night.

There was no sleep that night for Ferranini either. Why wasn't he worrying, thinking, making up his mind about something, he continued to ask himself. This lack of regret, this lack of purposefulness—it was more evidence of his typical failure to reflect. This trusting to fate, when twenty years ago, and he was just a young man, he had crossed the ocean with his heart cleft in two between missing what he was leaving and pride in what awaited him. Everything had been clear: his mission in the capitalist empire would begin in Boston, at the martyrs' tombs. Now it was all abdication and irony. In truth, if no one took him seriously and all he could do was envy Mazzola, was there any reason he should take himself seriously? However, a plan. An immediate program: to know what he would be doing when that visa expired, seven or eight days hence. Return to Rome? Come on! The thought made him shiver, like a man recalling the high fever he's just gotten over. Well then, supposing they didn't expel him immediately, he'd have to decide what to do, where to hide. Find a life, a job. Begin again. At the age of forty-six, disheartened, incredulous, incapable. Incapable even of worrying about Nancy, who'd asked for him to come and who was in danger.

Night behind him, night ahead. So the airplane flew, tracing its parabola, its trajectory between continents, but the plane had a route, it was going somewhere, and in the pilot's cabin all those blue lights burned, there was no night there. He was in the dark. Outcast and purposeless, like Lamoureux. Then a memory came to him. He remembered the warm and familiar darkness of their three attic rooms in Demarr's house, late at night when they would come in. A steep stairway up from one of the rooms not used by the Demarrs. The two of them would climb the stairs in the dark, and sometimes Nancy would go ahead, pretending to be afraid, with him behind, below her, pushing her up the creaky wooden stairs. The first times, they had to stop on the way.

"My legs. Feel my legs. The best legs in America have always been Irish."

Irish. One afternoon at the Soviet Academy of Sciences, an Irishman had been sitting beside him, Finetree, from Belfast. The session had ended and Finetree had said, We Westerners must recognize that while we possess all the appearance of reality, reality itself comes from the East. He, Walter Ferranini, was turning his back on reality. He was choosing appearances, he was making a beeline there at four hundred miles per hour. Comrade Ferranini, who had told the rail workers of Reggio that their city would one day be a capital of European Communism. Ferranini the pure, the resolute. What a joke. Just a few days—hours!—was all it had taken for him to lose his way. Or anyway, to lose his obedience, his prospects, his faith. Attention, American journalists, a Kravchenko is about to land in your country. Coming from the USSR? No, from Rome, where they didn't listen to him, didn't grant him the honors due. Good. Good for him, tomorrow he will ask for asylum in the land of freedom. And if not?

And if not, there was no going back. Fool, turncoat, whatever you like. But tired. Hopelessly tired. Utterly unable to go on. And was that so strange? There were priests who gave up the cassock. Enrico Caruso, in just three months, lost his voice. Someone's crazy in love, and then he isn't. Himself, for example. When that telegram came, he thought Nancy had died. The next morning getting ready to leave, he was unruffled. Of course he would get there in time. And why was that? Simple—because he was no longer in love. Love is a pessimist, love and jealousy, love and dread. Who was it who had said that? Oh yes, it was Nuccia. Nice try. Now he merely hoped, sincerely, that Nancy would recover, he needed her to recover. The enthusiasm of the past was no more. Had they told him in '46 or '47, Nancy is gravely ill, he would have lost his mind. When he went to the movies in those days, he always hoped there would be a girl in the film like her. He daydreamed of her voice when he walked down the street.

They were supposed to make a short stop at Gander, Newfoundland. Instead they were on the ground for three hours; the airplane's radio was malfunctioning. The weather report predicted snow halfway down the continent, from Hudson Bay to Washington. An airport official announced they were not yet certain that Idlewild Airport in New York was open. The good-looking Lamoureux stood beside the official, and imitating his way of speaking, said, "Ladies and gentlemen, we ask you not to draw any hasty conclusions about American efficiency from these mishaps."

What was he thinking, to joke about *efficiency*? One of the "appearances," as Finetree had put it, on which the West's reputation rested. At least that.

They landed in New York as planned, but at midday, rather than 9:00 a.m. He missed the connection for Boston and had to wait for the next flight at 3:00 in the afternoon. The telegram had come from Demarr's sister-in-law Rosaleen, or Rosy, with whom Nancy stayed when she was away from home. A widow, Rosy Gaven had always lived in Boston and Ferranini knew he would find Nancy with her. Nancy didn't like staying at her own house in Camden, and she certainly wouldn't have gone back there even if gravely ill, if old Demarr were still living there, or if he were dead. Only Aunt Rosy could have been asked to contact him. Nancy would never have confessed that belated change of heart to anyone in her own family.

Ferranini had recognized the address at the bottom of the telegram, West Brompton Terraces, his wife's mysterious dwelling toward which his jealous thoughts had often flown.

It was the gray, drowsy, even-more-silent-under-the-snow Boston of Sacco and Vanzetti—not so far away, he seemed to recall, from the prison where in a damp yard in the autumn of '39 he had paid tribute to their tombs. Two rows of small brick houses, each with a small, fenced-in rectangle of grass, like in the cemetery. The bell rang for a while, and then a neighbor appeared to say that Mrs. Gavan was out, but he could make himself at home all the same, the door wasn't locked. There was a rocking chair with a lacy cover near the cold fireplace. He waited there, in shadows that smelled of coal and lavender water, listening to the pendulum clock strike the hour.

Aunt Rosy was very courteous when (it was past 7:00 p.m.) she finally appeared.

"I thank you. My niece is better. She'll be delighted."

She'll be delighted. She didn't speak the usual *Americano* but an elegant, crisp, clear English. He'd envisioned her as tall, thin, dressed in dark colors, returning from some meeting at church, and instead here was a plump little perfumed lady in an electric-blue raincoat with pale blue hair. Coming from the editorial staff meeting of a literary review.

"I'm sorry to be home so late, I work at the *Literary Quarterly*. Very, very busy. For a couple of days now my niece has allayed our concerns somewhat, but we had reason to fear for her life. Nephritis, very advanced. I'll tell you about it. And then Demarr, her father, is also ill and can't leave his bed. You see. Poor Nancy, at the origin of everything was a terrible depression. Conflicts at work, a noble social mission that's been obstructed in every way, even at the highest levels and by some of the most influential elements in this country. I'll tell you about it. Recently she was living in Westchester outside New York. She was running a very combative magazine, *The Lower 48*, maybe you've heard of it—"

"Tell me right way," Ferranini interrupted her, "where is she?"

"In a hospital, obviously. I'm getting there. But first I have to explain." She glanced toward the front door to be sure it was closed. "Why do you think my niece wanted me to warn you? Why did she want you to come here before going to see her? To prepare you, that's why. She wants you to be informed."

"Take me there now. Please! Let's go."

He was in a hurry, he wanted the final chapter. He knew that for him, everything depended on that first meeting. Those first moments, the way she looked at him, would decide everything. Why did he need to babble on with this woman?

Rosaleen's eyes widened.

"Go? My friend, I'm sixty-three years old and you want me to set out like that, with no preparation? It's four hundred miles, and a night train."

"But where is she?" he howled. "Where is she?"

"In Philadelphia, my friend. Of course."

All of a sudden, the anticipation that had kept him together in the hours since he had landed collapsed—just as the time came to leave. There were no taxis, and he was lucky to catch one of the last buses in circulation. From the headlines of a newspaper he learned, as he got seated on the train, that a double disaster had befallen the Eastern states: an Arctic blizzard, and a strike of transportation workers (who were "scandalously underpaid," the paper said). Trains were still running, at least some. And in fact, by 1:00 p.m. he was back in New York. He hadn't known that the train he'd gotten off continued on to Washington and would have taken him to Philadelphia, and by the time someone told him, it was too late. He prepared himself to spend the night in Pennsylvania Station, immense and warm and strangely empty. He was resigned even to these wearying delays in various stations; they seemed inevitable and significant, marks of destiny. He was a rootless creature: the lives of others moved to the beat of the tender family obligations; his, to that of departure timetables. Every form of life, the biologists said, had evolved to occupy a particular habitat. His was a railway world, pending, contingent; some unknown evolutionary sin had condemned him to this.

He slept for two or three hours. Then he went to the restaurant and consoled himself eating, as he'd so often done. This time, however, paying particular attention to the intrinsic flavors of his food, frankfurters with mustard, so familiar to him from Chicago and his early immigrant days. He ate a lot, he ate passionately; nearby was a group of navy boys, noisy and cheerful, drinking California champagne. He felt for a moment that he had come back to the surface of things, was enjoying an effervescent new sensation, in a situation that was, yes, uncertain, but also open-ended. Wasn't Nancy getting better? He was going to see her. And he was free. He could have her back, start over. In the meantime he was enjoying a new awareness of something else, a particular smell he'd first noticed the morning he landed. It was the smell of America he'd so longed for, Virginia tobacco and with it a scent half chlorine, half ocean, or what? Maybe only the scent of distant chemical plants.

He got to Philadelphia in the early afternoon, aboard the only train traveling south.

Nancy was in John Morgan Hospital in Haddington, a neighborhood Ferranini seemed to remember. On the other side of town, beyond Fairmount Park where he used to take old Demarr to play golf. Memories began to resurface. Over there, inside the station, you went down to the subway. But the gate was closed. The strike. In the square outside (it was snowing), the people huddled by the wall taking shelter from the storm didn't move or reply. No taxis to be seen among the silent automobiles covered with snow. A dark day despite all this white around, said a policeman he'd asked about a taxi; apparently his question was absurd. He moved back under the roof of the entryway and tried approaching the drivers of two military vehicles for a ride. The first just laughed; the second man, a black, pretended to drive right at him, also jeering.

Now that he'd been restored to the city of his nostalgia, he was anxious to move quickly, he'd already wasted twenty-four hours of the few he'd been granted. He began to walk, his valise on his back. Walking to the hospital might take him two hours; it was four or five miles, no more. At 4:00 p.m. he'd be there.

After a long, straight hike, numb and half blind, he permitted himself a rest in what seemed to him to be Market Place. He calculated he had done about a quarter of the distance. The snow was coming down sideways, biting, dry; he could barely see but he had his bearings. He was still pretty good, after all those years. The route he needed to take was fairly clear in his mind; if he followed the other pedestrians along the course of the river, he should arrive at city hall, where he hoped to find some means of transportation or other. One evening he had met Nancy there on the street buying flowers (a Puerto Rican was selling cut flowers in a kiosk there), and that June evening Walter, taking one from the bunch, had put it in her hair. But city hall didn't materialize. He went into a large store where a man began trying to sell him, incongruously, a refrigerator; the man told him he was far from city hall, and in any case, to get to Haddington he had to cross the river and cut through the center of town toward the west. A woman shop assistant, to whom he'd explained he was looking for a hospital, took an interest in him. She went to ask, and informed him that a van making home deliveries was about to leave, and that it would be going near Fairmount.

She was quite courteous. Maybe, he thought, she was eager to please because she was a mulatto, because of her pale yellow skin. Ferranini forced himself to wait, but they didn't leave for another half hour, and the van had a long route to follow; it was already twilight when they let him out. He didn't go into Fairmount Park, afraid he would get lost. The blizzard was not letting up. He took the avenue along one side. There was a little group, kids let out of school, who were squealing with excitement at getting to walk for once, and Ferranini tried to keep up with them. He made his way up the great, curved, tree-lined street. The trees on one side formed a single mass with those of the park, and the light filtering through from the headlights did not prevent the place from looking primitive and fierce, a forest. The city beyond had vanished. Then the kids all left the avenue and turned onto a side street. As soon as he was alone he felt lost, and his arm began to hurt, worse than the cold and fatigue. It wasn't the right arm, carrying his valise; it was that quite different pain in the left forearm, running up his neck and the back of his head. And with it came the distressing image, even before he felt the void in his chest, of a strange, oppressive emptiness from diaphragm to throat. A premonition.

His breathing was still normal, though. Best not to think about it, distract himself, and meanwhile get some rest. Here and there along the avenue cars appeared, empty, snowed in. He rested on one, sweeping off snow with his hand to feel the metal underneath; the car felt like a surrogate human presence. He tried to calculate how far the hospital could be; he might have walked a mile and a half since getting out of the van, always keeping to the edge of the park. Therefore he had the same distance to go, or a bit more, close to an hour's walk.

He started up again, on the right side of the avenue, and noticed he was walking beside a clearing somewhat below the level of the street, where the snow was level. He recalled that somewhere there was a pond, and near it an old historic house from the War of Independence, and that after that there were buildings again. He stopped once more, put down the valise. He had gone to visit that house with Nancy, who had called it, in her somewhat high-flown way, "a shrine." He forced himself to plow through the murky air. No trace of the shrine. It was pointless to look for reference points. Behind him a column of cars, one after the other, was moving forward at low speed. He ran toward the road, but no one saw his frantic waving.

Here I am, *marooned*, he tried to joke to himself. Alone, in the middle of nowhere. America, in frontier times.

But if death was just a canceling out, he thought, why did he have to walk so much beforehand. Struggle, wear himself out, suffer.

He began to pull the valise behind him again, slowly, and this time he kept to the avenue. A car might stop and give him a lift. He had rediscovered America. He hadn't recognized it, after thirteen years of expectations, conscious or not. But he had found it. His last downstroke would not land him on via del Tritone in Rome, it had to be here. And here he was, right on the spot. What happened afterward was less important. By now, Nancy was nearby, and he understood that seeing her, speaking to her, was not indispensable. First, sleep. He needed to sleep, and if he wanted to find the hospital, perhaps it was because there were beds there. The snow seemed more familiar now that it was coming straight down, it wasn't flying into his face. It wasn't even that deep, only a bit more than knee-high. He sat on his bag, raised one leg, then the other; once in a while for a moment the headlights disappeared and it was utterly dark. He studied the shoe on his left foot; the stitching on the seam in back had given way, he hadn't noticed, and his heel came out easily, and the leather was shredded so that it left a reddish trace of color on the snow. He smiled at his foot, and he squeezed it, soaked and swollen around the ankle. It was begging not to have to walk any more.

He knew what there was in the valise under him: three shirts, a few handkerchiefs, the last two volumes of Nordenskiöld, yesterday's *l'Unità*, a sweater, a box of chocolates bought at Ciampino for Nancy. He was coming back to America not much wealthier than twenty years ago, when he'd landed as an immigrant. Once again a convoy of automobiles came down the street. From the window of one, pop music gushed out over the snow.

He resumed walking; it was night. The broad avenue continued, curving every so slightly, among majestic trees, centuries-old trees, not like with us, where a tree never got to twenty years, thirty years, because people were greedy and cut it down. Beeches, maples, elms, white, huge. America was a vast park, that was one of its beauties.

There along the borders of Fairmount, there should be a river, somewhere. That he remembered. But who could see it. Frozen, covered with snow. The parks were America's triumph, its symbol. America's Wonders. And if someone died inside? Well, tough for him. You didn't go walking in a park during a blizzard. Here the weather forecast came twelve hours ahead. Here, there was efficiency. Even the great Stalin acknowledged that. In his *Foundations of Leninism*. He says that Russian revolutionary sweep must be united with American efficiency. You think a Communist cannot admire America? Stupid Ferranini, who'd thought the two things were irreconcilable. Even Reparatore admired America; the American trade unions were technically the best in the world. But the newspaper had said the transport workers were *scandalously underpaid*. Tough luck for them. Reparatore knew what he was talking about; he had his reasons.

He was so tired, *porca matina*. Close my eyes for an instant and I'm done. The temptation to sleep grabbed him stupidly. Follow the ruts left by the wheels with his feet, walk and sleep. Close his eyes. But he had that ache in his neck, his shoulder, to help him stay awake. The pain was insistent, not terribly strong but regular, pulsing with his blood. He tossed the valise onto the snow, knelt down, took out the sweater and stuck it under his raincoat between his neck and his shoulder. He didn't have a scarf. He was hoping to find his bottle of Coramine in some corner of the bag, and instead he laid hands on his bible, the *Manifesto*. He closed the valise. *What is the family based on? On private capital.* The *Manifesto* said that, he knew it by heart, sentence by sentence. And wasn't that true? He had come in search of Nancy because Nancy represented private capital. Even more: the homeland of capitalism. President Leone had said he wished his wife well. Love of family meant something to Leone the Catholic: the man who loves his family loves order. Signor President, I am for order. But meanwhile he did not possess a scarf and had left the Coramine at home. The pain beat faster, the spasms branching out under his ear and behind it, shooting down his neck. He stood up, and the lights were gone. He turned, to look behind him. No lights, not even distant ones, just snow and silence. He trudged forward in the dark. My dearest Philadelphia, he thought.

Still, he might be in luck. When the lights returned—he'd been walking blindly for a while, stumbling over the car tracks—he saw that at a certain distance ahead the road forked. There, on the right, he saw that the trees thinned out and disappeared, while on both sides of the road the railings of a bridge could be made out. Maybe the river. After that, there might be houses. He reached the bridge; deserted, interminably long, whipped by the wind and by a hint of freezing water. Finally the road widened and descended, and the houses resumed.

Below, behind a barricade of abandoned automobiles, beside some dark, lifeless houses that looked abandoned, appeared a square. And something he hadn't even hoped for. A telephone.

The phone booth was lit and dry. He searched the phone book for the number with stiff fingers that struggled to separate the pages, then tormented himself trying to put together the English words he needed. His poor head was empty. The phone operator at the hospital didn't understand him. He tried speaking Italian. The operator refused to answer him.

Another man was waiting to telephone. He waved him toward the phone booth and pointed to the name of the hospital in the phone book. The man said, "It's nearby. Less than half a mile away." Ferranini traced the name Mrs. Demarr on the page with a pencil. The other man understood, called back, and said the name. He turned toward him to pass on the reply. No Mrs. Demarr in the hospital.

Ferranini went out. He leaned against the glass of the phone booth, and let himself sink to the ground with a groan of relief. The square vanished and everything turned black.

The man was shouting into the phone, he had lit a match. Ferranini, slouched down with his head on his chest, could hear every-thing (the man was speaking Spanish). He felt calm. His trial was over, there was no longer any need to keep going. Now I'll look in the bag again to see if I can find the Coramine, he thought. He didn't move.

The man came out and bent over Ferranini. He opened the glass door again and pushed him inside, bending his legs by force to close the door. Ferranini didn't react; he sat there alone, on the ground, in that small space.

After a while the man returned. He got into booth with difficulty, climbing over him. He lifted the receiver. Once again he shouted and cursed, in English now, and Ferranini listened, understanding everything. He had called the police, but they didn't take him seri-ously. He lit another match and tried another number, ranting into the phone, getting excited and crushing one of Ferranini's knees. "Strike and snow, *ves que malvado país*!" He was unleashing his anger against the stranger there at his feet, or maybe just talking to him-self; he probably thought the stranger was senseless, unconscious.

"You're croaking and they allow you to croak. *Como un perro*."

He was speaking a bastard language, he didn't care if anyone un-derstood. But Ferranini did understand every word and said to him-self, He's Puerto Rican.

"Downtown, in front of the Garden of Allah or the Roxy, you find the police. They go to get a taxi for the clients leaving. But you mustn't envy the people with money, no sir. In America all men are equal. All equal, and all alone."

Ferranini could feel the hem of the man's coat grazing his face in the dark, but it didn't bother him.

"All alone; here you have singles, not men. Each one a piece torn off from the rest, nothing to do with the life of the other. With their unions, their associations, their brotherhoods. For ten years I was a schoolteacher in the Southwest. In a village of Mexicans."

He was happy to have the man beside him. "Amigo," he mum-bled, and the other touched his face with a hand, perhaps amazed he was still alive.

"I taught my Mexicans to hold on tight to the machine. The machine that produces and consumes, and is all: family, humanity. However, sometimes the machine breaks down."

The pain in his neck and shoulder had returned. The back of his head. Now he was breathing hard. He tried to move the valise that was weighing on his chest. The man picked it up and put it between his legs.

"All it takes is a strike, a blizzard, even less. And a person is left with nothing, whether he's black or white, poor or rich, it's all in pieces. He has no connection to others, everyone thinks for himself and society falls apart, or rather, you see that it doesn't exist. All it takes is a major disaster, a fire. When there's a fire here, half of the people die."

Ferranini, quite clearheaded, was thinking: There are two of us in here consuming air. There's no more air. He understood that he would have to stand up to open the door. And that wasn't possible.

"When there's a fire the traffic doesn't stop, and the passersby just barely look up. In my hometown people don't die when their house burns down. I come from Spain, from Teruel. In my town people beat each other up at the tavern, they pick fights in church, but when I left the place I had to leave in secret because they didn't want me to go. Here instead your children, as soon as they start to earn some money, are no longer yours. I can tell you, I have three kids, three girls. If you get sick and have to leave your job, your workmate doesn't know you anymore. You're a foreigner. You'll learn."

Ferranini's breathlessness was getting worse, he was sucking in air with his mouth open. He recognized the smell of wet shoes, wet clothes, and another, pungent odor. Alcohol, it must be.

"You're a foreigner, you go and seek out your own kind. But they won't speak to you in your language, and before they accept you, they'll ask around in all the shops how many dollars you spend. *Y no tendrás voz a hablar.* Afterwards when you've found a place in the machine, and depending on what it is, they'll accept you. And if you don't find a place, they'll give you something to eat, but they won't treat you like a human being because you aren't. You especially will not feel you are a human being. Produce things, consume them, that is your life. Produce and consume, when you're no good for that you go back to being a spook. In the West, there are ghost towns. Cities, but cities that are empty, abandoned, that don't serve the machine anymore, and in the same way there are ghost people. You'll learn."

The man was talking and drinking. He would pull out the bottle and take a swig. Liquid spilled, wetting Ferranini. He's drunk, he thought vaguely.

"You see? The police are not coming. We've become savages. Worse. *Lo que yo llamo polvillo social.* Dust. Dirt of society. You and I are alone, abandoned this evening, alone as in the first forest, because there were primitive forests here where we stand, with a few frightened Indians in them. There are houses over there. But it's useless to go and knock. Everyone's in his little fortress, closed to all the others. Tomorrow they'll play upon level green fields, and you would think they were all friends. Tonight they don't know one another. They have every freedom, including this one: not to have to see your neighbor when it isn't convenient to see him. You are Polish, or Italian, or Yugoslav. You'll get used to this freedom, which didn't exist in your own land. Last summer there was an earthquake in Colorado. People got up at night, the tourists there, and drove off in their cars. A school collapsed, with many young boarders, children were screaming under the fallen walls, and the cars just drove by. The newspapers called it "panic." But what do you know, *pobre arrastrado*? Poor washed-up thing."

Ferranini moved a hand, touched the man's leg. He understood, the words were as if traced on a dark field in strange relief, and he seemed to read them rather than hear them. But he was quite sure he was not dreaming. The other, who seemed to be a big man, tried to bend down.

"Take it, try to drink."

Deeper in him beat an anxious thought (not a dream); it posed a question, and he felt he must choose. Choose again, a path, a solution, decide. But against that residue of his will, physical fatigue prevailed; resignation was easy and painless. Disengagement. His cheek was resting on the bottom of the glass panel, freezing. Next to his ear, snow fluttered down thickly.

The man bent over. He put the bottle to his face. "It will keep you from dying. Drink, you idiot."

John Morgan Hospital was not far away. A quarter of a mile.

They took him there without even loading him in the ambulance, and he was alert, attentive, sorry that they separated him from his companion of that night. In reality they'd been together less than two hours, and it wasn't yet 11:00 p.m. when they took him away. The emergency-room doctor's cursory diagnosis: ischemic cardiac event. The following morning that was revised by the head of department to which he'd been turned over. He hadn't slept well and gave no signs of improvement.

Dr. Wiener, awaiting further tests, wrote on his chart: "Circulatory collapse due to severe fatigue. Probable chronic heart disease." And, he added, "suspected alcoholism." Ferranini's wet clothes had smelled of alcohol. Wiener, a connoisseur, had hypothesized cheap Spanish brandy. As for his bag, it had already been examined by the hospital administration. It raised, along with other evidence, some doubts about whether the patient really was member of the Italian parliament, a status that had been deduced from the papers found on his person.

Elegant, gray-haired, a persistent cough, American of distant Swiss origins, Wiener had a visceral dislike for Italians. At the end of the war the army had "forgotten" him for eighteen months in Sardinia where he'd been treating malaria and trachoma.

Ferranini was alone in a two-bed room. As Wiener came in, he said loudly, "This man has a one-week visa. He has no intention of staying longer."

Walter shifted, and moaned. He would have liked to say: I'm going as soon as I can, even tomorrow. But he lacked the breath.

Later Wiener met his colleague Newcomer, the cardiologist, in the hallway. Newcomer had Ferranini's electrocardiogram in hand, the ink still damp. Wiener told him he'd already made things clear to the patient.

"It seems he's a politician. But it makes no difference, as far as I'm concerned, a foreigner's a foreigner."

Newcomer, younger, and as can happen, wiser, fixed his eyes on the other's face. "As far as I'm concerned, a sick person is a sick person. No matter where he comes from."

"Someone in his condition," Wiener shot back, "should not be traveling. We ought to get in touch with his consulate."

"The consulate has nothing to do with it. Nor does the FBI. A man's illness is a private matter that concerns the individual and us, so long as he's here."

There was no risk that news of Ferranini's unhappy adventure would cross the Atlantic.

A second consequence of their conversation was that Newcomer took number 203 under his direct supervision, with Wiener as his partner, something the older man tacitly accepted. For nearly the whole day, the patient's state of circulatory collapse resisted the forceful administration of cardiotonics. In severe respiratory distress, often barely conscious, Ferranini struggled over every breath, his left hand monotonously rowing back and forth, grazing his chest and then reaching out, falling back on his chest and then reaching out. For hours. There wasn't enough air for him. A canister of oxygen sat by the bed in its bamboo case but Newcomer, who had his ideas, didn't like to use oxygen, which offered relief but tired the heart, and he persisted with digitalis, an old remedy that he trusted. The patient's blood pressure had fallen sharply and there was an immediate risk of pulmonary edema, but Newcomer was not too worried about that. One symptom seemed auspicious, the sick man enjoyed eating. He sipped the orange juice avidly, swallowed the jello without being urged, and he followed the departing nurse with his eyes. Newcomer called her back and quite a few more spoonfuls went down.

"Damn, he was hungry," he observed. Before he left for the night, he had another fortunate insight—born of clinical experience, not textbook advice—and he ordered a large dose of soporifics. Wiener, who was present, disapproved. In fact, it was risky.

"I take the responsibility, let it be. He's a nervous type, and he must have had his highs and lows. He probably hasn't slept for a good long while."

By 9:00 p.m., there were already signs of improvement. For the first time Walter spoke. In English and in a voice that was not too faint.

"That man, where is he?"

"What man?"

Miss Joy, the nurse, had just come in.

"The one in the phone booth."

"You're speaking nonsense," the girl said, distracted.

No, he shook his head. No.

15

JOHN MORGAN Hospital was a collection of stone and brick buildings, not large and recently built. Neo-Georgian rusticity among the genuinely sylvan ash and maple trees. The building where Ferranini was hospitalized stood close to the Green Pavilion. It was scrupulously green, entirely covered with ivy and Virginia creeper, and between the two top floors ran a covered loggia.

Potted plants and armchairs sat between the radiators under the windows of the loggia. On that morning of February 28, snow partly covered the windows, but the sky had cleared and the sun was beginning to color the treetops red.

A love of ivy and Virginia creeper had led Nancy to ask to be transferred to the Green Pavilion when she'd begun to feel better. She'd always liked plants that made decorative patterns. Halfway down the loggia, peering out, she wondered which of the windows of the building nearby were Ferranini's.

She had finished breakfast and was smoking her first cigarette, a woman of about thirty-five, pale and drained after three weeks of illness but well on her way to recovery. A pleasing woman, and yet she had that off-putting quality of someone no longer interested in pleasure. Hands on her hips, dressing gown closed with care and something like primness, feet apart, solidly planted on the floor: there was dogged determination in her very waiting. The face, no; something uncertain and unstable kept it in motion. Some elusive, vague sentiment ready to fade away or contradict itself. Which might also be Irish *fickleness*; in America they said of the Irish first you bury them, then you fathom them—although maybe that was flattery. In other times Ferranini had thought, probably not wrongly, of his Nancy: Well, at least she's honest.

The evening before she had picked up the newspaper for the first time in a while and seen the story. Foreigner trapped by blizzard in phone booth, hospitalized at John Morgan in a state of exposure. The reporter noted that "the piquant detail is that this derelict Italian, saved by the timely action of police and the hospital, is apparently a member of the Italian parliament with the Communists, a big shot in the party across the Atlantic."

Nancy, rather sharper, thought to herself: The piquant detail is that this big-shot Communist was about to expire because of a strike called by the workers and their union. The shock was, all considered, bearable, and her immediate reaction was as follows:

"Do you have a Mr. Ferranini hospitalized here since yesterday?"

"Deputy Ferranini from Rome, Italy, I mean!"

The administrative office confirmed that they did.

"What's happened then? Mr. Ferranini comes four thousand miles to visit me, Mrs. Ferranini, and you don't even bother to notify me. Congratulations to your Department of Patients' Relations, if you have one. And if you don't, get one!"

The administration offered apologies; Nancy had a reputation as a journalist and a troublemaker, so they had to watch out. Then Nancy called Walter's ward and asked to speak to the chief physician.

"Where is Mr. Ferranini, and how is he doing? Is it possible to see him immediately? I should tell you that you're speaking to Mrs. Ferranini."

"Well, Ferranini's condition is serious," said Dr. Weiner. "You can't see him."

At that, she leapt out of bed. "I thought it was a simple case of exposure."

Wiener had no vocation for dealing with other peoples' troubles.

"It's circulatory collapse. The patient has regained consciousness, and therefore emotional reactions are to be avoided. Absolutely."

"He's my husband! We've been apart for thirteen years."

"So you can wait until tomorrow. Tomorrow morning I'll let you know."

Telephoning at 7:00 the next morning, Nancy had better news. After a few more calls, they gave her permission to visit. It was noon.

Ferranini had rested all night; he had actually slept for nearly ten hours, and Newcomer could be proud he had taken the calculated risk, doubling the sedative. The cardiac situation was improving and pulmonary edema had been averted. What surprised the doctors was how alert the patient was. Awake; they were feeding him. He asked if President Eisenhower had intervened in the transport strike.

"You're a leftist, aren't you?" said Newcomer, teasingly.

But in American, "leftist" meant something vaguer, more abstract, than what "man of the left" means in Italy. Remembering that, Ferranini replied, "I'm for the workers."

Wiener, severe, interrupted.

"Don't tire him. The man's pressure is at seventy."

"I was hoping it would be lower," said Ferranini, who had heard him. He stopped drinking his orange juice.

His comment didn't surprise Newcomer, the son and grandson of herring fishermen from the north Atlantic coast (from the sea where Kipling's *Captains Courageous* takes place), who, though not yet forty years old, had a good deal of human insight. Despite the patient's rapid improvement, Newcomer guessed that the man had little desire to get well, that he was already detached from life. Newcomer paid attention to his patients; he was alert and alive and open to them, however skeptical experience had left him about the humanity of his fellow men.

Wiener, meanwhile, had gone out with the nurse.

"You were hoping to get worse?" Newcomer asked Ferranini.

"A long time ago a doctor told me: Your heart is tired. Stay out in a blizzard and you'll meet your demise. And instead, I've survived."

Newcomer had asked for some tea, and he stood there, holding the cup. He took Walter's hand and squeezed it. Something happened to Ferranini that hadn't happened for a long time, not since childhood: tears came to his eyes.

"I lived for a while in India," said Newcomer. "Burma tea is the best in the world. Taste it, I'll get them to bring you some."

Ferranini received the tea with euphoria. He never drank tea.

Then Nancy arrived.

He looked at her, he studied her for a long time but said little.

"The other night," he said, when Nancy had sat down, "they told me you weren't here."

"What name did you give?"

"Mrs. Demarr."

"But I am Signora Ferranini," she said.

She said it in Italian. She had studied Italian and understood it fairly well. He spoke to her in Italian, while she used that well-modulated, educated Bostonian English to which she'd remained faithful. To Ferranini that voice and accent seemed to come from far, far away.

"Legally I can use my married name if I please," said Nancy. "And it pleases me to use it."

Ferranini was silent for a while, and then said, "You're better. It's obvious. But what did you have."

"Nephritis. Accidental intoxication. I just about kicked the bucket, you know."

"Really," he said softly, meditatively. He asked about her father.

"He's at home, in Camden. He can't go out. My brothers come. Mother, you know, died. In 1954."

Ferranini didn't know. No one had told him.

"Father had a stroke two months ago, at Christmas. It looked like he would die, but he's come back; he's stronger than any of us. The firm's now run by Salvatore. My brother. Business is going well, it seems. As always."

"And the farm?"

Nancy didn't understand him. He said again, with some effort, "The farm. Old Laurel Farm."

He shouldn't have said the words. Years ago in Reggio, when he still had passionate dreams of Old Laurel, he had already guessed, already known Nancy's reply.

"Not ours anymore."

Ferranini understood, darkly. And he understood that the reason he had come to see Nancy was above all this, to ask her this question. He had known the answer ahead of time, and still it hit him. Old Laurel, too, was finished. His hands went back and forth on the sheet between chin and chest, a tired gesture.

Pity, pain. Sorrow for the love that was trapped back there, in their season. Suddenly he was seized by the need to fight back. The sun beat on the window, and Old Laurel was not so far away as it was from Reggio, he could get there. Try to go back. Try. There was a stripe of sunlight on the bed. He had to move, to go.

His hands stopped moving.

Nancy saw that he was trying to pull himself up, his arms twisted, head sunk between his shoulders. Maybe he had worn himself out talking: she was afraid, she saw him white-faced, sucking in air with his mouth half closed. She rang the bell, but feeling it was not enough, ran to get the nurse.

"Don't worry," said Miss Joy, with a glance at him.

She helped to pull him up and gave him chloral hydrate. He forced himself to smile, to reassure her.

"It's nothing. I'm fine." He spoke in Italian and hadn't the strength to speak very loudly. Nancy didn't understand.

"Stay, please," she said to the nurse. "I have the feeling he's getting worse."

Newcomer didn't believe in the popular tranquilizers and sedatives, he called them *symptom suppressors*. He prescribed old-fashioned chloral hydrate, which attacked emotional excitability, including affections, even the most sincere and heartfelt, at the humble organic root, the brain and spinal cord. Ferranini swallowed two fingers of water with thirty grams of chloral hydrate, and Old Laurel sank back into the mists of Lake Erie. It would regain its place among the tolerable memories. He ate some noodles in broth and the jello brought to him by the nurse. Then he dozed off. Nancy put the two sprigs of Japanese allspice she'd taken from her room into two glasses. She handled the plants tenderly, sending an affectionate and even connubial glance in Walter's direction from time to time. Finally she left, for she too was convalescent and the doctor on her ward needed to know where she was.

In the afternoon she was back. Ferranini had slept and eaten; his heart beat more regularly and his blood pressure had recovered to the point that Newcomer had said cheerfully, "But you were just starving and in need of sleep." Ferranini received her happily.

"Oh, thanks for coming," he said in English.

He seemed not to remember she had been there that morning. Once again he asked her why she'd been hospitalized.

"As you see," he told her, "I came as soon as you called."

"And it was so good of you. It's not as if I've done all that much to deserve it."

That was the end of that. But she did find his reappearance (trapped in the snow, passed out in the phone booth) "terribly sweet."

"You're still the same old Walter. Only you could pull that off."

She talked. She had done a lot of things, "pursued many paths." In '47 she'd been in Canada, Quebec, and as she got to know the Canadians she found that a number of them liked the idea of political union with the United States. And so she threw herself into the annexation cause with enthusiasm. She founded a Daughters of the American Revolution chapter and attracted more than four hundred members. Between '49 and '52 she'd been a newspaper correspondent in Anchorage, Alaska. There she'd run into Francis, also a journalist, and it was marvelous, a great romance. Love and mutual spiritual understanding, neither one prying too much into the other's business.

"You wouldn't understand, Walter, you're Italian. Three years together and no promises, no vows. No arguments. Reasonable concessions on either side; I lived at the hotel and Francis had a small apartment. Weekends together. Francis a bit younger than me, a leftist, quite convinced, and a musicologist, writing a book about Schoenberg. I was interested in social matters, sociology. We helped each other, encouraged each other. Definitely. Maybe hard for you to fathom."

True, he couldn't fathom it. Sometime between '49 and '52 he had met Nuccia, and seen that she cared for him. From their very first meetings what was important to him was to have found someone he could talk with about America and Nancy.

"Nothing to say? Don't tell me you're jealous of Francis."

Jealous. In all those years of thinking about her, the idea that she might have taken a lover had never once crossed his mind.

"What's that smell?" he said.

"I don't know, darling."

"Flowers. Did you bring them? The smell's too strong."

They were the same powerfully fragrant winter flowers Nancy had in her room that day he went to visit her at her boarding school in Meadville. She meekly took the two flowerpots out into the hallway. Ferranini looked around him for the first time. He noticed the oxygen canister near the bed. Newcomer, making his afternoon rounds, could see right away on entering the room that 203 was improving. But he made it clear that the visitor should leave, because he needed to examine the patient. "See you tomorrow."

"Yes, we were ready to give you oxygen, we were even ready to bid you farewell. Your myocardiopathy is a textbook case, my friend, and I don't suppose this is the first time you've been told that. What you need is a very peaceful life, you know. But you are ruled by your nervous system, and while relationships are dangerous for you, you obviously need them."

It was true: now that Nancy was gone, Walter felt weaker. His mouth gaped open, hungry for air, and his head fell back and began to bob again. Newcomer, from the chair beside the bed, kept a sharp eye on him. This patient of his must have suffered badly and worked very hard, probably in his youth. Studying his face you could see traits of naiveté and stubbornness, a kind of exotic primitive idealism that had struck Newcomer in the faces of Stakhanovites and other heroes of labor glimpsed in photographs.

"Tell me. You are a Communist; do you believe that ideology is so ingrained today as to modify human appearance? Is there, say, a Marxist physiognomy and another for the neo-capitalist?"

Ferranini turned slowly toward him. Clever doctor, this New-comer, I'm having trouble breathing and so he's trying to distract me. "You know," Ferranini said, "I may not deserve to call myself a Communist."

Smiling, Newcomer leaned forward and gave him a tap on the foot. "Very good, Ferranini! Like all men of faith, you're troubled by doubts. You feel unworthy. Here you are, tended by heathens, a guest in the wicked Babylon of the anti-Marxists. Have no fear, we don't intend to take you prisoner. And remember that your wife is here, two steps away."

He struggled for words to reply. When you didn't feel well, having to speak a foreign language was a chore.

"Don't laugh, doctor. I must leave within four days. Hardly a prisoner."

Leaving, he thought, made sense. He was ready and in four days he'd be back on his feet. His problem was different. Leave for where? For what? Some Communist. If Newcomer only knew.

And Nancy. "Your wife." Who had actually called him darling!

"Tell them to give me something good to eat, doctor. You need to get me back in shape. Make me eat."

"Try not to think too badly of America," said Newcomer, his stethoscope on the patient's ribs. A pinpoint of sunlight that had pierced the icy windows now played on the nape of his neck. "As you see, we let devotees of Communism come in. We tolerate the Beat poets, we allow our blacks to convert, or convert back, to Islam."

Ferranini was touched by the man's warmth and vitality; he felt regretful but not bitter. The strong neck and shoulders, the pleasant voice that came out clearly even as Newcomer leaned awkwardly over the bed, his evident and easy self-possession—with that cordial hint of irony in his speech and thinking—he was sorry their communication was limited to these minutes of prodding and poking. Newcomer spoke to distract him, the better to get a normal reading of his pulse and pressure. He treated him like what he was: a poor, sick, impressionable creature.

"Don't take me too seriously," Newcomer went on. "I know the case for the other side. Our tolerance, our liberty, is merely formal. A freedom that doesn't alter the effective subservience of the individual in the least. Up and down the social ladder. The estrangement, the alienation. Now, Ferranini," he said, straightening up, "I was going after an intermittent extrasystole that could be heard very clearly the other day. This morning, it seems it's not there."

He removed the stethoscope from his ears.

"I know those objections, and not only do I know them, I appreciate them. I share them. I'm not an admirer of the state of things in this country. I'll say more. If I knew that things worked better elsewhere, I'd be inclined to leave. Yes, yes, that's right, the place you're thinking of. But I'm not confident I will find better elsewhere. Bear with me another minute while I take your blood pressure. Did you know that this device was made by an Italian? Riva Rocci was the name. Is that too tight? As I said, I'm not very confident. Both here and *there*, technology is galloping forward, even if here we also have plutocracy. I'd say there are hidden analogies between the two countries. Do you know America?"

"I'm beginning to."

"I speak from empirical evidence, you know; I don't have a theory. There's a dominant social type I would call the Ungregarious American. His personality, his inner life, is asocial, superficial, not very empathetic. Contacts between individuals are subordinated to organizational functions, to the status the individual derives from his organizational role. Contacts outside that don't survive. Nor do they get formed until organizational roles are defined. The difficulties you've experienced are not the only problems the system has. The extraneous element is first isolated and identified before it's integrated into the system. You know about that, don't you?"

Ferranini didn't reply. Yes, he did. But what was the point of bringing it up? He'd lost any desire to talk about it and he wouldn't have known how.

"But there's an even more serious difficulty, I'd say. Which is the tenuous nature of all relationships, which are always conditional, always reversible. Apparent," Newcomer continued. "While the organization, by contrast, is absolute. Man serves the organization and not vice versa. It wouldn't be a bad idea to leave this country, not at all. But to go where? Over to the other side, where opposite premises have produced similar results. Obviously you don't agree! Another solution? I don't believe there is a third option, I see only two. Ferranini, do you believe in the third world?"

"I've never liked what's in-between."

"I think I know what you mean. And so I stay put. I don't bother to look further. How do you explain the fact that there's no third world?"

"Well, there are only two poles, the positive electric charge and the negative. The physical world is bipolar."

Newcomer didn't believe that social reality could be interpreted using the laws of physics. He had another explanation, which he cloaked in genteel understatement.

"I'm a dilettante, I speak as a dilettante. Perhaps we could put it this way, that a third world, a third way, must be an improvement, an advance, and an advance requires not merely a middle stage but a new stage. Which is not to say that one day we won't discover it. But meanwhile, better to wait."

"There won't be a new stage," Ferranini replied. "What you say makes Marxism one point in a historical dialectic. While instead it is the end point."

"I knew you'd say that!" a cheerful Newcomer exclaimed. "It was the lesson I was expecting. And I'm ready to admit that reality disproves my thesis. I lived for a number of years in India. That is a country that could hold its own, with a newly minted ideology that is antithetical to the two great systems. And yet, India is gravitating toward one. Nehru and company, with their theoretical elaboration of Gandhism, have already taken sides, and today the country, where it is not still in the Middle Ages, draws inspiration from the capitalist New Deal."

The visit was finished. He announced the patient's blood pressure—110—and on his way out said, "Wait till around noon to get out of bed. You can stay up until four. Your wife is very eager to talk to you on the phone. Today I'll let her do so. Your phone here has been blocked, but I'll have it activated."

Ferranini raised a hand to stop him. "I'm not used to having a phone by the bed, it will annoy me. Leave it blocked." Right, he thought, people here think we're not just husband and wife but actual lovebirds.

Nancy came around 4:00 just as he, tired out, was undressing to return to bed. Earlier, getting dressed, he'd even put on a jacket and tie. He was relieved to get back in bed. Nancy offered to help him take off his clothing.

"No!" he said, surly. "What's got into you? Go outside and I'll let you know when I'm done."

Staggering in front of the window, sock in hand, he looked out and shivered: the trees were stiff with frost in spite of the sun, which had not yet gone down. He ruminated, partly in English. Nancy's changed. Too bad, I've changed too. Who knows, though, whether I've changed or whether it's just that I'm sick? As for her, you'd think she loved me. And her face hasn't changed, she's still the same pretty girl.

But Nancy's eyes, still green and pretty, had grown lifeless, they didn't sparkle. Her face and neck were chalky white. Ferranini didn't notice, it was her tone that struck him, attentive and even slightly humble. Perhaps now was the moment. With stubborn tenderness she had brought him more flowers. Carnations, odorless, so they wouldn't bother him.

They talked. But she only reminisced about the years that had passed. Of all of it, what she remembered most fondly was Alaska. But not because of Francis! No. Because Alaska was a new, clean America without poverty. Without classes.

In Anchorage there was next to no disparity between rich and poor. Median annual temperature 46 degrees Fahrenheit, 8 degrees Celsius: cold sterilized the place against privilege. The Alaskan spoke of the States as "the lower 48." When Nancy returned to Boston she founded a biweekly by the same name. In *The Lower 48*, a handful of brave polemicists, all of them intellectuals, waged war on

the government and the elite groups, prodding America to add social justice to its many distinctions. In that somewhat irregular
group of "intellectuals" there was Francis; the actress Erica Stein, an
old friend of Nancy's from Canadian days; Joseph O'Connor, who
did TV skits; and of course Rosy Gavan. At sixty, the aunt from
Boston had discovered a knack for social inquiry, that is, "demo-
scopic research": stopping people in shops, church, the subway,
wherever, and interviewing them about a wide variety of personal
matters. In fact, the review had a double purpose. Politically, to create a movement or party that Nancy, the soul of the operation, liked
to call "National Laborism"; intellectually, to promote the use of
"practical sociology." However, the review was no more. They had
ceased to publish six months ago.

"Everything bores you so quickly," said Ferranini, eyes closed.

Poor Nancy's white face flushed with color. "Oh, Walter. Don't
say that! It wasn't my fault. The review was honorable, it was a much-
needed dose of medicine for Americans. You have no idea how igno-
rant people here are about the socioeconomic situation. They think
the United States is not only the richest nation in the world but that
the whole nation is rich. Every last person. Yes, we do have thirty
percent of the world's wealth and only five percent of the population. Still, a third of the inhabitants of this country live in poverty.
Understand? Darling, do you follow me?"

Ferranini had an intense need for silence. A need that intensified
whenever Nancy was around. A confused desire to go back, to understand. Without speaking, perhaps looking at her, but in silence.

But that (keen, ardent) flow of chatter kept coming. She went on:
"One twentieth of the U.S. population, that is, at least eight million
men and women, live in absolute poverty, they would be poor even
in the underdeveloped part of the world. Venezuela, Bolivia, Greece,
Italy. Can you imagine? This is why I gave up the *National Review*,
the American Heritage movement, and the Daughters of the American Revolution, and took up National Laborism. You didn't know,
but for two years, in '56 and '57, I subscribed to your hometown
newspaper. From Reggio Emilia."

"What?"

"Yes, Walter. I would look for your name and read the speeches you gave, and your articles. I was close, very close to you. You can't deny that our beliefs have a strong affinity. You're a socialist; I'm a National Laborist."

Oh, please. This was all he needed. His eyes ran over her unbuttoned dressing gown, under which the arms, waist, bosom were broader and plumper than those of his Nancy. Where on earth had she gone, his Nancy?

"Are there no national roads to socialism?" she went on. "We are very close, darling, even spiritually. The silly and frivolous girl of the past is gone, and in her place is a woman worth your esteem. A woman who can stand at your side and do you honor—here, in Reggio Emilia, wherever. Do you want to hear how my conversion happened?"

"Your conversion," he said, and felt terribly sad.

"Well, it was shame. I was ashamed to think that the most powerful nation on earth, which claims to be a moral guide to all humanity (and is!), had as much social injustice as any of the others. One day a mother wrote to me. Hers was a family of ten, with her husband, seven children, and the grandmother, and to get by they farmed eighteen acres, a piece of land not much bigger than the grounds of this hospital. They had to borrow against the year's crop: twenty dollars a week at ten percent. Am I making a mistake to talk about America's dirty linen? I'm destroying your illusions. Is it a mistake?"

She was sitting in the chair beside the bed, her toes tucked between the two mattresses, fanning herself with the newspaper and studying him. Sincere, uncertain, wanting to know.

"Ring for the nurse," said Ferranini. "I asked for some milk; I need sustenance. They don't seem to understand that I need to eat."

The nurse came and they asked for milk.

"I see you don't want to answer me," she started up again.

Ferranini waved a hand vaguely. "Do you honestly care what I think?"

He was about to add: You haven't once asked what I've been doing all these thirteen years.

"You talk," he said. "Go ahead, you have a lot to say."

"Yes, there is a lot," she said in that earnest way that made him smile, though he didn't feel like it. (Tired and sweaty, Nancy's face was aged, lined. She was beginning to look like her mother.)

She'd learned so many new, unexpected things that now she had "a different perspective on the world," she had changed. "I'm not the same person, if you only knew": it was three days she'd been saying that and studying him to be sure he was listening and believed her. She had been in the South, the Deep South with its unfathomable human contradictions. She had lived for a few months in Alabama, where the rural social structure hadn't changed since the antebellum years. Human beings, both high and low, whose minds were utterly set. Hostile to progress, as if their entire sense of self depended on maintaining their beliefs, even against their own interests. A sub-feudal world trapped in the past.

From her description—objective, competent—it was clear Nancy was familiar with the problems. Her diagnosis was a tribute to the Nicholson-Murray school of sociology. Poverty produced deep-rooted psychological weaknesses, and that was one of the reasons it endured. Nancy had met people who were poor and attached to their condition, who were loyal to those responsible for their poverty. She'd met Charles Cutler, seventy-five years old, who lived with his wife in a wood hut with a leaking roof. And no toilet! Nancy had been scandalized. The old man was proud of his hovel and determined never to leave. Meanwhile he was paying ninety dollars a month rent to the owner, the wealthy wife of a Texas hotshot, a Democratic party leader, one Lyndon Johnson.

She returned to her old self for a moment. "But the nature down there is just fascinating. The Southern forests are so different from our woods. The Everglades, in Florida. Twenty varieties of orchids, wild orchids I mean, and all marvelous!"

"Some people might call you self-absorbed," Walter observed.

"But you have a real political temperament, that's the truth, and you've gotten involved here. And how!"

"You don't like that," said Nancy, discouraged.

"No! Actually I envy you. Your personal interests mean less to you than the political ones. You're great. Not like me."

The rooms at John Morgan were tidy and antiseptic, but in Ferranini's an out-of-season spider turned up, something he couldn't explain because he'd forgotten there was a huge green park below. The spider had fallen into his glass of water and now he was trying to push it under with a spoon, that is, kill it. The thing had no intention of dying and kept bobbing up; it was a crime any patient might commit, but when Miss Joy, the attractive nurse from Texas, caught Ferranini doing the dirty deed, she took the glass away. All innocence, she asked, "So is it true that Italians detest animals?" Yes, he had said—maybe because we can't take it out on the blacks.

Later he found himself thinking that perhaps Miss Joy was not entirely wrong, and that he and the spider were equally stupid to hold on so desperately to a last little bit of life, beyond its season. He had even said to Newcomer that morning, "So when will you let me out of here?" If there was someone without any reason to get out, someone unworthy to stay afloat, that was him. "I'm empty. They've taken everything out. I don't have a single idea that's worth knocking against another," he thought, and apart from ideas, he had no hopes or prospects to light his way. Nothing mattered anymore, he felt no impulse to look into himself, or to look back to see what might be left of him.

His conscience—difficult convalescent!—wasn't really dark and murky so much as sleepy, reluctant. A house may fall down, but when you visit it looking for something you've lost, it's still a house. For Ferranini, though, even the ruins had been razed by those last days in Rome, the leap across the Atlantic, the dizzying encounter with this desolate new America. What had he lost? He no longer had a name for it; all he could say was: Rome. But the moral and physical distress were both old; they had been growing for a while (not that he'd noticed, where in his simple soul had it hidden?). To say "Rome" was not really enough. His whole world was coming down. Many things, some deduced with pain and difficulty, had brought it down, and yet they remained hard to define. At most they were vaguely, instinctively felt.

Everything had become white. No outlines, no color, no relief. His mind refused to go there. Just one thought emerged: I will not begin again. No.

Okay, one day he would think about it. Put order in his mind. One of these days. Explain (to himself, certainly not to others, who would that be?) how it happened. Begin again, no.

This interval in hospital had come at just the right time, and it was foolish to be in a hurry to leave. It was a deferment. An excuse not to live, for a man who had left life behind him. And then, there was Nancy.

Poor thing. She was doing her part, and even doing it well. It was worth having met her all those years ago if only for that. For the good turn she was doing him. Her speeches, her diligent accounts, explanations, justifications. Alaska, Alabama, Francis ("You're not jealous!"), American populism, a second New Deal. All that foolishness, the illusions of a no-longer-young lady who had never gotten pleasure from anything else and would never have anything else.

That morning for the first time he tried to look after Nancy with goodwill. Newcomer had the day off, and Ferranini asked Wiener to get detailed information about Nancy's health from her doctor. Wiener must have gone right to work because the phone rang at 10:00 a.m. It was the department head of the Green Pavilion, Nancy's doctor.

"You are her husband?"

"I'm her husband," he said coolly. What difference did it make? He had said crazier things, he'd been forced to say many.

"Well then, your wife's situation: She's fully recovered from the accidental intoxication that brought her here. There remains an acute state of anxiety, accompanied by depression as happens in these cases. Your wife has slept badly the last few days. She is agitated."

"And it is my fault," said Ferranini.

"I expect so. In a way."

"I understand, doctor. I'll take care of it."

He should have thought of this; his presence wasn't good for her. Maybe it was for the best that he was getting ready to leave. He asked her not to come down; he would go to her. "Oh Walter, I'm pleased. Come to my room." He told her he'd prefer to meet halfway, in the covered passageway between the two pavilions, and he waited until 4:00 p.m. to get up. At 4:30, he thought, I'll just say goodbye and come back to my room. He'd been four full days in bed but he took the stairs up the one flight; he felt strong enough. Nancy was sitting in a chair with her newspapers still folded in her lap (she never forgot her papers). Her face was wet with tears.

"You're so good, you've always been so good to me."

"You've said that before, don't get upset."

The loggia was not much used. They were alone.

"Walter, you're so sweet. Do you remember that night when, before we went to sleep, I told you that I felt another calling, that I wasn't born for family life, and you said: 'Maybe not for family life but for love, yes, for my love'?"

She had unbuttoned the neck of her dressing gown quite naturally, and a sliver of flesh was visible. He took her hands and squeezed them.

"Darling, I treated you badly. In '45. When I went to Boston."

"You've already said so; let's not talk about it."

Just then the young Demarrs came to pay a visit—a good thing, Ferranini thought. All three of them appeared: Salvatore, Nicola, Carmelo. The elder Demarr had baptized his sons with Italian, or rather Pugliese names. And the three, who all looked a lot like him, also shared his expansive, somewhat distracted manner. They embraced Ferranini. Nicola (who was never going to be a proper WASP) told him flatly that he looked ghastly, he should take care of himself.

Carmelo, the youngest, nearing twenty, brought out half a dozen fresh eggs from the dairy near home for Nancy to drink. Carmelo didn't remember Ferranini but the others did and treated him like an unexpected, somewhat pathetic elderly relative. Salvatore, in his thirties, was running the family business; Nicola was a doctor. They told him about their father, who was feeling better and now wanted to buy himself a trailer and head South. He would end up in some "cemetery for elephants," he told them. One of those cities of the old, where the retired are kept in segregation until they die.

Salvatore spoke of the trials and successes of Demarr Incorporated, which had recently expanded into pharmaceuticals, and his plans to move the main office from Camden to Philadelphia. Already, Nancy had regained her smile. She laughed with Carmelo over the eggs and gave out advice to Salvatore. Her command of the business amazed Ferranini.

It's me who depresses her, he thought. Her mood had changed just like that.

The arrival of the brothers had raised his spirits too. He gathered that they had been trying to convince her to join the firm, and she was resisting.

"I'm not cut out for business, fellows."

Nicola, the doctor, seemed to have most authority.

"Nancy is the eldest," he said, "we should make her manager." And then he said (Ferranini was sure he'd understood this part), "The main thing is to keep the medicine cabinet under lock and key."

Now things were clear. When the brothers left, he didn't beat around the bush.

"Your accidental intoxication, that was sleeping pills, right? You tried to kill yourself. Why didn't you tell me?"

This time Nancy didn't adopt a maudlin tone. She was calm and straightforward. "It's true."

"Why? What happened? Was it Francis?"

He was quite serious, anything but ironic. She said, "If anything it was Erica Stein. She was part of my group, a great friend and a supporter of the review. Last year she took a revolver and shot herself."

"And you wanted to follow her?"

"I'll tell you. Erica had been working for two years on Broadway, as the star in a musical. She got laryngitis, lost her voice completely, and they replaced her. Two months away from the stage, and she had lost her fans, friends, contract, and even her lover. They found her with a note that said, 'For the rest of the world I'm already dead anyway.' Do you understand what that means?"

"No!"

"It means that here, if you cease to carry out a given economic role, you no longer exist. As a human being. Understand? I had never thought about it and it hit me, it made a terrifying impression on me. Does that seem so strange, darling?"

"A person doesn't hang on to life because another person's hanging on. And a person doesn't kill herself because another person did."

"It was a bad time for me, I have to tell you. They were waging war on me for the review. The review that I founded and directed."

"When was this?"

"They attacked me right from the beginning—and my brother Salvatore was one of the ones who disapproved. I was famous; you don't know. The Baltimore paper wrote an article urging the Un-American Activities Committee to investigate me. Me, who's fighting for this country's honor. You're not supposed to mention certain things, and my crime was that I did. I said that America is powerful but lacks justice."

Although she hadn't quite become famous, Nancy Demarr had in fact gained a certain dangerous notoriety on the East Coast. For months several newspapers had deluged her with sarcasm and nasty comments and there were letters, not always signed, not at all respectful, from indignant good citizens who frequently invited her to "move to Greenwich Village" or "go to Russia."

Senator McCarthy had made heated allusions to her little review, and he had endorsed demands to outlaw the Socialist Workers' Party, accused, wrongly, of financing her publication. In a TV debate organized by the inglorious John Birch Society, a boorish opponent, facing Nancy under the lights of the cameras, had pointed a finger at her and shouted, "Any man here want to offer himself to this ... female? Maybe that'll cure her!" Some of the hostility, although less brutal, was more effective. The company that distributed the review carried out hidden sabotage. The company that printed it was forced by its own employees to rescind the contract. Up until then the review had broken even, with a print run that sometimes reached forty thousand copies, but now they were short of funds and Nancy began to invest her own. They struggled on for another six months before folding.

The story came to an end.

"I came down to Camden for Christmas and didn't move from here. I was always tired, could barely stand on my two feet, and was very anxious. On the one hand I was pleased to see my family again, after so many years of that do-it-yourself thing, one room with kitchenette, owning nothing, no means of support. But I had taken too much of a beating. I had come to feel afraid of everything, everybody. I was ill."

Ferranini, deep in his armchair under the window, stroked his knees with his hands, and said nothing.

"You feel sorry for me. Don't you, Walter?"

He raised his arms and made a circle. "*Tutto mi fa pena. E schifo.*" He would have said the words in English, but he didn't know them. Nancy understood all the same. He felt sorry about everything. And disgusted.

After a moment of silence, she said, "I knew you'd blame this country. This country and this system. And I didn't want you to." She went on. "I would have liked you to be happy to be here. Do you know why?"

"Why?"

Nancy's usual light tone returned, and so did her smile. "Guess." But Ferranini was not the least bit curious.

The following day, which was supposed to be his last day at Morgan, she arrived in his room before 8:00 a.m. With her, the usual bunch of carnations.

"Are you crazy, getting up at this hour when you're supposed to be resting?"

"Sorry, darling. I didn't sleep a wink."

"And if you go on like this, you'll just get worse. I'm doing you no favor by staying here."

He persuaded her to go back to bed, and promised her that later he would come to see her.

Newcomer came in as he was packing his bag and advised him not to leave. If it was about the visa, the hospital could arrange an extension.

"And your wife? You cross the Atlantic to see her and then leave right away?"

"Nancy," said Ferranini, astonished by the ease with which the words came, "Nancy was just a pretext for me to flee."

There might be some truth to that, so why regret having said it? Newcomer was a man. A man who sympathized with him and had treated him intelligently.

"My hope," said the doctor, "is that you'll take another week to improve. Allow me to speak as a friend, if I may. You must have a little more respect for yourself. You are wrong to value your life so little."

"I've recovered, I feel fine. Now it's Nancy who is getting worse, and very likely it's my fault. I'm going away tomorrow without saying anything to her; you'll tell her yourself afterwards. I hope you'll do me that favor, Newcomer."

"Walter," Nancy had begun that evening of their last meeting, in the loggia, "do you remember my school in Meadville? To please me you made friends with the French nuns. You, the atheist. Near the lake there one of them grew flowers in a hothouse—she was called Villiers. A specialist in grafting rhododendrons. We went there the day before we were married. One day, when you arrived in Meadville you said to me in Italian, 'The Chevy, I wrung its damn neck! It took me less than four hours to get here from Camden.' Remember?"

"Forget it, Nancy. What's the point?"

She had thought about it, and after a few moments replied, "The point is to remind us that life exists. What do you think life's made of? The substance of life is the past."

"Are you that old?" he had said, teasing her for once.

"Listen. When did you stop loving Nancy?" she asked.

"Hmm. When my youth departed."

"Good. That's the right answer, Walter," she said. That evening she was calmer, less insistent. She looked better too.

On the train to New York, Ferranini went over that last conversation. He was happy there had been no farewells, that he'd left unannounced, just as he'd arrived. The whole episode, Philadelphia, the John Morgan, so strange and improbable, could not have ended otherwise. The certainty that he was not necessary to Nancy (that he'd been a negative intrusion in her life) now pressed his new perceptions into a reassuring and well-worn shape, like some comfortable article of clothing.

The fact was, there was always something morbid about Nancy when she was operating in the private, personal realm. It wasn't normal for her, she needed an impersonal bond with people, some kind of collectivity, on which to exert her influence. It was the calling of a missionary, which she executed faithfully, trying to set an example to others, and not just to women. A generous Don Quixote of a woman, little made for love (and finally, Ferranini thought without bitterness, not that much of a woman).

He hadn't thought to suggest the Peace Corps or the UN agency for displaced persons. A pity, they were big, American-made contrivances where, after her ugly experiences, she might have found a place. A way back from subversive patriotism to bourgeois patriotism. She was a missionary, but not inclined to waste much time on ideological consistency, so a change of program wouldn't cost her much, he reckoned. In short, Ferranini thought, she's even more of a stray than I am! So why, before he left the hospital, had he gone back to peer at the loggia where she had always waited for him. Her voice, softening to say his name, still rang in his ears.

Rainy countryside, a coastline where the high, green sea hit the sand in silence. The train ride seemed long. Hoping to fill the void inside, Ferranini allowed himself to think about this woman he'd never see again. What he needed to avoid thinking about above all was himself; for years train rides had served as one of those rare occasions to take personal stock of things. And to arrive at decisions. Decisions were essence of life and its purpose, he now recognized with sorrow and dismay.

What he wanted was a deferment, a suspension. Another interval like his hospital stay, but one that would last. To be neither here nor there (impossible, but he was so weary!). A balance he had been looking for, without knowing it, when he left Rome with the illusion he was escaping. Freedom not to plant his feet on the earth. A foolish thought pestered him: the bourgeoisie had invented so many pointless freedoms—why not this one? Well, because this was not merely a formal liberty, freedom in name alone. He rose and went to see where he could find a newspaper. He hadn't read one for nearly two weeks. He came back with the papers, mechanically opened his bag, and stuffed them in. Hid them.

This trip must never finish: if only the plane would come to a halt in the middle of the Atlantic, drop into the ocean. Leaving him stuck there, betwixt and between. Thus resolving Newcomer's problem. A third geographic world, given that there wasn't a real one.

Newcomer. He'd said that high altitudes were no good for Ferranini. Take the ocean route; it's restful. But he had the return ticket in his pocket. Throw it away? He didn't like the idea.

Yes, pain prompted powerful reactions that then made common cause with the most petty, even miserly logic. But the psychic economy, you had to admit, depended on curious currency, although—no, let's not bring Marx into this—although there was that old problem of the "mystery" of money worship, money fetishism. Ferranini took out his wallet to see how much money he had left. He had quite a bit.

At the hospital, they had been strangely uninterested in payment. He hadn't spent money on anything else either, and so pretty much all of the cash he'd brought from Rome was still in the envelope. He sat back in his seat, calmer.

Along with the cash was an expenses sheet to account for the advance on his pay at the chamber. The form unaccountably made him think of the thick lenses and blunt manner of President Leone. He'd advised him to notify his parliamentary group before setting off from Rome.

He hadn't notified anyone. There would be time to send a telegram at the next stop, or when he got to New York. If he wanted to, but then, what for? He could even send two words to Nuccia. Right, Nuccia. He owed her more than he owed the PCI group. It was the first time he had given her a thought.

But when he got to New York at 3:00 p.m., he forgot to telegraph. He came out of the station into a large street, and though he tired quickly, he didn't mind walking. It was Eighth Avenue, and he didn't stop walking until he reached the park, a half-hour walk, and sat down (it was raining) on a bench near the Mayflower Hotel, a point he must have passed before, since it looked familiar. He recognized the entrance to the park, the statue of Christopher Columbus. Some hundred people were crowded around the base of the statue, listening to a guy making a speech. Women and girls, holding up anti-Communist and anti-Soviet placards. "We like the American way of life." "Watch out, Commies, this war could become hot."

A street peddler offered him some postcards. He chose one with the skyline of New York at night, to send to Fubini. But not to Reggio, not to the Federation. He'd send it to Vimondino where his old comrade went every week.

He walked back downtown to recover his valise; Eighth Avenue was dark and teeming with people (rush hour, hurry to the trains, the breathless end to the day) and he thought of Vimondino. He could go to his hometown. He could ask to change his destination from Rome to Milan. Then Milan to Mantua, Mantua to Guastalla, back to Vimondino from Guastalla on "his" train line, avoiding Reggio. Go to Fubini's. (Fubini's mother had always been good to him, she'd take him in.) Wait for Fubini to come home and talk to him. Explain to him. Oscar's a good kid, after all, he's fond of me. As soon as he arrived, get into bed, that was for sure. Get them to call the doctor. (Morganti, if he's still there, Morganti can give me a doctor's excuse for the chamber.) Maybe Fubini would like to go down to Rome, to listen in. Inform himself.

And thus from mighty Eighth Avenue to the streets of Vimondino, 1,700 inhabitants. A leap. Yes, Fubini, better him than Nuccia. Nuccia would have a hundred thousand questions, a hundred thousand stories to tell. Better for her, too. He'd write to her afterwards, or call her. If she wanted to, she could come visit for a short time. Later, sometime later.

Cross the Po River, his Po, familiar and wild, hidden by poplars. His melancholy Po. (He must call the interprovincial committee that was meeting about the river. The Po, my friends, has no bridges. Our river is good for nothing but flooding. We are *padanians*, people of the Po first, before we are natives of Emilia, or Lombardy, or Italy.)

He heard himself thinking, incredulous. For the length of a block, one corner to the next, a couple of minutes, and again he heard that internal "No." Send Oscar to Rome to find out what? To obtain what? In any case, Ferranini would never be the man he'd been before. Ready to join the ranks again out of discipline, abnegation . . . or resignation? Because he couldn't think of anything better to do? The district medical officer Morganti certifies that Ferranini is *resigned*. Apathetic, deeply indifferent, was this the same man who had always been an eager, unquestioning participant? The crowd heading toward the trains went with him, and when they stopped at the lights they formed a compact front. People beside him, people behind, they moved forward again, men and women, with that five-in-the-afternoon midtown pace (rapid, orderly). As they flowed, he felt his inertia had found an excuse, a prop.

Still, he was in a hurry, and Eighth Avenue was interminably long (from Columbus Circle to Pennsylvania Station). He remembered that he hadn't reserved a seat on that evening's flight.

Without any trouble, they found him a seat, and on the flight to Milan. A very nice woman at the desk telephoned and took care of everything. She spoke to him in Italian. In her makeup bag on her desk was a lipstick, a golden cylinder with a bullet-shaped point. Patting his pocket he felt Nuccia's lipstick, which he'd picked up in Rome on leaving the bookstore. I can tell Nuccia I traveled with a souvenir of her, he thought vaguely. They were on the bus, on the way to Idlewild. Nuccia would come to see him, he could count on that, he hadn't actually done her any wrong. There was a traffic jam on the East River, and they were stuck there for a long time, halfway across the bridge. The night sky flickered with a million lights, and soon enough Ferranini was thinking that no, he couldn't count on it. There was her husband. There was Lonati. Who knew what Lonati would get up to. Ferranini would be easy to hit back at. A man in liquidation—in practice, out. His enemies must be rubbing their hands with glee.

Lonati wanted Nuccia back, and maybe Nuccia was thinking: Walter with his wife, me with my husband. Four happy people. Nuccia was now more distant, more uncertain than Nancy. Everything was upside down. It was all so strange, unbelievable to him. Nuccia, a memory? Nuccia and all that? All what?

Something bigger and more important than Nuccia, or Rome, or Oscar Fubini was coming unstuck from him. He must let it go, finally, or else grab it back: this was his life, and yet his consciousness was failing him, he couldn't focus. He need to straighten things out and yet he wouldn't, couldn't. His troubled, elusive thoughts were coming together. But they were useless, angry. His position. Liquidated? By whom. How. President Leone had said: Your mandate comes from the electorate. Right was on his side. Liquidate Ferranini? Let them go to Reggio and find out what kind of man he was. And observe that after thirty years when the Catholics were in command, there was now a progressive administration in Vimondino. And there were a lot of other Vimondinos in the province. Hadn't he achieved results? Hell if he hadn't! He'd brought a couple of dozen cooperatives to the party, and several thousand members, and sympathizers, had brought backers and votes.

His old valise sat on his knees, and he pounded on it with both fists. Back when he was a believer, he'd known how to spread the

faith. He'd been a driving force. Sure, he had left Rome without no-
tifying anyone. For eight days, an emergency, family reasons. Eight
days, it was no crime. In any case he'd let them know at the chamber,
he had warned them. President Leone had been informed. The president's office might have told his group.

"Back when he was a believer." That was well said. And now?

The bus had started to move again, slowly, and the East River
disappeared behind them. The eight days were finished and he was
returning, on time. According to the stipulations of the American
authorities and in agreement with what he had promised. There
could be no objections. Returning? They were moving very slowly,
and in the dim half-light, some uneasy passengers shifted; they
might be late arriving at the airport. Returning, was he?

Next to him, an Italian was complaining. After protesting to the
bus staff, he turned on Ferranini, who hadn't backed him up.

"You, do you even care whether you take off or not?"

Yes, he cared. He was keen to depart. Depart, that was it. Nobody
was waiting for him on the other side, he had no plans. His bag was
there with him; it held everything he had, everything he needed. He
was free, independent. What was bothering him at that moment
was the stink of cigarettes. Chesterfields, Lucky Strikes. Virginia tobacco. Once upon a time he'd liked the smell.

Getting off the bus, and later, waiting on the strip to board the
plane, he shivered in the cold, the wind tossing freezing rain in his
face. It was raining on his already sopping raincoat, the gabardine
with the dusty, dandruff-strewn velvet collar. That morning in the
hospital, Miss Joy had noticed it and brought him a brush, which he
had rudely tossed on the bed. The rain bounded off the cement as
they squeezed around the stairs up to the plane. Fourteen years ago
he had also departed shivering, and in the same unpleasant weather,
and back then, flying hadn't been as safe: he had taken an old aircraft
owned by an Irish company with a holy card of Saint Patrick on the
door to the pilot's cabin. This time things were different. Before they
announced the takeoff, he searched the plane from back to front.

He would have been pleased to find Lamoureux onboard. His

memory of the trip westward made him smile. And for a moment he thought he saw him; a tall, young, sun-tanned passenger who had taken off his jacket to replace it with a pajama top that was tight across his broad shoulders.

He sat down in his seat again. Took out the newspapers. Finally he felt like reading them. It was Friday, the paper said, and he thought: Tomorrow Fubini will be home, he goes back home on Saturday night. He had *The New York Times* and *The Philadelphia Inquirer* with him; he saw there was an editorial on Algeria, reports from Argentina, Saudi Arabia, and twenty other countries, and not even the briefest word from Italy. As usual. He pushed the papers away and buckled his seat belt. He thought: I'll eat, then I'll sleep.

1964–1965

NOTES

CHAPTER 1

3   *president of the chamber, Leone:* Giovanni Leone (1908–2001) was a prominent politician in the Christian Democratic Party.

5   *Italy's Kiev:* The Emilia-Romagna region, in the 1950s widely devoted to agriculture, was one of Italy's Reddest. It was one of the places where the cooperative movement, nascent socialism in Ferranini's eyes, flourished.

    legge-truffa: The "scam law," as the left-wing opposition called it, was a new electoral law of 1953 assigning the winning party a large bonus of seats in parliament.

7   *Palmiro Togliatti:* Togliatti (1893–1964) was the general secretary of the Italian Communist Party (PCI) from 1927 to 1964.

9   *Il Migliore:* "The Best," as Togliatti was known.

11   *between March and May 1915:* The months just before Italy entered World War I.

13   ras *Italo Balbo:* The term *ras* (from the Amarico, meaning an Ethiopian nobleman) made its way into Italian during the colonial period to describe an Italian political boss, thus the Fascist Italo Balbo. The attempt on his life referred to here appears to be a novelistic invention.

    Turati: Filippo Turati (1857–1932), the leader of Italy's Socialist Party, which was founded in 1892. The party split in 1921 when the Communists broke off. The Communists considered Turati's followers mere reformists.

    Anna Kuliscioff: Kuliscioff (1857–1925), who was born in Russia, was Turati's partner and one of the leaders of the Italian Socialist Party.

14 *Abyssinia awaited, and perhaps Spain:* In 1935–1936 Italy fought a brutal war in Ethiopia before annexing the territory to its East Africa Colony. Some 50,000 Italian "volunteers" were sent by Mussolini to fight with Franco in the Spanish Civil War. Other Italians went of their own accord to back the Republicans.

16 *Bosciàn:* It's unclear if the name refers to any historical figure. During the 1930s and '40s, the preeminent Soviet agronomist was the regime-backed anti-Mendelian Trofim Lysenko (1898–1976).

 Oparin: Alexander Oparin (1894–1980) was a Soviet biochemist who formulated a pioneering theory of how life originates from carbon-based molecules in a primordial soup.

 Lepeshinskaya: The biologist Olga Lepeshinskaya (1871–1963) maintained that life could come forth from inanimate matter via spontaneous generation.

18 Qualunquista!: Politically apathetic, someone who "doesn't give a damn" about ideological consistency.

CHAPTER 2

25 *Cope, de Vries, Mark Baldwin:* The American paleontologist and anatomist Edward Cope (1840–1897); Hugo de Vries (1848–1935), a Dutch biologist who expounded the anti-Darwinist theory of mutationism; and James Mark Baldwin (1861–1934), an American psychologist who proposed that learned behavior influences reproductive success and thus guides natural selection.

 Camden, New Jersey: Morselli identifies the city as Camden, Pennsylvania, when from the context it is clear he is writing about Camden, New Jersey.

35 *Marcinelle, to the mines in Belgium:* In 1956, 262 miners, the majority of them Italian immigrants, died in a coal-mine fire near this Belgian city.

CHAPTER 3

37 porca vita, porca matina: "Swine of a life," "swine of a morning," minced oaths with a strong edge of blasphemy.

49 *Camillo Prampolini:* Prampolini (1859–1930), born in Reggio Emilia, was an early socialist.

50 *People's Train:* A special weekend train (*treno popolare*) created by the Fascists for popular tourism and leisure.

CHAPTER 4

60 *anti-blasphemy laws:* Morselli writes of an apocryphal "Blasphemy Act, a federal law."

65 *Academy of Saint Thérèse of Lisieux:* The name Morselli gives the school translates as Garden of Lisieux, a slightly improbable name for an American Catholic school.

68 *"Americanism":* The term Morselli uses, in English in the original, is "Americanhood."

73 National Review: In fact, the magazine was not founded until 1955.

CHAPTER 5

81 *American army rifle company:* Morselli refers to a nonexistent American "27th Rifles."

83 *CGIL:* Italian General Confederation of Labor, the largest Italian labor union association; the majority of its membership was traditionally Communist.

89 *Nenni:* Pietro Nenni (1891–1980) was a longtime leader of the Italian Socialist Party.

92 *Luigi Longo:* Longo (1900–1980) was the deputy secretary of the PCI under Togliatti, and later became the general secretary. In early editions of the novel he is identified by a pseudonym, Mauro, but real names were reinstated for both Togliatti (pseudonym, Maccagni) and Longo in the collected *Romanzi* (Adelphi, 2002), following corrections to the manuscript added in 1966 and 1967 when the novel was edited by Rizzoli (but never published). For unspecified reasons Longo is called Giuseppe Longo in the 2002 edition.

93 *if there's a second attack let's hope they shoot at me:* In 1948 Togliatti was shot and gravely wounded, but he recovered.

CHAPTER 6

102 *Di Vittorio:* Giuseppe Di Vittorio (1892–1957) was a legendary Italian trade unionist and anti-Fascist.

107 *the big man Valletta:* Vittorio Valletta (1883–1967) was the president of Fiat from 1946 to 1966. The Agnelli family owned the company.

109 *Gramsci's* L'Ordine Nuovo, *in which Tasca:* The Communist intellectual Antonio Gramsci (1891–1937) founded the socialist review *L'Ordine Nuovo* in 1919 along with Angelo Tasca (1892–1960). Gramsci and Tasca were also among the founders of the Italian Communist Party, which split from the Socialists in 1921. In 1929, Tasca was expelled from the PCI for anti-Stalinism.

CHAPTER 7

122 *you're not the most attractive bunch in the chamber:* The handsome parliamentarians Nuccia cites are actual politicians—Giolitti, Alessandrini, Moro, Colombo—not fictional characters.

131 *Huxley:* Julian Huxley (1887–1975) was a British biologist and geneticist.

134 *Marx praised Darwin:* Morselli mistakenly attributes that praise to Hegel, who died almost thirty years before *On the Origin of Species* was published.

136 *the famous balcony:* Mussolini's office was in Palazzo Venezia and he made his public orations from its balcony overlooking Piazza Venezia.

140 *the 17th and a Friday to boot:* Seventeen is an unlucky number in Italian folklore, and Friday the 17th is considered a most unlucky day.

144 *Togliatti's also out of line:* The party secretary Togliatti, who was married, had a long-standing affair with a leading party official, Nilde Iotti (1920–1999).

145 *Alexandra Kollontai:* A Russian revolutionary, Kollontai (1872–1952) joined the Bolsheviks in 1915 and became commissar for social welfare in 1917. A proponent of free love, she was an early champion of Soviet women's rights.

CHAPTER 8

159 *the errors of a Blanqui:* The French socialist Louis Auguste Blanqui (1805–1881) held that a socialist revolution should be carried out by a small group of secret conspirators who take over the state, in contrast to Marx's emphasis on the guiding role of the proletariat.

162 *next number of* Nuovi Argumenti: A left-leaning review of literature and politics, in fact founded in 1953 by Alberto Moravia (1907–1990).

CHAPTER 9

171 Lunik: Unmanned Soviet spacecraft first sent to the moon in the late 1950s.

182 *Father Gapon:* Georgy Gapon (1870–1906), a Russian Orthodox priest and the leader of working-class protests during the 1905 revolution, was executed by the Socialist Revolutionary Party for being a police spy.

He turned toward the Forum: Morselli writes "Foro Italico," a Fascist-era complex very far from via delle Botteghe Oscure, a street near the Roman Forum from where Ferranini is setting out on foot. Probably a mere error of Roman geography.

CHAPTER 10

189 *apply Modugno's blue:* The reference is to Domenico Modugno's 1958 hit love song "Nel blu dipinto di blu" (In the sky painted blue), better known as "Volare."

190 *Fascist of the first hour:* As the earliest followers of Mussolini are known. Morselli uses the somewhat more recondite term *Sansepolcristi* after Mussolini's founding rally in Milan's Piazza San Sepolcro in 1919.

Dino Grandi: Dino Grandi (1895–1988) was one of the leading lights of Fascism in Emilia. As Morselli says here, a number of committed Fascists joined the PCI after 1945.

204 *ARMIR:* Some 235,000 Italian soldiers fought alongside Hitler in Russia and Ukraine in 1942 in the Armata Italiana in Russia, the Italian Eighth Army. After a notorious, crushing defeat by the Soviets in the winter of 1942–1943, ARMIR withdrew. Many Italians died.

205 *Chebutykin's* History of Scientific Thought *tucked under his arm:* This invented text suggests a possible ironic reference to Dr. Ivan Chebutykin, an alcoholic doctor unashamed of his ignorance who is a celebrated character in Chekhov's "Three Sisters."

CHAPTER 13

252 *Labriola:* The philosopher Antonio Labriola (1843–1904) was an Italian expert on Marxism.

261 *The 'Curia':* The term comes from Catholicism, where the Curia is the church's central administration that keeps the machine running (just as here it is the PCI equivalent). Italians often compare the PCI to the Italian church and its political sympathizers, the Christian Democrats, the two parties having been the main political-ideological structures of postwar Italy.

CHAPTER 14

273 *Kravchenko:* The Soviet diplomat Victor Kravchenko (1905–1966), a famous defector to the United States in 1944.

CHAPTER 15

291 *where Kipling's* Captains Courageous *takes place:* Morselli's geography is slightly off; he identifies the setting of the novel as Nantucket.

310 *Peace Corps:* Morselli is writing about 1959, but the organization was not created until 1961.

TITLES IN SERIES

For a complete list of titles, visit www.nyrb.com or write to:
Catalog Requests, NYRB, 435 Hudson Street, New York, NY 10014

* *Also available as an electronic book.*